ALSO BY P. D. JAMES

A CERTAIN JUSTICE

A
CERTAIN JUSTICE

P. D. JAMES

ALFRED A. KNOPF   NEW YORK   1997

THIS IS A BORZOI BOOK
PUBLISHED BY ALFRED A. KNOPF, INC.

Copyright © 1997 by P. D. James

http://www.randomhouse.com/

Published in Great Britain by Faber and Faber Limited, London.

Library of Congress Cataloging-in-Publication Data

James, P. D.
A certain justice / P. D. James. — 1st American ed.
p.   cm.
ISBN 0-375-40109-1
1. Dalgliesh, Adam (Fictitious character)—Fiction.
2. Police—England—Fiction.   I. Title
PR6060.A467C45   1997b
823'.914—dc21   97-36889
CIP

Manufactured in the United States of America
First American Trade Edition

A signed first edition of this book has been privately
printed by the Franklin Library.

To my grandchildren with love

Katherine, Thomas, Eleanor, James and Beatrice

CONTENTS

AUTHOR'S NOTE

I am very grateful to a number of friends in medicine and the law who have given up valuable time to help me in writing this book, and in particular to Dr. Caroline Finlayson and her colleagues and to Alderman Gavyn Arthur, whose timely advice on procedure at the Old Bailey has saved me from a number of embarrassing errors. If any remain, the responsibility is solely mine.

In a poor return for this kindness I have brutally demolished part of Fountain Court in the Middle Temple to erect my imaginary Pawlet Court, and have peopled it with maverick lawyers. Some of the places in the novel, including the beautiful and historic Temple Church, are manifestly real; all of the characters are fictitious and are not based in any way on living persons. In particular only the perfervid imagination of a crime novelist could possibly conceive that a member of the Honourable Society of the Middle Temple could harbour uncharitable thoughts towards a fellow member.

I am told that this customary disclaimer gives little protection in law, but I make it nevertheless because it is the truth, the whole truth and nothing but the truth.

P. D. JAMES, 1997

BOOK ONE

COUNSEL FOR THE DEFENCE

1

Murderers do not usually give their victims notice. This is one death which, however terrible that last second of appalled realization, comes mercifully unburdened with anticipatory terror. When, on the afternoon of Wednesday, 11 September, Venetia Aldridge stood up to cross-examine the prosecution's chief witness in the case of *Regina* v. *Ashe,* she had four weeks, four hours and fifty minutes left of life. After her death the many who had admired her and the few who had liked her, searching for a more personal response than the stock adjectives of horror and outrage, found themselves muttering that it would have pleased Venetia that her last case of murder had been tried at the Bailey, scene of her greatest triumphs, and in her favourite court.

But there was truth in the inanity.

Court Number One had laid its spell on her since she had first entered it as a pupil. She had always tried to discipline that part of her mind which she suspected could be seduced by tradition or history, yet she responded to this elegant wood-panelled theatre with an aesthetic satisfaction and a lifting of the spirit which was one of the keenest pleasures of her professional life. There was a rightness about the size and proportions, an appropriate dignity in the richly carved coat of arms above the dais, and the glittering seventeenth-century Sword of Justice suspended beneath it, an intriguing contrast between the witness box, canopied like a miniature pulpit, and the wide dock, in which the accused sat level-eyed with the judge. Like all places perfectly designed for their purpose with nothing wanting, nothing super-fluous, it induced a sense of timeless calm, even the illusion that the passions of men were susceptible to order and control. Once from curiosity she had gone into the public gallery and had sat for a minute looking down at the empty court and it had seemed to her that only here, where the spectators sat close-packed, was the air knotted with decades of human terror, hope and despair. And now she was once more in the place where she belonged. She hadn't expected the case to be heard in the Old Bailey's most famous court or to be judged by a High Court Judge, but a previous trial had collapsed and the judge's sittings and court allocation had been reorganized. It was a happy omen. She had lost in Court One, but the memories of defeats there were not bitter. More often she had won.

Today, as always in court, she reserved her gaze for the judge, the jury, the witnesses. She seldom conferred with her junior, spoke to Ashe's solicitor seated in front of her or kept the court waiting even momentarily while she searched in her papers for a note. No defending counsel went into court better prepared. And she rarely glanced at her client, and then, when possible, without too obviously turning her head towards the dock. But his silent presence dominated her mind as she knew it did the court. Garry Ashe, aged twenty-one years and three months, accused of murdering his aunt, Mrs. Rita O'Keefe, by cutting her throat. One clean single slash, severing the vessels. And then the repeated frenzied stabs at the half-naked body. Often, particularly with a murder of great brutality, the accused seemed almost pathetically inadequate in his ordinariness, his air of hapless incompetence at variance with the violent dedication of the deed. But there was nothing ordinary about this accused. It seemed to Venetia that, without turning, she could remember every detail of his face.

He was dark, the eyes sombre under straight thick brows, the nose sharp and narrow, the mouth wide but thin-lipped, unyielding. The neck was long and very slender, giving the head the hieratic appearance of a bird of prey. He never fidgeted, indeed seldom moved, sitting very upright in the centre of the dock, flanked by the attendant officers. He seldom glanced at the jury in their box to his left. Only once, during the prosecution counsel's opening speech, had she seen him look up at the public gallery, his gaze ranging along the rows with a slight frown of disgust, as if deploring the quality of the audience he had attracted, before turning his eyes again to rest them on the judge. But there was nothing tautly anxious about his stillness. Instead he gave the impression of a man accustomed to public exposure, a young princeling at a public entertainment, to be endured rather than enjoyed, attended by his lords. It was the jury, the usual miscellany of men and women assembled to judge him, who looked to Venetia like an oddly assorted group of miscreants herded into the box for sentence. Four of them, in open-necked shirts and jumpers, looked as if they were about to wash the car. In contrast, the accused was carefully dressed in a navy-blue striped suit with a shirt so dazzling that it looked like an advertisement for a washing powder. The suit was well pressed but poorly cut, the over-padded shoulders giving the vigorous young body some of the gangling tenuity of adolescence. It was a good choice, the suit hinting at a mixture of self-respect and vulnerability which she was hoping to exploit.

She had a respect, but no liking, for Rufus Matthews, who was prosecuting. The days of flamboyant eloquence in court were over and had in any case never been appropriate to the prosecution, but Rufus liked to win. He would make her fight for every point gained. Opening the prosecution case, he had recounted the facts with a brevity and an unemphatic clarity which left the impression that no eloquence was necessary to support a case so self-evidently true.

Garry Ashe had lived with his maternal aunt, Mrs. Rita O'Keefe, at 397 Westway for a year and eight months before her death. His childhood had been spent in care, during which he had been placed with eight foster parents between periods in children's homes. He had lived in two London squats and had worked for a time in a bar in Ibiza before moving in with his aunt. The relationship between aunt and nephew could hardly be called normal. Mrs. O'Keefe was in the habit of entertaining a variety of men friends, and Garry was either compelled, or consented, to photograph his aunt and these various men engaged in the sexual act. Photographs which the accused had admitted taking would be shown in evidence.

On the night of the murder, Friday, 12 January, Mrs. O'Keefe and Garry were seen together from six o'clock to nine in the Duke of Clarence public house in Cosgrove Gardens, about one and a half miles from Westway. There was a quarrel and Garry left shortly after nine, saying that he was going home. His aunt, who was drinking heavily, stayed on. At about ten-thirty the licensee refused to serve her any more and she was helped into a taxi by two of her friends. At that time she was drunk but by no means incapable. Her friends judged that she was able to get home on her own. The cab-driver deposited her at Number 397 and watched her enter through the side gate at about ten-forty-five.

At ten minutes past midnight a call was made to the police by Garry Ashe from his aunt's house to say that he had returned from a walk to discover her body. When the police arrived at twelve-twenty they found Mrs. O'Keefe lying on a single divan in the front sitting-room, practically naked. Her throat had been cut and she had been slashed with a knife after death, a total of nine wounds. It was the opinion of the forensic pathologist who saw the body at twelve-forty that Mrs. O'Keefe had died very shortly after her return home. There was no evidence of a break-in, and nothing to suggest that she had been entertaining or expecting a visitor that night.

A smear of blood, later identified as Mrs. O'Keefe's, had been found on the headpiece of the shower above the bath in the bathroom, and two spots of her blood on the stair carpet. A large kitchen knife had been discovered under the privet hedge of a front garden less than a hundred yards from 397 Westway. The knife, which had a distinctive triangular chip in the handle, had been identified both by the accused and by the cleaning woman as having come from the drawer in Mrs. O'Keefe's kitchen. It had been cleaned of all fingerprints.

The defendant had told the police that he had not gone straight home from the public house, but had walked the streets behind Westway and down as far as Shepherd's Bush before returning after midnight to discover his aunt's body. The court would, however, hear evidence from the neighbour living next door that she had seen Garry Ashe leaving 397 Westway at eleven-fifteen on the night of the murder. It was the case for the Crown that Garry Ashe had, in fact, gone straight home from the Duke of Clarence public house, that he had waited for his aunt to return and that he had killed her with the kitchen knife, probably himself in a state of nakedness. He had then taken a shower, dressed and left the house at eleven-fifteen to walk the streets in an attempt to establish an alibi.

Rufus Matthews's final words were almost perfunctory. If the jury were satisfied on the evidence put before them that Garry Ashe had murdered his aunt, it would be their duty to return a verdict of guilty. If, however, at the end of the case they were left with a reasonable doubt of his guilt, then the accused was entitled to be acquitted of the murder of Mrs. Rita O'Keefe.

The cross-examination of Stephen Wright, landlord of the Duke of Clarence, on the third day of the trial had presented Venetia with little difficulty and she had expected none. He had entered the witness box with the swagger of a man determined to show that he wasn't intimidated by wigs and scarlet robes, and had taken the oath with a nonchalance which made only too plain his opinion of this archaic ritual. Venetia had met his slightly salacious smile with a long cool glance. The prosecution had called him to add weight to their case that relations between Ashe and his aunt had quickly descended into acrimony when they were in the pub together, and that Mrs. O'Keefe had been frightened of her nephew. But he had been an unconvincing and prejudiced witness and had done little to shake the evidence of the other pub witnesses that Ashe had, in fact, said little and had drunk less. "He used to sit very quiet," said Wright, seduced by hubris into folly and turning to confide in the jury. "Dangerous quiet, if you ask me. And he'd stare at her with that look he has. He didn't need drink to make him dangerous."

Venetia had enjoyed her cross-examination of Stephen Wright and, by the time he was released, couldn't resist a glance of commiseration at Rufus as he rose to try to undo some of the harm. Both knew that more had been lost during the last few minutes than one witness's reliability. Every time a prosecution witness was discredited the whole case for the Crown became tainted with distrust. And she knew that she had had from the start one great advantage: there was no instinctive sympathy for the victim. Show the jury pictures of the violated body of a dead child, tender as a fledgeling, and some atavistic voice within always whispered, "Someone ought to pay for this." The need for vengeance, so easy to confuse with the imperatives of justice, always worked for the prosecution. The jury didn't want to convict the wrong man, but they did need to convict someone. The prosecution evidence was always weighted with the need to believe it true. But here those stark police photographs of the victim, the flabby pendulous belly and the spreading breasts, even the severed vessels, so horribly reminiscent of a pig's carcass hung on a butcher's hook, evoked disgust rather than pity. Her character had been effectively destroyed. It was seldom difficult in a murder case; the victim, after all, was not there to defend herself. Rita O'Keefe had been a drunken, unattractive, quarrelsome fifty-five-year-old with an insatiable appetite for gin and sex. Four of the jury were young, two only just of the qualifying age. The young were not indulgent towards age and ugliness. Their silent inner voices would be muttering a very different message: "She had it coming to her."

And it was now, in the second week and seventh day of the trial, that they had reached what, for Venetia, was the critical cross-examination of a prosecution witness: Mrs. Dorothy Scully, neighbour of the victim, a widow aged sixty-nine, the woman who had told the police, and now the court, that she had seen Garry Ashe leaving Number 397 at eleven-fifteen on the night of the murder.

Venetia had watched her during the examination-in-chief, noting her strengths, assessing her vulnerability. She knew what she needed to know about Mrs. Scully; she had made that her business. The woman was poor, but not desperately so, a widow managing on her pension. Westway had, after all, been relatively prosperous, a comfortable enclave of the respectable, reliable, law-abiding lower-middle class who owned their houses and took a pride in clean lace curtains and carefully tended front gardens, each a small triumph of individuality over the drab conformity. But their world was crashing down with their houses, rising in great choking clouds of ochre dust. Only a few houses were now left standing as the work on the road-widening went inexorably ahead. Even the painted slogans of protest on the boards which separated the vacant lots from the road were beginning to fade. Soon there would be nothing but tarmac and the ceaseless roar and screech of traffic thundering westward out of London. In time even memory would be powerless to conjure up what once had been. Mrs. Scully would be one of the last to leave. Her memories would be built on air. She had brought with her into the witness box her soon-to-be-obliterated past, her uncertain future, her respectability and her honesty. It was an inadequate armoury with which to confront one of the country's most formidable cross-examiners.

Venetia saw that she had purchased no new coat for this court appearance. A new coat was a major extravagance; only the onset of a particularly cold winter, or the wearing out of the old coat, could justify that expenditure. But the hat was obviously bought for the occasion, a pale-blue felt with a small brim, adorned with a huge white flower, imposing a note of discordant frivolity above the serviceable tweed.

She had taken the oath nervously, her voice almost inaudible. Twice during her evidence the judge had bent forward to ask her in his courteous old voice to speak up. She had, however, become more at ease as the examination proceeded. Rufus had tried to make it easy for her by occasionally repeating a question before she replied, but Venetia thought that his witness had found this more confusing than helpful. She guessed, too, that Mrs. Scully had disliked his over-loud, slightly hectoring upper-class voice and his habit of addressing his remarks to the air some few feet above the heads of the jury. Rufus had always been at his most effective when cross-examining a hostile witness. Mrs. Scully, old, pathetic, a little hard of hearing, brought out the bully in him. But she had been a good witness, answering simply and convincingly.

She had spent the evening from seven o'clock having supper and then watching a video of *The Sound of Music* with a friend, Mrs. Pierce, who lived five doors down the road. She didn't herself have a video recorder but her friend would hire a video each week, and usually invited her to spend the evening so that they could watch it together. She didn't normally leave the house at night but Mrs. Pierce lived so close that she didn't mind walking the short distance home and the road was well lit. She was certain of the time. When the film ended both she and her friend had said how much later it was than either of them had expected. The clock on her friend's mantelpiece had shown ten minutes past eleven and she had looked at her own watch because of her surprise that the time had passed so quickly. She had known Garry Ashe since he had come to live with his aunt. She had no doubt that it was he whom she had seen leaving Number 397. He had walked swiftly down the short garden path and had turned left on Westway, walking quickly away from her. She had stood watching him until he was out of sight, surprised that he was leaving the house so late. She had then let herself into Number 396. She couldn't remember whether there were any lights showing from the house next door. She rather thought that it had been in darkness.

It was towards the end of Rufus's examination-in-chief that the note was passed to Venetia. Ashe must have signalled to his solicitor, who went over to the dock. The note was handed from him to Venetia. It was written in a black ballpoint in a firm, small, upright hand. There was nothing impulsive or scrawled about this message. "Ask her what spectacles she was wearing on the night of the murder."

Venetia was careful not to look at the dock. It was, she knew, one of those moments of decision which could decide the outcome of the trial. And it went straight to that first rule of cross-examination learned when she was a pupil: never ask a question unless you already know the answer. She had five seconds to decide before she must rise to cross-examine. If she asked this question and the answer was wrong, Ashe would go down. But she was confident of two things. The first was that she did already know the answer; Ashe would not have written that note unless he was certain. The second was as vital. She had, if at all possible, to discredit Mrs. Scully. The woman's evidence, given with such obvious honesty, such certainty, had been damning.

She slipped the note under her papers as if it were an unimportant matter which she could attend to at leisure and took her time getting to her feet.

"Can you hear me clearly, Mrs. Scully?"

The woman nodded and whispered "Yes." Venetia smiled at her briefly. It was enough. The question, the encouraging smile, the warmth of the voice said it all: I'm a woman. We're on the same side. These pompous men don't frighten us. You've nothing to fear from me.

Venetia went over the evidence quietly so that when she was ready to move in for the kill the victim was happily compliant. The rows she had heard from next door, one male voice, the other, strongly Irish, recognizably that of Mrs. O'Keefe. Mrs. Scully had thought it had been the same male voice each time. But Mrs. O'Keefe was always entertaining her men friends. Perhaps a more accurate word would be "clients." Could she be certain that the voice was Garry's? Mrs. Scully could not be sure. The suggestion was skilfully planted that a natural animus against the aunt could have spilled over to include the nephew. They were not the kind of neighbours Mrs. Scully was used to.

"We come now, Mrs. Scully, to your identification of the defendant as the young man you saw leaving Number 397 on the night of the murder. Did you often see Garry leaving the house by the front door?"

"No, he usually used the back door and the garden gate because of his motorbike."

"So you would see him leaving, wheeling his bike out by the garden gate?"

"Sometimes. I could see from my bedroom window at the back."

"And as he kept his motorcycle in the garden, then that would be the natural way for him to leave?"

"I suppose so."

"Did you sometimes see him leaving by the back gate even when he hadn't the bike with him?"

"Once or twice, I suppose."

"Once or twice in all, or once or twice a week? Don't worry if you can't be absolutely precise. It isn't, after all, something you'd make a note of."

"I suppose I saw him leaving by the back door about two or three times a week. Sometimes with his bike, sometimes not."

"How often did you see him leaving by the front door?"

"I can't remember. Once when he had a taxi call for him. He left by the front door then."

"As one would expect. But did you often see him use the front door? You see, what I'm trying to find out here, because I think it will help the jury, is whether Garry normally used the front door or the back door when he left the house."

"I think they mostly used the back door, both of them."

"I see. They mostly used the back door." Then, still quietly, still in the same interested, sympathetic voice: "The spectacles you are wearing today, Mrs. Scully, are they new?"

The woman put up her hands to the frames as if uncertain that she was still wearing them. "Quite new. I got them on my birthday."

"Which was?"

"February 16th. That's how I remember."

"And you are quite sure about the date?"

"Oh yes." She turned to the judge as if anxious to explain. "I was going to have tea with my sister and I went into the shop to collect them on the way. I wanted to know what she thought about the new frames."

"And you are quite sure of the date, February 16th—five weeks after the murder of Mrs. O'Keefe?"

"Yes, quite sure."

"Did your sister think that the new glasses suited you?"

"She thought they were a bit fancy, but I wanted a change. You get tired of the same old frames. I thought I'd try something different."

And now the dangerous question, but Venetia knew what the answer would be. Women who are struggling on a low income don't pay for an eye test unnecessarily or see their spectacles as a fashion accessory.

She asked: "Is that why you changed the spectacles, Mrs. Scully? Because you wanted to try different frames?"

"No, it wasn't. I couldn't see properly with the old spectacles. That's why I went to the oculist."

"What couldn't you see specifically?"

"Well, the television really. It was getting so that I couldn't see the faces."

"Where do you watch the television, Mrs. Scully?"

"In the front sitting-room."

"Which is the same size as the one next door?"

"It must be. The houses are all alike."

"Not a large room, then. The jury have seen photographs of Mrs. O'Keefe's front room. About twelve feet square, would you say?"

"Yes, I suppose so. About that."

"And how far do you sit from the screen?"

The first sign of slight distress, an anxious look at the judge, then she said: "Well, I sit by the gas fire, and the telly's in the opposite corner, by the door."

"It's never comfortable to have the screen too close, is it? But let's see if we can be more definite." She looked at the judge, "If I may, my Lord," and received his confirming nod. Then she leaned forward to Ashe's solicitor, Neville Saunders. "If I ask this gentleman to move slowly towards his Lordship, will you tell me when the distance between them is roughly the same as the distance between you and the set?"

Neville Saunders, a little surprised but setting his features into the gravity appropriate to taking a more active part in the proceedings, got up from his seat and began his slow game of grandmother's footsteps. When he was ten feet from the bench, Mrs. Scully nodded. "About there."

"Ten feet or a little less."

She turned again to the witness. "Mrs. Scully, I know that you are an honest witness. You are trying to tell the truth to help the court and you know how important that truth is. The freedom, the whole future of a young life depends on it. You have told the court that you couldn't comfortably see your television set at ten feet. You have stated on oath that you recognized the defendant at twenty feet on a dark night and by the light of overhead street lighting. Can you be absolutely sure that you weren't mistaken? Can you be confident that it wasn't some other young man leaving the house that night, someone of roughly the same age and the same height? Take your time, Mrs. Scully. Think back. There's no hurry."

There were only eight words the witness needed to speak: "It was Garry Ashe. I saw him plainly." A professional criminal would have said them, would have known that in cross-examination you stick to your story doggedly, without alteration, without embellishment. But professional criminals know the system; Mrs. Scully was under the disadvantage of honesty, of nervousness, of the wish to please. There was a silence, then she said: "I thought it was Garry."

To leave it there or to go one step further? This was always the danger in cross-examination. Venetia said: "Because it was his house, he lived there. You would expect it to be Garry. But could you really see plainly, Mrs. Scully? Can you be sure?"

The woman stared at her. At last she said: "I suppose it could have been someone like him. But I thought at the time it was Garry."

"You thought at the time it was Garry, but it could have been someone like him. Precisely. It was a natural mistake, Mrs. Scully, but I suggest to you that it was a mistake. Thank you."

Rufus, of course, could not leave it like that. Entitled to re-examine on a point requiring clarification, he got portentously to his feet, hitched up his gown and surveyed the air above the witness box with the puzzled frown of a man expecting a change in the weather. Mrs. Scully looked at him with the anxiety of a guilty child who knows that she has disappointed the grown-ups. Rufus attempted with some success to modify his tone.

"Mrs. Scully, I am sorry to keep you but there is one point on which I think that the jury may be somewhat confused. During your examination-in-chief you said that you had no doubt that it was Garry Ashe whom you saw leaving his aunt's house at a quarter past eleven on the night of the murder. However, during cross-examination by my learned friend you have said—and I quote—"I suppose it could have been someone like him. But I thought at the time it was Garry." Now, I'm sure you will realize that these two statements can't both be right. The jury may find it difficult to understand what precisely it is you are saying. I confess I find myself somewhat confused. So I have just the one question. The man you saw leaving Number 397 that night, who do you believe he was?"

And now she was anxious only to be let out of the witness box, no longer to feel that she was being pulled between two people who both wanted a clear answer from her, but not the same answer. She looked at the judge, as if hoping that he would answer for her, or at least help her to a decision. The court waited. Then the answer came and it came with the desperation of truth.

"I believe that it was Garry Ashe."

Venetia knew that Rufus had little choice but to call his next witness, Mrs. Rose Pierce, to confirm the time at which Mrs. Scully had left her house. Time was of the essence. If Mrs. O'Keefe had been killed immediately or shortly after arriving home from the pub, Ashe would have had thirty minutes in which to kill, shower, dress and set out on his walk.

Mrs. Pierce, plump, red-cheeked, bright-eyed and padded in a black woollen coat topped with a flat hat, fitted comfortably into the witness box like Mrs. Noah ensconced in the cabin of her ark. No doubt, thought Venetia, there were places which Mrs. Pierce might find intimidating but the premier court at the Old Bailey was not among them. She gave her profession as retired children's nurse, "A nanny, my Lord," and gave the impression that she was as capable of dealing with the adult nonsenses of the male sex as she had been with their childhood delinquencies. Even Rufus, facing her, seemed to be visited by uncomfortable memories of nursery discipline. His examination was brief and her answers were confident. Mrs. Scully had left her house just before Mrs. Pierce's carriage clock, given to her by one of her employers, had chimed quarter past eleven.

Venetia rose at once to ask her single question.

"Mrs. Pierce, can you remember whether Mrs. Scully complained that she had difficulty in seeing the video that evening?"

Mrs. Pierce was surprised into unexpected loquacity.

"Funny you should ask that, learned counsel madam. Dorothy complained at the time that the picture wasn't clear. Mind you, that was when she had her old specs. She'd been saying for some time that she ought to have her eyes tested and I told her the sooner the better and we had a chat over whether she'd stick to the same frames or try something different. Try something new, I told her. Be a devil. You only live once. Well, she got the new specs on her birthday and she's had no trouble since."

Venetia thanked her and sat down. She felt a little sorry for Rufus. The night of the murder could so easily have been the one on which Mrs. Scully had made no complaint of poor sight. But only the most naïve believed that luck played no part in the criminal-justice system.

On the next day, Thursday, 12 September, Venetia stood up to open the case for the defence. She had already effectively made that case in her cross-examination. Now, by the early afternoon, she had only one witness left to call: the accused.

She knew that she had to put Ashe in the box. He would have insisted.

She had recognized early in their professional relationship the vanity, the mixture of conceit and bravado, which might even now undo all the good achieved by her cross-examination of the Crown witnesses. He wasn't going to be cheated out of this final public performance. All those hours of sitting patiently in the dock were for him a prelude to the moment when at last he could answer for himself and the case would be won or lost. She knew him well enough to be sure that what he had most hated was the knowledge that he had to sit while others spoke, others argued their case. He was the most important person in that courtroom. It was for him that a High Court judge in his scarlet robe sat to the right of the carved royal arms, for him that twelve men and women sat there listening patiently for hour after hour, for him that the distinguished members of the Bar in their wigs and gowns questioned, cross-questioned and argued. Venetia knew that it was easy for the accused to feel that he was merely the ineffectual object of others' concerns, that the system had taken him over, was using him, that he was on display so that others could demonstrate their cleverness, their expertise. Now he would have his chance. She knew that it was a risk; if the conceit, the bravado proved stronger than his control then they were in trouble.

Within minutes of her examination-in-chief she knew that she needn't have worried. His performance—and she had no doubt that it was that—was beautifully judged. He was, of course, prepared for her first question, but she had not been prepared for his answer.

"Garry, did you love your aunt?"

A short pause, and then: "I was very fond of her, and I was sorry for her. I don't think I know what people mean by love."

They were the first words he had spoken in court except for that plea of not guilty spoken in a firm low voice. The court was absolutely silent. The words fell on the quiet expectant air. Venetia could sense the reaction of the jury. Of course he didn't know, how could he? A boy who had never known his father, had been thrown out by his mother before he was eight, been taken into care, shunted from foster parent to foster parent, transferred from one children's home to another, seen as a nuisance from the moment he was born. He had never known tenderness, security or disinterested affection. How could he know the meaning of love?

She had an extraordinary sense during his examination of their working together like two actors who had played opposite each other for years, recognizing each other's signals, judging each pause for its effectiveness, being careful not to spoil the other's most powerful moment, not because of affection or even mutual respect, but because this was a double act and its success depended on that instinctive understanding in which each contributed to the desired end. His story had the merit of consistency and simplicity. What he had first said to the police he now told the court without alteration or embellishment.

Yes, his aunt and he had had a disagreement while they were at the Duke of Clarence. It had been a resurgence of the old argument: she wanted him to go on taking photographs of her when she and her customers were having sex, he wanted to stop. It had been a disagreement rather than a violent quarrel, but she had been drunk and he had thought it wise to get away, to walk alone through the night to think out whether it was time for him to move on.

"And is that what you wanted, to leave your aunt?"

"Part of me wanted that, part of me wanted to stay. I was fond of her. I think she did need me, and it was home."

So he had walked through the streets behind Westway as far as Shepherd's Bush before returning. There were people passing, but not many. He had noticed no one in particular. He wasn't even sure which streets he had walked. He had arrived home just after midnight to find his aunt's body lying on the single divan in the sitting-room and had at once telephoned the police. No, he had not touched the body. He could see as soon as he entered the room that she was dead.

He was unshaken in cross-examination, ready to say in reply to questions that he could not remember or was not sure. He never once looked at the jury, but they in their box to the right of him kept their eyes on him. When he finally left the witness box she wondered why she had ever doubted him.

Her final speech for the defence took each of the prosecution's points one by one and persuasively demolished them. She spoke to the jury as if she were confiding to them the truth of a matter which, with good reason, had caused both them and her concern, but which could now be seen in its true, its reasonable, its essentially innocent light. Where was his motive? It had been suggested that he hoped to be his aunt's heir, but all Mrs. O'Keefe had in prospect was the money for the compulsory sale of her house, when it came through, and that was insufficient to cover her debts. Her nephew knew that she spent lavishly, particularly on drink, that her creditors were pressing, that debt-collectors called at the house. What could he expect to receive? By her death he had gained nothing and lost a home. Then there was that single small splash of Mrs. O'Keefe's blood on the head of the shower and the two spots on the stairs. It had been suggested that Ashe had killed his aunt naked and had showered before leaving the house to take a walk designed to provide an alibi. But a visitor, particularly if he were a regular client, would have known the house, known that the tap of the bathroom washbasin was stiff and gave an uncertain flow of water. What more natural than that he should wash his bloody hands under the shower?

The prosecution had relied largely on one witness, the neighbour, Mrs. Scully, who said in her examination-in-chief that she had seen Garry leaving the house by the front door at quarter past eleven. The jury had seen Mrs. Scully in the witness box. She may have struck them, as surely she did everyone who had heard her, as an honest witness trying to tell the truth. But what she had briefly seen was a male figure at night under the high sodium lights designed to shine brightly on the busy road, but apt to throw confusing shadows over the fronts of the houses. At the time she was wearing spectacles through which she couldn't even clearly see the faces on her television screen at less than ten feet. In cross-examination she had told the jury: "I suppose it could have been someone like him. But I thought at the time it was Garry." The jury might feel that Mrs. Scully's identification of Garry Ashe, central to the prosecution's case, could not be relied upon.

She ended: "Garry Ashe has told you that he went for that night walk because he couldn't face his aunt when she returned home from the Duke of Clarence pub, drunk, as he knew she would be. He needed time to think about their life together, about his future, whether it was time to leave. In his own words in the witness box: 'I had to decide what I was going to make of my life.' Remembering those obscene photographs, which I am sorry you had to see, you may wonder why he didn't leave before. He has told you why. She was his only living relation. The home she provided was the only home he had ever known. He thought that she needed him. Members of the jury, it is hard to walk out on someone who needs you, however inconvenient, however perverse that need.

"So he walked unseeing and unseen through the night and returned to the horror of that blood-splattered sitting-room. There is no forensic evidence to link him with the crime. The police found no blood on his clothes or his person, his fingerprints were not on that knife. Any one of her numerous clients could have called that night.

"Members of the jury, no one deserves to be murdered. A human life is a human life whether the victim is a prostitute or a saint. In death as in life we are all equal before the law. Mrs. O'Keefe did not deserve to die. But Mrs. O'Keefe, like all prostitutes—and that, members of the jury, is what she was—put herself peculiarly at risk because of her lifestyle. You have heard what that lifestyle was. You have seen the photographs which her nephew was induced or compelled to take. She was a sexually rapacious woman who could be affectionate and generous but who, in drink, was abusive and violent. We do not know who it was she let in that night or what happened between them. The medical evidence is that no sexual act took place immediately before death. But is it not overwhelmingly likely, members of the jury, that she was murdered by one of her clients, killed out of jealousy, rage, frustration, hatred or the lust to kill? It was a murder of great brutality. Half drunk, she opened her door to her murderer. That was her tragedy. It is also a tragedy for the young man who is in the dock in this court today.

"My learned friend, in his opening address, put the matter to you quite clearly. If you are convinced beyond reasonable doubt that my client murdered his aunt, then your verdict must be one of guilty. But if, after considering all the evidence, you have a reasonable doubt that it was indeed his hand that struck down Mrs. O'Keefe, then it will be your duty to return a verdict of not guilty."

All judges are actors. Mr. Justice Moorcroft's forte, a part which he had played for so many years that it had become instinctive, was a courteous reasonableness occasionally enlivened with shafts of mordant wit. During his summing up it was his habit to lean well forward towards the jury, a pencil delicately spanning the first finger of each hand, and address them as equals who had kindly agreed to give up their valuable time to assist him with a problem which had its difficulties, but, as with all human concerns, was susceptible to reason. The summing up, as always with this judge, was exemplary in its comprehensiveness and fairness. There could be no appeal in a court of law on the grounds of misdirection; with this judge there never had been.

The jury listened with impassive faces. Watching them, Venetia thought, as she often did, that it was a curious system but one which worked remarkably well provided that your first priority was the protection of the innocent rather than the conviction of the guilty. It wasn't designed—how could it be?—to elicit the truth, the whole truth and nothing but the truth. Even the Continental inquisitorial system couldn't do that. It would have gone hard with her client if it had.

There was nothing more that she could do for him now. The jury were given their charge and filed out. The judge rose, the court bowed and waited, standing, until he had left. Venetia heard above her the murmuring and shuffling as the public gallery emptied. She had nothing to do now but to await the verdict.

2

In Pawlet Court, on the western boundary of the Middle Temple, the gas lamps were glowing into light. Hubert St John Langton, Head of Chambers, watched from his window as he had on every evening when he had been working in Chambers, for the last forty years. It was the time of the year, the time of day, that he loved best. Now the small court, one of the loveliest in the Middle Temple, took on the soft refulgent glow of an early-autumn evening, the boughs of the great horse chestnut seeming to solidify as he watched, the rectangles of light in the Georgian windows enhancing the atmosphere of ordered, almost domestic, eighteenth-century calm. Beneath him the cobbles between the pavements of York stone glistened as if they had been polished. Drysdale Laud moved up beside him. For a moment they stood in silence, then Langton turned away.

He said: "That's what I'm going to miss most, the lighting of the lamps. But it's not quite the same now they're automatic. I used to like watching for the lamplighter to come into the court. When that stopped, it seemed as if a whole era had gone for ever."

So he was going, he'd actually made up his mind at last. Laud carefully kept from his voice either surprise or regret. He said: "This place is going to miss you."

There could hardly, he thought, have been a more banal exchange over a decision he had been awaiting with increasing impatience for over a year. It was time for the old man to go. He wasn't very old, not yet seventy-three, but in the last year Laud's critical anticipatory eyes had seen the gradual but inexorable draining of powers physical and mental. Now he watched as Langton seated himself heavily at his desk, the desk that had been his grandfather's and which he had hoped one day might be his son's. That hope, like so many others, had been swept away in that avalanche above Klosters.

He said: "I suppose the tree will have to go eventually. People complain that it shuts out too much light in summer. I'll be glad not to be here when they take the axe to it."

Laud felt a small surge of irritation. Sentimentality was something new for Langton. He said: "It won't be an axe, it will be a heavy-duty chainsaw, and I don't suppose they'll do it. The tree is protected." He waited for a moment, then asked with studied unconcern: "When were you thinking of leaving?"

"At the end of the year. Once these decisions are made there's no point in dragging things out. I'm telling you now because we need to give thought to my successor. There's the Chambers meeting coming up in October. I thought we might discuss it then."

Discuss? What was there to discuss? He and Langton had run Chambers between them for the last ten years. The two archbishops—wasn't that how Chambers spoke of them? Colleagues might use the words with an undertone of slight resentment, even of derision, but they expressed a reality. He decided to be frank. Langton had become increasingly vague and indecisive, but surely not about this. He had to know where he stood. If there was going to be a fight it was better to be prepared.

He said: "I'd rather thought that you wanted me to succeed you. We work together well. I thought that Chambers had come to take it for granted."

"That you were crown prince? I expect they have. But it might not be as straightforward as I expected. Venetia is interested."

"Venetia? This is the first I've heard of it. She's never shown the slightest interest in becoming Head of Chambers."

"Not until now. But I've heard a rumour that she's changed her mind. And she is, of course, the senior. Only just, but there it is. She was called a term before you."

Laud said: "Venetia made her position perfectly plain four years ago, when you were off for two months with glandular fever and we had a Chambers meeting. I asked her then whether she wanted to take the chair. I remember her reply perfectly. 'I have no ambition to occupy that seat either temporarily or when Hubert decides to vacate it.' What part has she ever played in running this place, in the more tedious chores, even in the finance? All right, she comes to Chambers meetings and protests at whatever other people propose, but what does she actually do? Her own career has always come first."

"Perhaps this is about her career. I've been wondering if she might not have an ambition to become a judge. She's apparently enjoying sitting as an assistant recorder. If so, succeeding me as Head of Chambers would be important to her."

"It's important to me. For God's sake, Hubert, you can't let her cut me out because I happened to have appendicitis at the wrong time. The only reason she's senior to me is because I was in the operating theatre on the day she was called. It put me a term behind. I don't think Chambers is going to choose Venetia because she was called in the Michaelmas term and I was forced to wait until the Lent."

Langton said: "But it does make her senior. If she wants the job it will be embarrassing to reject her."

"Because she's a woman? I thought we'd come to that. Well, it may terrify the more timid members of Chambers but I think they'll put fairness over political correctness."

Langton said mildly, "But it isn't exactly political correctness, is it? We do have a policy. There is a code of practice on sexual discrimination. That's what it's going to look like if we pass her over."

Trying to control the mounting anger in his voice, Laud said: "Has she spoken to you? Has she actually said she wants it?"

"Not to me. Someone—I think it was Simon—said she'd hinted at it to him."

It would be Simon Costello, thought Laud. Number Eight, Pawlet Court, like all Chambers, was a hotbed of gossip, but Simon's contribution to it was notorious for inaccuracy. If you wanted reliable news you didn't go to Simon Costello.

He said: "It's pure guesswork. If Venetia wanted to initiate a campaign she'd hardly begin with Simon. He's one of her *bêtes noires.*" He added: "It's important to avoid a contest if it's at all possible. It'll be fatal if we descend to personalities. Chambers could become a bear garden."

Langton frowned: "Oh, I hardly think so. If we have to vote, that's what we'll do. People will accept the majority decision."

Laud thought with some bitterness: And you no longer care. You won't be here. Ten years of working together, of covering up your indecision, of advising without appearing to advise. And you do nothing. Don't you realize that defeat would be, for me, an intolerable humiliation?

He said: "I can't think she'll have much support."

"Oh I don't know. She's probably our most distinguished lawyer."

"Oh, come off it, Hubert! Desmond Ulrick is our most distinguished lawyer beyond question."

Langton stated the obvious. "But Desmond won't want it when the time comes. I doubt whether he'll even notice the change."

Laud was calculating. He said: "The people at the Salisbury Annexe and those who work mainly from home probably care less than those physically in Chambers, but I doubt whether more than a minority will want Venetia. She's not a conciliator."

"But is that what we need? There are going to have to be changes, Drysdale. I'm happy I shan't be here to see them, but I know they'll come. People talk about managing change. There'll be new people in Chambers, new systems."

"Managing change. That fashionable shibboleth. Venetia might well manage change, but will they be the changes that Chambers want? She can manage systems; she'd be disastrous at managing people."

"I thought you liked her. I've always seen you—well, I suppose as friends."

"I do like her. In so far as she has a friend in Chambers, I'm that friend. We share a liking for mid-twentieth-century art, we go occasionally to the theatre, we dine out about once every two months. I enjoy her company, presumably she enjoys mine. That doesn't mean I think she'll make a good Head of Chambers. Anyway, do we want a criminal lawyer? They're a minority here. We've never looked to the criminal Bar for the Head of Chambers."

Langton answered an objection understood but not stated. "Isn't that rather a snobbish view? I thought we were getting away from that. If law has to do with justice, with people's rights, their liberty, their freedom, isn't what Venetia does more important than Desmond's preoccupation with the minutiae of international maritime law?"

"It may be. We're not discussing relative importance, we're choosing the Head of Chambers. Venetia would be a disaster. And there are one or two other matters which we'll have to discuss at Chambers meeting on which she'll be difficult. What pupils to take on as tenants, for example. She won't want Catherine Beddington."

"She's Catherine's sponsor."

"That will make her objections more compelling. And there's another thing. If you're hoping to get Harry an extension of his contract, forget it. She wants to do away with the Senior Clerk and appoint a practice manager. That'll be the least of the changes if she gets her way."

There was another silence. Langton sat at his desk as if spent. Then he said: "She seems to have been a bit on edge in the last few weeks. Not herself. Is anything wrong, do you know?"

So he had noticed. That was the difficulty with premature senility. You could never be sure when the gears in the mind might not engage again, the old Langton disconcertingly assert himself.

Laud said: "Her daughter's home. Octavia left boarding school in July and I gather she's done nothing since. Venetia's let her have the basement flat so they shouldn't be on top of each other, but it isn't easy. Octavia's not yet eighteen, she needs some control, some advice. A convent education is hardly the best preparation for running around London unsupervised. Venetia's over-busy, she can do without the worry. And they've never got on. Venetia isn't maternal. She'd be a good enough mother to a beautiful, clever, ambitious daughter, but that's not the kind she's got."

"What happened to her husband after the divorce? Is he still in the picture?"

"Luke Cummins? I don't think she's seen him for years. I'm not sure he even sees Octavia. I believe he's married again and lives somewhere in the West Country. Married to a potter or a weaver. A craftsperson of some kind. I've got a feeling they're not well off. Venetia never mentions him. She's always been ruthless in writing off her failures."

"I suppose that's all that's wrong, worry about Octavia?"

"It's enough, I should have thought, but I'm only guessing. She doesn't talk to me about it. Our friendship doesn't extend to personal confidences. The fact that we go to an occasional exhibition together doesn't mean that I understand her—or any other woman, come to that. It's interesting, though, the power she exerts in Chambers. Has it ever occurred to you that a woman, when she is powerful, is more powerful than a man?"

"Powerful in a different way, perhaps."

Laud said: "It's a power partly based on fear. Perhaps the fear is atavistic, memories of babyhood. Women change the nappy, give the breast or withhold it."

Langton said with a faint smile: "Not now, apparently. Fathers change nappies and it's usually a bottle."

"But I'm right, Hubert, about power and fear. I wouldn't say it outside these walls, but life in Chambers would be a great deal easier if Venetia fell under that convenient Number 11 bus." He paused, and then asked the question to which he needed an answer. "So I have your support, have I? Can I take it that I'm your choice to succeed you as Head of Chambers?"

The question had been unwelcome. The tired eyes looked into his and Langton seemed to shrink back in his chair as if bracing himself against a physical attack. And when he spoke Laud didn't miss that quavering note of petulance.

"If that is the will of Chambers, of course you will have my support. But if Venetia wants it I don't see how she can reasonably be rejected. It goes by seniority. Venetia is the senior."

It wasn't enough, thought Laud bitterly. By God, it wasn't enough.

He stood looking down at the man he had thought was his friend and, for the first time in that long association, it was a look more judgemental than affectionate. It was as if he were seeing Langton with the critical, un-clouded eyes of a stranger, noting with detached interest the first ravages of merciless time. The strong regular features were losing flesh. The nose was sharper and there were hollows under the jutting cheekbones. The deep-set eyes were less clear and beginning to hold the puzzled acceptance of old age. The mouth, once so firm-set, so uncompromising, was slackening into an oc-casional moist quaver. Once his had been a head formed, or so it seemed, to be topped by a judge's wig. And that surely was what Langton had always hoped for. Despite the success, the satisfaction in succeeding his grandfather as Head of Chambers, there had always hung about him the uncomfortable whiff of hopes unrealized, of a talent which had promised more than it had achieved. And like his grandfather, he had stayed on too long.

Both, too, had been unlucky in their only sons. Hubert's father had re-turned from the First World War with lungs half destroyed by gas and a mind tormented by horrors of which he was never able to speak. He had had energy enough to father his only child, but had never effectively worked again and had died in 1925. Hubert's only son, Matthew, as clever and am-bitious as his father, sharing his father's enthusiasm for the law, had been killed by an avalanche while skiing two years after being called to the Bar. It was after that tragedy that the final spark of ambition had seemed to flicker, then die in his father.

Laud thought, "But it hasn't died in me. I've supported him for the last ten years, covered his inadequacies, done his tedious chores for him. He may be opting out of responsibility but, by God, he's not going to opt out of this."

But he knew with a sickness of the heart that this was mere posturing. There was no way in which he could win. If he forced a contest Chambers would be embroiled in an acrimonious dissent which would be publicly scandalous and could last for decades. And if he won by a narrow margin, what legitimacy would that confer? Either way, he wouldn't easily be for-given. And if he didn't make a fight for it, then Venetia Aldridge would be the next Head of Chambers.

3

It was never possible to estimate how long the jury would be out. Sometimes a case which had seemed so strong as to admit no possible question of the accused's guilt resulted in a wait of hours, while one of apparent doubt and complexity produced a verdict with astonishing speed. Counsel had different ways of occupying the dead hours. The occasional sweepstake on the time the jury would take to arrive at their verdict provided at least a diversion. Some played chess or Scrabble, others went down to the cells to share the suspense with their clients, to encourage, sustain, perhaps warn, while others reviewed the evidence with their colleagues and meditated possible lines for an appeal if the case went against them. Venetia preferred to spend the waiting time alone.

As a junior she had walked the corridors of the Bailey, moving from the Edwardian baroque of the old building to the simplicity of the new, then down to the marbled splendour of the Great Hall to pace under the dome between its lunettes and blue mosaics and contemplate once again the familiar monuments while she emptied her mind of the things she might have done better, those she could have done worse, and prepared herself for the verdict.

Now this perambulation had become for her too obvious a defence against anxiety. She preferred to sit in the library, and her insistence on solitude ensured that she was almost always alone. She took a volume from the shelf without noticing its title and carried it over to a table with no intention of reading.

"Garry, did you love your aunt?" The question brought to mind a similar question asked—when?—eighty-four years earlier, in March 1912, when Frederick Henry Seddon had been found guilty of the murder of his lodger, Miss Eliza Barrow. "Seddon, did you like Miss Barrow?" And how could he convincingly answer that, of the woman he had cheated out of her fortune and had buried in a pauper's grave? The Frog had been fascinated by the case. He had used that question to demonstrate the devastating effect which one question could have on the result of the trial. The Frog had come up with other instances too: the expert witness for the defence in the Rouse burning-car case whose evidence had been discredited because he couldn't give the coefficient of expansion of brass; the judge, Mr. Justice Darling, leaning forward to intervene in the trial of Major Armstrong to ask why the defendant, who claimed that the arsenic he had bought was for the destruction of dandelions, had parcelled it up into small portions. And she, a fifteen-year-old, sitting in that small, under-furnished bed-sitting-room, had said: "Because a witness forgets a scientific fact or the judge decides to intervene? Is that justice?"

The Frog had for a moment looked pained, because he needed to believe in justice, he needed to believe in the law. The Frog. Edmund Albert Froggett. Improbably a bachelor of arts, obtained by external study at some unspecified university. Edmund Froggett, who had made her a lawyer. She acknowledged this truth with gratitude to that odd, mysterious, pathetic little man, but he seldom came into her mind as an invited guest. The memory of the day when their relationship ended was so painful that gratitude was subsumed in embarrassment, fear and shame. If she thought of him it was because, as now in this moment, some trick of memory intruded on the present and she was fifteen again, sitting in the Frog's bed-sitting-room listening to his stories, learning about the criminal law.

They would be seated one each side of his small hissing gas fire with only one section burning because the Frog had to put coins into the meter and the Frog was poor. But there was a gas ring beside the fire, and he would make cocoa for them both, strong and not too sweet, just as she liked it. She must have been there with him in summer surely, in spring and in autumn, but in memory it was always winter, the unlined curtains drawn, the noise of the school muted now that the boys were in bed. Her parents, in their sitting-room in the main part of the house, were unworried about her, because she was supposed to be in her bedroom finishing her homework. At nine o'clock she would break off their talk and go downstairs to say good-night, to answer the predictable questions about how her work had gone, the timetable for the next day. But she would return always to the only room in the house in which she had ever been happy, to the hiss of the fire, the armchair with the broken springs which was made comfortable because the Frog would take a pillow from his bed and put it at her back, to the Frog sitting opposite her in the upright chair with his six volumes of *Notable British Trials* piled on the floor by his side.

He had been the least regarded, the most exploited of the teachers at her father's suburban prep school, Danesford, where he had been employed to teach English and history throughout the school, but was required to undertake almost any job at the headmaster's whim. He was a neat, delicately boned little man, snub-nosed, with small bright eyes behind the pebble glasses and a fringe of ginger hair. Inevitably he was nicknamed the Frog by the boys. He could have been a good teacher, given the chance, but the small barbarians could smell out a natural victim in their juvenile jungle, and the Frog's life was a patiently borne hell of noisy insurrection and calculated cruelty.

If a friend or acquaintance asked Venetia about her childhood—and few did—she had an answer ready, always in the same words, always spoken with a tone of casual acceptance which somehow still managed to prohibit further curiosity.

"My father kept a boys' prep school. Not exactly the Dragon or Summerfields. One of those cheaper places which parents send their children to when they want them out of the way. I don't know who disliked it most, the pupils, the staff or I. But I suppose being brought up with a hundred small boys wasn't a bad preparation for a criminal lawyer. Actually, my father taught rather well. The pupils could have done worse."

She herself could hardly have done worse. The school, the pretentious red-brick residence of a nineteenth-century local worthy and former mayor, had originally been built some two miles outside the pleasant Berkshire town which had then been little more than a village. By the time Clarence Aldridge bought the school in 1963, using a legacy from his father, the village had grown into a small town, though still with an individual character and a sense of identity. Ten years later it had become a dormitory suburb, spreading over the green fields in a creeping cancer of red brick and concrete, executive estates, small shopping precincts, office buildings and blocks of flats. The fields between Danesford and the town had been bought by the local council for housing, but when the money ran out with only part of the estate developed, the ground remaining had been left vacant, a junk-strewn wilderness of scrub and broken trees, the playground and the rubbish tip of the surrounding estate. She would cycle through it on her way to the high school, a journey she came to dread but invariably took because the alternative route was twice as long and by way of the main road, and her father had forbidden her to use it. Once she had disobeyed him and had been seen by one of his friends as his car sped past. Her father's anger had been dreadful, painful and long-lasting. The weekday journey across the scrubland, over the railway bridge which divided it from the town, and through the housing estate was an ordeal. Daily she ran the gauntlet of taunts and shouted obscenities, provoked by the sight of her school uniform. Daily she tried to judge the roads which were most clear, on the watch for the larger, more frightening boys, accelerating or slowing down to miss the waiting mob, despising herself and hating her tormentors.

The high school was a refuge from more than the estate. She was happy there, or as happy as she was capable of being. But her life was so separate from her life at Danesford as her parents' only child that all her schooldays she had the sensation of living in two worlds. One she would prepare for when she put on the dark-green uniform and knotted her school tie, and would physically take possession of when she dismounted and wheeled her bicycle through the school gates. The other would receive her back each late afternoon, a world composed of boys' voices, feet ringing on boards, the slamming of desktops, the smell of cooking, drying clothes and young inadequately washed bodies and, overlaying all, the scent of anxiety, incipient failure and fear. That, too, had its solace. She sought it out every evening in the Frog's small, under-furnished bed-sitting-room.

He used his six volumes of the *Notable British Trials* series as textbooks and training exercises, he putting the case for the prosecution, she for the defence, and then changing roles. Every character in the trial became familiar to her, every murder projected an image as powerful as it was vivid, feeding an imagination which was fertile but circumscribed always by a sense of reality, the need to know that those desperate men and women, some buried in lime in the prison yard, weren't the creatures of her imagination but had actually lived, breathed and died, that their tragedies could be analysed, discussed and made sense of. Alfred Arthur Rouse, with his blazing car flaming like a fatal beacon in a Northampton lane; Madeleine Smith proffering a cup of cocoa, and perhaps arsenic, through the bars of a Glasgow basement; George Joseph Smith playing the harmonium in a Highgate lodging house while the woman he had seduced and murdered lay dead in the bath upstairs; Herbert Rowse Armstrong holding out the scone dosed with arsenic to his rival with the words "Excuse fingers"; William Wallace making his conscientious way through the suburbs of Liverpool to find the non-existent Menlove Gardens East.

The Seddon case was one which they found particularly fascinating. The Frog would briefly recount the facts before they turned once again to the transcript of the trial.

"The year: 1910. The accused: Seddon, Frederick Henry. Rapacious, miserly, obsessed with money and profit. Lives with his wife, Margaret Anne, and their five children, his elderly father and a servant girl at Torrington Park in Islington. In a healthy way of business with the London and Manchester Industrial Insurance Company. Owns his house and has acquired a chain of small properties in different parts of London. And then, on 25th July 1910, he acquires a lodger. Eliza Mary Barrow is forty-nine, unattractive in character and personal habits, but she does have money. She also has an eight-year-old orphan, Ernie Grant, the child of a friend, who moves in with her and shares her bed. He probably loved her, no one else did. Ernie's uncle, Mr. Hook, and his wife also moved into the Seddon house but didn't stay long. They left after a quarrel with Miss Barrow and a scene with Seddon, whom they accused of trying to get hold of Miss Barrow's money. And over a period of little more than a year he did just that. It was worth having. We are talking of 1910, remember. One thousand six hundred in three-and-a-half-per-cent India stock, the leasehold interest in a public house and a barber's shop. Two hundred and twelve on deposit in a savings bank, and cash in gold and notes which she kept under the bed. All was transferred to Seddon in return for a promised annuity of just over a hundred and fifty pounds per year. An annuity means that Seddon took all the money and promised to pay her in return that amount each year for the rest of her life."

Venetia said: "She was asking to be murdered, wasn't she? Once he'd got his hands on all her cash she was just a liability."

"Certainly no lawyer would have advised such a show of trust. But being cold-blooded and greedy for money doesn't make a man a murderer. You must try to keep an open mind if you're going to make a speech for the defence."

"You mean I have to believe he didn't do it?"

"No, what you believe isn't at issue. Your job is to convince the jury that the Crown failed to make out its case against the prisoner beyond reasonable doubt. But you should never reach a decision about anything without first examining the facts."

"How did he do it? All right, how did the prosecution allege that he did it?"

"With arsenic. On 1st September 1911 Miss Barrow complained of stomach pains, sickness and other unpleasant symptoms. A doctor was called and was in regular attendance for two weeks, but early in the morning of 14th September Seddon called at the doctor's house to tell him that his patient was dead."

"Didn't the doctor order a post-mortem?"

"I suppose he saw no reason for one. He issued a death certificate showing that Miss Barrow had died from epidemic diarrhoea. That same morning Seddon arranged for her to be buried in a common grave for four pounds and demanded a commission from the undertaker for introducing the business."

"The common grave was a mistake, wasn't it?"

"So was the way he treated Miss Barrow's relations when they began inquiries. He was arrogant, unfeeling and offensive. Not surprisingly, they became suspicious and decided to communicate with the Director of Public Prosecutions. Miss Barrow's body was exhumed and arsenic was found. Seddon was arrested, and his wife six months later; they were jointly charged with murder."

She had said: "But wasn't he hanged because he was avaricious and greedy, not because the Crown really had a case? He was supposed to have sent his fifteen-year-old daughter, Maggie, to buy the arsenic for him, but she denied it. I don't think that chemist's evidence—Mr. Thorley, wasn't it?—can be relied upon. Do you think you could have got him off?"

The Frog had given a little smile, but not without satisfaction. He had his small vanities and sometimes she amused herself by provoking them.

He had said: "You're asking me if I could have done better than Edward Marshall Hall. Now, there was a marvellous advocate. I would like to have heard him, but of course he died in 1927. Not a great lawyer, he was said to dread the Court of Appeal. But one of the great advocates, wonderfully eloquent, an astonishing flow of language. Of course, it wouldn't do today. That kind of histrionic, dramatic advocacy hasn't a place in a modern court. But there was something he said I have never forgotten. I'll write it down for you. 'I have no scenery to help me and no words are written for me to speak. There is no curtain. But out of the vivid dream of somebody else's life I have to create an atmosphere—for that is advocacy.' Out of the vivid dream of somebody else's life. I like that."

She had said: "I like that too."

The Frog had said: "I think you're going to have the right kind of voice. Of course, you're young yet. It may not develop."

"What kind of voice is that?"

"Attractive to listen to. Not strident. Versatile, warm, perfectly modulated and controlled. Persuasive—above all persuasive."

"Is that so very important?"

"It's vital. Norman Birkett had a voice like that. I wish I'd had a chance to hear it. Voice is as important to an advocate as it is to an actor. I might have been a lawyer if I'd had a voice. I'm afraid mine lacks strength. It wouldn't carry as far as the jury box."

Venetia had bent her head over the *Notable Trials* volume so that he wouldn't see her smile. It wasn't only his voice—high, pedantic, with that occasional disconcerting rodent squeak; even to picture a wig atop that dry thatch of ginger hair or a gown on that diminutive, graceless body was risible. And she had overheard her father's dismissive comments on the Frog's lack of qualifications too often to have any doubt that he had had few chances in life. But she enjoyed his praise, and the game they played together had become an addiction. It satisfied her need for order and certainty. The Frog's bed-sitting-room with its faint smell of the gas fire and the two ragged chairs, provided a refuge more reassuring even than her desk at the high school. Each gave what the other needed; he was a wonderful teacher and she was an intelligent, enthusiastic pupil. Night after night she would hurry through her homework and choose her moment to slip unobserved from the main schoolhouse, across to the annexe and up the lino-covered stairs to his room, to listen to his stories, to indulge in their common obsession.

The game ended three days after her fifteenth birthday. The Frog had borrowed from the local library an account of the trial of Florence May-brick, which they were to discuss that evening. He had left the book with her overnight, but she was anxious not to carry it to school or to leave it in her room, where it could invite the curiosity of one of the school's two maids, or be discovered by her parents. She had very little faith that her privacy was ever respected. She decided to leave the volume in the Frog's room. Her knock was perfunctory; she hardly expected to find him in. It was seven-thirty and he would be supervising the boys' breakfast. The door, as she expected, was unlocked.

To her astonishment the Frog was there. There was a large canvas suit-case on the bed, its battered lid open. The counterpane was covered with a tumble of shirts, pyjamas and underclothes, only his socks were neatly twisted into balls. It seemed to her that she was simultaneously aware of his look of horror at her eruption into the room and of the pair of pants, soiled at the crotch, which, following her gaze, he shoved with trembling hands under the lid of the suitcase.

She said: "Where are you going? Why are you packing? Are you leaving?"

He turned away from her. She could only just hear his words. "I'm sorry if I distressed you. I didn't mean . . . I didn't realize . . . I can see now that it was unwise, selfish of me."

"What do you mean, distress me? What was unwise?"

She came into the room and, shutting the door, leaned against it, forcing him by an act of will to turn and look at her. But when he did, she saw on his face ashamed embarrassment and a desperate appeal for pity, which she knew was as much beyond her understanding as it was beyond her power to help. She was filled with a terrible apprehension, a fear for herself, which made her voice sharper than she realized.

"Distress me? You haven't distressed me. What's all this about?"

He said with a pathetic formality: "It seems that your father has misunderstood the nature of our relationship."

"What has he been saying to you?"

"It doesn't matter, nothing can be done. He wants me out of here. I'm to be gone before school starts."

She said, knowing as she spoke that the words were empty, the promise meaningless: "I'll speak to him. I'll explain. I'll put it right."

He shook his head. "No. Please no, Venetia. It would only make matters worse." He turned away and she watched as he folded a shirt and placed it in the case. She saw the trembling of his hands and heard the tone of ashamed acceptance in his voice. "Your father has promised me a good reference."

Of course, the reference. Without that he would be without hope of another teaching job. It lay within her father's power to do more than throw him out. There was nothing else to be said and nothing she could do, but she still lingered, feeling the need for some gesture, some word of farewell, some hope that they might meet again. But they never would meet again, and what she was feeling now was not affection but fear and shame. He was packing his volumes of the *Notable Trials*. The case was already over-full; she wondered if it would hold the extra weight. One volume still lay on the bed and he handed it to her. It was the Seddon case. He said without looking at her: "Please take it. I'd like you to have it."

Still without looking at her, he whispered, "Please go. I'm sorry, I didn't realize."

Memory was like a film of sharply focused images, the set arranged and brightly lit, the characters formally disposed, the dialogue learnt and unchangeable, but with no linking passages. Now, sitting with a book on contract law open but unread before her unfocused eyes, she was again in her place opposite her father in that over-furnished dining-room, smelling the pungent morning aroma of coffee, toast and bacon. Here again was that solid oak table with the drop leaf, which could be lifted to increase its length, pressing uncomfortably against her knees, the mullioned windows which excluded rather than admitted light, the sideboard with its ornate back and bulbous legs, the hot-plates and covered dishes. Her father had once seen a play in which the upper classes helped themselves to breakfast from a side table. It had seemed to him the epitome of gracious living, and he had introduced it at Danesford, although the choice was never more than bacon and egg or bacon and sausage. How odd that she should still be able to feel a prick of resentment at the silliness of the pretension and the extra work it had made for her mother.

She helped herself to bacon, sat down and forced herself to look at her father. He was eating solidly, his eyes moving from the heaped plate to *The Times* neatly folded beside it. His mouth, beneath the small scrubby moustache, was pinkly moist. He would cut off small squares of toast, spread them with butter and marmalade, and then cast them into that raw pulsating gap which seemed to have a voracious life of its own. His hands were square and strong, the backs of the fingers spiked with black hair. She was sick with fear of him. She had always been frightened of him and had known that she couldn't look to her mother for support; her mother's fear was greater than her own. He had beaten her as a child for every infraction of his petty household rules, his laid-down standard of behaviour and achievement. The beatings hadn't been severe but they had been unbearably humiliating. Each time she would resolve not to cry out, terrified that the boys might hear. But the attempt at courage was futile; he would continue the punishment until she did. Worst of all, she knew that he enjoyed it. When she reached puberty he did stop. It was a small sacrifice on his part. After all, he still had the boys.

Now, sitting in silence in the library, she could see his face again, the cheekbones broad and mottled under eyes from which she could never recall receiving a look of tenderness or kindness. One of the mistresses at school, after she had received her speech-day prizes, had told her that her father was very proud of her. It had seemed an extraordinary statement at the time and it still did so now.

She had tried to keep her voice calm, unfrightened. "Mr. Froggett says he's leaving."

Still her father didn't look up. He said, with his mouth chomping, "You were not meant to see him before he left. I trust you have made no promise to write or get in touch."

"Of course not, Daddy. But why is he leaving? He said it was something to do with me."

Her mother had stopped eating. She cast one frightened, imploring glance at Venetia, then began breaking her toast into crumbs. Her father still didn't look up. He turned a page of his paper.

"I'm surprised that you need to ask. Mr. Mitchell thought it right to inform me that my daughter was spending literally every evening until late in the bedroom of a junior master. If you had no sense of your own position in this school, you might at least have considered mine."

"But we weren't doing anything, just talking. We talked about books, about the law. And it isn't a bedroom, it's his sitting-room."

"I don't wish to discuss it. I'm not even asking what went on between you. If you have anything to confide I suggest that you speak to your mother. As far as I'm concerned the affair is now closed. I don't wish to hear Edmund Froggett's name mentioned in this house again, and from now on you will do your homework here on this table, not in your room."

Was it that day, she wondered, or later that she first realized what it had all been about? Her father had been looking for an excuse to get rid of the Frog. He worked hard, but he was a poor disciplinarian, unpopular with the boys, an embarrassment at school events. He was cheap, but not cheap enough. The school was losing money; only later did she realize how much. Someone had to go and the Frog was expendable. And her father had been clever. His accusation, unspecific no doubt in its details but horribly clear in its essentials, was one the Frog would never dare publicly to refute.

She had never seen him again, nor had she heard from him. The gratitude for what she acknowledged he had given her was overlaid always with the shame of her weakness and betrayal. She had been fascinated by the game they had played but never by him as a man. And she knew she would have been ashamed if any of her classmates had seen them together.

The knowledge that she hadn't fought for him, hadn't defended him with vigour, let alone passion, that she had felt more shame for herself and fear of her father than she had felt compassion, stayed with her to taint the memory of those evenings together. He came now only rarely into her mind. Sometimes she found herself wondering if he were still alive, and would have disconcerting and surprisingly vivid pictures of his hurling himself from Westminster Bridge with incredulous passers-by straining over the parapet at the seething river, or would watch as he crammed the aspirin tablets into his mouth and washed them down with cheap wine, sitting on the single bed in some attic bed-sitting-room.

What, she wondered, had that fifteen-year-old child felt for him? Not love, certainly. There had been affection, need, companionship, stimulation and the sense that she herself was needed. Perhaps she had been lonelier than she realized. But she knew with shame what she had always known, that she had been using him. If she had met him in the street walking with her few friends after school, she would have pretended not to see him.

To a superstitious mind it might have seemed a judgement that after the Frog's departure the school's decline accelerated. It might have survived, however, might even have recovered some prosperity as parents, increasingly disenchanted with the local state school and seeking some imagined prestige, discipline and a show of good manners, saw Danesford as a reasonably cheap solution to family problems. But the suicide put an end to hope. The stretched neck of the young body hanging from the banisters in the annexe, the carefully written note with the spelling of "ahsamed" scrupulously corrected, as if the headmaster's anger dominated even this last act of pathetic rebellion, were not things which could be covered up or explained away. It seemed to Venetia that, with the severing of that taut pyjama cord, more than the body was cut down. The weeks that followed, the inquest, the burial, the comments in the papers, the allegations of beatings and over-severity, became subsumed in the picture of departing cars, of small boys clutching their bulging cases and making their way, shame-faced or triumphant, to the waiting vehicles. The school died in a sickroom stench of scandal, tragedy and, by the end, almost relief that the agony was over, the undertaker's van at last at the door.

The family moved to London. Perhaps, she thought, her father, like so many before him, had seen the great city as an urban jungle where loneliness at least walked with the safety of anonymity, where no questions were asked unless invited and where the predators had more satisfying prey than a disgraced schoolmaster. The school premises, now to be converted into a roadhouse and a motel, provided sufficient cash to buy a small terraced house behind Shepherd's Bush and to furnish an income which augmented the pittance he occasionally managed to earn from casual work. After a few months he found an underpaid job marking papers for a correspondence school, a job which he did conscientiously, as he did all his teaching. When the correspondence school failed he advertised for pupils. A few recognized the quality of his teaching, others found too dispiriting the small dark front room, which neither Aldridge nor his wife found the energy to do anything about, and which Venetia wasn't allowed to touch.

She walked daily to the local comprehensive school. It was one of the first established in London and was intended as a showcase for the new educational policy. Although the first heady years of doctrinaire optimism had been overtaken by the usual problems of a large urban school, it was one in which a clever industrious child could do well. For Venetia the change from the long-established provincial single-sex high school, with its slightly snobbish conventions and local traditions, was less traumatic than she had expected. It was as easy to be a loner at the new school as it had been at the old. She coped with the few bullies by a tongue which could lash them into silence; there was, after all, more than one way of making oneself feared. She worked hard in school, harder still at home. She knew precisely where she wanted to go. The three top-grade A levels gained her an Oxford place.

The first-class degree was followed by an equally brilliant academic success in her Bar examinations. By the time she went up to Oxford she thought she knew all she needed to know about men. The strong could be devils; the weak were moral cowards. There might be men she would sexually desire, even admire, come to like and even want to marry. But never again would she put herself at the mercy of a man.

The door opened, recalling her to the present. She looked at her watch. Nearly two hours. Had it really been so long since the jury went out? Her junior tried to control his excitement.

"They're back."

"With a question?"

"Not a question. We've got a verdict."

4

Slowly and with a careful avoidance of drama or obvious anxiety the court reassembled, waiting for the jury and the appearance of the judge. It was at this moment that Venetia remembered her pupil-master. He had been a traditionalist to whom the picture of a woman in a wig was an anachronism to be borne with stoicism, provided the face beneath the wig was pretty, the manner sweetly deferential and the brain no challenge to his own. There had been general surprise in Chambers when he had accepted a woman pupil; it could only be in penance for an infraction too grievous to be atoned for by less draconian means. When she remembered him it was with respect rather than affection, but he had given her two pieces of advice for which she was grateful.

"Keep all your blue notebooks after trial. Not just for the specified time, for always. It's useful to have a record of cases and you can learn from early mistakes."

The second had been equally useful: "There are moments when it is essential to look at the jury, moments when it is advisable to do so, and moments when you should avoid even a glance. One of the last is when they return with the verdict. Never betray anxiety in court. And if you've put up a good fight and they're going against you, looking at them will only embarrass them."

The latter advice was difficult to follow in Court One at the Bailey, where the jury box was immediately facing the barristers' benches. Venetia fixed her eyes on the judge's seat and didn't glance across the court when, following the usual preliminaries, the Clerk to the Court asked the foreman of the jury to stand. A middle-aged, scholarly-looking man, more formally dressed than the others, got to his feet. He had, thought Venetia, been a natural choice for foreman.

The Clerk asked: "Have you arrived at your verdict?"

"We have, sir."

"Do you find the accused, Garry Ashe, guilty or not guilty of the murder of Mrs. Rita O'Keefe?"

"Not guilty."

"And that is the verdict of you all?"

"It is."

There was no sound in the body of the court, but she heard from the public gallery a low murmur, somewhere between a groan and a hiss, which could have been surprise, relief or disgust. She didn't look up. It was only after the verdict had been given that she gave a thought to the audience, to those closely packed benches where the relations and friends of the accused and the victim, the aficionados of murder, the casuals and the regulars, the morbid and the curious had sat and looked down impassively while, below them, the court played out its stately measure of advance and retreat. Now it was over and they would jostle down that bleak uncarpeted stairway and breathe the untainted air and relish their freedom.

She did not glance at Ashe, but she knew that she would have to see him. It was difficult to avoid at least a few words with a client who had been acquitted. People needed to express their pleasure, occasionally their gratitude, although she suspected that gratitude never lasted long, and for some no longer than the presentation of her bill. But it was only for the convicted clients that she felt even a trace of affection or pity. In her more analytical moments she wondered whether she might not be harbouring a subconscious guilt which after a victory, and particularly a victory against the odds, transferred itself into resentment of the client. The thought interested but did not worry her. Other counsel might see it as part of their job to encourage, to support, to console. She saw her own in less ambiguous terms; it was simply to win.

Well, she had won, and there came, as there so often did after the momentary exhilaration of triumph, a draining tiredness which was as much physical as emotional. It never lasted long but sometimes, after a case which had dragged on for months, the reaction of triumph and then exhaustion would come close to overpowering her and it would take an effort of will to collect her papers together, get to her feet and respond to the murmured congratulations of her junior and the solicitors. Today it seemed to her that the congratulations were muted. Her junior was still young and found it difficult to rejoice in a verdict which he thought wrong. Yet for once the tiredness was only momentary; she could feel the surge of energy and strength returning to muscles and veins. But never before had she felt such repugnance for a client. She hoped never to have to see him again, but this last encounter was unavoidable.

And now he came forward with his solicitor, Neville Saunders, in attendance, the latter wearing his usual schoolmaster's expression of disapproval, as if about to warn his client against a recurrence of the events which had brought them together. Smiling his wintry half-smile, he held out his hand and said: "Congratulations." Then, turning to Ashe: "You're a very fortunate young man. You owe Miss Aldridge a great deal."

The dark eyes looked into hers and she thought she detected for the first time a glint of humour. The unspoken message was clear: We understand each other. I know what got me off, and so do you.

But all he said was: "She'll get what she's owed. I'm on legal aid. That's what it's for, remember."

Saunders, his face flushed, opened his mouth to expostulate, but before he could speak Venetia said, "Good afternoon to you both," and turned away.

She had less than four weeks left of life. And she did not ask him then or later how he had known what spectacles Mrs. Scully had been wearing on the night of the murder.

5

On the same evening Hubert Langton left his Chambers at six o'clock. It was his usual time, and in recent years he had become obsessional about the small comforting rituals of life. But this evening there seemed no possible reason to return home, to the long lonely hours which stretched ahead. Almost without conscious thought he turned right, crossed Middle Temple Lane and passed under the arch by Pump Court and through the Cloisters to the Temple Church. It was open, and he entered through the great Norman doorway to the sound of the organ. Someone was practising. The music was modern, abrasive to his ears, but he sat himself in the stall on the cantoris side in which he had sat Sunday after Sunday for nearly forty years, and let the weariness and ennui which had threatened him all day take undisputed possession.

"Seventy-two is not old." He spoke the words aloud but they fell on the unencumbered air less as a small defiant affirmation than as a thin wail of desperation. Was it really possible that that appalling moment over the road in Court Twelve only three weeks earlier could have robbed him of so much in one moment? The memory of it, the agony of it, was with him almost every waking minute. Now his body became stiff with remembered terror.

He had been in the middle of his closing arguments in a case which had been more forensically interesting than difficult, a lucrative brief from an international company, and a case concerned as much with establishing a point of law as with any dramatic conflict of interests. In one second, with no warning, language deserted him. The words he next wanted to speak were not there, neither in his mind nor on his tongue. The familiar court in which he had appeared for over forty years became an alien cockpit of terror. He could remember nothing, not the name of the judge or of the parties, not the name of his junior or of opposing counsel. There was a half-minute when it seemed that every breath was stilled, every eye in the court was bent on him with surprise, contempt or curiosity. He managed somehow to finish his sentence and sit down. At least he could still read. The written words still conveyed a meaning. He took up his brief with hands which were shaking so violently that they must have signalled his distress to the whole court. But no one spoke, nothing was said. After a little pause and a glance at him, the opposing counsel got to his feet.

But it mustn't happen again. He couldn't live again through that embarrassment, that panic. He had been to his general practitioner, had spoken in general terms of lapses of short-term memory, of a fear that this could be a symptom of something worse. He had forced himself to speak the dreaded word, Alzheimer's. The subsequent physical examination revealed nothing abnormal. The doctor spoke reassuringly about overwork, the need to take things more gently, the advisability of a holiday. The connectors of his brain were getting less efficient with age; that was to be expected. He was reminded of the words of Dr. Johnson: "If a young man mislays his hat he says he has mislaid his hat. The old man says, 'I have lost my hat. I must be getting old.' " He suspected that this anecdote was offered as reassurance to all elderly patients. He had received no reassurance; he had expected none.

Yes, it was time to retire. He hadn't intended to commit himself to Drysdale Laud, had regretted the words as soon as they were spoken. He had been precipitate. But he had been wiser than he knew. It was right to give way to a younger man as Head of Chambers. Or a younger woman. Drysdale or Venetia, it hardly mattered to him which of them succeeded him. And how much did he himself want to go on? Even Chambers had changed. It was now less a band of brothers than the convenient, if over-crowded, set of rooms in which men and women lived their separate professional lives, sometimes not meeting for weeks. He lamented the old days, when he was first a member and there was less specialization, when colleagues would saunter into each other's rooms to discuss a brief or the nicer points of law, to seek advice and rehearse arguments. A gentler world. Now the systems men had taken over with their calculators, their technology, their managerial obsession with results. Wouldn't he be better out of it? But where was he to go? For him there was no world elsewhere, no place except that quadrilateral of narrow streets and courts where the ghost of a small boy, with his romantic dreams, his naïve ambitions, walked through the Middle Temple.

His grandfather, Matthew Langton, had from his birth intended him to be a lawyer. Despite the name, with its overtones of ecclesiastical eminence, the family had been poor; his great-grandfather had kept a small hardware shop in Sudbury in Suffolk, his great-grandmother had been in service with an aristocratic Suffolk family. They managed, but there was never money to spare. But their only child had been highly intelligent, ambitious and determined to be a lawyer. Scholarships had been won, sacrifices made, the family at the great house where his mother had worked had given their patronage. At the age of twenty-four Matthew Langton had been admitted to the Middle Temple.

And now memory, like a searchlight, moved with seemingly deliberate intent over the wasteland of Hubert's life, paused to illumine with shadowless clarity a moment in time which for a second was fixed and motionless and then, as if activated by some click of recollection, moved on again. Himself at the age of ten, walking through Middle Temple Gardens with his grandfather, trying to match his steps to the old man's longer stride, hearing the roll call of famous names, men who had been members of their ancient society: Sir Francis Drake, Sir Walter Raleigh, Edmund Burke, the American patriot John Dickinson, the Lord Chancellors, the Lord Chief Justices, the writers—John Evelyn, Henry Fielding, William Cowper, De Quincey, Thackeray. He and his grandfather would pause at every building to identify it by the badge assigned to the Templars: the Paschal Lamb carrying the banner of innocence set in a red cross on a white nimbus ground. He remembered his triumph when he discovered it above a door or on a water pipe. He was told the history, the legends. Together they counted the goldfish in the pool in Fountain Court and stood hand in hand under the four-hundred-year-old double hammer-beamed roof of Middle Temple Hall. And here, in those childhood years, he had imbibed the history, the romance, the proud traditions of this ancient society, and had known that one day he would be part of it.

He must have been aged eight, perhaps even younger, when his grandfather first showed him the Temple Church. They had walked together between the thirteenth-century effigies of the knights, and he had learned their names by heart as if they were friends: William Marshall, Earl of Pembroke, and his sons William and Gilbert. William the Marshall had been adviser to King John before Magna Carta. Geoffrey de Mandeville, Earl of Essex, with his cylindrical helmet. Hubert would recite the names in his high childish voice, pleasing his grandfather by this act of memory and, greatly daring, laying small hands on the cold stone as if these flat impassive faces held some secret to which he was heir. The church had outlived them and their turbulent lives as it would outlive him. It would survive the ceaseless battering of the millennium against its walls as it had survived that night of 10 May 1941, when the flames had roared with the tongues of an advancing army, the chapel had become a furnace, the marble pillars had cracked and the roof had exploded in a burst of fire to fall in blazing shards over the effigies. Then it had seemed that seven hundred years of history were falling in flames. But the pillars had been replaced, the effigies repaired, new stalls were ranked in collegiate order where once there had been Victorian woodwork, and Lord Glentanar had given his splendid Harrison organ to replace the one destroyed.

Now in his own old age, Hubert suspected that his grandfather had tried to discipline his passionate pride in the career he had achieved, his veneration for the ancient society of which he was part, and that only with the child had he felt free to express emotions, of the strength of which he was half ashamed. He had told his stories with little embellishment, but as the fervid imagination of adolescence had replaced the simple acceptance of childhood, Hubert had clothed history with romance. He had felt his jacket brushed by the gorgeous robes of Henry III and his nobles as they processed into the Round Church on Ascension Day in 1240 for the consecration of the magnificent new choir; had heard the weakening moans as a condemned knight starved to death in the five-foot-long Penitential Chamber. The eight-year-old had found the story more interesting than horrific.

"What had he done, Grandfather?"

"Broken one of the rules of the Order. Disobeyed the Master."

"Are people put in the cell today?" He had stared at the two window slits, imagining that he could see desperate eyes peering down.

"Not today. The Templars Order was dissolved in 1312."

"But what about the lawyers?"

"I'm happy to say that the Lord Chancellor is satisfied with less draconian measures."

Hubert smiled, remembering, sitting still and silent as if he, too, were carved in stone. The organ music had ceased, he couldn't remember when any more than he could remember how long he had been sitting there. What had happened to those years? Where had they gone, the decades since he had walked between the stone knights with his grandfather, had sat with him Sunday after Sunday for matins? The simplicity and ordered beauty of the service, the splendour of the music had seemed to him to represent the profession into which he had been born. He still attended every Sunday. It was as much a part of his routine as buying the same two Sunday newspapers at the same stall on his way home, the luncheon taken from the fridge and heated up in obedience to Erik's written instructions, the short afternoon walk through the park, then the hour of sleep and the evening of television. The practice of his religion, which, it seemed to him now, had never been more than a formal affirmation of a received set of values, was now little more than a pointless exercise designed to give shape to the week. The won-der, the mystery, the sense of history—all had gone. Time, which took so much away, had taken that as it was taking his strength and even his mind. But not, please God, his mind. Anything but that. He felt himself praying with Lear: "O! let me not be mad, not mad, sweet Heaven! Keep me in temper. I would not be mad!"

And then there came into his mind a more accepting, more submissive prayer. "Hear my prayer, O Lord, and with thine ears consider my calling. For I am a stranger with thee, and a sojourner, as all my fathers were. O spare me a little, that I may recover my strength before I go hence, and be no more seen."

6

It was four o'clock on Tuesday, 8 October, when Venetia hitched her gown more firmly on her shoulders, shuffled her papers together and left a court in the Old Bailey for what was to be the last time. The 1972 extension with its rows of leather-covered benches was empty. The air held the expectant calm of a normally busy concourse now cleansed of discordant humanity and settling into its evening peace.

The trial had made few demands on her, but she felt unexpectedly weary and wanted nothing more than to get to the lady barristers' robing-room and to put aside her working clothes for yet another day. She hadn't expected this case to come on at the Bailey. The trial of Brian Cartwright on the charge of grievous bodily harm had originally been scheduled for Winchester Crown Court but had been transferred to London because of local prejudice against the defendant. He had been more chagrined than gratified by the change, complaining bitterly throughout the two weeks' trial of the inconvenience of the venue and the time lost in travelling from his factory to London. She had won and, for him, all inconveniences were forgotten. Volatile and indiscreet in victory, he had no intention of hurrying away. But for Venetia, anxious to see the last of him, it had been an unsatisfactory case, ill-prepared by the prosecution, presided over by a judge who she suspected disliked her—and who had made his disapproval of the majority verdict only too apparent—and made tedious by a prosecuting counsel who could never believe that a jury could take in any fact that hadn't been explained to them three times.

And now Brian Cartwright was at her shoulder and scurrying beside her down the corridor with the bumbling persistence of an over-affectionate dog, euphoric with a victory which even with his optimism he had hardly dared to expect. Above the crisply laundered collar, the carefully knotted old school tie, the large pores of his strong red face oozed sweat as greasy as ointment.

"Well, we did for those buggers! Good work, Miss Aldridge. I did all right in the box, didn't I?"

He, the most arrogant of men, was suddenly like a child avid for her approval.

"You managed to answer questions without betraying your strong dis-like of the anti–blood-sports lobby, yes. We won because there was no clear evidence that it was your whip which blinded young Mills, and because Michael Tewley was seen as an unreliable witness."

"Unreliable he bloody well was! And Mills was only blinded in one eye. I'm sorry for the lad, of course I am. But these people are keen enough to at-tack others and then scream when they get hurt themselves. Tewley hates my guts. There was animus, you said so yourself, and the jury agreed. Animus. Those letters to the press. The telephone calls. You proved that he was out to get me. You tied him up properly, and I liked that last bit, when you were making the speech for the defence. 'If my client has such an ungovernable temper, such a reputation for unprovoked violence, you may find it surpris-ing, members of the jury, that at the age of fifty-five he has never had a crim-inal conviction.' "

She began moving away, but he was at her shoulder. Venetia thought she could smell his triumph.

"I don't think we need re-fight the case, Mr. Cartwright."

"You didn't say that I'd never before appeared in a court of law, though, did you?"

"That would have been a lie. Counsel don't lie to the court."

"But they can be economical with the truth, can't they? Not guilty, then, this time and not guilty the last time. Lucky for me. It wouldn't have been a good thing to come before the court with form. I don't suppose the jury no-ticed the actual words you used." He laughed. "Or didn't use."

She thought, but did not say: The judge did. So did prosecuting counsel.

As if he had read her mind, he went on: "They couldn't say anything, though, could they? I was found not guilty." He lowered his voice and glanced round at the almost empty hall. He paused. "You remember what I told you about the last time, how I got off?"

"I remember, Mr. Cartwright."

"I haven't told another soul but I thought you'd like to know. Knowledge is power."

"Some knowledge is dangerous. I hope in your own interest that you'll keep this particular knowledge to yourself. You'll get my fee-note in due course. I don't need additional payment in the form of private information."

But the piggy bloodshot eyes were sharp. He was a fool about some things but not about everything. He said: "You're interested, though. Thought you might be. After all, Costello's in your Chambers. And don't worry. I've kept it to myself for four years. I'm not a blabbermouth. You don't get to build up a successful business if you don't know when to keep your mouth shut. Hardly the sort of thing I'd sell to the Sunday tabloids, is it? Not that they'd ever get proof. I paid well the last time and I don't mind paying well for this. I said to the lady wife, 'I'm getting the best criminal lawyer in London. I'll pay what it takes. Never economize on necessities. We'll see these bastards off.' Urban vermin, that's what they are. They haven't got the guts to ride a seaside donkey. I'd like to put them up on a hunter. They don't know anything about the countryside. They don't care about animals. What they hate is seeing people enjoy themselves. Malice and envy, that's what it's about." He added, with a tone of surprised triumph, as if the words were inspired: "They don't love foxes, they hate humans."

"Yes, I've heard that argument before, Mr. Cartwright."

He seemed now to be pressing himself against her. She could almost smell the disagreeable warmth of his body through the tweed. "The rest of the hunt won't be too pleased with the verdict. Some of them want me out. They wouldn't have minded seeing that saboteur win. They didn't exactly leap into the box as witnesses for the defence, did they? Well, if they want to hunt across my land they'd better get used to seeing me in a pink coat."

How predictable he was, she thought, the stereotype of the hard-riding, hard-drinking, womanizing, would-be country gentleman. Wasn't it Henry James who had said, "Never believe that you know the last thing about any human heart"? But he was a novelist. It was his job to find complexities, anomalies, unsuspected subtleties in all human nature. To Venetia, as she grew into middle age, it seemed that the men and women she defended, the colleagues she worked with became more, not less, predictable. Only rarely now was she surprised by an action totally out of character. It was as if the instrument, the key, the melody were settled in the early years of life, and however ingenious and varied the subsequent cadenzas, the theme remained unalterably the same.

Yet Brian Cartwright had his virtues. He was a successful manufacturer of parts for agricultural machinery. You didn't build up a business from nothing if you were a fool. He provided jobs. He was said to be a generous, open-handed employer. What hidden talents and enthusiasms, she wondered, might lie under that carefully tailored tweed jacket? He had at least had the sense to dress soberly for his appearance in the witness box; she had feared that he might appear in over-bold checks and breeches. Had he perhaps a passion for lieder? For growing orchids? For baroque architecture? Unlikely. And what in God's name did the lady wife see in him? Was it significant that she hadn't been in court?

Venetia had reached the door of the lady barristers' robing-room. At last she would be free of him. Turning, she risked once more the vise-like grip of his hand, then watched him go. She hoped never to see him again, but that was what she felt about the defendant in every successful case.

A court attendant had come up. He said: "There's quite a crowd of antihunt saboteurs outside. They're not happy with the verdict. It might be wise to leave by the other door."

"Are the police there?"

"There's a couple of officers. I think they're more noisy than violent—the crowd, I mean."

"Thank you, Barraclough. I'll leave as I usually leave."

It was then, passing along the concourse to the main staircase, that she saw them. Octavia and Ashe. They were standing together beside the statue of Charles II, looking fixedly down the wide hall towards her. Even from this distance she could see that they were together, that this was no chance meeting but a deliberate encounter, a time and place they had chosen. There was a stillness about them, unusual in her daughter but known and recognized in Ashe. For a second, no more, her steps faltered, and then she walked steadily towards them. As she came within speaking distance she saw Octavia move her hand towards Ashe's and then, as he made no response, as quietly withdraw it, but her daughter's eyes did not fall.

Ashe was wearing a white shirt which looked newly starched, blue jeans and a denim jacket. Venetia could see that the jacket had not been cheap; somehow he had got hold of money. Beside his stylish self-confidence, Octavia looked very young and rather pathetic. The long cotton shift which she habitually wore over a T-shirt was cleaner than usual, but still made her look like a Victorian orphan newly released from a children's home. Over the T-shirt she was wearing the jacket of a tweed suit. The cumbersome trainers on her feet looked too heavy for her narrow ankles and thin legs, adding to the impression of a vulnerable child. The thin knowing face, which could so easily assume a look of fatuous slyness or mutinous resentment, now looked peaceful, almost happy, and for the first time in years she looked steadily at her mother with the rich deep-brown eyes which were the only feature they shared in common.

Ashe was the first to speak. Holding out his hand, he said: "Good afternoon, Miss Aldridge, and congratulations. We were in the gallery. We were impressed, weren't we, Octavia?"

Venetia ignored his hand but knew that this was both what he expected and what he wanted. Without looking at him, keeping her eyes on her mother, Octavia nodded.

Venetia said: "I should have thought you'd had enough of the Bailey to last a lifetime. I take it that you know each other."

Octavia said simply: "We're in love. We're thinking of getting engaged."

The words came out in a rush in her high childish voice but Venetia didn't miss the unmistakable note of triumph.

She said calmly: "Indeed? Then I suggest you unthink it. You may not be particularly intelligent, but presumably you have some sense of self-preservation. Ashe is totally unsuitable to be your husband."

There was no outburst of protest from Ashe, but, then, she hadn't expected one. He stood regarding her with the same half-smile, ironic, challenging, tinged with contempt.

He said: "That's for Octavia to decide. She's of age."

Venetia ignored him and spoke directly to her daughter. "I'm walking back to Chambers. I want you to come with me. Obviously we have to talk."

She wondered what she would do if Octavia refused, but Octavia looked at Ashe.

He nodded and said: "Shall I see you tonight? What time would you like me to come round?"

"Yes please. Come as soon as you can. Six-thirty. I'll cook something for supper."

Venetia recognized the invitation for what it was, a declaration of defiance. Ashe took her hand and raised it to his lips. Venetia knew that the mock formality of the exchange, the play-acting, was for her benefit, as was the kiss. She was seized with an anger and revulsion so strong that she had to clasp her hands to prevent herself slapping his face. People were passing, barristers she knew and was acknowledging with a brief smile. They had to get out of the Bailey.

Venetia said, "Right. Shall we go?" and without looking again at Ashe, led the way.

Outside, the street was almost empty. Either the protesters had grown tired of waiting for her or had been content to heckle Brian Cartwright. Still without speaking, she and Octavia crossed the road.

It was Venetia's habit to walk back to Chambers when she had finished a case at the Bailey. Occasionally she would vary the route. More often she would turn off Fleet Street at Bouverie Street, then down Temple Lane to enter the Inner Temple by the Tudor Street entrance. She would then walk down Crown Office Row and across Middle Temple Lane to Pawlet Court. This afternoon, as always, Fleet Street was busy and noisy, the pavement so crowded that it was difficult for her and Octavia to walk abreast and impossible to hear comfortably above the grind and rumble of the traffic. This wasn't the time to begin a serious talk.

Even when they were in the comparative peace of Bouverie Street she waited. But once in Inner Temple she said, without turning to Octavia: "I've got thirty minutes to spare. We'll walk in the Temple Gardens. All right, tell me about this. When did you meet him?"

"About three weeks ago. I met him on 17th September."

"He picked you up, I suppose. Where? Some pub? A club? You're not going to tell me that you were formally introduced at a meeting of the Young Conservatives?"

She realized as soon as the words were out of her mouth that they were a mistake. In her confrontations with Octavia she had never been able to resist the cheap gibe, the easy sarcasm. Already she realized with the familiar sinking of the heart that their conversation—if you could call it that—was doomed to acrimonious failure.

Octavia didn't reply. Venetia said, keeping her voice calm: "I'm asking where you met him."

"He crashed his bicycle at the end of our road and asked me if he could leave it in the basement area. He couldn't get it on a bus and he hadn't enough money for a taxi."

"So you lent him ten pounds and—surprise, surprise!—he came back next day to repay it. And what happened to the bicycle?"

"He threw it away. He doesn't need it. He's got a motorbike."

"The cycle had served its purpose, I suppose? Something of a coincidence, wasn't it, crashing it outside my house?"

My house, not our house. Another mistake. Again Octavia was silent. Had it been a coincidence? Stranger ones had happened. You couldn't be a criminal lawyer without encountering almost weekly the capricious phenomenon of chance.

Octavia said sulkily: "Yes, he came back. And after that he came back again because I invited him."

"So you met him less than a month ago, you know nothing about him, and you're telling me that you're engaged. You're not stupid enough to believe he loves you. Even you couldn't be that deluded."

Octavia's voice was like a cry of pain. "He does love me. Just because you don't, doesn't mean no one else ever will. Ashe loves me. And I do know about him. He's told me. I know more about him than you do."

"I doubt that. How much has he told you about his past, his childhood, what he's been doing for the last seven years?"

"I know that he hasn't a father and that his mother chucked him out when he was seven and made the local authority look after him. She's dead now. He was in care until he was sixteen. They call it being taken into care. He said it was being taken into hell."

"His mother chucked him out because he was unmanageable. She told the local authority that she was frightened of him. Frightened of a seven-year-old. Doesn't that tell you something? His life has been a series of unsuccessful fostering and children's homes which moved him on as soon as they could persuade someone else to take him. None of it is his fault, of course."

Octavia's head was bent; her words were hardly audible. "I expect you would have liked to do the same with me, put me in care. Only you couldn't because people would have talked, so you sent me to boarding school instead."

Venetia willed herself to stay calm. "You two must have had an enjoyable three weeks together, sitting in the flat provided for you by me, eating my food, spending money I have earned and exchanging horror stories about your suffering. Has he told you about the murder? You do know, I suppose, that he was accused of slashing his aunt to death and that I defended him? You do realize that the murder happened only nine months ago?"

"He told me he didn't do it. She was a horrible woman who was always having men in the house. One of them killed her. He wasn't near the place when it happened."

"I'm aware of the defence. I conducted it."

"He's innocent. You know he's innocent. You told the court that he didn't do it."

"I didn't tell the court that he didn't do it. I've explained all this to you before, only you've never been interested enough to listen. The court isn't concerned with what I think. I'm not there to give them my opinion. I'm there to test the prosecution's case. The jury had to be convinced of his guilt beyond reasonable doubt. I was able to show that there was a reasonable doubt. He was entitled to be acquitted and he was acquitted. You're perfectly right, he's not guilty, at least of that crime. Not guilty in law. That doesn't mean that he's a suitable husband for you—or for any woman. His aunt wasn't a pleasant woman but something held them together. Almost certainly they were lovers. He was one of many, but in his case, no doubt, it came free."

Octavia cried: "It isn't true. It isn't true. And you can't stop us marrying. I'm over eighteen."

"I know I can't stop you. What I can do, and have a duty to do as your mother, is to point out the dangers. I know this young man. I make it my job to find out as much as I can about my clients. Garry Ashe is dangerous. He may even be evil, whatever that word means."

"So why did you get him off?"

"You haven't understood a word I've said, have you? So let's be practical. When do you propose to marry?"

"Soon, in a week maybe. Perhaps two, perhaps three. We haven't decided."

"Are you having sex? But of course you are."

"You haven't any right to ask that."

"No, I'm sorry. You're quite right. You're of age. I haven't any right to ask that."

Octavia said sulkily, "Anyway, we're not. Not yet. Ashe thinks we ought to wait."

"How very clever of him. And how does he propose to support you? As he's to be my son-in-law I suppose I do have a right to ask that question."

"He'll work. I've got my allowance. You've settled that on me. You can't take it away. And we may sell our story to the papers. Ashe thinks they would be interested."

"Oh, they'll be interested all right. You won't get a fortune but you'll get something. I can imagine the line he'll take. 'Disadvantaged young man unjustly accused of heinous crime. Brilliant defence lawyer. Triumphant acquittal. The dawn of young love.' Yes, it could make you a pound or two. Of course, if Ashe is prepared to confess to his aunt's murder you might even ask for six figures. And why not? He can't be tried again."

They paced together through the gathering dusk, heads bent close yet distanced. Venetia found herself physically shaking with emotions which she was powerless to make sense of or control. He would sell the story if a paper made it worth his while. He felt no loyalty to her, any more than she had felt liking for him. He had needed her; perhaps they had needed each other. And afterwards, in that brief interview, she had seen the contempt in his eyes, his conceit, and had sensed that he felt for her not gratitude but resentment. Oh yes, he would gladly humiliate her if he had the power. And he did have the power. But why was it worse to contemplate the sentimentality and the vulgarity of that press exposure, the pity and amusement of her colleagues, than it was to face the thought of his marriage to Octavia? Did she really with part of her mind—that mind in which she took such pride—care more for her reputation than for her daughter's safety?

She had to make one more effort. They were turning out of the garden now.

After a moment she said: "There's something he did, not perhaps the worst thing, but one which for me is crucial. It explains why I think of him as evil, which isn't a word I normally care to use. When he was fifteen he was in a children's home outside Ipswich. There was a residential social worker there—his name is Michael Cole—who really cared for Ashe. He spent a great deal of time with him, believed he could help him, perhaps loved him. Ashe tried to blackmail him. He said that if Coley, as he called him, didn't hand over a proportion of his weekly wage he'd accuse him of assaulting him sexually. Cole refused and was denounced. There was an official inquiry. Nothing was proved, but the authorities thought it prudent to move Cole into another post not working with children. He'll be under suspicion for the rest of his professional life—if he still has a professional life. Think of Coley before you commit yourself to marriage. Ashe has broken the heart of everyone who has tried to help him."

"I don't believe it. And he won't break my heart. Perhaps I'm like you. Perhaps I haven't got one."

Suddenly she had turned away and was running through the gardens towards the Embankment gate, moving clumsily like a distraught child, the legs thin as sticks above the heavy trainers, the jacket flying open. Turning to watch her, Venetia felt a momentary spasm of an emotion which had some of the tenderness of pity. But it passed, and was replaced with a burning anger and a sense of injustice as physical as a hard knot of pain under the heart. It seemed to her that Octavia had never given her a moment of unalloyed satisfaction, let alone joy. What, she wondered, had gone wrong? When and how? Even as a baby she had resisted her mother's attempts to cuddle and caress her. The sharp-featured little face, always an adult face, twisting into a bawling purple mask of hatred, the baby legs, surprisingly strong, clamped against her stomach thrusting her away, the body arched and rigid. And then at school it had seemed that every emotional crisis had been deliberately timed to make Venetia's professional life more difficult. Every speech day, every school play had been arranged on a day when it was impossible for her to get away, increasing Octavia's resentment, her own nagging guilt.

She remembered now the time when she had been engaged in one of the most complicated cases of fraud she had ever defended, and had been called immediately after the court rose on a Friday to cope with Octavia's expulsion from her second boarding school. She could remember clearly every word of the conversation with Miss Egerton, the headmistress.

"We haven't been able to make her happy."

"I didn't send her to you to be made happy. I sent her to be educated."

"The two aren't incompatible, Miss Aldridge."

"No, but it's as well to know which has priority in your scheme of things. So the convent takes your failures?"

"There is no formal arrangement but we do recommend it to parents from time to time. I don't want you to gain the wrong impression. It isn't a school for problem children, quite the reverse. And the examination results at A level are respectable. Pupils do go on to university. But it caters for girls who need a more pastoral, less academic education than we are able to provide."

"Or are willing to provide."

"This is a highly academic school, Miss Aldridge. We educate the whole girl, not only the mind, but the girl who does best here is usually highly intelligent."

"Spare me the school prospectus, I've read it. Did she tell you why she did it?"

"Yes. To get expelled."

"She admitted that?"

"Not in those words."

"In what words, Miss Egerton?"

"She said, 'I did it to get away from this fucking school.' "

Venetia had thought: So at last I've got an honest answer out of her.

Miss Egerton had said: "The convent is run by Anglo-Catholic nuns but I don't think you need fear religious indoctrination. The Mother Superior is scrupulous about respecting parental wishes."

"Octavia can genuflect before the blessed sacrament day and night if it gives her any satisfaction and gets her a couple of decent A levels."

But the interview had given her hope. A girl who could use that word to Miss Egerton at least had spirit. Perhaps on some bleak unwatered scrubland of the mind she and Octavia might yet find a common meeting-place. Perhaps there could be respect, even liking, even if there couldn't be love. But it had only taken the drive home to show that nothing had changed. Octavia's eyes still met hers with that same blank stare of obstinate antagonism.

The convent had coped in the sense that Octavia had stayed there until she was seventeen, achieved four modest passes in her O levels. But Venetia had always been ill at ease on her few visits to the convent, particularly with the Reverend Mother. She remembered that first interview.

"We have to accept, Miss Aldridge, that Octavia, as the child of divorced parents, will be disadvantaged all her life."

"Since that is a disadvantage she shares with thousands of other children, she'd better learn to cope."

"That is what we shall try to help her to do."

Venetia had curbed an outward show of irritation with difficulty. Was this sponge-faced woman with the small implacable eyes behind steel-rimmed spectacles daring to take upon herself the role of prosecuting counsel? Then she realized that no criticism was intended, no defence awaited and no mitigation invited. It was simply that the Reverend Mother lived her life by rules, and one of them was that actions had consequences.

Now, obsessed with this latest emergency, angry with Octavia and herself, faced with a calamity to which she could find no answer, she hardly remembered the short walk through Pawlet Court to Chambers. Valerie Caldwell was at her desk in the reception booth and looked up stony-faced as Venetia entered.

Venetia asked: "Is Mr. Costello in his room, do you know?"

"Yes I think so, Miss Aldridge. He came in after lunch and I don't think he's left. And Mr. Langton asked me to let him know when you came in."

So Langton wanted to see her. She might as well go to his room now. Simon Costello could wait.

When she entered Hubert's room she found Drysdale Laud with him. That didn't surprise her; the archbishops usually acted together.

Laud said, "It's about the Chambers meeting on the thirty-first. You are coming, Venetia?"

"Don't I usually attend? I don't think I've missed more than one Chambers meeting since you made them twice yearly."

Langton said: "There are a couple of matters on which we thought it might be helpful to know your mind."

"You mean, to indulge in a little preliminary lobbying in the interests of getting through the meeting with the minimum of dissension? I shouldn't be too optimistic."

Drysdale Laud took over. He said: "First we have to decide who to take on as tenants. We agreed that we could usefully find places for two more. It isn't an easy choice."

"Isn't it? Come off it, Drysdale! Don't tell me you haven't reserved a place for Rupert Price-Maskell."

Langton said: "He's got an excellent reference from his pupil-master and he's popular in Chambers. He's academically outstanding, of course, Scholar of Eton, Scholar of King's, First-Class Honours."

Venetia said: "And he's the nephew of a Law Lord, his great-grandfather was Head of these Chambers and his mother is the daughter of an earl."

Langton frowned. "You aren't suggesting that we're being . . . we're being . . ." He paused, his face for a moment a mask of embarrassment. Then he said, "That we're being over-influenced?"

"No. It's as illogical and indefensible to discriminate against Etonians as it is to discriminate against any other group. It's convenient that the candidate you want happens to be the one best qualified. You don't have to persuade me to vote for Price-Maskell; I was going to do so anyway. He'll be as pompous as his uncle in twenty years' time, but if we take incipient pomposity into account we'd never appoint a member of your sex. I take it that Jonathan Skollard has the second place? He's less obviously brilliant, but I'm not sure he won't prove to have the better mind, more staying power."

Laud walked over to the window. He said in a voice unemphatic and unworried: "We were thinking of Catherine Beddington."

"Men in Chambers spend a great deal of time thinking of Catherine Beddington, but this isn't a beauty contest. Skollard is the better lawyer."

This, of course, was what it was all about. She had known from her first entry into Hubert's room.

Langton intervened: "I don't think Catherine's pupil-master would necessarily agree. He's given her a very satisfactory report. She's got an excellent brain."

"Of course she has. She wouldn't have been given pupillage in these Chambers if she were stupid. Catherine Beddington will be a decorative and efficient member of the Bar, but she isn't as good a lawyer as Jonathan Skollard. I am her sponsor, remember. I've taken an interest in her and I've seen some of her work. She isn't as impressive as Simon makes out. For example, when I'm in conference discussing points of law in manslaughter I do rather expect a pupil to see the relevance of *Dawson* and *Andrews*. Those are cases she should have learned before she entered Chambers."

Laud said lightly: "You terrify the child, Venetia. She's perfectly competent with me."

"If she's terrified by me I pity her when she has to stand up before Mr. Justice Carter-Wright on a day his piles are giving him hell."

How long, she thought, were they going to pussyfoot around the real issue? How they hated any argument in Chambers, any genuine dissent. And how typical that Hubert had needed Drysdale's support, the two archbishops acting in concert, as always. And wasn't it a way of letting her know that Drysdale was heir apparent, that she might as well give up hope of succeeding Hubert as Head of Chambers? But at least in this matter they knew that her voice would be influential—more than influential, it would probably carry the day.

She saw their quick glances at each other, then Drysdale said: "Isn't it a question of balance? I thought we'd agreed—at a Chambers meeting in the spring of '94, wasn't it?—that if we had two candidates for a Chambers vacancy, one male, one female, and they were equally qualified . . ."

Venetia broke in. "They never are equally qualified. People aren't clones."

Laud went on as if she hadn't interrupted. "If we decided that there was nothing to choose between them, then in the interests of balance we'd take the woman."

"When people say there's nothing to choose, they mean that they want to avoid the responsibility of choosing."

Langton's voice held a note of obstinacy. "We agreed that we would take the woman." He paused, then added: "Or the black, if we had a black pupil."

This was too much. Venetia's carefully controlled anger spilled out. "Woman? Black? How convenient to bracket us together. Pity we haven't a black, lesbian, unmarried mother with a disability. That way you could satisfy four politically correct requirements at one go. And it's bloody condescending to me. Do you think successful women want to be made to feel that we've got where we are because men were kind enough to give us an unfair advantage? Jonathan Skollard is the better lawyer, and you know it. So does he. Do you think it will help Catherine Beddington's career if he's able to go about saying he was cheated out of a place here because we wanted it for a less able woman? What does that do for the cause of equal opportunity?"

Langton glanced at his colleague, then went on: "I'm not sure that it does the reputation of Chambers any good if we are seen to be a coterie of misogynists out of touch with changes in society and in the profession."

"Our reputation is founded on professional excellence. These are small Chambers but we haven't a dud. On the contrary, we've got some of the best people in their fields in London. And what are you frightened of? Has someone been getting at you?"

There was a pause. Langton said: "Informal representations have been made."

"Oh have they! Might I ask from whom? Anyway, it won't be that female pressure group, Redress. It's the women they go after, the ones they judge aren't doing enough to give their sex a chance. Bankers, businesswomen, lawyers, publishers, top consultants. They're compiling a list of women who don't do enough to help the sisterhood. Not surprisingly, I'm on it. I suppose someone sent you a copy of their rag, *Redress*. There's a mention of me in the latest issue. It could be libellous. I'm taking advice from Henry Makins. If he advises that it's actionable, I'll sue."

Laud said: "Is that wise? You'll get nothing unless they're insured. Are they worth the time or the trouble?"

"Probably not, but with the press as mean-minded and vicious as some of it is today it's unwise to let the idea get around that you can't be bothered to sue. You know as well as I that the litigious generally get left alone. Look at Robert Maxwell. And I can afford Henry Makins, Redress can't. If you are worried about the reputation of the law, why don't you apply your minds to that inequality? What is it that you currently charge for an hour of your time, Drysdale? Four hundred pounds, isn't it? Five hundred? That effectively puts justice out of the reach of most people. Doing something about that is rather more difficult than pushing a few women into jobs for which they are under-qualified, in the interests of balance. . . ."

She paused. Neither of the men spoke. Then she said: "So what's your other problem? You said there were two. It's Harry Naughton's retirement, I suppose."

Langton said: "Harry's sixty-five at the end of the month. His contract ends then but he'd very much like another three years. His boy, Stephen, has got a place at university—Reading. He's just started on his first year. It's a big thing for them. But it means, of course, that the boy won't be earning and naturally they're worried. They can manage but it would be easier if Harry could carry on here for a year or two."

Laud added: "He's good for another three years at least. Sixty-five is young for a healthy man to be pensioned off if he wants to go on working. We could give him an extension, renewed annually, and see how it goes."

Venetia said: "He's a perfectly competent Senior Clerk. He's conscientious, methodical, accurate and he gets the money in on time. I have no complaint about Harry, but things have changed since he succeeded his father here. He's made no attempt to come to terms with the new technology. All right, so the junior clerks, Terry and Scott, have. It comes easily to their generation. We haven't lost out. And I sympathize with Harry. I rather like his wall chart and personal files and his little flags showing where we're appearing. But he should go when he's due to go. We all should. You know my views. What we need is a Chambers manager. If we're going to expand—and we are expanding—the office and services need modernizing."

"He'll take it very hard. He's given thirty-nine years to these Chambers and his father was Senior Clerk before him."

Venetia cried: "For God's sake, Hubert, you're not sacking the man! He's had thirty-nine good years and he's reached retirement age. He'll get his pension and no doubt a little present to go with it. Of course you want him to stay on. That way you can postpone another difficult decision. You won't have to decide for another three years what Chambers really needs and set about putting it in place. And now, if you'll excuse me, I've got work to do. You've had your answers. If I've any influence in Chambers then Jonathan Skollard will get the second vacancy and Harry won't get an extension. And for God's sake, both of you, show some guts! Why not make a decision on its merits for a change?"

They watched her without speaking as she went to the door. God, she thought, what an awful day. What a horrible day. And now she had to tackle Simon Costello. That, of course, could wait but she was in no mood to let it wait, no mood to show mercy to any man. But there was one thing more to be said to the archbishops. She turned at the door and looked at Laud.

"And if you're worried that Chambers may be getting a reputation for misogyny, relax. I'm the senior member after Hubert. Having a woman as next Head of Chambers should put that right."

7

He had said that he would be with her at Pelham Place by six-thirty, and by six Octavia was ready and waiting, moving restlessly from her small galley kitchen to the left of the door into the sitting-room, where she could gaze from the window up through the basement railings. It would be the first meal she had cooked for him, the first time he had entered the flat. Until now he had called for her, but when she had invited him in, he had said mysteriously, "Not yet." She wondered what he had been waiting for. Some greater certainty, some more positive commitment, the right moment to make a symbolic entrance into her life? But she couldn't be more committed to him than she was now. She loved him. He was her man, her person, her lover. They had never made love, but that would come. There would be a right time for that too. Now it was sufficient for her that she could rejoice in the assurance that she was loved. She wanted the whole of the world to know. She wanted to take him back with her to the convent, to show him off, to let those despised and arrogant girls know that she, too, could get a man. She wanted the conventional things: a ring on her engagement finger, a wedding to be planned, a home to make for him. He needed looking after, he needed love.

And he had another power over her, and one she only half-acknowledged. He was dangerous. She didn't know how dangerous or in what way, but he wasn't of her world. He wasn't of any world that she had ever known or expected to know. With him there was not only the urge and excitement of growing desire, there was a *frisson* of danger which satisfied the rebel in her, made her feel for the first time in her life fully alive. This wasn't just a love affair, it was a comradeship-in-arms, an alliance, offensive and defensive, against the conforming world of home, against her mother and all her mother stood for. The motorcycle was part of that Ashe. Her arms round his waist, she would feel the rush of cold night air, see the road spinning like a grey ribbon under their wheels, want to shout with exhilaration and triumph.

She had never known anyone like him. His behaviour to her was punctilious, almost formal. He would bend and kiss her cheek when they met, or lift her hand to his lips. Otherwise he never touched her, and she was beginning to want him with a need which increasingly she found it hard to hide. She knew that he didn't like to be touched but she could barely keep her hands from him.

He never told her where he was taking her, and she had been content not to know. Invariably it was to a country pub; he seemed to dislike London pubs and they went to them seldom. But he despised the smart country pubs with rows of Porsches and BMWs carefully parked outside, the hanging baskets, the bar with its open fire and artfully arranged objects to provide a synthetic rusticity, the separate restaurant serving predictable food, the sound of confident, braying upper-class voices. He stopped always at the quieter, less fashionable places where the country people drank, and he would settle her in a corner seat, fetch the medium sherry or half-pint of lager for which she asked, and his own half-pint of beer. They would eat bar food, usually cheese or pâté and French bread, and she would talk while he listened. He told her little about himself. She sensed that he was both willing that she should know how awful those early years had been, and yet unable to tolerate her pity. If she questioned he would reply but briefly, sometimes with a single word. The impression he gave was of someone in control, who had always been in control, staying with each foster parent for as long as he had decided to stay and no longer. She learned to know when she was treading on dangerous ground. After the meal they would walk for half an hour in the country, he striding ahead, she scurrying to keep up with him, before setting back for London.

Sometimes they went on to the coast. He liked Brighton and they would roar out on the Rottingdean road with its wide view of the Channel, find a small café, eat, then drive on over the Downs. Although he disliked fashionable places, he was fussy about his food. A roll which wasn't fresh, cheese which was dry, rancid-tasting butter would be pushed aside.

He would say: "Don't eat this muck, Octavia."

"It's not too bad, darling."

"Don't eat it. We'll buy some chips on the way home."

She liked that best of all, sitting on the verge while the traffic swished past, the smell of chips and warm greaseproof paper, the excitement of being free and untrammelled, on the move, and yet of being secure in their private world. The purple Kawasaki was both the means of their freedom and its symbol.

But today she was to cook for him for the first time. She had decided on steak. Surely all men like steak. She had bought filet at the butcher's suggestion, and now the two thick lumps of red flesh lay on a plate, ready to be put under the grill at the last minute. She had been to Marks and Spencer and bought ready-washed and prepared vegetables—peas, small carrots, new potatoes. They were to have a lemon tart as a pudding. The table was laid. She had bought candles and borrowed two silver candlesticks from the drawing-room. She carried them with her into the ground-floor kitchen, where her mother's housekeeper, Mrs. Buckley, was scraping potatoes, and said without preamble: "If my mother wants to know where her candlesticks are, I've borrowed them."

Without waiting for a response she went over to the drinks cupboard and took out the first bottle of claret to hand, outstaring Mrs. Buckley's disapproving gaze. The woman opened her mouth to protest, thought better of it and bent again to her task.

Octavia thought: "Silly old cow, what's it to do with her? She'll probably be peering through the curtains to watch who arrives. Then she'll sneak to Venetia. Well, let her. It can't matter now."

Standing at the door with the candlesticks in one hand, the bottle of wine in the other, she said: "Perhaps you'd open the door for me. Can't you see I've got my hands full?"

Without a word Mrs. Buckley came over and held open the door. Octavia swept out and heard the door close behind her.

Downstairs, in her own sitting-room, she surveyed the table with satisfaction. The candles made all the difference. And she had even remembered to buy flowers, a bunch of bronze chrysanthemums.

The sitting-room, which she had never liked, looked festive and welcoming. Maybe this evening they would make love.

But when he arrived, on time, unsmiling as always, and she opened the door, he still didn't come in.

He said: "Get into your bike things. There's something I want to show you."

"But, darling, I said I'd cook supper for you. I've got steak."

"It'll wait. We'll have it when we get back. I'll cook it."

When she returned a few minutes later, carrying her helmet and zipping up her leather jacket, she said: "Where are we going?"

"You'll see."

"You make it sound important."

"It is important."

She asked no more questions. Fifteen minutes later they were at the Holland Park roundabout and turning onto Westway. Another five minutes and he drew up outside of one of the houses and she knew where they were.

It was a scene of utter desolation, made more unreal and bizarre by the glare of the overhead lights. On either side of them the houses stretched, boarded up with what looked like sheets of rust-coloured metal. They were identical, semi-detached with side entrances and recessed porches. There were three-paned bay windows on the ground and upper floors and a triangular gable crossed with dark wooded slats. The windows and doors were barred. The fences of the front gardens had been wrenched away and the small patches of scrub, some with the torn and broken branches of rose-bushes and shrubs, were open to the pavement.

He wheeled the bike down the side entrance of Number 397 and she followed. He said, "Wait here," and, pulling himself up onto the wall with one easy swing, climbed over the gate. A second later she heard the bolt drawn back. She held the gate open while he wheeled the bike into the back garden.

She said: "Who lived next door?"

"A woman called Scully. She's gone now. This is the last house to be cleared."

"Does it belong to you?"

"No."

"But you live here?"

"I do for now. Not much longer."

"Is there electricity on?"

"There is at present."

She could see little of the garden. There was the outline of a small shed. Perhaps, she thought, this was where he kept the bike. She thought she could see a round white plastic table, overturned, and the spiky outline of garden chairs broken and on their sides. There had been some kind of tree, but now there was only a splintered black trunk, its jagged spears sharp against the lurid blue and crimson of the evening sky. The air was dusty, clogging her nostrils, and smelt strongly of brick dust, rubble and charred wood.

Ashe took a key from his pocket and opened the back door, then put out his hand for the light. The kitchen sprang into view, unnaturally bright. She saw a small stone sink, the cheap dresser with half of its hooks missing, the table with its stained plastic top peeling, the four insubstantial chairs. And here the smell was different, older, staler, the smell of years of inadequate cleaning, of rotting food, of unwashed dishes. She could see that he had made attempts to clean up. She knew how meticulous he was about order. How this place must have disgusted him. He had used disinfectant—the stink of it lingered. But the other smells were not so easily wiped away.

She didn't know what to say, but he seemed to expect no comment and made none. Then he said: "Come and see the hall."

The hall light was from a single bulb hung high and unshaded. When Ashe pressed down the switch, Octavia gave a gasp of wonder. The walls on both sides of the passage had been pasted with coloured pictures obviously cut out from books and magazines, a rich collage of shiny images which, as she gazed amazed from side to side, seemed to close in on her in vibrant, shimmering colour. Pasted over the gentle views of mountains, lakes, cathedrals, piazzas, were naked women, legs parted, naked breasts and buttocks, pouted lips, and male torsos with the genitalia caged in shiny black pouches, the whole superimposed on garlands of summer flowers, formal gardens with their vistas and sculptures, cottage plots, animals, and birds. And there were faces, grave, gentle and arrogant, cut from reproductions of the world's great paintings, faces so placed that they seemed to regard the jumble of crude sexual images with distaste or patrician disdain. No inch of the walls was uncovered. Ahead was the front door, its glass panel boarded from outside. The door was fitted with heavy bolts at top and bottom, inducing in Octavia a moment of claustrophobic unease.

After the first shock of surprise, she said: "It's crazy, but it's wonderful. Did you do all this?"

"Auntie and I did it. I worked out the pattern but it was her idea."

It was odd the way he spoke always of Auntie, no name, just Auntie. Something about the way he said it struck a note of subtle disparagement, of falsity, of a stronger emotion carefully controlled. And there was something more: he spoke the word as if it were a warning.

She said: "I like it. God, it's clever. It's really clever. We could do something like this in the flat. But it must have taken months."

"Two months and three days."

"Where did you get all the pictures?"

"Magazines mostly. Auntie's men brought them in for her. Some I stole."

"From libraries?"

She remembered reading about two men who had done that, a playwright and his lover. They had covered their flat walls with prints from stolen library books and had been found out. Hadn't they gone to prison?

He said: "Too risky. I stole the books from bookstalls. Safer, easier and it takes less time."

"And soon they'll be pulling it all down. Doesn't that worry you? I mean, after all this work."

She could picture it, the great ball swinging against the walls, the billows of grit and dust rising in a choking cloud, the images cracking apart like a broken jigsaw.

He said: "It doesn't worry me. Nothing about this house worries me. It's time it was pulled down. Look in here. This was Auntie's room."

He opened a door to the right and put out his hand for the switch. The room was bathed in a red light. It came not from a central bulb but from three lamps fitted with ruched shades of scarlet satin and set about the room on low tables. The air was suffused with redness. It was like breathing blood. When she glanced down at her hands she expected to see the flesh stained pink. The heavy curtains drawn across the barred windows were of red velvet. The walls were covered with a patterned paper of pink roses. The long sagging sofa in front of the window and the two armchairs on each side of the gas fire were covered with throws of Indian cotton in rich reds, purple and gold. Against the wall opposite the fire was a divan covered with a grey blanket, a single sombre piece among the garish extravaganza. On a low table in front of the fire was a pack of playing-cards and a glass globe.

He said: "Auntie told fortunes."

"For money?"

"For money. For sex. For amusement."

"Did she have sex in this room?"

"On that couch. This was her place. Everything happened here."

"Where were you? What did you do? I mean, where were you when she was in here having sex?"

"I was here too. She liked me to be here. She liked me to watch. Didn't your mother tell you? She knew. It came out at the trial."

It was impossible to tell from his voice what he was feeling. She shivered. She wanted to say, "And did you like that? Why did you stay? Were you fond of her? Did you love her?" But she couldn't have spoken that word. Love. She had never been sure what it meant, only that until now she had never known it. What she did know was that it had nothing to do with this room.

She asked, almost in a whisper: "Is this where it happened? Is this where she was killed?"

"On the couch."

She looked at it, fascinated, and said with a kind of wonder: "But it looks so clean, so ordinary."

"It was covered in blood, but they took away the mattress cover with the body. If you lift that blanket you can still see the stains."

"No thank you." She tried to make her voice light. "Did you cover it with that blanket?"

He didn't reply but she was aware that he was looking at her. She wanted to move close to him, to touch him, but she sensed that this would be unwise, and perhaps more than unwise, that he might even repel her. She was aware of her own quickened breathing, of a mixture of fear and excitement, and something else which was as exhilarating as it was shameful. She wanted him to carry her over to that couch and make love to her. She thought, I'm frightened but at least I'm feeling something. I'm alive.

He was still looking at her. He said: "There's something else I could show you. Upstairs, in the dark-room. Do you want to see?"

Suddenly she needed to get out of the sitting-room. The redness was beginning to hurt her eyes.

She said casually: "OK. Why not?" Then added: "This was your home, where you lived. I want to see everything."

He led the way upstairs. The stairs were carpeted in an indistinguishable pattern, the pile matted with grime and in parts worn through, so that once she caught her foot in a tear and had to grasp the banister to save herself from stumbling. Ashe didn't look back. She followed him into a room at the rear of the house, small enough to be a box room but perhaps meant to be a bedroom. The single high window was covered with a thick black cloth nailed to the wooden frame. Beneath it were three shelves. To the right, mounted above a bench, was a large piece of equipment, which reminded her of a giant microscope. The bench itself held three rectangular plastic trays filled with liquid. She was aware of the smell, a mixture of ammonia and vinegar, slightly gaseous.

He said: "Seen a room like this before?"

"No. It's the dark-room, isn't it? I don't know what it's for."

"Don't you know anything about photography? Didn't you have a camera? Your kind always has a camera."

"The other girls at school did. I didn't want one. What was there to photograph?"

She had always hated those special days—speech days, the summer fête, the Christmas-carol service, the annual play. She could picture the garden in high summer with Reverend Mother laughing with two of the parents, old girls with daughters now at the school, the jostle round them of jumping children with the cameras pointed. "Look this way, Reverend Mother. Oh please! Mummy, you're not looking at the camera." Venetia hadn't been there; Venetia was never there. There was always a court attendance, a meeting in Chambers, something which couldn't be put off. She hadn't even been part of the audience when Octavia had been chosen to play Paulina in *The Winter's Tale*.

She said: "We didn't have a dark-room at school. The pictures went off to Boots or somewhere to be developed. Did your aunt give you this?"

"That's right. Auntie paid for the camera, and the room, and the equipment. She wanted me to take pictures."

"What sort of pictures?"

"Pictures of her having sex with her lovers. She liked to look at them afterwards."

She said: "What happened to them, the pictures you took?"

"My solicitor had them. They were exhibits for the defence. I don't know where they are now. They were used to prove that Auntie had lovers. And the police saw them. They tried to trace the men to exclude them from the inquiry. They only found one of them and he had an alibi. I don't think they looked very hard for the others. They'd got me, hadn't they? They'd built up their case. They weren't going to waste time looking for evidence they didn't want to find. That's how the police work. They make up their minds and then they look for the evidence."

She had a sudden picture, vivid, indecent but shamefully exciting, of that garish sitting-room beneath them, of two naked bodies humping and groaning on the couch, of Ashe standing above them adjusting the lens, moving around, crouching, to get the pictures he wanted. She almost said, "Why did you do it? How could she make you?" but she knew that they were questions which she couldn't ask. She was aware that he was looking at her closely with a concentrated, unsmiling gaze.

He rested his hand on the equipment and asked: "Know what this is?"

"Of course not. I told you, I don't understand about photography."

"It's an enlarger. Do you want to see how it works?"

"If you like."

"We'll be in the dark for a time."

"I don't mind the dark."

He moved over to the door and switched off the light, then came back to where she stood and lifted his arm. A red bulb glowed, a stocky candle of translucent scarlet staining his fingers. Now another light, small and white, shone from the enlarger. He took from his pocket an envelope and withdrew a short strip of film, a single negative.

He said: "Thirty-five millimetre. I'm putting it into a frame and the frame into the enlarger."

An image which she couldn't decipher fell on a white board crossed by bands of black metal like rulers. She couldn't make sense of it, while he peered at it through what looked like a small telescope.

She said: "What is it? I can't see anything."

"You will presently."

He switched off the enlarger light and now they were in darkness except for that glimmering red pillar. She watched while he took a sheet of paper from a box on the lowest shelf and fitted it into the frame, adjusting the black rods.

She said: "Go on, tell me what you're doing. I want to know."

"I'm deciding on the size."

He switched on the light in the enlarger, it seemed for only six or seven seconds. Then he quickly put on a pair of plastic gloves, lifted the frame and tossed the paper into the first bath, gently agitating the fluid. It began swaying and moving, snake-like, as if it were alive. She gazed at it fascinated.

"Now watch. Keep looking." The words were a command.

And almost at once the image began to come up, a pattern in stark black and white. There was the couch, but covered now with a bedspread patterned in squares and circles. And on the couch was the body of a woman. She was lying on her back, naked except for a thin négligé which had fallen open to reveal the black smudge of pubic hair and breasts white and heavy like giant jellyfish. The hair was a tangled frizz against the whiteness of the pillow. Her mouth was half open, the tongue slightly protruding, as if she had been strangled. The eyes were open, black and staring, but they were dead eyes. The knife wounds in the chest and belly gaped like mouths from which the blood was oozing like black sputum. There was a single gash across the throat. And here the blood had gushed, seemed as she looked to be gushing still, a spurting fountain of blood flowing over the breasts, dripping from the divan to the floor. The image pulsated in the tray until she could almost believe that the blood was seeping from it to stain the fluid red.

Octavia could hear the rhythmic thudding of her heart. Surely he must hear it too. It seemed to power the claustrophobic little room like a dynamo. She said in a whisper: "Who took it?"

He didn't reply for a moment. He was scrutinizing the print as if to check its quality.

Still gently agitating the fluid, he said quietly: "I did. I took it when I got back and found her."

"Before you phoned the police?"

"Of course."

"But why did you want it?"

"Because I always photographed Auntie on that couch. That's what she liked."

"Weren't you afraid that the police would find it?"

"A strip of film is easy to hide, and they had the photographs they wanted. They weren't looking for it. They were looking for the knife."

"Did they find it?"

He didn't reply. She asked again: "Did they find it, the knife?"

"Yes, they found it. He'd chucked it in a front garden four houses down, hidden under the privet hedge. It was a cooking knife from the kitchen."

With his gloved hands he took the print from the fluid, dropped it into the second dish and then immediately transferred it to the third. He switched on the overhead light. Taking the print from the dish, he held the dripping edge over a canister and almost ran with it out of the room. She followed him into the bathroom next door. Lying in the bath was another dish and flowing gently into it was cold water from a rubber shower hose attached to the tap.

He said: "I have to use the bathroom. There's no water laid on next door."

"Why do you use gloves? Is that fluid dangerous?"

"It's not the stuff to get on your hands."

They stood together as the picture in its stark uncompromising horror swayed and shifted under the cleansing stream. He set all this up before he called for me this evening, Octavia thought. He must have done. He wanted me to see it. He meant it as a test.

She turned her eyes away and tried to concentrate on the room, the narrow, comfortless little cell, its stained bath with its rim of dirt and grease, the curtainless window of opaque glass, the brown linoleum curling round the base of the lavatory pedestal. But always her eyes came back to that gently moving image. She thought: But she was old. Old, ugly, horrible. How could he bear to live with her? She remembered her mother's voice. "His aunt wasn't a pleasant woman but something held them together. Almost certainly they were lovers. He was one of many, but in his case, no doubt, it came free." She thought: It isn't true. She was saying it to turn me against him. But there's nothing she can do now. He's shown me this, he trusts me, we belong together.

Suddenly there were voices, loud shouting, a crash from the back door as if someone were trying to kick it in. Without a word, Ashe rushed downstairs. Octavia, in panic, grabbed the print and dropped it into the lavatory bowl. Under the water she tore it in two, then tore again, and jerked down the handle of the flush. There was a gurgle, a thin trickle, then nothing. With a sob of desperation she jerked the handle again. After a second the water gushed and the segments with their glossy image swirled out of sight. With a gasp she ran downstairs.

In the kitchen Ashe was forcing a young boy against the wall, holding a kitchen knife to his throat. The boy's eyes swivelled to hers in a mixture of terror and appeal.

Ashe said: "If you or your mates get over that fence again I shall know. And next time I cut. I know a place where I can bury your body and no one will ever find it. Do you understand?"

The knife moved a fraction from the throat. The boy, terrified, nodded. Ashe released him and he disappeared out of the kitchen so quickly that he skidded into the doorpost.

Ashe calmly replaced the knife in a drawer. He said: "One of the kids from the estate. They're all barbarians." And then he saw Octavia's face. "God, you look terrified. Who did you think it was?"

"The police. I tore up the picture, flushed it down the loo. I was afraid they'd find it. I'm sorry."

Suddenly she was frightened of him, of his displeasure, of his anger, but he shrugged and gave a short mirthless laugh. "It wouldn't matter if they did see it. I could sell it to a Sunday paper and there's nothing they could do. You can't be tried twice for the same offence. Didn't you know that?"

"I suppose I did know. I just didn't think. I'm sorry."

He came over to her and, taking her head in his hands, bent and kissed her on the lips. It was the first time. His lips were cold and surprisingly soft, but the kiss was firm, his mouth closed. She remembered other kisses and how she had hated them: the slobbery taste of beer and food, the wetness, the tongue thrusting down her throat. This kiss, she knew, was an affirmation. She had passed the test.

Then he took something from his pocket and lifted her left hand. She felt the coldness of the ring before she saw it, a heavy band of old gold with a blood-red stone encircled with clouded pearls. Octavia gazed down at it while he waited for her response, and then she shivered and caught her breath as if the air had become icy cold. Her veins and muscles tightened with fear, and she could hear the thud of her heart. Surely she had seen the ring before, on his dead aunt's little finger. The photograph swam up again before her eyes, the gaping wounds, the slashed throat.

She knew that her voice sounded cracked. She made herself say: "It wasn't hers, was it? She wasn't wearing it when she died?"

But now his voice was softer, gentler than she had ever before heard it.

"Would I do that to you? She had one like it but with a different-coloured stone. I bought this especially for you. It's an antique ring. I thought it was one you'd like."

She said: "I do like it." She turned it on her finger. "It's a little loose."

"Wear it on the middle finger for now. We'll get it made smaller."

"No," she said: "I don't want to take it off, ever. And I won't lose it. It's on the right finger. It shows that we belong together."

"Yes," he said. "We belong together. We're safe. Now we can go home."

8

Simon Costello knew that the purchase of the house in Pembroke Square had been a mistake within a year of his and Lois's moving in. A possession which can only be afforded by the exercise of stringent and calculated economy is best not afforded at all. But at the time it had seemed a sensible, as well as a desirable, move. He had had a run of successful cases and the briefs were coming in with reassuring regularity. Lois had returned to her job at the advertising agency within two months of the birth of the twins, and had been given a rise which took her salary to thirty-five thousand. It was Lois who had argued the more strongly for a move, but he had put up little resistance to arguments which at the time had seemed compelling: the flat wasn't really suitable for a family; they needed more room, a garden, separate accommodation for an au pair. All these, of course, could have been achieved in a suburb or in a less fashionable part of London than Pembroke Square, but Lois was ambitious for more than additional space. Mornington Mansions had never been an acceptable address for an up-and-coming young barrister and a successful businesswoman. She never gave it without a sense that even speaking the words subtly diminished her standing, socially and economically.

She had, he knew, a vivid mental picture of their renewed life together. There would be dinner parties—admittedly prepared by outside caterers or based on ready-cooked meals from Marks and Spencer—but elegant, carefully managed, the guests chosen to provide stimulating and amusing conversation, the whole a culinary celebration of marital harmony and professional success. It hadn't turned out like that. Both of them were too tired by the end of the working day to face more than a quickly prepared meal eaten at the kitchen table, or sitting with a tray in front of the television. And neither of them had had any idea of the demands made by the twins as they grew out of that first swaddled, cradle-bound, milky acquiescence into rumbustious eighteen-month-olds whose claims to be fed, comforted, changed and stimulated seemed insatiable.

A succession of au pairs of varying degrees of competence dominated his and Lois's life. It sometimes seemed to him that they were more preoccupied with the comfort and happiness of the au pair than they were with each other's. Most of their friends were childless; the occasional warnings they had been given about the difficulty of finding reliable help had seemed more motivated by unacknowledged envy of Lois's pregnancy than by personal experience. But they had proved only too accurate. Sometimes it seemed that the au pair, so far from lessening their responsibilities, made them greater: another person in the house to be considered, fed and propitiated.

When the girl was satisfactory they worried constantly that she would leave. Inevitably she did; Lois was an over-demanding employer. When it was necessary to get rid of an au pair they argued over who should be the one to do it and agonized about the difficulty of finding a replacement. They lay in bed constantly discussing the defects and foibles of the girl-in-post, whispering in the darkness as if they feared that the criticisms could be heard two floors above, where she slept in the room next to the nursery. Was she drinking? One could hardly mark the level of the bottles. Did she have boyfriends in during the day? Impossible to inspect the sheets. Were the children left alone? Perhaps one of them ought to come home unexpectedly from time to time to check. But which one? Simon protested that he couldn't walk out of court. Lois couldn't possibly take time off; the rise in salary was being dearly earned by longer hours and more responsibilities. There was a new boss whom she didn't like. He would be only too glad to say that married women with children were unreliable.

Lois had decided that a necessary economy was for one of them to travel by public transport. Her firm was in Docklands; obviously Simon must be the one to economize. The over-crowded tube journey, started in a mood of envious resentment, had become an unproductive thirty minutes of brooding on present discontents. He would recall his grandfather's house in Hampstead, where he had stayed as a boy, the decanter of sherry placed to hand, the smell of dinner from the kitchen, his grandmother's insistence that the returning breadwinner, tired from his exhausting day in court, should be given peace, a little gentle cosseting and relief from every petty domestic anxiety. She had been a Chambers wife, indefatigable in legal good causes, elegantly present at all Chambers functions, apparently content with the sphere of life which she had made her own. Well, that world had passed for ever. Lois had made it plain before their marriage that her career was as important as his. It had hardly needed saying; this was, after all, a modern marriage. The job was important to her and important to them both. The house, the au pair, their whole standard of living depended on two salaries. And now what they were precariously achieving could be destroyed by that bloody self-righteous interfering bitch.

Venetia must have come straight from the Bailey to Chambers and she had been in a dangerous mood. Something or someone had upset her. But the word "upset" was too weak, too bland for the intensity of furious disgust with which she had confronted him. Someone had driven her to the limit of her endurance. He cursed himself. If he hadn't been in his room, if he'd only left a minute earlier, the encounter wouldn't have taken place, she would have had the night to think it over, to consider what, if anything, she ought to do. Probably nothing. The morning might have brought sense. He remembered every word of her angry accusations.

"I defended Brian Cartwright today. Successfully. He told me that when you were his counsel four years ago you knew before trial that he had suborned three of the jury. You did nothing. You went on with the case. Is that true?"

"He's lying. It isn't true."

"He also said that he passed over some shares in his company to your fiancée. Also before trial. Is that true?"

"I tell you, he's lying. None of it's true."

The denial had been as instinctive as an arm raised to ward off a blow and had sounded unconvincing even to his own ears. His whole action had been one of guilt. The first cold horror draining his face was succeeded by a hot flush, bringing back shameful memories of his housemaster's study, of the terror of the inevitable beating. He had made himself look into her eyes and had seen the look of contemptuous disbelief. If only he'd had some warning. He knew now what he should have said: "Cartwright told me after the trial but I didn't believe him. I don't believe him now. That man will say anything to make himself important."

But he had told a more direct, more dangerous lie, and she had known that it was a lie. Even so, why the anger, why the disgust? What was that old misdemeanour to do with her? Who had sent Venetia Aldridge to be guardian of the conscience of Chambers? Or of his, come to that? Was her own conscience so clear, her behaviour in court always so immaculate? Was she justified in destroying his career? And it would be destruction. He wasn't sure what exactly she could do, how far she was prepared to go, but if this got about, even as a rumour, he would never take silk.

As soon as he opened his front door the bawling met him. An unknown girl was coming down the stairs holding Daisy in unpractised arms. He had an instantaneous conviction of her dangerous incompetence; the spiked red hair, the grubby jeans, the studs implanted in the side of her ear, the precarious balance of the high-heeled sandals on the uncarpeted stairs. He ran up and almost snatched the screaming Daisy from her arms.

"Who the hell are you? Where's Estelle?"

"Her boyfriend fall off bike. She go to see him in hospital. Very bad. I look after babies till Mrs. Costello come."

A familiar smell confirmed one cause of the crying: the child needed changing. Holding her almost at arm's length, he carried her up to the nursery. Amy, still in her daytime dungarees, was standing in her cot, clutching at the bars and grizzling.

"Have they been fed?" He might have been talking of animals.

"I give milk. Estelle say wait for Mrs. Costello."

He dumped Daisy in her cot and her bawling increased. It was, he thought, less distress than anger. Her eyes were slits through which she glared at him with concentrated malevolence. Amy, not to be outdone by her twin, began a more piteous sobbing which soon broke into loud crying.

He heard with relief the sharp closing of the front door and Lois's feet on the stairs. Going to meet her, he said: "For God's sake, cope in there. Estelle's off with some injured boyfriend and she's left a freak in charge. I need a drink."

The drinks cupboard was in the drawing-room. Throwing his coat over a chair, he poured himself a large whisky. But the sounds penetrated: Lois's angry voice becoming shrill, the crying children, feet on the stairs, more voices in the hall.

The door opened. "I've got to pay her off. She wants twenty quid. Have you got a note?"

He took out two tens and handed them silently over. The front door was decisively closed, and after a few minutes there was a blessed silence, but it was forty minutes before Lois finally reappeared.

"I've got them settled. You weren't a lot of use. You could at least have changed them."

"I hadn't time. I was going to when you came in. What's happened about Estelle?"

"God knows. I've never even heard of this boyfriend. She'll reappear sometime, I suppose, probably in time for supper. Oh, this is the last straw! She'll have to go. God, what a day! Pour me a drink, will you? Not whisky. I'd like a gin and tonic."

He took the drink over to where she sat slumped in the corner of the sofa. She was wearing what he thought of as her working clothes. He hated them:

the black skirt with the centre slit, the well-cut jacket, the soft gleam of the silk shirt, the plain court shoes. They represented the Lois from whom he felt increasingly alienated and a world which was as important to her as it was threatening to him. Only a moistness of the skin, a receding flush of the forehead betrayed the recent struggle. How odd, he thought, that one could get used to beauty. Once he had thought that any price would be worth paying if he could possess it, know it to be exclusively his, feed on it, be comforted, exalted, even sanctified by it. But you couldn't possess beauty any more than you could possess another human being.

She drained the glass quickly, then, getting up, said: "I'll go and get changed now. We'll have spaghetti bolognese for supper, and if Estelle comes back I don't want to tackle her till I've eaten."

He said: "Don't go for a moment. There's something I've got to tell you."

It wasn't a good time to break the news, but when would the time be right? Better get it over. He told her the facts baldly.

"Venetia Aldridge came into my office before I left. She'd just defended Brian Cartwright. He told her that I knew three of the jurors had been bribed when I defended him in that assault case in 1992. He also told her about the Cartwright Agricultural Company shares he passed over to you before trial. I don't think she's going to let it rest."

"What do you mean, she isn't going to let it rest?"

"I suppose at worst she could report me to the Bar Council or my Inn."

"Well she can't. It's over. It's nothing to do with her."

"She seemed to think it is."

"I suppose you denied it?" Her voice sharpened: "You did deny it, didn't you?"

"Of course I denied it."

"Then that's all right. She can't prove anything. It's your word against Cartwright's."

"It isn't as simple as that. She could find proof about the shares, I imagine. And Cartwright will probably give her the jurors' names if pressed."

"It's hardly in his interest to, is it? Why the hell did he tell her, anyway?"

"God knows. His way of handing out a tip for services received, I suppose. Conceit perhaps. Wanted to boast, to tell her that it was his cleverness, not counsel's, that got him off last time. Why do people do these things? What does it matter why he did it? He did it."

"So what? Even if he does give the names, it's still his and their word against yours. And why shouldn't he give me the shares? You know how it was. I came to see you in Chambers just as he was leaving and we had a chat. We took to each other. You stayed on and I shared a taxi with him. I rather liked him. We talked about investments. A week later he wrote and gave me the shares. It was nothing to do with you. We weren't even married."

"We were a week later."

"But he gave them to me. Me personally. There's nothing illegal in a friend giving me some shares, I suppose. It was nothing to do with you. He would have handed them over even if we hadn't been engaged."

"Would he?"

"Anyway, I could say that you never knew about the shares. I never told you, so that's all right. And you could say that you didn't believe Cartwright about the bribery. You thought it was his idea of a joke. No one could prove anything. Isn't the law all about proof? Well there isn't any. Venetia Aldridge will see that herself. She's supposed to be such a brilliant lawyer, isn't she? She'll let it drop. And now I need another drink."

Lois had never understood the law. She liked the prestige of being married to a barrister and in the early days of their married life she had occasionally attended his cases, until boredom drove her away.

He said: "It isn't as simple as that. She doesn't actually need proof, not the kind that would stand up in court. If this gets about I can say goodbye to any chance of taking silk."

Now she was worried. She turned to him sharply, gin bottle in hand. She said, her voice incredulous: "You mean that Venetia Aldridge could actually stop you becoming a QC?"

"If she wanted to take the trouble, yes."

"Then you'll have to stop her." He didn't reply. She said: "Someone will have to stop her. I'll speak to Uncle Desmond. He'll tackle her. You always said that he's the most highly regarded lawyer in Chambers."

Now his voice was sharp. "No. No, Lois. You're not to say a word to him. Can't you see what that would mean? This is the last thing that Desmond Ulrick would be sympathetic to."

"Not sympathetic to you, perhaps. Sympathetic to me."

"I know you think that Desmond would do anything for you. I know he's besotted with you. I know you borrowed money from him."

"We borrowed money. We wouldn't have this house if he hadn't helped with that loan. Interest-free. The Cartwright shares and Uncle Desmond's loan, that's what paid the deposit, and don't you forget it."

"I'm not likely to. Fat chance we've got of paying it back."

"He doesn't expect to be paid back. He called it a loan to save your pride."

It hadn't saved his pride. Even in this, his extremity of worry, the old jealousy, irrational but ever-present, pricked him like the twinge of a familiar pain. Ulrick was besotted with her, that he could understand—who better? What he found repugnant was her exploitation of it, her exultation in it.

He said again: "You're not to say a word to him. I forbid you, Lois. The worst thing would be to confide in anyone about this, particularly someone in Chambers. Our only hope is to keep it quiet. Cartwright won't spread it around. He hasn't done so for the last four years. It isn't in his interest, anyway. I'll speak to Venetia."

"You'd better, and soon. You can't go on relying on my salary."

"I don't rely on it, we rely on it. And you're the one who's been most insistent on working."

"Well, I'm not as insistent as I was. I'm fed up with Carl Edgar. He's becoming intolerable. I'm looking for another job."

"Still, you'd better stick to the one you've got for the present. This is hardly the time to start handing in your notice."

"It's too late, I'm afraid. I've done so already, this afternoon."

They gazed at each other appalled, then she said again: "So you'd better do something about Venetia Aldridge, hadn't you? And quickly."

9

The call came through to Mark Rawlstone's Pimlico house just as the nine o'clock news on the BBC was drawing to an end. There had been nothing of importance in the House and, with a speech to work on for next week's debate, he had dined at home alone. Lucy was visiting her mother in Weybridge and would be staying the night. Mother and daughter had, after all, things to talk over, particularly now. But as usual she had left his dinner ready, a duck casserole which he had only needed to reheat, a simple salad, prepared except for the dressing, fruit and cheese. He was half-expecting a telephone call and this could be it. Kenneth Maples was dining at the House, but had said that he might drop in later for coffee and a chat. He would ring to confirm. Ken was in the Shadow Cabinet; the chat could be important. Everything that happened between now and the election could be important. This might be Ken confirming that he was on his way.

Instead, with a mixture of disappointment and irritation, he heard Venetia's voice. She said: "I'm glad I got you. I did try at the House. Look, I need to see you urgently. Can you come over for half an hour?"

"Can't it wait? I'm expecting someone to ring me later."

"No, it can't wait. I shouldn't have rung if it could wait. Leave a message on the answerphone. I won't keep you long."

The first spurt of irritation had given way to resignation. "All right," he said ungraciously, "I'll take a cab."

Putting down the receiver, he reflected that it was unusual for Venetia to ring him at home. Indeed, he couldn't remember the last occasion. She had been as punctilious as he about keeping separate their love affair and their private lives, just as obsessive about secrecy and security—not because she had as much to lose as he, but through a fastidious dislike of knowing that her sexual life was the subject of Chambers gossip. It had helped that he was a member of Lincoln's Inn, not the Middle Temple, helped too that an MP's life, with its unpredictable and long hours, the journeys to and from his Midlands constituency, afforded opportunities for secret meetings, even occasionally for nights together at Pelham Place. But during the last six months the meetings had become less frequent, the first move towards them coming more often from Venetia than from himself. The affair now was beginning to have some of the longueurs of marriage, but with none of marriage's reassuring safety and comfort. It wasn't only that the excitement had gone. It was difficult now to recall those first heady weeks when their affair had first started, impossible to recapture that mixture of sexual enthralment spiced with danger, the exhilarating self-confidence of knowing that a beautiful and successful woman found him desirable. Did she still? Hadn't it become a matter of habit for them both? Everything, even illicit passion, had its natural end. At least this affair, unlike some of his earlier, ill-advised escapades, could be ended without acrimony.

He had been meaning to end it even before Lucy had told him of her pregnancy. It was becoming too dangerous, the word "sleaze" altogether too fashionable. The British public, and in particular the press with their usual genius for hypocrisy, had decided that a sexual licence which journalists might permit themselves was disgraceful and unforgivable in a politician. The breed, never popular, must now be made uncomfortable by the imposition of an irreproachable sexual virtue. And he had no doubt his affair would rate the front page if the story broke on a dull day: rising young Labour MP tipped for junior-minister rank, devout Roman Catholic wife, a mistress who was one of the country's leading criminal lawyers. He wasn't going to take part in the usual demeaning charade, the public double act complete with photograph of the repentant adventurer, the loyal little wife nobly standing by her delinquent husband. He wouldn't put Lucy through that, not now, not ever. Venetia would see sense. He wasn't dealing with a jealous, vindictive, self-absorbed exhibitionist. One advantage of choosing an intelligent independent woman as a mistress was the certainty that an affair could always be ended with dignity.

Lucy had waited until the pregnancy was certain and well established before she told him. It was typical of her, the ability to wait, to know what she meant to do, to think out precisely what she meant to say. He had taken her into his arms, had felt the resurgence of a half-forgotten passion, an old protective love. Their childlessness had been a grief to her, a regret to him. In that moment he had realized overwhelmingly that he, too, had wanted a child with something of her desperation, that it was only because failure had always been intolerable that he had suppressed a hope which he had come to believe would never be fulfilled. Freeing herself from his arms, Lucy had given her ultimatum.

"Mark, this makes a difference to us, to our marriage."

"Darling, a child always makes a difference. We'll be a family. My God, it's wonderful! It's wonderful news! I don't know how you kept it to yourself for four months."

He realized before the sentence was out of his mouth that this could be a mistake. It wasn't a secret that she would have found so easy to keep in the days when they were close. But she let it pass.

She said: "I mean it makes a difference to us now. Whoever it is you've been seeing—I don't want to know her name, I don't want to hear anything about it—but it has to end. You do see that?"

And he had said: "It has ended. It wasn't important. I've never loved any woman but you."

At that moment he believed it. He still believed it; in so far as he was capable of loving, she had his heart.

There had been an unspoken codicil to their concordance and both of them knew it. The dinner party planned for Friday night was part of it. Lucy would do what was expected of her and would do it well. She was little interested in politics. The world in which he strove, with its intrigues, its strategies for survival, its coteries and rivalries, its frenetic ambition, was alien to her fastidious mind. But she had a genuine interest in people, seeming unconscious of class or rank or importance, and they had responded always to that gentle, inquiring gaze, felt at ease in her drawing-room, knew themselves to be safe. He told himself that his world needed Lucy; he needed Lucy.

When the taxi turned into Pelham Place, he saw that a young man on a motorcycle was just leaving Venetia's house. Some friend of Octavia's, presumably. He had forgotten that she was now living in the basement. That was another reason for ending the affair. At least when she had been at school they could be sure of privacy for most of the year. She was an unattractive child. He didn't want her even vicariously in his life.

He rang the bell. Venetia had never given him a key even when their affair was at its most intense. He told himself, not without a touch of resentment, that there had always been privacies Venetia would never surrender. He had been admitted to her bed but not to her life.

It was she, not the housekeeper Mrs. Buckley, who opened the door and led him upstairs to the drawing-room. The whisky decanter was already set out on the low table in front of the fire. He thought, as he had done before but now with a more positive reaction, that he had never really liked her drawing-room, never enjoyed or liked her house. It lacked comfort, individuality, a sense of welcome. It was as if she had decided that a Georgian town house must be formally furnished and had gone round the auction houses bidding for the minimum of appropriate pieces. Nothing in the room, he suspected, had come from her past; nothing had been bought because she deeply cared for it—the padded chaise longue which looked good but wasn't really comfortable, the silver table with a few choice pieces which he knew she had bought one afternoon in the Silver Vaults. The one picture, a Vanessa Bell over the mantelpiece, at least witnessed a personal taste: she was fond of twentieth-century paintings. But there were never flowers. Mrs. Buckley had other things to do and Venetia was too busy to buy and arrange them.

He realized afterwards that he mishandled their meeting from the first moment. Forgetting that it was she who had called him for advice, he said: "I'm sorry, I can't stop, I'm expecting Kenneth Maples. But I've been meaning to call in to see you. Life has rather fallen around my ears in the past few weeks. There's something I think I ought to say. I don't think we should see each other again. It's getting too dangerous, too difficult for us both. I've had a feeling for some time that you've been thinking along the same lines."

She never drank whisky, but there was a decanter of red wine on the silver tray. Now she poured herself a glass. Her hand was perfectly steady, but the dark treacle-brown eyes stared into his with a look of such accusing contempt that instinctively he recoiled. He had never seen her like this. What was wrong with her? Never before had he felt that she was maintaining a precarious self-control.

She said: "So that's why you've condescended to come here, even at the risk of missing Kenneth Maples. You're telling me you want to end our affair."

He said: "I thought you were feeling much the same. After all, we haven't seen a great deal of each other in recent weeks."

To his horror he heard in his voice a tone of almost humiliating appeal. He went on with a kind of desperate assurance.

"Look, we had an affair. I made no promises, neither of us did. We never pretended to be madly in love. It wasn't on those terms."

"What terms, precisely, did you think it was on? No, tell me, I'm interested."

"The same as you, I imagine. Sexual attraction, respect, affection. I suppose habit really."

"A very convenient habit. A sexual partner available as and when required whom you could trust because she had as much to lose as you, and whom you didn't have to pay. It's a habit your sex find it easy to acquire, especially politicians."

"That's unworthy of you. It's also unfair. I thought I made you happy."

And now there was a harshness in her voice which chilled his blood.

"Did you, Mark? Did you really? Are you that arrogant? Making me happy isn't as easy as that. It requires more than an impressive prick and a modicum of sexual technique. You didn't make me happy, you've never made me happy. What you did was to provide from time to time—when it was convenient, when your wife didn't need you to entertain guests, when you had a spare evening—an instant of sexual pleasure. I could have done as much for myself, if less effectively. Don't call that making me happy."

Trying to find a foothold in what seemed a morass of irrationality, he said: "If I treated you badly, I'm sorry. I didn't want to hurt you. That's the last thing I wanted."

"You just don't understand, do you, Mark? You don't listen. You haven't the capacity to hurt me. You aren't that important to me, no man is."

"Then what are you complaining about? We had an affair. We both wanted it. It suited us. Now it's over. If I wasn't important to you, where's the hurt?"

"I'm complaining about the extraordinary way in which you think you can treat women. You deceived your wife because you wanted variety, sex spiced with danger, and because you knew I was discreet. Now you need Lucy. Suddenly she's important. You need respectability, a dutiful loving wife, a political asset. So Lucy promises to overlook the infidelity, support you through the election, be the perfect MP's wife, in return, no doubt, for your promise that our affair is over. 'I'll never see her again. It never really meant anything. It was always you I loved.' Isn't that how philanderers reconcile themselves to the little woman?"

Suddenly he found the comfort of anger. He said: "Leave Lucy out of this. She doesn't need your concern or your bloody patronizing sympathy. It's a bit late to start setting yourself up as a champion of the female sex. I'll look after Lucy. Our marriage has nothing to do with you. Anyway, it wasn't like that. Your name wasn't mentioned. Lucy doesn't know about our affair."

"Doesn't she? Grow up, Mark. If she doesn't know it was me, she knows it was someone, wives always do. If Lucy kept quiet it was because she knew it was in her interests to keep quiet. You weren't going to break up the marriage, were you? It was just a little diversion on the side. Men do these things."

"Lucy's pregnant."

He didn't know what had made him say it, but now the words were out.

There was a pause. Then she said calmly: "I thought Lucy couldn't have children."

"That's what we thought. We've been married eight years. You do tend to give up hope. Lucy wouldn't go through the paraphernalia of infertility testing and treatment, she thought it would be too humiliating for me. Well, it wasn't necessary. The baby's due on 20th February."

"How convenient. All done by prayer and lighting candles, I suppose. Or was it an immaculate conception?"

She paused, holding out the whisky bottle. He shook his head. She filled her own glass with wine, then said, her voice deliberately casual: "Does she know about the abortion? When you had that reconciling little talk, did you think to mention that twelve months ago I aborted your child?"

"No, she doesn't know."

"Of course not. That's one sin you wouldn't dare to confess. A little sexual misdemeanour, something on the side, that's forgivable, but killing an unborn child? No, she wouldn't be so charitable about that. A devout Roman Catholic, well-known supporter of the Pro-Life movement and now pregnant herself. That interesting piece of information would overshadow the months between now and February, wouldn't it? Wouldn't there be for her a silent, reproachful, invisible sibling growing up with your son or daughter, isn't that how she'd see it? Wouldn't she feel the ghost of that aborted baby every time you held your child?"

"Don't do that to her, Venetia. Have some pride. Don't talk like a cheap blackmailer."

"Oh, not cheap, Mark, not cheap. Blackmail is never cheap. You're a criminal lawyer. You should know that."

And now he was reduced to pleading, hating himself, hating her.

"She's never harmed you. You wouldn't do that to her."

"Probably not, but you'll never be certain, will you?"

He should have left it at that. Afterwards he cursed his folly. It wasn't only in cross-examination that you had to know when to stop. He should have disciplined his pride, made a final appeal to her and left. But he was angered by the injustice of it all. She was talking as if the responsibility was his alone, that she'd been forced into aborting the child.

He said: "It was you who got it into your head that the Pill was harmful and that you'd better come off it for a time. It was you who took the risk. And you were as keen on the termination as I was. You were horrified when you found you were pregnant. An illegitimate child would have been a disaster. Any child would, you said so yourself. And you never wanted another child. You don't even care for the one you have."

She wasn't looking at him now. Her angry eyes gazing past him were suddenly appalled and he turned to follow her glance. Octavia was standing silently at the door, clutching a pair of silver candlesticks. No one spoke. Mother and daughter were frozen into a tableau. He muttered, "I'm sorry. Sorry," and, pushing past Octavia, almost ran down the stairs. There was no sign of Mrs. Buckley, but the door had been left on the Yale and he was saved the ignominy of waiting to be let out.

It was only when he was yards from the house and breaking into a run, desperate to hail a taxi, that he realized that he had never asked Venetia what she had wanted to say to him.

10

Drysdale Laud was aware that his friends thought, not without a touch of resentment, that he had his life pretty well organized. It was a view with which he agreed and for which he took some credit. As a successful lawyer specializing in libel, his profession gave him ample opportunity to witness the mess some people made of their lives, messes that he viewed with proper professional sympathy, but with a greater wonder that human beings, given the choice between order and chaos, reason and stupidity, could behave with such a lack of self-interest. If challenged he would have admitted that he had always been fortunate. He was the indulged only child of prosperous parents. Intelligent and exceptionally good-looking, he had progressed at school and Cambridge from success to expected success, achieving a first-class degree in classics before studying law. His father, although not a lawyer, had friends in the law. There was no difficulty in finding a suitable pupillage for young Drysdale. He had become a member of Chambers at the expected time and had taken silk at the first reasonable opportunity.

His father had now been dead for ten years. His mother, left comfortably off, imposed on him no onerous filial duty, requiring only that he spend one weekend each month at her house in Buckinghamshire, during which she would arrange a dinner party. His part of the unstated bargain was to be present, hers was to produce excellent food and guests who wouldn't bore him. The visits also provided cosseting from his ex-nanny, who had remained with his mother as general factotum, and the opportunity for a round of golf or a vigorous country walk. A bag of soiled shirts would be washed and beautifully ironed. It was cheaper than taking them across the road to the nearest laundry and saved time. His mother was a keen gardener and he would take flowers, fresh fruit and vegetables in season back to his flat on the South Bank of the Thames, near Tower Bridge.

He and his mother had an affection for each other which was based on a respect for the other's essential selfishness. Her only criticism of him, hinted at rather than explicit, was his dilatoriness in getting married. She wanted grandchildren; his father would have expected him to carry on the family name. A succession of suitable girls was invited to her dinner parties. Occasionally he obliged by seeing one of them later. Less frequently the dinner party led to a brief affair, though it usually ended in recriminations. When the last candidate had demanded bitterly through her angry tears, "What is your mother? Some kind of pander?" he decided that the mess and emotional turmoil were disproportionate to the pleasure, and returned to his former satisfactory arrangement with a lady who, although highly expensive, was discriminating in her choice of clients, imaginative in the personal services rendered and entirely discreet. But these things had to be paid for. He had never expected to get his pleasures cheaply.

He knew that his mother, who retained an old-fashioned prejudice against the divorced especially when they had children, and who had found Venetia unsympathetic on the one occasion they had met, had been afraid that he might marry her. The thought had once crossed his mind, but only for an hour. He suspected that Venetia already had a lover, although he had never been curious enough to take the trouble to discover his name. He knew that their friendship was a source of gossip in Chambers, but they had, in fact, never been lovers. He wasn't physically attracted to successful or powerful women, and would occasionally tell himself with a wry smile that sex with Venetia would be too like an examination in which his performance would be subject to subsequent rigorous cross-examination.

Once a month his mother, an energetic and still-handsome sixty-five-year-old, came up to London to meet a friend, shop, see an exhibition or have a beauty treatment, and would then come on to the flat, as she had this evening. They would have dinner together, usually at a riverside restaurant, and afterwards he would put her into a taxi for Marylebone and her usual train. It was, he thought, typical of her independence that she was beginning to question whether the detour was sensible at the end of a heavy day. Tower Bridge was inconvenient to reach from the West End and in winter particularly she disliked being late home. He suspected that the arrangement wouldn't last much longer and that for both of them its ending would be a source of only mild regret.

The telephone rang as he re-entered the flat. Answering, he heard Venetia's voice. She sounded peremptory.

"I need to see you, tonight if possible. Are you alone?"

He said cautiously: "Yes. I've just seen my mother into her taxi. Can't it wait? It's eleven."

"No it can't. I'll be with you as soon as I can."

Half an hour later he let her in. It was the first time she had been in his flat. Invariably punctilious in these matters, he called for her at her house when they had a date and took her home afterwards. But she entered his sitting-room without the slightest sign of interest either in the room, or in the wide expanse of shining water outside the windows and the glittering floodlit wonder of Tower Bridge. He felt a moment's irritation that a room over which he had taken such trouble should be so disregarded. Ignoring the spectacular view which normally drew visitors to the windows, she flung off her coat and handed it to him as if he were a servant.

He said: "What will you drink?"

"Nothing. Anything. What you're having."

"Whisky."

It was a drink he knew she disliked. She said: "Red wine, then. Anything you've got open."

He had nothing open, but he fetched a bottle of Hermitage from the wine cupboard, poured her a glass and set it down on the low table in front of her.

Ignoring the drink, she said without preamble: "I'm sorry to come at such short notice but I need your help. You remember that boy Garry Ashe I defended three or four weeks ago?"

"Of course."

"Well, I saw him at the Bailey after my case today. He's taken up with Octavia. According to her they're engaged."

"That's quick. When did they meet?"

"After the trial, of course, when else? Obviously it's a put-up job on his part and I want it stopped."

He said carefully: "I can see that it's unwelcome, but I don't see how you can stop it. Octavia's of age, isn't she? Even if she weren't you'd have some difficulty. What could you allege against him? He was acquitted."

His unspoken words were so obvious that he might as well have said them aloud: "Thanks to you."

He asked: "You've spoken to Octavia?"

"Of course. She's adamant. Well, she would be. Part of his attraction is the power he gives her to hurt me."

"Isn't that a little unjust? Why should she want to hurt you? She could be genuinely fond of him."

"For God's sake, Drysdale, be realistic. Besotted maybe. Intrigued perhaps. Liking the spice of danger—I can understand that, he is dangerous. But what about him? You're not telling me that Ashe is in love, and after three weeks. This is deliberate, and one or both of them engineered it. It's directed against me."

"By Ashe? Why should it be? I'd have expected him to be grateful."

"He isn't grateful and I don't expect or want his gratitude. I want him out of my life."

Drysdale said quietly: "Isn't he rather more in Octavia's life than yours?"

"I've told you, this is nothing to do with Octavia. He's using her to get at me. They're even thinking of going to the press. Can you imagine that? A sentimental picture of them in the Sunday tabloids with his arm around her. 'Mummy Saved My Boyfriend from Prison. Top QC's Daughter Tells the Story of Their Love.' "

"She wouldn't do that, surely?"

"Oh yes she would."

Drysdale said: "If you don't interfere it'll probably pass. One or the other will get tired of it. If he chucks her she'll be hurt in her pride, but that'll be all. Isn't the important thing not to antagonize her? To make her feel that you'll be there if she needs you? Haven't you a family friend, solicitor, GP, someone like that? An older person she respects who could talk to her?"

He could hardly believe that it was he who was speaking. He thought: I sound like some agony aunt handing out the predictable pabulum to rebellious daughters and their disaffected mothers. The flood of resentment against Venetia surprised him by its intensity. He was the last person who could help with this kind of problem. All right, they were friends, they enjoyed each other's company. He liked being seen in public with a beautiful woman. She never bored him. Heads turned when they entered a restaurant together. He liked that, even while he faintly despised himself for so easy, so commonplace a vanity. But they had never been involved in each other's private lives. He seldom saw Octavia, and when he did he found her unresponsive, moody, antagonistic. She had a father somewhere. Let him take responsibility. It was ludicrous of Venetia to expect him to get involved.

She was saying: "One thing could stop him. Money. He thought he was going to inherit from his aunt. She liked to give the impression that there was money and she spent freely enough. On him, too. The photographic equipment, his motorbike—none of it was cheap. But she died in debt. She'd borrowed heavily against the compensation money for the compulsory purchase of the house. The bank will take most of it. He won't get a penny. Incidentally, they were almost certainly lovers."

He said: "None of that came out in the trial, did it, that Ashe and his aunt were lovers?"

"There were a number of things about Garry Ashe that didn't come out in the trial." She looked him full in the face. "I thought you might see him and find out how much he wants, buy him off. I'd be willing to go to ten thousand pounds."

He was appalled. The idea was fantastic. It was also dangerous. That she could even think of it showed the measure of her desperation. That she should seriously expect him to involve himself was demeaning to them both. There were things which friendship had no right to demand.

He kept his voice calm: "I'm sorry, Venetia. If you want to pay him off you'll have to do it yourself or get your solicitor to try. I can't be involved. I'd probably do more harm than good anyway. And if you're afraid of publicity, think of the press coverage if this went wrong. 'Top Lawyer's Man Friend Tries to Buy Off Daughter's Lover.' They'd have a field day."

She put down her glass and got up.

"So you won't help?"

"Not won't. Can't."

Unwilling to meet the angry contempt in her eyes, he went over to the windows. Below him the river was running strongly, its swirls and eddies fired with dancing tongues of silver light. The bridge with its towers and struts outlined with light looked, as always at night, as shimmering and unsubstantial as a mirage. It was a view with which, glass in hand, he had solaced himself after a busy day night after night. Now she had spoilt it for him and he felt some of the petulant resentment of a child.

Without looking round, he said quietly: "How much does this really matter to you? How much would you be willing to give up for it? Your job? Being Head of Chambers?"

There was a pause, then she said quietly: "Don't be ridiculous, Drysdale. I'm not bargaining."

He turned. "I didn't say you were. I was just wondering about your priorities. What is really important to you when the chips are down? Octavia or the career?"

"I don't intend to sacrifice either. I do intend to get rid of Ashe." Again there was a pause, then she said: "You're telling me you won't help?"

"I'm sorry, I can't get involved."

"Can't or won't?"

"Both, Venetia."

She reached for her coat. "Well, at least you've had the guts to be honest. Don't disturb yourself. I'll make my own way out."

But, following her to the door, he asked: "How did you come? Can I call a taxi?"

"No thank you. I'll walk across the bridge and pick one up there."

He went down in the lift with her, then stood for a moment looking after her as she walked along the waterfront under the glitter of the lights. She didn't look back. Her stride, as always, was vigorous, confident. And then, as he watched, it seemed to him that she faltered. Her body sagged and he realized, with the first genuine pity he had felt since her arrival, that he was watching the walk of an old woman.

BOOK TWO

DEATH IN CHAMBERS

11

At seven-thirty on Thursday, 10 October, Harold Naughton left his house in Buckhurst Hill, walked the quarter-mile to Buckhurst Hill Station and caught a train just before seven-forty-five which would take him on the Central Line direct to Chancery Lane. It was a journey he had taken for nearly forty years. His parents had lived in Buckhurst Hill and when he was a boy the suburb had still held some of the self-contained distinctiveness of a small country town. Now that it was just one of the dormitory outposts of the metropolis it still retained, in its leafier streets and lanes of cottage-like houses, a measure of rural peace. He and Margaret had begun their married life in what was then one of the few blocks of modern flats.

He had married an Essex girl; Epping Forest was her countryside, Southend Pier her sight and smell of the sea, the Central Line to Liverpool Street and beyond carried her only rarely to the dangerous delights of London. His father had died within a year of retirement and after his mother's death, three years later, he had inherited the small house where he had been brought up in the claustrophobic, over-protected world of an only child. But he was becoming successful, there were Stephen and Sally needing rooms of their own, Margaret hoped for a larger garden. The family house was sold and the money used for the deposit on the modern semi-detached house on which Margaret had set her ambitions. The garden was long and had been enlarged a few years later, when their elderly neighbour, needing money and finding his patch too large to cope with, had been glad to sell.

To this home, to his comfort, to the bringing up of their children, to the garden and greenhouse, to the local church and her patchwork quilts, Margaret had happily given her life. She had never wanted to take a job and he had valued his domestic comfort too highly to encourage her to look for one. When, at a difficult time, his income from Chambers had fallen, she had tentatively suggested that she might brush up her secretarial skills. He had said, "We'll manage. The children need you here."

And they had managed. But today, as the train rattled into the darkness of the tunnel after the momentary brightness of Stratford Station, he sat, his *Daily Telegraph* still folded, and wondered how he would manage now. By the end of the month, after the Chambers meeting, he would know whether he was to be given an extension of his contract, three years if he were lucky, or one year, perhaps renewable. If the answer were no, what would there be for him? For nearly forty years Chambers had been his life. He had given, out of his need more than theirs, an absolute commitment of time, energy and dedication. He had no hobbies; there hadn't been time for hobbies except at weekends, and those were spent sleeping, watching television, taking Margaret for drives into the country, cutting the lawn and helping with the heavier jobs in the garden. And what hobbies could he find? There might be something useful to be done in the church, but Margaret was already on the parochial church council, a member of the flower and cleaning rotas, part-time secretary of the Women's Wednesday Fellowship. He was repelled by the thought of going to the vicar, an embarrassing supplicant: "Please find me a job. I'm getting old. I'm unskilled. I've nothing to offer. Please make me feel useful again."

There had always been the two worlds, his and Margaret's. His world— she had come to believe or had decided to believe—was a mysterious masculine enclave of which her husband, after the Head of Chambers, was the most important member. It required nothing from her, not even her interest. She never complained about its demands on her husband, the early start to the day, the late arrival home. He was meticulous about telephoning before he left the office if the delay was unusual, and she timed to the minute the heating of the casserole, the moment when the joint could be taken out of the oven to rest, the lighting of the gas under the vegetables so that they were precisely as he liked them. His job was important and must be served because he provided the income without which her world would collapse.

But what place was there for him in that world? His and Margaret's only shared interest had been in the bringing up of the children, though even that had been mainly Margaret's responsibility. Sally and Stephen had been in bed by the time he got home. It was Margaret who gave them their supper, read them the bedtime story and, when they were old enough for school, listened to their tales of small triumphs or of woe. When they had needed him—if they ever needed him—he hadn't been there. They were still a shared anxiety, children always were. Stephen had only just achieved the A-level grades necessary to gain his place at Reading and they worried that he might not survive the first year. Sally, the elder, had trained as a physiotherapist and was working in a hospital in Hull. She rarely came home, but telephoned her mother at least twice weekly. Margaret, wanting grandchildren, worried there might not be a man in Sally's life, or that there was a man, but not one Sally felt she could bring home to introduce to her parents. When the children were at home, Harold got on well with them both. He had never found it difficult to get on well with strangers.

His father, when he had made the same journey from Buckhurst Hill, had got off the train at Liverpool Street Station and taken a bus along Fleet Street to Middle Temple Lane. He preferred to go three stations further and walk down Chancery Lane. He loved the early-morning freshness of the City, the first stirring of life, as if a giant were just waking and beginning to stretch his limbs, the comforting smell of coffee as the cafés opened for the early workers or those coming off night shifts. The familiar shop fronts and public buildings in Chancery Lane were like old friends: the London Silver Vaults; Ede and Ravenscroft, wig- and robemakers, with the royal arms over the door, the window dignified with ceremonial scarlet and ermine; the impressive Public Record Office, which he could never pass without recalling that it housed Magna Carta; the offices of the Law Society with the iron railings and gilded lions' heads.

His normal route was across Fleet Street to enter Middle Temple Lane through the Wren Gatehouse. He never passed under its portal without glancing upwards at the badge of the Paschal Lamb holding the banner of innocence. It was his one superstition, the momentary lifting of his eyes to the ancient symbol. Sometimes he thought that it was his only prayer. But for the last few months the Fleet Street entrance to Middle Temple Lane had been closed for rebuilding and he had had to walk on to the narrow lane opposite the Royal Courts of Justice, by the George pub, to the small black door set in the wider gate.

This morning, as he reached the lane, he felt that he wasn't ready to face the working day and, almost without pausing, he walked briskly on towards Trafalgar Square. He needed time to think, needed, too, the physical release of walking while he tried to make sense of this muddle of anxiety, hope, guilt and half-formulated fears. If the offer to stay on were made, should he accept it? Wouldn't it be merely a cowardly postponement of the inevitable? And what did Margaret really want? She had said, "I don't know how Chambers will manage without you, but you must do what you think best. We can manage on the pension, and it's time you had some life of your

own." What life? He loved her, he had always loved her, although it was difficult now to believe that they were the same people who, in those early days
of marriage, had longed only for bedtime, for that falling into each other's
arms. Now even love-making had become a habit, as comfortable, reassuring and unstressful as the evening meal. They had been married for thirty-
two years. Did he really know so little about her? Was he really telling
himself that life at home with Margaret would be intolerable? A snatch of
random conversation overheard after last Sunday's sung eucharist fell like a
stone into his mind: "I said to George, You have to find something to do. I
don't want you under my feet all day."

But Margaret was right, they could manage on his pension. Had it been
honest, that suggestion to Mr. Langton that they couldn't? He had never before lied to Mr. Langton. They had entered Chambers at the same time, Mr.
Langton as a newly qualified barrister, he as assistant to his father. They had
grown old together. He couldn't imagine Chambers without Mr. Langton.
But something was wrong. The force, the confidence, even the authority of
Head of Chambers seemed to have seeped out of him in the last few months.
And he didn't look well. Something was worrying him. Could it be that he
was concealing a mortal illness? Or was he planning to retire and facing the
same problem of an unknown and useless future? And if he did retire, who
would succeed him? If Miss Aldridge took over would he really wish to stay
on? No, that at least was certain. He wouldn't want to be Senior Clerk if
Miss Aldridge were Head of Chambers. And she wouldn't want him. He
knew that the one voice speaking against him would be hers. It was not, he
felt, that she disliked him personally. Despite a slight fear of her, of that
quick, authoritative voice, that demand for instant response, he didn't really
dislike her, although he wouldn't want to serve under her as Head of Chambers. But it wouldn't be Miss Aldridge, the thought was ridiculous. Chambers only had four criminal lawyers and they would want a non-criminal QC
to take over. The obvious candidate was Mr. Laud; after all, the two archbishops already ran Chambers between them. But if Mr. Laud took over,
would he be strong enough to stand up to Miss Aldridge? If Mr. Langton retired then Miss Aldridge would get her way, would press even more strongly
for the appointment of an office manager, for new methods, new technology.
Was there a place for him in this modern world, where systems mattered
more than people?

He had been walking for over half an hour. He had only a confused recollection of the route he had taken, but could remember pacing restlessly
back and forward along the Embankment, then past Temple Place before

striking northwards up an unremembered street to the Aldwych and along the Strand to the Royal Courts of Justice. And now it was time to start the working day. He had at last made up his mind. If invited, he would stay on for a further year but no longer, and in that year he would make up his mind what he wanted to do with the rest of his life.

Pawlet Court was deserted. Only a few ground-floor windows of adjoining chambers showed a pattern of light where clerks as punctilious as himself had already started their working day. The air smelt mistier than it had in the Strand, as if the small court still held some of the raw dampness of the October night. Round the great trunk of a horse chestnut the first fallen leaves lay in sluggish disorder. He took out his bunch of keys and felt for the straight edge of the one for the Banham security lock, and then the smaller Ingersoll above it, which he turned to open the door. Immediately the alarm system gave out its insistent high-pitched warning. He moved unhurriedly, knowing to a second how long he had to switch on the light in the reception office and insert his smallest key in the control panel to turn off the alarm. Beside the panel was a wooden board with the names of members of Chambers lettered on sliding panels to show whether they were in or out. The board showed that all were absent. The members were not always conscientious in their use of the board, but the theory was that the last member out should slide his peg across and then set the alarm. Mrs. Carpenter and Mrs. Watson, the cleaners, arriving at half past eight at night, were usually the last people in Chambers. Both were scrupulous in ensuring that the alarm was set before they left at ten o'clock.

He cast his eye critically over the reception room, which was also a waiting area. Valerie Caldwell's word processor under its cover was precisely placed in the middle of her desk. The two-seater sofa, the two armchairs and the two upright chairs for visitors were in place, the magazines on the table neatly arranged on the highly polished mahogany. All was as he had expected to find it, with one small difference: it looked as if neither Mrs. Carpenter nor Mrs. Watson had vacuum-swept the carpet. The office machine, bought six months previously, was as formidable in power as it was in noise, and usually left telltale lines on the carpet pile. But the floor looked clean. Perhaps one of them had run the carpet-sweeper over it. It wasn't his job to oversee the cleaners and, with women from Miss Elkington's admirable agency, no supervision was normally necessary, but he liked to keep an eye on things. The reception room was a visitor's introduction to Chambers and first impressions mattered.

Next he looked briefly into the library and conference room, to the right of the front door. Here, too, all was in order. The room had something of the atmosphere of a gentlemen's club, but without its comfortable intimacy. Even so, it had its graces. To the left and right of the marble fireplace the leather spines of books gleamed behind the glass of the eighteenth-century bookcases, each topped with a marble bust, on the left of Charles Dickens and on the right of Henry Fielding, both members of the Honourable Society of the Middle Temple. The fitted unglazed bookcases on the wall facing the door held a more utilitarian library of law reports, bound statutes, *Halsbury's Laws of England* and books on various aspects of criminal and civil law. Ranged on the lower shelves were red leather-bound volumes of *Punch* from 1880 to 1930, a parting gift from a previous member of Chambers whose wife reputedly had insisted on their disposal before moving to their smaller retirement home.

The four leather armchairs were placed about the room with an eccentric disregard for the conveniences of intimate conversation. Much of the floor space was occupied by a large, rectangular table in old oak, almost black with age, with ten matching chairs. The room was seldom used for Chambers meetings; Mr. Langton preferred to hold them in his own room and, if there were insufficient chairs, colleagues would carry in their own and sit informally in a circle. But occasional suggestions that the conference room should be given over to a new member of Chambers in the interest of productive use of space were always resisted. The table, which had once been owned by John Dickinson, was the pride of Chambers and no other room could suitably accommodate it.

There were double doors opening from the reception room into the clerk's office, but they were seldom used and the normal entrance was from the hall. As he entered he could hear the occasional bleep of the fax machine spewing out yesterday's judgements. He went over to read the messages, then took off his coat and hung it on the wooden coat hanger bearing his name on the peg behind the door. Here in this cluttered, over-furnished but ordered space was his sanctum, his kingdom, the powerhouse and very heart of Chambers. Like all clerks' rooms he had ever seen, it was cramped and over-furnished. Here was his desk and the desks of his two junior clerks, each with its word processor. Here was the computer to which he had at last become accustomed, although he still missed the early-morning walk over to the Law Courts, the chat with the listing officer. Here was his wall chart, setting out in his small meticulous handwriting the court appearances of each member of Chambers who worked from Pawlet Court. Here, tied up in the large cupboard against the wall, were the rolled briefs, the red ribbon for defence, the white for prosecution. The room, its smell, its organized clutter, the chair on which his father had sat, the desk on which his father had worked, were more familiar to him than his own bedroom.

The telephone rang. It was unusual for anyone to want him so early. The voice was unfamiliar to him, a woman's voice, high, anxious and with a faint note of incipient hysteria.

"It's Mrs. Buckley speaking. I'm Miss Aldridge's housekeeper. I'm so glad there's someone there. I did try even earlier. She always told me that you opened the office just after eight-thirty, if there was something important."

He said defensively: "Chambers are not open at eight-thirty but I am usually here by that time. Can I help you?"

"It's Miss Aldridge. Is she there please?"

"No one has arrived in Chambers yet. Did Miss Aldridge say that she'd be in early?"

"You don't understand." The voice now held a definite note of hysteria. "She didn't come home last night, that's why I'm so worried."

He said: "Perhaps she spent the night with a friend."

"She wouldn't do that, not without telling me. And it was ten-thirty when I went off duty—and up to my room. She wasn't expecting to stay out all night. I did listen for her but she's always very quiet coming in so sometimes I don't hear her. I took up her tea at half past seven and the bed hasn't been slept in."

He said: "I think it's rather early to become seriously worried. I don't think she's here. There were no lights on in the front when I arrived, but I'll go and have a look. Wait for a moment, will you please?"

He went up to the front room on the first floor, which Miss Aldridge occupied. The heavy oak outer door was locked. This was not in itself particularly surprising; members of Chambers who wanted to leave important papers on their desks did sometimes lock their rooms before leaving. But it was more usual to leave the oak unlocked and to secure only the inner door.

He went back to his own room and picked up the receiver. "Mrs. Buckley? I don't think she's in her room but I'll just unlock the door. I won't be long."

He had a spare key to each room, jealously guarded, tagged and kept in the bottom drawer of his desk. The key to Miss Aldridge's room was there. It opened both the oak and the inner door. Again he went up the stairs, this time aware of the first prickings of anxiety. He told himself that it was unnecessary. A member of Chambers had chosen to spend a night otherwise than in her own home. That was her affair, not his. Probably even now she was putting the key in her front door.

He unlocked the oak door and turned his key in the inner door. Instantaneously he knew that something was wrong. There was a smell in the room, alien and faint but still horribly familiar. He put out his hand to the switch and four of the wall lights came on.

What met his eyes was so bizarre in its horror that for half a minute he stood rooted in disbelief, his mind rejecting what his eyes so plainly saw. It wasn't true. It couldn't be true. For those few seconds of disorientated incredulity he was incapable even of terror. But then he knew it was true. His heart leapt into life and began a pounding which shook his whole body. He heard a low incoherent moaning and knew that this strange disembodied sound was his own voice.

He moved slowly forward as if drawn by the inexorable pull of a thread. She was sitting well back in the swivel chair behind her desk. The desk was to the left of the door, facing the two tall windows. Her head was slumped forward on her chest, her arms hung loosely over the curved arms of the chair. He couldn't see her face but he knew that she was dead.

On her head was a full-bottomed wig, its stiff curls of horsehair a mass of red and brown blood. Moving towards her, he put the back of his right hand against her cheek. It was ice-cold. Surely even dead flesh couldn't be as cold as this. The touch, gentle as it had been, dislodged a globule of blood from the wig. He watched, horrified, as it rolled in slow spurts over the dead cheek to tremble on the edge of her chin. He moaned in terror. He thought: Oh God, she's cold, she's dead cold, but the blood is still tacky! Instinctively he clutched at the chair for support and to his horror it swung slowly round until she was facing the door, her feet dragging on the carpet. He gasped and drew back, looking appalled at his hand as if expecting it to be sticky with blood. Then he leaned forward and, stooping, tried to look into her face. The forehead, the cheeks and one eye were covered with the congealed blood. Only the right eye was unsullied. The dead unseeing stare, fixed on some far enormity, seemed, as he gazed at it, to hold a terrible malice.

Mesmerized, he slowly backed away from her. Somehow he managed to get out of the door. With shaking hands, he closed and locked both doors behind him carefully and quietly, as if a clumsy move could wake that terrible thing within. Then he pocketed the key and made his way to the stairs. He felt very cold and he wasn't sure that his legs could support him, but somehow he staggered down. And at least his brain was clear, miraculously clear. When he picked up the phone he knew what he had to do. His tongue felt too swollen and unyielding for a mouth grown suddenly taut and dry. The words came, but the sounds were harshly alien.

He said, "Yes, she is here, but she can't be disturbed. Everything's all right," then he put down the receiver before she could answer or ask any further questions. He couldn't tell her the truth, it would be all over London. She would know all about it in good time. Now there was a higher priority; he would have to telephone the police.

He reached again for the receiver and then hesitated. He had a sudden vivid picture of police cars racing up Middle Temple Lane, of loud masculine voices, of members of Chambers arriving to find the court cordoned off. There was a higher priority even than the police; he had to ring the Head of Chambers. The phone was answered quickly by a male voice. Mr. Langton had left for Chambers fifteen minutes earlier.

He felt an immense weight lifted from his shoulders. It would only be about twenty minutes before the Head of Chambers arrived. But the news would be horribly shocking to him. He would need some help, some support. He would need Mr. Laud. Harry telephoned the flat at Shad Thames and heard the familiar voice.

He said: "It's Harry Naughton, sir, ringing from Chambers. I've just telephoned Mr. Langton. Could you come at once, please? Miss Aldridge is dead in her room. It isn't a natural death, sir. I'm afraid it looks as if she's been murdered." He was surprised that his voice could be so strong, so steady. There was silence. He wondered for a moment whether Mr. Laud had taken it in, or whether shock had rendered him speechless, whether he had even heard the message. He began again tentatively: "Mr. Laud, it's Harry Naughton . . ."

And then the voice answered. "I know. I heard you, Harry. Tell Mr. Langton when he arrives that I'm coming immediately."

He had telephoned from the reception room, but now went back into the hall and waited. There were footsteps, but heavier than those of Mr. Langton. The door opened and Terry Gledhill, one of his junior clerks, came in, carrying as usual a bulging briefcase which contained his sandwiches, a thermos and his computer magazines. He took one glance at Harry's face.

"What's up? You all right, Mr. Naughton? You look as white as that door."

"It's Miss Aldridge. She's dead in her room. I found her when I arrived."

"Dead? Are you sure?"

Terry went towards the stairs but Harry moved instinctively to block his path.

"Of course I'm sure. She's cold. No point in going up. I've locked the door." He paused and said: "It wasn't . . . it wasn't natural, Terry."

"Christ! You mean she was murdered? What happened? How do you know?"

"There's blood. A lot of blood. And, Terry, she's cold. Ice-cold. But the blood is tacky."

"You're sure that she's dead?"

"Of course I'm sure. I told you, she's cold."

"Have you rung the police?"

"Not yet. I'm waiting for Mr. Langton."

"What can he do? If it's murder you want the police, and we ought to ring them now. No point in waiting till all the staff arrive. They could muck up the scene, destroy clues. The police will have to be called, and the sooner the better. It'll look pretty odd if you don't ring them at once. And we'd better warn security."

The words were an uncomfortable echo of Harry's own misgivings. But he heard in his voice the note of obstinate self-justification. He told himself that he was Senior Clerk, he didn't have to explain his actions to his staff. He said: "Mr. Langton is Head of Chambers. He ought to be told first, and he's on his way. I rang his flat and I've rung Mr. Laud too. He'll be as quick as he can. It's not as if anyone can help Miss Aldridge."

He added, more sharply: "You'd better get into the office, Terry, and start the day. No point in holding up the work. If the police want us all out when they arrive, no doubt they'll say so."

"More likely to want us all here for questioning. Look, shall I make a cup of tea? You look as if you could do with it. Christ! Murder, and in Chambers."

He put his hand on the banister and looked up the stairs with a horrified, half-curious fascination.

Harry said, "Yes, make some tea. Mr. Langton will need something when he arrives. Better make it fresh for him, though."

Neither of them heard the approaching footsteps. The door opened and Valerie Caldwell, the Chambers secretary, closed it behind her and leaned against it. Her eyes settled first on Harry's face and then on Terry's with what seemed like questioning deliberation. None of them spoke. It seemed to Harry that the moment was frozen in time: Terry with his hand on the banister; himself staring in horrified dismay, like a schoolboy caught out in some juvenile mischief. He knew with an appalling certainty that nothing needed to be said. He watched while the blood drained from her face and it changed, grew old and unfamiliar, as if he were watching the very act of dying. He could take no more.

He said: "You tell her. Make that tea. I'm going upstairs."

Harry had no idea where precisely he was going or what he was going to do. He only knew that he had to get away from them. But he had barely reached the landing before he heard a soft thud and heard Terry's voice.

"Give me a hand, Mr. Naughton. She's fainted."

He came down and together they lifted Valerie into the reception room and lowered her onto the sofa. Terry put his hand on the back of her neck and forced her head down between her knees. After about half a minute, which seemed much longer, she gave a little moan.

Terry, who seemed to have taken control, said: "She'll do now. Better get a glass of water for her, Mr. Naughton, and then I'll make that tea—good and sweet."

But before either of them could move they heard the sound of the front door closing and, looking up, saw Hubert Langton standing in the doorway. Before he could speak, Harry took his arm and gently led him across the hall and into the conference room. Surprised into acquiescence, Langton was as docile as a child. Harry closed the door and spoke the words which he had already mentally rehearsed.

"I'm sorry, sir, but I have something very shocking to tell you. It's Miss Aldridge. When I arrived this morning her housekeeper rang to say that she hadn't been home last night. Both doors of her room here were locked but I've got the spare key. I'm afraid that she's dead, sir. It looks like murder."

Mr. Langton didn't reply. His face was a mask betraying nothing. Then he said: "I'd better look. Have you rung the police?"

"Not yet, sir. I knew you were on your way so I thought it would be better to wait. I've telephoned Mr. Laud and he said he'd come immediately."

Harry followed Mr. Langton up the stairs. The Head of Chambers held on to the banisters but his feet were steady. He waited calmly, his face still expressionless, while Harry took the key from his pocket and unlocked the doors, then held them open.

For a second, as the key turned, he had been seized with an irrational conviction that it would all prove to be a mistake, that the blood-bloated head had been a sick fantasy and that the room would be empty. But the reality was even more horrible than on the first sight. He dared not look at Mr. Langton's face. Then he heard him speak. His voice was calm, but it was the voice of an old man.

"This is an abomination, Harry."

"Yes, sir."

"And this is how you found her?"

"Not quite, Mr. Langton. She was facing the desk. I touched the chair, inadvertently really, and she swung round."

"Have you told anyone else—Terry, Valerie—about the blood and the wig?"

"No, sir, just that I found her dead. I did say it looked like murder. Oh, and I did tell Terry that there was fresh blood. That's all I told him."

"That was sensible of you. Keep the details to yourself. The media will make a meal of this if it gets out."

"It's bound to get out sooner or later, Mr. Langton."

"Then let it be later. I'll ring the police now." He moved towards the desk telephone, then said: "Better do it from my room. The less we touch in here the better. I'll take charge of the key."

Harry handed it over. Langton turned out the light and locked both doors. Watching him, Harry thought that the old man was taking the shock more calmly than he had dared to hope. This was the Head of Chambers he remembered: authoritative, calm, taking control. But then he looked at his companion's face and knew with a rush of pity what this calmness was costing him.

He said: "What shall I do about the rest of the staff, sir? And then there are the members of Chambers. Mr. Ulrick always comes in early on Thursday if he's in London. They'll want to get to their rooms."

"I've no intention of preventing them. If the police want Chambers closed for the day, that will be for them to decide. Perhaps you'd come with me while I telephone, then you'd better stay on the door. Tell the staff as they arrive as little as possible. Try to keep them calm. Ask any members of Chambers to have the goodness to see me immediately in my room."

"Yes sir. There's Mrs. Buckley, the housekeeper. She'll be fussing. And then there's the daughter. Someone will have to tell her."

"Oh yes, the daughter. I'd forgotten about the daughter. We'll leave that to the police and to Mr. Laud. He knows the family."

Harry said: "Miss Aldridge was due at Snaresbrook Crown Court at ten. She was expecting the case to end by this afternoon."

"Her junior will have to cope. It's Mr. Fleming, isn't it? Ring him at home. You'd better tell him that Miss Aldridge has been found dead in her room, but say as little as possible."

They were in Mr. Langton's room now. Hubert stood for a moment with his hand hovering on the telephone. He said with a kind of wonder: "I've never had to do this before. Dialling 999 hardly seems appropriate. I'd better try the Commissioner's office—or there is someone I know at the Yard, not well, but we have met. It may not be for him, but if it isn't, he'll know what has to be done. He's got a name that's easy to remember—Adam Dalgliesh."

12

The appointment for Detective Inspectors Kate Miskin and Piers Tarrant to take their qualifying test at the West London shooting range had been made for eight o'clock. Anticipating some difficulty in parking, Kate set out from her Thames-side flat at seven and arrived at seven-forty-five. She had completed the preliminaries, handed over her pink card showing the record of her previous shoots, and had made the required declaration that she hadn't taken alcohol in the last twenty-four hours and wasn't on any prescribed drugs, before she heard the sound of a lift and Piers Tarrant came unhurriedly through the door precisely on time. They greeted each other briefly but there was no conversation. It was unusual for Piers to be silent for long, but Kate had noticed on their practice shoot a month earlier that he had said nothing throughout the whole shoot except to congratulate her briefly at the end. She approved of his silence; talking was not encouraged. The shooting gallery wasn't the place for chatter or badinage. There was always about it the heightened atmosphere of incipient danger, of serious men engaged in a serious purpose. The officers of Commander Dalgliesh's squad shot at West London by special arrangement. The gallery was normally used only by officers on royal- and personal-protection duties. More than one life could depend on the speed of their reactions.

Kate was apt to judge her male colleagues by their behaviour when shooting. Massingham could never bear to be outscored by her and seldom was. The qualifying shoot was not intended to be competitive; officers were supposed to be concerned only with their own achievement. But Massingham had never been able to resist a quick glance at her score and had made no attempt at generosity if she outscored him. To him success at the shooting range had been an affirmation of masculinity. He had been brought up with guns and had found it intolerable that a woman, and one with Kate's urban background, could handle a weapon effectively. Daniel Aaron, on the other hand, had seen the practice shoots as a necessary part of the job and had cared little whether he scored higher than Kate provided he qualified. Piers Tarrant, who had succeeded him three months earlier, had already shown himself a better shot than either of his predecessors. She had yet to learn how much that mattered to him, how important it was that she could still outscore him.

It was one of many things which she had not yet learned about him. Admittedly they had only worked together for three months and no major case had broken, but she still found him puzzling. He had come to Dalgliesh's team from the Arts and Antiques Squad set up to investigate the theft of stolen works of art. It was generally considered an élite squad but Tarrant had apparently asked for a transfer. She knew something about him. Policing was a job in which it was difficult to safeguard personal privacy. Gossip and rumour soon provided what reticence hoped to keep private. She knew that he was twenty-seven, unmarried, and lived in a flat in the City from which he cycled to New Scotland Yard, saying that he had more than enough of cars in the job without using one to get to work. He was rumoured to be knowledgeable about the Wren churches in the City. He took policing light-heartedly, more casually than Kate's dedication sometimes found appropriate. She was intrigued, too, by his occasional swings of mood between a gently cynical amusement and, as now, a self-contained quietude which had none of the depressing contagion of moodiness but had the effect of making him unapproachable.

She stood at the door of the authorized firearms officer's glass-fronted office and watched Piers as he completed the preliminaries, assessing him as if she were seeing him for the first time. He wasn't tall, less than six feet, but although he walked lightly there was a streetwise toughness about the shoulders and long arms which made him look like a boxer. His mouth was well shaped, sensitive and humorous. Even when set firm, as now, it suggested an inner, barely contained amusement. There was the faintest suggestion of the comedian about the slightly pudgy nose and deep-set eyes under slanting eyebrows. His mid-brown hair was strong, an undisciplined strand falling across his forehead. He was less handsome than Daniel, but she had been aware from their first meeting that he was one of the most sexually attractive officers with whom she had ever worked. It had been an unwelcome realization, but she had no intention of letting it become a problem. Kate believed in keeping her sexual and professional lives separate. She had seen too many careers, too many marriages, too many lives messed up to go down that dangerously seductive path.

A month after he joined the squad, on impulse, she had asked: "Why the police?" It was unlike her to force a confidence, but he had answered without resentment.

"Why not?"

"Come off it, Piers! Oxford degree in theology? You're not the typical copper."

"Do I have to be? Do you have to be? What is the typical copper anyway? Me? You? AD? Max Trimlett?"

"We know about Trimlett. A foul-mouthed sexist bastard. Trimlett likes power and thought joining the police was the easiest way to get it. He certainly hasn't the intelligence to get it any other way. He should have been chucked out after that last complaint. We're not talking about DC Trimlett, we're talking about you. But if you don't like the question, that's OK. It's your life. I'd no right to ask."

"Think of the alternatives. Teaching? Not with today's young. If I'm going to be bashed by louts, I'd rather be bashed by an adult lout when I can do some bashing back. The law? Over-crowded. Medicine? Ten years' hard labour and at the end you sit handing out prescriptions to a surgery of dispirited neurotics. Anyway I'm too squeamish. I don't mind dead bodies, I just don't fancy watching them die. The City? Precarious and I can't add up. The Civil Service? Boring and respectable, and anyway they probably wouldn't have me. Any suggestions?"

"You could try male modelling."

She thought she might have gone too far, but he had answered: "Not photogenic enough. What about you? Why did you join?"

It was a fair question, and she could have answered: To get away from that flat on the seventh floor of Ellison Fairweather Buildings. My own money. Independence. The chance of pulling myself out of poverty and mess. To get away from the smell of urine and failure. The need to do a job which offered opportunities, and which I believe is one worth doing. For the security of order and hierarchy. Instead she said: "To earn an honest living."

"Ah, that's how we all begin. Maybe even Trimlett."

The instructor checked that they were to fire not Glocks but the six-shot .38-calibre Smith and Wessons, issued them earmuffs, their weapons and the first bullets for hand-loading, holster and ammunition pouch and jet-loader, then watched from his window as they went through to the shooting gallery, where his colleague was waiting. Still without speaking, they cleaned their weapons with a four-by-two rag and loaded the first six bullets into the chambers by hand.

The authorized firearms officer said: "Right, ma'am? Right, sir? Seventy-round classifying shoot from three metres to twenty-five, two-second exposure."

They fitted the earmuffs and joined him on the three-metre line, standing one on each side of him. Against the dark-pink wall was the row of eleven target figures, stark black, forward-crouching, guns in hand, with a white line encircling the central visible mass which was the target area. The figures were reversed to show only the blank white backs. The AFO barked out his command, the crouching figures swung back into view. The air crackled with gunfire. Despite the earmuffs that first explosion of sound always surprised Kate by its reverberating loudness.

When the first six rounds had been fired they moved forward to inspect the targets, sticking white circles on each hole. Kate saw with satisfaction that hers were nicely grouped in the centre of the visible target area. She always wanted to achieve a neat, concentric pattern and had occasionally come close to it. Glancing across at Piers busy with his white markers, she saw that he had done well.

They moved back to the next line and, finally, to twenty-five metres, shooting, checking the hits, reloading, checking again. At the end of the seventy rounds they waited while the instructor added up and recorded their scores. Both had qualified, but Kate had scored the higher.

Piers spoke for almost the first time. "Congratulations. Go on like this and you'll get seconded for royal protection. Think of all those Buck House garden parties."

They checked in their weapons and equipment, received their signed cards and had almost reached the lift when they heard the telephone.

The AFO put his head out of his office and called: "It's for you, ma'am."

Kate heard Dalgliesh's voice: "Is Piers with you?"

"Yes, sir. We've just completed the qualifying test."

"There's a suspicious death at Eight, Pawlet Court, in the Middle Temple. A woman QC at the criminal Bar, Venetia Aldridge. Collect your murder bags and meet me there. The manned gate from Tudor Street will be open and they'll show you where to park."

Kate said: "The Temple? Isn't that for the City, sir?"

"Normally, yes, but we're taking it with City back-up. An exercise in co-operation. Actually the boundary between Westminster and the City runs through the middle of Number Eight. Lord Justice Boothroyd and his wife have their flat on the top floor and Lady Boothroyd's bedroom is said to be half in Westminster and half in the City. Both she and the judge are out of London, which saves one complication."

"Right, sir, we're leaving now."

Going down in the lift, she put Piers in the picture. He said: "So we're to work with those giants from the City. God knows where they recruit their six-footers. Probably breed them. Why is this for us, anyway?"

"Senior barrister murdered, judge and his wife living upstairs, sacred precincts of the Middle Temple. Not exactly your usual scene of crime."

Piers said: "Not exactly your usual suspects. Add to which the Head of Chambers probably knows the Commissioner. It'll be pleasant for AD. Between grilling members of the Bar he'll be able to contemplate the thirteenth-century effigies in the Round Church. Should even inspire a new slim volume of verse. It's time he gave us one."

"Why don't you suggest it? I should like to see his reaction. Do you want to drive or shall I?"

"You, please. I want to get there safely. All that banging away has unsettled my nerves. I hate loud noises, especially when I'm making them myself."

Clicking on her seat belt, Kate said on impulse: "I wish I knew why I always look forward to a shoot. I can't imagine wanting to kill an animal, let alone a man, but I like guns. I like using them. I like the feel of the Smith and Wesson in my hand."

"You like shooting because it's a skill and you're very good at it."

"It can't only be that. It's not the only thing I'm good at. I'm beginning to think that shooting is addictive."

He said: "Not for me, but, then, I'm not as good as you. Anything we're good at gives us a sense of power."

"So that's what it amounts to, power?"

"Of course. You're holding something that can kill. What else does that give you but a sense of power? No wonder it's addictive."

It hadn't been a comfortable conversation. With an effort of will Kate put the shooting range out of her mind. They were on their way to a new job. As always she felt, along the veins, that fizz of exhilaration that came with every new case. She thought, as she often did, how fortunate she was. She had a job which she enjoyed and knew she did well, a boss she liked and admired. And now there was this murder with all it promised of excitement, human interest, the challenge of the investigation, the satisfaction of ultimate success. Someone had to die before she could feel like this. And that, too, wasn't a comfortable thought.

13

Dalgliesh arrived first at Number Eight, Pawlet Court. The court lay quiet and empty in the strengthening light. The sweet-smelling air was pricked with a faint mist, presaging another unseasonably warm day. The great horse chestnut was still weighted with the heaviness of high summer. Only a few of the leaves had stiffened into the brown and gold of their autumn decrepitude. As Dalgliesh entered the court, carrying his murder bag which looked so deceptively like a more orthodox case, he wondered how a casual watcher would see him. Probably as a solicitor arriving for a consultation about a brief. But there were no watchers. The court lay open to the morning in an expectant calm, as removed from the grinding traffic of Fleet Street and the Embankment as if it were a provincial cathedral close.

The door of Number Eight opened as soon as he reached it. They were, of course, expecting him. A young woman whose smeared and puffy face showed that she had recently been crying ushered him in with an inaudible welcome and disappeared through an open door to the left, where she seated herself behind the reception desk and stared into space. Three men came out of a room to the right of the hall and Dalgliesh saw with surprise that one of them was the forensic pathologist, Miles Kynaston.

Shaking hands, he said: "What's this, Miles? Premonition?"

"No, coincidence. I had an early consultation at E. N. Mumford's Chambers in Inner Temple. They're calling me for the defence in the Manning case at the Bailey next week."

Turning, he introduced his companions. Hubert Langton, Head of Chambers, and Drysdale Laud, both of whom Dalgliesh had briefly met before. Laud shook hands with the wariness of a man who is uncertain how far it would be prudent to acknowledge the acquaintanceship.

Langton said: "She's in her room on the first floor, just above this. Do you want me to come up?"

"Later perhaps. Who found her?"

"Our Senior Clerk, Harry Naughton, when he arrived this morning. That was at about nine. He's in his office with one of the junior clerks, Terry Gledhill. The only other member of staff in Chambers is the secretary-receptionist, Miss Caldwell, who let you in. Other people, staff and members of Chambers, will be arriving soon. I don't think I can keep members of Chambers out of their rooms, but I suppose the staff could be sent home."

He looked at Laud as if seeking guidance. Laud's voice was uncompromising: "Obviously we shall co-operate. But the work has to go on."

Dalgliesh said calmly: "But the investigation of murder—if this is murder—takes precedence. We shall have to search Chambers and the fewer people here the better. We don't intend to waste time, ours or yours. Is there a room we can use temporarily for interviews?"

It was Laud who replied: "You can have mine. It's two floors up at the back. Or there's the reception room. If we close Chambers for the morning that will be free."

"Thank you. We'll use the reception room. In the meantime it would be helpful if you could stay here together until we have had a preliminary look at the body. Detective Inspectors Kate Miskin and Piers Tarrant are on their way with the back-up team. We may have to tape off a part of the court but I hope not for long. Meanwhile I'd be glad to have a list of all occupants of Chambers with their addresses, and a plan of the Middle and Inner Temple with all the entrances marked, if you have one. It would also be helpful to have a plan of this building showing which rooms the members occupy."

Langton said: "Harry has a map of the Temple in his office. I think it has all the entrances marked. I'll get Miss Caldwell to type out the list of members for you. And the staff, of course."

Dalgliesh said: "And the key. Who has it?"

Langton took it from his pocket and handed it over. He said: "I locked both the outer and inner doors after Laud and I had seen the body. This one key opens both."

"Thank you." Dalgliesh turned to Kynaston. "Shall we go up, Miles?"

It interested but did not surprise him that Kynaston had waited for him to arrive before examining the body. As a forensic pathologist Miles had all the virtues. He came quickly. He worked without fuss or complaint however inconvenient the terrain or repellent the decomposing corpse. He spoke little, but always to the point, and he was blessedly free of that sardonic humour with which some of his colleagues—and not always the least distinguished—attempted to demonstrate their imperviousness to the more gruesome realities of violent death.

He was dressed now as he always was whatever the season, in a tweed suit with a waistcoat and a thin wool shirt with the collar ends buttoned down. Mounting the stairs behind his stumbling gait, Dalgliesh wondered again at the contrast between this graceless solidity and the precision and delicacy with which Kynaston could insinuate his fingers, gloved in their second skin of white latex, into the body's unresisting cavities, the reverence with which he laid those dreadfully experienced hands on violated flesh.

The four rooms on the first floor had outer doors of stout oak banded with iron. Behind the outer oak of Venetia Aldridge's room was an inner door with a keyhole but no push-button security system. The key turned easily and as they entered Dalgliesh put out his hand to the left of the door and switched on the light.

The scene that met their eyes was so bizarre that it might have been a tableau in Grand Guignol, deliberately contrived to confront, astonish and horrify. The desk chair in which she sat slumped had swung round so that she was facing them as they entered, the head a little forward, the chin pressed against the throat. The top of the full-bottomed wig was covered with blood, leaving only a few stiff grey curls visible. Dalgliesh moved close to the body. Blood had flowed down over the left-hand side of the face to soak the fine wool of her black cardigan and stain with reddish brown the edges of a cream shirt. The left eye was obscured with globules of viscous blood which, as he watched, seemed to tremble and solidify. The right eye, glazed with the dull impassivity of death, was fixed beyond him as if his presence was unworthy of notice. Her forearms rested on the arms of the chair, the drooping hands with the two middle fingers a little lowered frozen into a gesture as graceful as a ballet-dancer's. Her black skirt had rucked up above the knees, and knees and legs were held close together and slanted to the left, a pose reminiscent of the deliberate provocation of a fashion model. The fine nylon tights sheened the knee bones and emphasized every plane of the long elegant legs. One black court shoe with its medium heel had fallen or been kicked off. She was wearing a narrow wedding ring, but no other jewellery except for an elegant, square-faced gold watch on the left wrist.

There was a small table to the right of the door. It was covered with papers and briefs tied with red tape. Dalgliesh went over and placed his murder bag in the only clear space, then took out and put on his search gloves. Kynaston had, as always, taken his from his suit pocket. He tore off the end of the envelope and put them on, then drew very close to the body, Dalgliesh at his shoulder.

He said: "I'll state the obvious. Either the blood was poured over the wig within the last three hours or it contains an anticoagulant." His hands moved about the neck, gently rotated the head, touched the hands. Then with extreme care he lifted the wig from her head, bent low over her hair, sniffed as if he were a dog and as gently replaced the wig. He said: "Rigor well developed. Probably dead twelve to fourteen hours. No obvious wound. Wherever it came from, the blood isn't hers."

With extraordinary delicacy the stubby fingers undid the buttons of her cashmere cardigan to reveal the shirt. Dalgliesh saw that there was a narrow, sharp-edged cut just below a button on the left side. She was wearing a bra. The swell of the breasts looked very white against the creamy sheen of the silk. Kynaston placed his hand underneath the left breast and gently released it from the bra. There was a puncture wound, a narrow slit about one inch long, a little depressed and with some superficial oozing but no blood.

Kynaston said: "A thrust to the heart. He was either very lucky or very skilled. I'll confirm it on the table, but death must have been almost instantaneous."

Dalgliesh asked: "And the weapon?"

"Long, thin, rapier-like. A narrow dagger. Could be a thin knife, but that's unlikely. Both sides were sharp. Could be a steel paper-knife provided it's sharp, pointed, strong and at least four inches long in the blade."

It was then that they heard the running footsteps and the door was flung open with force. They turned towards it, their bodies shielding the corpse. The man who stood in the doorway was literally shaking with anger, his face a white mask of outrage. He was holding a pouch like a clear plastic hot-water bottle, and now he shook it at them.

"What's going on here? Who has taken my blood?"

Dalgliesh, without replying, stood to one side. The result in other circumstances would have been risible. The newcomer stared at the body in a wide-eyed parody of disbelief. He opened his mouth to speak, thought better of it, moved quietly, cat-like, into the room as if the corpse were a figment of his imagination which would disappear if only he could bring himself to confront it. When he did speak he had his voice under control.

"Someone has a curious sense of humour. And what are you doing here?"

Dalgliesh said: "I would have thought that was obvious. This is Dr. Kynaston, who is a forensic pathologist. My name is Dalgliesh. I'm from New Scotland Yard. Are you a member of these Chambers?"

"Desmond Ulrick. And yes, I am a member of these Chambers."

"And you arrived when?"

Ulrick's gaze was still fixed on the body but with a look which Dalgliesh thought held more fascinated curiosity than horror. He said: "My usual time. Ten minutes ago."

"And no one stopped you?"

"Why should they? As I have said, I'm a member of these Chambers. The door was closed, which is unusual, but I have a key. Miss Caldwell was at her desk as usual. No one else was around as far as I could see. I went down to my room. It's in the basement at the back. A few minutes ago I opened my refrigerator to take out a carton of milk. The stored blood was missing. The blood was drawn three days ago and was being stored for a minor operation I'm due to have on Saturday."

"When did you put it in the refrigerator, Mr. Ulrick?"

"On Monday, at about midday. I came straight from the hospital."

"And who knew it was there?"

"Mrs. Carpenter, the cleaner. I left a note warning her not to touch it. I told Miss Caldwell in case she wanted to put her milk in my fridge. I have no doubt she passed the news round Chambers. Nothing is secret here. You had better ask her." He paused and then said: "I take it from the presence of you and your colleague that the police are treating this as an unnatural death."

Dalgliesh said: "We are treating it as murder, Mr. Ulrick."

Ulrick made a movement as if about to approach the body, then turned to the door.

"As you no doubt know, Commander, Venetia Aldridge was much concerned with murder, but she could hardly have expected to be so intimately involved. She will be greatly missed. And now, if you will excuse me, I'll get down to my room. I have work to do."

Dalgliesh said: "Mr. Langton and Mr. Laud are in the library. I would be glad if you would join them. We shall need to examine your room and to dust for fingerprints. I'll let you know as soon as it's free."

He thought for a moment that Ulrick was about to protest. Instead he held out the pouch.

"What am I supposed to do with this? It's no use to me."

Dalgliesh said, "I'll take it, thank you," holding out his gloved hands.

He carried it by the corner over to the table and, taking out an exhibit bag, placed the pouch inside. Ulrick watched, seeming suddenly reluctant to leave.

Dalgliesh said: "While you are here, perhaps you could tell me something about the wig. Is it yours?"

"No. I have no ambitions to be a judge."

"Did it belong to Miss Aldridge, do you know?"

"I shouldn't think so. Few barristers own a full-bottomed. She'll have worn one once before, when she became a QC. It's probably Hubert Langton's. It used to belong to his grandfather and he keeps it here in Chambers to lend to any member who takes silk. It's kept in a tin box in Harry Naughton's office. Harry's our Senior Clerk. He'll be able to check for you."

Kynaston was peeling off his gloves. Ignoring Ulrick, he said to Dalgliesh: "I can't do anything more here. I have a couple of PMs this evening at eight. I could fit her in then."

He turned to go but found the doorway temporarily blocked by Kate Miskin. She said: "The SOCOs and the photographers are here, sir."

"Good, Kate. Take over here, will you. Is Piers with you?"

"Yes, sir. He's with Sergeant Robbins. They're taping off this part of the court."

Dalgliesh turned to Ulrick. "We shall need to search your room first. Perhaps you would be good enough to join your colleagues in the library."

More meekly than Dalgliesh had expected, Ulrick went out, almost colliding with Charlie Ferris in the doorway. Charlie Ferris, inevitably nicknamed the Ferret, was one of the most experienced of the Met's scene-of-crime officers, reported to be able to identify by sight threads normally discernible only under a microscope, and to smell out a decaying body at a hundred yards. He was wearing the search garb which in the last few months had replaced his former, somewhat eccentric, outfit of white shorts, with the legs cut to the crotch, and a sweat-shirt. He now wore a tight-fitting cotton jacket and trousers and white plimsolls, and his customary plastic swimming-cap, tight-fitting to prevent the contamination of the scene with his own hairs. He stood for a moment in the doorway as if assessing the room and its potential before beginning his meticulous kneeling search.

Dalgliesh said: "The carpet is scuffed just to the right of the door. It's possible she was killed there and dragged to the chair. I'd like that patch photographed and protected."

Ferris muttered, "Yes, sir," but did not take his eyes from the part of the carpet he was examining. He wouldn't have missed the scuffmark and would get to it in time. The Ferret had his own way of working.

The photographers and fingerprint officers had arrived now and went silently about their business. The two photographers were an efficient couple, used to working together, who wasted no time on the niceties but did their job and got out. As a young detective sergeant Dalgliesh used to wonder what they made of it, this almost daily recording of man's inhumanity to man, and whether the photographs they took when they were off duty, the innocent holiday pictures and records of family occasions, were overlaid by the images of violent death. Taking care to keep out of their way, Dalgliesh began his examination of the room, Kate at his shoulder.

The desk was not modern, a solid mahogany partner's desk, leather-topped, the wood showing the patina of years of polishing. The brass handles on the two sets of three drawers were obviously original. In the top left-hand drawer was a handbag in soft black leather with a gold clasp and a narrow strap. Opening it, Dalgliesh saw that it contained her cheque book, a thin wallet of credit cards, a purse with twenty-five pounds in notes and a few coins, a clean folded handkerchief in white linen and a bunch of miscellaneous keys. Examining them, he said: "It looks as if she kept her house and car keys on a separate ring from her keys to Chambers' front door and this room. It's odd that the killer locked these two doors and took away the keys. You'd expect him to leave the door open if he wanted this to look like an outside job. But he could get rid of them easily enough. They're probably in the Thames or dropped through a grating."

He drew open the two bottom drawers and found little of immediate interest. There were boxes of writing-paper and envelopes, notepads, a wooden box containing a collection of ballpoint pens and, in the bottom drawer, two folded hand towels and a toilet bag containing soap, a toothbrush and toothpaste. A smaller zipped bag held Venetia Aldridge's make-up, a small bottle of moisturizer, a compact of pressed powder, a single lipstick.

Kate said: "Expensive but minimal."

Dalgliesh heard in her voice what he himself had so often felt. It was the small chosen artefacts of daily life which produced the most poignant *memento mori*.

The only paper of interest in the top right-hand drawer was a copy of a thin pamphlet, inexpertly printed, and headed *Redress*. It was apparently distributed by an organization concerned with opportunities for women in senior posts in the professions and industry, and consisted mainly of comparative figures for some of the most prominent corporations and companies, showing the total number of women employed and those who had achieved directorships or senior managerial posts. The four names printed beneath the name *Redress* meant nothing to Dalgliesh. The secretary was a Trudy Manning with an address in North-East London. The pamphlet consisted of only four pages; the last bore a brief note:

"We find it surprising that the chambers of Mr. Hubert Langton at Eight, Pawlet Court, Middle Temple, employ only three women barristers from a total of twenty-one members. One of them is the distinguished criminal lawyer Miss Venetia Aldridge, QC. May we suggest to Miss Aldridge that she shows a little more enthusiasm than she has to date for ensuring fair treatment for her own sex."

Dalgliesh took out the pamphlet and said to Ferris: "Put this among the exhibits, will you, Charlie."

Venetia Aldridge had obviously been working when she was killed. There was a brief on the desk supported by a thick wodge of papers. A cursory glance at the brief showed Dalgliesh that it was a case of grievous bodily harm set down for the Bailey in two weeks' time. The only other papers on the desk were a copy of the *Temple News Letter* and the previous day's *Evening Standard*. It looked untouched, but Dalgliesh noted that the pink financial insert, "Business Day," was missing. A stout manila envelope, neatly slit and addressed to Miss Venetia Aldridge, QC, was in the waste-paper basket to the right of the desk. Dalgliesh thought it had probably held the *Temple News Letter*.

The room, about fifteen feet square, was sparsely furnished for a barrister's chambers. Along the left-hand side a long elegant bookcase, also mahogany, stretched almost the whole length of the wall facing the two Georgian windows, each with its twelve panes. The bookcase contained a small library of law books and bound statutes, with beneath them a row of barristers' blue notebooks. Drawing one or two out at random, Dalgliesh saw with interest that they covered the whole of her professional career and were meticulously kept. On the same shelf was a volume of the *Notable British Trials* series dealing with the trial of Frederick Seddon. It was a somewhat incongruous addition to a library otherwise completely dedicated to statutes and criminal statistics. Opening it, Dalgliesh saw a brief dedication in a small cramped hand. "To VA from her friend and mentor, EAF."

He moved over to the left-hand window. Outside, in the morning light which was beginning already to hold the promise of sunshine, he saw that part of the court had been taped off. No one was about, yet he seemed to sense the presence of watching eyes behind blank windows. Briefly he surveyed the rest of the furniture. To the left of the door there was a four-drawer metal filing cabinet and a narrow mahogany cupboard. A coat hanger held a coat in fine black wool. There was no red robe bag. Perhaps she was in the middle of a case and had left her wig and gown in the locker room of the Crown Court. In front of the windows was a small conference table with six chairs, while the two leather high-backed chairs in front of the marble fireplace suggested a more comfortable ambience for consultation. The only pictures were a line of *Spy* cartoons of nineteenth-century judges and barristers in wig and gown and over the fireplace an oil by Duncan

Grant. Under an impressionistic late-summer sky it showed a haystack and wagon with low farm buildings and a corn field beyond, the whole painted in clear bold colours. Dalgliesh wondered whether the cartoons had been there when Miss Aldridge took over the room. The Duncan Grant suggested a more personal taste.

The photographers had finished for the present and were ready to go, but the fingerprint officers were still occupied with the desk and the jamb of the door. Dalgliesh thought it unlikely that any useful prints would be found. Anyone in Chambers would have had legitimate access to the room. He left the experts to their task and went to join the company waiting in the library.

There were now four men present. The addition to the company, a large red-haired man, powerfully built, was standing in front of the fireplace.

Langton said: "This is Simon Costello, a member of Chambers. He wanted to stay and I wasn't prepared to keep any member of Chambers out of this building."

Dalgliesh said: "If he stays in this room he won't be in the way. I had rather assumed that busy men would prefer to work elsewhere for the morning."

Desmond Ulrick was seated in a high-backed chair by the fireplace. A book lay open on his lap and, with his thin knees pressed together, he looked as docile and absorbed as an obedient child. Langton was standing at one of the two windows, Laud at the other, and Costello had begun a restless pacing as soon as Dalgliesh entered. All except Ulrick fixed their eyes on him.

Dalgliesh said: "Miss Aldridge was stabbed in the heart. I have to tell you that we are most certainly dealing with a case of murder."

Costello's voice was roughly belligerent: "And the weapon?"

"Not yet found."

"So why almost certainly? If the weapon isn't there how can it be anything else but murder? Are you suggesting that Venetia stabbed herself and someone else conveniently removed the weapon?"

Langton sat down at the table as if his legs had suddenly lost power. He looked at Costello, silently imploring him to be tactful.

Dalgliesh said: "Theoretically Miss Aldridge could have stabbed herself and the weapon have been removed later by someone else, perhaps the person who put the wig on her head. I don't for a moment believe that's what happened. We are treating the case as murder. The weapon was a sharp stiletto-like blade, something like a small thin dagger. Has any of you seen such a thing? The question may seem absurd, but obviously it has to be asked."

There was silence. Then Laud said: "Venetia had something very like it.

A paper-knife, but it wasn't intended as a paper-knife. It's a steel dagger with a brass handle and guard. It was given to me by a grateful if undiscriminating client when I took silk. I think he had it specially made and imagined it was something like the Sword of Justice. An embarrassing object. I was never sure what I was expected to do with it. I gave it to Venetia about two years ago. I was in her office when she was opening her letters and her wooden paper-knife snapped, so I went down to my room and brought up the dagger. I'd put it at the back of one of my desk drawers and had almost forgotten about it. Actually it made a very effective paper-knife."

Dalgliesh said: "Was it sharp?"

"God yes, extremely sharp, but it had a sheath. That was in black leather with a brass tip and a kind of brass rose on it, as far as I remember. And the paper-knife itself had my initials engraved on the blade."

Dalgliesh said: "It isn't in her office now. Can you remember when anyone here last saw it?"

There was no reply. Laud said: "Venetia used to keep it in her top right-hand drawer unless she was actually opening letters. I don't think I've seen her with it for weeks."

But she had opened that stiff envelope the night before and the flap had been sliced, not torn.

Dalgliesh said: "We shall have to find it. If it was the weapon, the killer may, of course, have taken it away with him. If it is found, obviously it will be tested for prints. That means that we need the prints of anyone who was or could have been in Chambers yesterday evening."

Costello said: "For elimination purposes. And afterwards, of course, they will be destroyed."

"You're a criminal lawyer, aren't you, Mr. Costello? I think you know the law."

Langton said: "I'm sure I speak for the whole of Chambers when I say that we shall co-operate in every way we can. Obviously you'll need our prints. Obviously, too, you'll need to search Chambers. We'll be glad to have the use of our rooms as soon as possible but we do understand the need for delay."

Dalgliesh said: "I'll ensure that it's kept to the minimum. Who is the next-of-kin, do you know? Have the family been told?"

The question was treated with embarrassment, almost, he thought, with dismay. Once more no one responded. Langton looked again at Laud.

Laud said: "I'm afraid that what with shock and the need to call you in as soon as possible we hadn't thought about next-of-kin. There's an ex-husband, Luke Cummins, and an only child, Octavia. Venetia had no other family as far as I know. She's been divorced for eleven years. Her ex-husband has remarried and lives in the country. Dorset, I think. If you want his address I expect it will be among Venetia's papers. Octavia lives in the basement flat at her mother's house. She's young, only just eighteen. Actually she was born on the first minute of the first day of October; hence the name. Venetia always liked life to be rational. Oh, and there's the housekeeper, of course, Mrs. Buckley, who rang Harry this morning. I'm surprised she hasn't been on to us again."

Langton said: "Didn't Harry say that he'd told her that Miss Aldridge was here? She'll probably be expecting her home for dinner as usual."

Dalgliesh said: "The daughter should be told as soon as possible. I don't know whether a member of Chambers would wish to do that? I should in any case want to send two of my officers to the house."

Again there was an embarrassed pause. Again the other three seemed to be looking to Laud for a lead. He said: "I knew Venetia better than anyone else in Chambers, but I've hardly met the daughter. None of us knows Octavia. I don't think she's ever set foot in Chambers. When we did meet I sensed that she didn't much care for me. If we had a woman colleague here, we could send her, but we haven't. It might be better if one of your people told her. I don't think the news would come well from me. I'm here, of course, if I can help." He looked round at his colleagues. "We all are."

Dalgliesh asked: "Did Miss Aldridge normally work late in Chambers?"

Once more it was Laud who replied. "Yes, she did. Occasionally she'd be here as late as ten. She preferred not to work at home."

"And who was the last person to see her yesterday?"

Langton and Laud glanced at each other. There was a pause and then Laud replied. "Probably Harry Naughton. Harry says that he took a brief up to her at six-thirty. The rest of us had left by then. But one of the cleaners may have seen her, Mrs. Carpenter or Mrs. Watson. We get them from Miss Elkington's domestic agency, and they both come from eight-thirty to ten on Mondays, Wednesdays and Fridays. On the other two days Mrs. Watson works alone."

A little surprised that Laud should know these domestic details, Dalgliesh asked: "And one or both of them has a key?"

Again it was Laud who replied: "To the main door? Both of them, and Miss Elkington. They're extremely reliable women. They set the alarm before they leave."

Langton broke his silence. He said: "I have every confidence in the reliability and integrity of the cleaners. Every confidence."

There was an embarrassed silence. Laud seemed about to speak, changed his mind and then looked straight at Dalgliesh. "There's something I ought perhaps to mention. I'm not saying it's got anything to do with Venetia's death but it could be a factor in the situation. I mean, it's something your officers might find it helpful to know before they see Octavia."

Dalgliesh waited. He was aware of a heightened interest in the room, an almost perceptible tightening of tension. Laud said: "Octavia's taken up with Garry Ashe, the boy Venetia defended a month ago. He was accused of murdering his aunt in a house on Westway. You'll remember the case, of course."

"I remember."

"Apparently he made contact with Octavia almost as soon as he was released. I don't know how or why, but Venetia thought it was contrived. Obviously she was desperately worried. She told me they were actually thinking of getting engaged, or were already engaged."

Dalgliesh asked: "Did she say whether they were lovers?"

"She thought not, but she wasn't sure. That was the last thing she wanted, of course. Well, that would be the last thing any parent would want. I've never seen Venetia so upset. She wanted me to help."

"In what way?"

"By buying him off. Yes, I know it's absurd, I had to tell her so. But there it is, or rather there he is."

"In the house?"

"In Octavia's flat most of the time, I believe."

Langton said: "I thought that Venetia was in a very odd mood when she got back from the Bailey on Tuesday. I suppose she was worried about Octavia."

It was then that Ulrick looked up from his book. He said to Laud: "I'm interested in why you should think this is—how did you describe it?—a factor in the situation."

Laud said curtly: "Garry Ashe was accused of murder; this is murder."

"A convenient suspect, but I can't see how either he or Octavia could have known about the blood in my refrigerator, or where the full-bottomed wig was stored. I have no doubt you are right to bring the matter to the attention of the police, but I fail to see why Venetia was so worried. After all, the young man was found not guilty. A brilliant defence, I believe. Venetia should have been gratified that he obviously wished to maintain his links with the family."

He returned to his book. Dalgliesh said, "Excuse me," and drew Kate outside.

He said: "Tell Ferris what we're looking for, then get the Aldridge address from Harry Naughton and take Robbins with you. If there's a chance of finding out what the girl and Ashe were doing last night without upsetting her too much, do so. And I want the cleaners here, Mrs. Carpenter and Mrs. Watson. As they work at night there's a good chance one of them will be at home. Oh, and leave a WPC and a man at the house, will you, Kate? The girl may need some protection from the press. And speak to the housekeeper, Mrs. Buckley, in private if you get a chance, she could be helpful. But don't spend too long. We'll need to go back later and the real questions can wait until the daughter's over the shock."

Kate wouldn't, he knew, resent the instructions or see this chore as an irritating interruption in the real detection. Nor would she resent the fact that this was regarded as a woman's job. It was always better to send a woman to another woman, and women, with some notable exceptions, were better at breaking bad news than men. Perhaps down the centuries they had had more practice. But Kate, even as she comforted, would be watching, listening, thinking, assessing. She knew as well as any police officer that the first encounter with the bereaved was, as often as not, the first encounter with the killer.

14

The address given by Harry Naughton for Miss Aldridge was in Pelham Place, sw7. Checking her list of addresses and consulting the map before driving off, Kate said to Sergeant Robbins: "After we've seen Octavia Cummins, assuming she's at home, we'll try Mrs. Carpenter at Sedgemoor Crescent. That's in Earls Court. The other cleaner, Mrs. Watson, lives in Bethnal Green. Earls Court will be quicker. But we need to talk to one or both of the women as soon as possible. We could telephone and check if they're at home but it's better to break the news face to face."

Pelham Place was a quiet attractive street of equally attractive period terraces, identical three-storeyed gleaming houses with elegant fanlights, railed front gardens and basements. The street and the houses had a perfection which was almost intimidating. Surely no weed, thought Kate, would dare to push its unsanctified tendrils through these carefully tended small lawns and flower beds. There was a noticeable absence of cars and the street lay in a morning calm with no sign of life. Kate parked in front of Miss Aldridge's house with an uneasy feeling that she might well find the car clamped or missing when she and Robbins returned. Looking up at the glistening façade, the two tall windows at first-floor level with their ironwork balcony, Robbins said: "Nice house. Pleasant road. I didn't think members of the criminal Bar did that well for themselves."

"It depends on the barrister. Venetia Aldridge didn't just rely on legal aid—not that legal-aid cases are as badly paid as some lawyers make out. But she's always had a number of wealthy private clients. There were those two cases last year, one of criminal libel and the other fraud against the Inland Revenue. The second lasted three months."

Robbins said: "She didn't win it, though, did she?"

"No, but that doesn't mean she wasn't paid."

She wondered why Venetia Aldridge had chosen this particular street and then thought that she knew why. The South Kensington underground station was within a few minutes' walk with only six stops from there to the Temple. Miss Aldridge could be in Chambers in about twenty minutes, whatever the congestion on the roads.

Robbins put up his hand to a gleaming bell-push. They heard the thin scrape of the chain and an elderly woman peered anxiously out at them.

Kate showed her warrant card. She said, "Mrs. Buckley? I'm Detective Inspector Miskin and this is Sergeant Robbins. May we come in?"

The chain was released and the door opened. Mrs. Buckley was revealed as a slight, nervous-looking woman with a small, precisely formed mouth between bulging cheeks, which gave her the appearance of a hamster, and an air Kate had noticed before in the insecure: a somewhat desperate respectability tempered by an attempt at authority.

She said: "The police. You'll be wanting Miss Aldridge, I expect. She isn't here. She's at her Chambers in Pawlet Court."

Kate said: "It's about Miss Aldridge that we've come. We have to see her daughter. I'm afraid there's bad news."

At once the anxious face paled. She said: "Oh God, so there is something wrong." She stood to one side shaking, and, as they entered, pointed soundlessly to the door on the right.

As they came in, she whispered: "She's in there—Octavia and her fiancé. Her mother's dead, isn't she? That's what you've come to tell us."

"Yes," said Kate, "I'm afraid she is."

Surprisingly, Mrs. Buckley made no attempt to precede them but left Kate to open the door, then followed last behind Sergeant Robbins.

They were met immediately by a strong breakfast smell of bacon and coffee. A girl and a young man were seated at the table but got up as they entered and stared at them with unwelcoming eyes.

It could only have been a couple of seconds before Kate spoke, but in that brief moment her keen eyes had taken in the girl, her companion and the layout of the room. It had obviously originally been two but a dividing wall had been taken down to make one long dual-purpose room. The front part was the dining-room with an oblong table in polished wood, a sideboard to the right of the door and, opposite, a period fireplace with fitted shelves on either side and an oil painting above. At the garden end was the kitchen, and Kate noted that the sink and stove had been fitted to the left-hand wall so that the window gave an unimpeded view of the garden. Small details impinged upon her eyes and mind. The row of terra-cotta pots of herbs under the far window, an assortment of porcelain figures, discordant in size and period, placed rather than arranged on the display shelves, the smear of grease on the mahogany table left by the discarded plates.

Octavia Cummins was skinny but full-breasted, with the face of a knowing child. Her eyes, the irises a rich chestnut brown, were narrow and slightly slanted under thin brows which looked as if they had been plucked. They gave an exotic distinction to a face which might have been thought interesting if not pretty, were it not for the sullen downturn of the over-long mouth. She was wearing a long sleeveless cotton dress, patterned in red, over a white shirt. Both were in need of washing. Her only jewellery was a ring, a red stone surrounded by pearls, on her engagement finger.

In contrast to her grubbiness, the young man looked aggressively clean. He could have sat for a portrait in black and white: dark, almost black hair, black jeans, a pale face and a very white open-necked shirt. The dark eyes stared at Kate with a look half insolent, half appraising, but which, as their eyes held, became disconcertingly blank as if, for him, she had suddenly ceased to exist.

Kate said: "Miss Octavia Cummins? I'm Detective Inspector Kate Miskin and this is Detective Sergeant Robbins. I'm afraid we have some very bad news. Miss Cummins, I think it would be better if you sat down."

It was always a useful warning of impending disaster, this convention that bad news should never be taken standing up.

The girl said: "I don't want to sit down. You can if you like. This is my fiancé. His name is Ashe. Oh, and this is Mrs. Buckley. She's the housekeeper. I don't think you want her, do you?"

Her voice held an unmistakable note of bored contempt, and yet, thought Kate, it was surely impossible that she should have no realization of the significance of their visit. How often did the police come bearing good news?

It was the housekeeper who spoke. "I should have known. I should have rung the police last night when she didn't come home. She's never stayed out all night without telling me. When I rang this morning that man, the clerk, said she was there in Chambers. How could she be there?"

Kate kept her eyes on the girl. She said gently: "She was there, but I'm afraid she was dead. The clerk, Mr. Naughton, found her body when he arrived for work. I'm very sorry, Miss Cummins."

"Mother's dead? But she can't be dead. We saw her on Tuesday. She wasn't ill then."

"It wasn't a natural death, Miss Cummins."

It was Ashe who spoke. "You're telling us that she was murdered."

It was a statement, not a question. His voice puzzled Kate. It was superficially ordinary enough, yet it struck her as artificial, one of many voices he could summon up at will. It was not, she thought, the voice he had been born with, but, then, was hers? She was not the Kate Miskin who had lugged her grandmother's shopping up seven urine-smelling flights of stairs at Ellison Fairweather Buildings. She didn't look the same. She didn't sound the same. She sometimes wished that she didn't feel the same.

She said: "I'm afraid it looks like that. We shan't know the details until the post-mortem." She turned again to the girl. "Is there anyone you would like to have with you? Shall I ring your doctor? Do you want a cup of tea?"

A cup of tea. That English remedy for grief, shock and human mortality. She had made tea in so many kitchens during her career as a policewoman: in squalid stinking pits where the sink was piled with unwashed plates and rubbish spilled from the bin; in neat suburban kitchens, small shrines of domesticity; in elegantly designed rooms in which it was difficult to believe that anyone ever cooked.

Mrs. Buckley glanced towards the kitchen and said, looking at Octavia: "Shall I?"

The girl said: "I don't want tea. And I don't want anyone else. I've got Ashe. And I don't need a doctor. When did she die?"

"We don't yet know. Sometime last night."

"Then you won't be able to pin it on Ashe like you did last time. We've got an alibi. We were down in my flat and Mrs. Buckley cooked dinner for us. The three of us were there all the evening. Ask her."

This was information Kate wanted, but she had had no intention of asking for it yet. One does not break the news to a daughter of her mother's murder and at the same time inquire whether she and her boyfriend have an alibi. But she couldn't resist raising an interrogative eyebrow at Mrs. Buckley. The woman nodded. "Yes, that's true. I cooked a meal in the kitchen downstairs and we were together all evening until I went up to my room. That was after I'd washed up. It must have been ten-thirty or a little after. I remember thinking that it was half an hour after my usual time."

So that put Ashe and the girl in the clear. They could hardly have got to the Temple in under fifteen minutes, even by a fast motorcycle and assuming the roads were unusually clear. The time could be checked but why bother? Venetia Aldridge had been dead long before ten-forty-five.

Octavia said: "So there you are. Hard luck. This time you'll have to find the real murderer. Why not try her lover? Why not question bloody Mr. Mark Rawlstone, MP? Ask him what he and my mother were quarrelling about on Tuesday night."

Kate controlled herself with difficulty. Then she said calmly, "Miss Cummins, your mother was murdered. It's our job to find out who was responsible. But at the moment I'm more concerned to make sure that you're all right. Obviously you are."

"That's what you think. You don't know anything about me. Why don't you go away?"

Suddenly she collapsed onto one of the dining-chairs and burst into a loud sobbing, as uncontrolled and spontaneous as the bawling of a small child. Kate instinctively made a move towards her, but Ashe intervened and stood silently between them. Then he moved to the back of the chair and placed his hands on her shoulders. At first, seeing a small convulsive twitch, Kate thought that Octavia would shrug him away, but she submitted to the controlling hands and after a little time the howls subsided into a low sobbing. Head slumped forward, the tears fell in a steady stream over the clenched hands. The dark expressionless eyes again met Kate's over the girl's head.

"You heard what she said. Why don't you go away? You're not wanted here."

Kate said: "When the news breaks there may be unwelcome media attention. If Miss Cummins needs protection, let us know. We shall want to talk to you both. Will you be in later today?"

"I expect so, here or in Octavia's flat. That's in the basement. You could try your luck in either place about six."

"Thank you. It would be helpful if you could make an effort to be here. It will save us wasting time by having to come back."

Kate and Sergeant Robbins left, followed by the housekeeper. At the door Kate turned to her.

"We shall need to talk to you later. Where can we find you?"

The woman's hands were shaking; her eyes looked into Kate's with a mixture of fear and appeal which was all too familiar. She said: "Here, I suppose. I mean, I'm usually here from six onwards to cook Miss Aldridge's dinner when she's in London. I have a small bed-sitting-room and bathroom at the top of the house. I don't know what's going to happen now. I suppose I'll have to move out. Well, I won't want to work for Miss Cummins. I suppose she'll sell the house. It sounds awful thinking about myself, but I don't know what I'll do. I've got a lot of my things here, small things really. A desk, some of my late husband's books, a cabinet of china I'm fond of. I put the heavier furniture in store when Miss Aldridge took me on. I can't believe she's dead. And like that. It's horrible. Murder—it changes everything, doesn't it?"

"Yes," Kate said. "Murder changes everything."

She had already decided that it would have been inappropriate to question the daughter until later, but Mrs. Buckley was different. It wasn't possible to say much while lingering on the doorstep, but the housekeeper, as if anxious to prolong the interview, moved with them towards the car.

Kate said: "When did you last see Miss Aldridge?"

"Yesterday morning at breakfast. She likes—she liked to get her own. Just orange juice, muesli and toast. But I always came down to ask about the day, what meals she would be in for, any instructions. She left just before eight-thirty to go to the Crown Court at Snaresbrook. She usually told me if she'd be out of London in case she was wanted urgently and they rang here instead of Chambers. But that wasn't the last time I spoke to her. I rang Chambers at seven-forty-five last night."

Kate was careful to keep her voice calm. She said: "Are you sure of the time?"

"Oh, quite sure. I told myself that I'd wait until seven-thirty before I worried her. And then, when seven-thirty came, I lifted the receiver but put it down again. I waited until a quarter to eight. I'm quite sure of the time. I looked at my watch."

"Did you actually speak to Miss Aldridge?"

"Oh yes, I spoke to her."

"How did she seem?"

Before Mrs. Buckley could answer they heard footsteps and, turning, saw Octavia Cummins running down the garden path, glaring like an angry child.

She shouted: "She rang my mother to complain about me! And if you want to talk to my housekeeper, do it inside, not on the street."

Mrs. Buckley gave a startled exclamation, and without another word turned and scurried into the house. The girl took one last look at Kate and Robbins, then followed her. The door was firmly closed.

Fastening her seat belt, Kate said: "We mismanaged that, at least I did. Disagreeable little beast, isn't she? Makes you wonder why people bother to have kids."

Sergeant Robbins said: "The tears were genuine." He added quietly: "Never the easiest part of our job, breaking the bad news."

"Tears of shock, not grief. And was it such bad news? She's an only child. She'll get it all—house, money, furniture and that expensive oil over the fireplace. And no doubt a lot of the same upstairs in the drawing-room."

Robbins said: "You can't judge people by their reaction to murder. You can't know what they're thinking or feeling. Sometimes they don't know themselves."

Kate said: "All right, Sergeant, we all know you're the humane face of policing, but don't lay it on too thick. Octavia Cummins never even bothered to ask exactly how her mother died. And think of her first reaction. All she worried about was that we wouldn't be able to pin it on to her fiancé, so-called. That's an odd set-up. Young people today don't have fiancés, they have partners. And what exactly is he after, d'you suppose?"

Robbins thought for a moment, then he said: "I think I know who he is. Garry Ashe. He was acquitted about four weeks ago of murdering his aunt. The woman was found with her throat slashed in her house off Westway. I remember the case because a friend of mine was a detective constable working on it. And there's something else that's interesting: Venetia Aldridge was defending counsel."

The car had been halted at a traffic light. Kate said: "Yes, I know. Drysdale Laud told us. I should have mentioned it on the way here, before we got to the house. Sorry, Sergeant."

She felt angry with herself. Why on earth hadn't she told Robbins? It was hardly the kind of information which slipped the mind. Admittedly she hadn't been expecting to find Garry Ashe at the house but that was no excuse. She said again: "Sorry."

The car moved on. They were travelling now along the Brompton Road. There was a silence, then Robbins said: "D'you think there's a chance of breaking that alibi? Mrs. Buckley struck me as honest."

"Me too. No, she was telling the truth. Anyway, how could Ashe or the girl have got into Chambers? And what about the wig and the blood? Would they know where to find either? We've been told that Octavia never showed her face in Chambers."

"What about this supposed lover? Spite or truth?"

"A bit of both, I imagine. Obviously, he'll have to be seen. He isn't going to like it. Up-and-coming MP. Not in the Shadow Cabinet but a possible candidate for junior office. Majority of under a thousand to defend."

"You know a lot about him."

"Who doesn't? You can hardly catch a political programme without seeing him pontificating. Take a look at the map, will you? These roads are tricky. I don't want to miss the turning into Sedgemoor Crescent. Let's hope that we find Mrs. Carpenter at home. The sooner we talk to these women, the better."

15

Dalgliesh and Piers saw Harry Naughton in his office. It seemed to Dalgliesh that the clerk would be more at ease there, in the room where he had worked for nearly forty years. Terry Gledhill, the Junior Clerk, had been questioned and told that he could go home; Naughton would stay to deal with anything urgent. He sat now at his desk, hands on his knees, like a man in the extremes of exhaustion. He was of medium height and build but seemed smaller, the tired anxious face looking older than his body. The thinning grey hair was carefully brushed back from a lumpy forehead. There was a strained look in the eyes which Dalgliesh thought was more long-standing than the result of the day's tragedy. But there was in his bearing the innate dignity of a man who is at ease with his work, does it well and knows that he is valued. He was carefully dressed. The formal suit was obviously old but the trousers were immaculately creased, the shirt was freshly laundered.

Dalgliesh and Piers had taken the other two chairs and they sat among the usual apparently disorganized clutter of the clerk's room, the heart of Chambers. Dalgliesh knew that the man before them could probably tell him more about what went on in Number Eight, Pawlet Court, than any of the tenants; whether he would choose to do so was more debatable.

On the floor between them was the tin which had held the full-bottomed wig. It was about two feet high, very battered, and with the initials J.H.L. painted on the side beneath a coat of arms now almost indecipherable. The tin was lined with pleated fawn silk with a central padded column to support the wig. The lid was open and the tin empty.

Naughton said: "It's always been kept in the clerk's office as long as I've been here, and that's as long as Mr. Langton—nearly forty years. It belonged to his grandfather, who was given it by an old friend when he took silk. That was in 1907. There's a photograph of him wearing it in Mr. Langton's room.

It was always lent to members of Chambers when they took silk. Well, you can see, sir, from the photographs."

The framed photographs, some old in black and white and the most recent in colour, were hung to the left of Naughton's desk. The faces, all but one male, grave, self-satisfied, broadly smiling or with a more controlled satisfaction, gazed at the camera above the silk and the lace, some with their families, one or two obviously taken in Chambers with Harry Naughton, rigid with vicarious pride, at their side. Dalgliesh recognized Langton, Laud, Ulrick and Miss Aldridge.

He said: "Was the tin kept locked?"

"Not in my time. There didn't seem a need. It was locked in old Mr. Langton's time. Then the clasp got broken, I think about eight years ago, maybe more, and there didn't seem any point in getting it mended. It's always kept closed to preserve the wig and isn't usually opened until a new QC is appointed. And sometimes a QC will borrow it if he's invited to the Judges' Annual Service."

"And when was it last worn?"

"Two years ago, sir. That's when Mr. Montague took silk. He works from the Salisbury Annexe. We don't often see him here in Chambers. But that wasn't the last time I saw the wig. Mr. Costello was in the office last week and he tried it on."

"When was that?"

"Wednesday afternoon."

"And how did it happen?"

"Mr. Costello was looking at the photograph of Miss Aldridge. Terry, my assistant, said something like 'You'll be next, sir.' Mr. Costello asked whether we still had Mr. Langton's wig. Terry dragged it out of the cupboard and Mr. Costello opened it to look, then he tried it on. It was only on his head for a moment. He took it off and put it back almost at once. I think it was intended as a humorous gesture, sir."

"And as far as you know the tin hasn't been opened since?"

"Not to my knowledge. Terry put it back in the cupboard at once and no more was said."

Piers asked: "Didn't you think it odd that Mr. Costello should ask whether you still had the wig? I thought it was generally known in Chambers that the wig was kept in your office."

"I think it was generally known. Mr. Costello was probably speaking lightly. I can't be absolutely sure of the exact words. He may have said: 'You've still got the full-bottomed wig here, haven't you?' Something like that. He'll be able to be more accurate, I expect."

They then went over Naughton's first account of the finding of the body. He had recovered from the worst of the initial shock, but Dalgliesh noticed that his hands, which had been resting on his knees, began a restless plucking at the trouser creases.

Dalgliesh said: "You acted with great sense in an appalling situation. You realize that we are still anxious that the business of the blood and the wig shouldn't be spoken of by the few people who've seen the body?"

"It won't be spoken of by me, sir." He paused and then said, "It was the blood, that's what got me. The body was cold, stone-cold. It was like touching marble. And yet the blood was wet, tacky. That's when I nearly lost my head. I shouldn't have touched the body, of course. I realize that now. I suppose it was kind of instinctive, to make sure she was dead."

"It didn't occur to you that the blood must be Mr. Ulrick's?"

"Not then. Not later either. I should have realized at once that it couldn't be Miss Aldridge's blood. It seems odd now, but I think I tried to put the picture out of my mind, not to think about it."

"But you knew that Mr. Ulrick had a pint of blood stored in his fridge?"

"Yes I knew. He told Miss Caldwell and she told me. I think it was generally known in Chambers—among the staff, that is—by the end of Monday. Mr. Ulrick was always very careful about his health. Terry said something like 'Let's hope he never needs a heart transplant or God knows what we'll find in his fridge.' "

Piers said: "People tended to make a joke about it?"

"Not a joke exactly. It just seemed an odd idea, taking your own blood into hospital."

Dalgliesh seemed to rouse himself from a reverie. He asked: "Did you like Miss Aldridge?"

The question was as unexpected as it was unwelcome. Naughton's pale face flushed. "I didn't dislike her. She was a very fine lawyer, a respected member of these Chambers."

Dalgliesh said gently: "But that isn't really an answer, is it?"

Naughton looked at him. "It wasn't my job to like or dislike, only to see that she got the service she was entitled to. I know of no one who wished her ill, sir, and that includes me."

Dalgliesh said: "Can we go back to yesterday? Do you realize that you may have been the last person to see Miss Aldridge alive? When was that?"

"Just before half past six. Ross and Halliwell, the solicitors who gave her a great deal of work, had sent round a brief. She was expecting it and rang to ask me to bring it up as soon as it arrived. I did that. Terry had run out to get a copy of the *Evening Standard* just after six and I took that up too."

"And the *Standard* was complete? No one had extracted part of it?"

"Not that I noticed. It looked untouched."

"What happened?"

"Nothing, sir. Miss Aldridge was seated at her desk working. She seemed perfectly all right, just as usual. I said good-night and left her. I was the last of the staff to leave but I didn't set the alarm. I could see a light in Mr. Ulrick's office downstairs, so I knew he'd be leaving after me. The last person out usually sets the alarm and then when the cleaners arrive they disconnect it while they're working."

Dalgliesh asked him about the cleaning arrangements. Naughton confirmed what Laud had already told him. The work was in the hands of Miss Elkington's Domestic Agency. Miss Elkington specialized in the cleaning of lawyers' offices and employed only the most reliable women. Their two cleaners were Mrs. Carpenter and Mrs. Watson. They would have been there last night, arriving at their usual time of eight-thirty. The hours were eight-thirty until ten on Mondays, Wednesdays and Fridays.

Dalgliesh said: "We shall, of course, be speaking to Mrs. Carpenter and to Mrs. Watson. One of my officers is fetching them now. Do they clean the whole of the building?"

"Except, of course, for the upstairs flat. They have nothing to do with Mr. Justice Boothroyd and Lady Boothroyd's flat. And sometimes they can't get into one of the rooms here if a member of Chambers chooses to lock it. This is very rare, but it can happen if there are highly sensitive papers about. Miss Aldridge did occasionally lock her door."

"Which has, of course, a key, not a security device."

"She disliked those press-button systems. She said they spoilt the look of Chambers. Miss Aldridge always had a key and I had a duplicate. I keep duplicate keys to all the rooms in this cupboard here."

During their interview there had been intermittent messages coming through by fax. Now Naughton glanced anxiously towards the machine. But there was a last question before they let him go.

Dalgliesh said: "You have earlier described exactly what happened this morning. You left your house in Buckhurst Hill at seven-thirty to catch your usual train. You would expect to be in the office by about eight-thirty, but it was nine before you rang Mr. Langton. There seems to be about thirty minutes unaccounted for. What were you doing in that time?"

The question, with its implication of facts withheld, of a long-established routine inexplicably broken, could not have been more unwelcome, however gently put. Even so, the response was surprising.

Naughton looked for a moment as guilty as if he had been accused of the murder. Then he recovered himself and said: "I didn't come straight into the office. When I got to Fleet Street there were things I needed to think over. I decided to go on walking for a time. I can't remember exactly where I went, but it was along the Embankment and then up to the Strand."

"Thinking about what?"

"Personal things. Family matters." He added, "Mostly about whether I'd accept a year's extension here if it were offered."

"And will it be?"

"I'm not sure. Mr. Langton did talk about it, but of course he couldn't promise anything before it was discussed at Chambers meeting."

"But you expected no difficulty?"

"I can't say. You had better ask Mr. Langton, sir. There may have been members who thought it was time for a change."

Piers asked: "Was Miss Aldridge one of them?"

Naughton turned and looked at him. "I think her idea was to have a practice manager instead of a clerk. One or two chambers have appointed them and I believe it's working well."

"But you hoped to stay on?" Piers persisted.

"I thought I did, as long as Mr. Langton was Head of Chambers. He and I came here the same year. But it's different now. Murder changes everything. I don't suppose he'll want to stay on. This could break him. It's a terrible thing for him, a terrible thing for Chambers. Terrible."

The enormity of it seemed suddenly to have overwhelmed him. His voice broke. Dalgliesh wondered whether he was about to cry. They sat in silence. It was broken by the sound of hurrying footsteps and Ferris came in.

Keeping his voice controlled, he said: "Excuse me, sir, but I think we've found the weapon."

16

The four members of Chambers waited together in the library, for the most part without speaking. Langton had taken the chair at the head of the table, more from habit than from any wish to preside. He caught himself glancing at each of his colleagues' faces with a momentary intensity which he was half afraid they would detect and resent. He saw them as if for the first time, not as three familiar faces, but as strangers involved in a common catastrophe, stranded in some airport lounge, wondering how each would react, curious about the circumstances that had so fortuitously thrown them together. He found himself thinking: I'm Head of Chambers and these are my friends, my brothers in the law, and I don't even know them. I have never known them. He was reminded of a day when he was fourteen—it had been his birthday—and he had for the first time looked in the bathroom glass and subjected every detail of his face to a long unsmiling scrutiny and had thought: This is me, this is what I look like. And then he had remembered that the image was reversed and that never in all his life would he see the face that others saw, and that perhaps it was more than his features that were unknowable. But what could one tell from a face? "There's no art to find the mind's construction in the face. He was a gentleman on whom I built an absolute trust." *Macbeth*. The unlucky play, or so actors claimed. The play of blood. How old had he been when they had studied it at school? Fifteen? Sixteen? How odd that he could remember that quotation when so much else had been forgotten.

He glanced across the table at Simon Costello. He was sitting at the far end and continually pressing back his chair as if to rock himself into equanimity. Langton looked at the familiar pale square face, the eyes which now seemed too small under the heavy brows, the red-gold hair which could flame in high sunlight, the powerful shoulders. He looked more like a professional rugger player than a lawyer, though not when he wore his wig.

Then the face became an impressive mask of judicial gravitas. But, thought Langton, wigs metamorphose us all; perhaps that's why we're so unwilling to get rid of them.

He looked across at Ulrick, at the slight, delicate face, the undisciplined brown hair falling across the high forehead, the eyes keen and speculative behind the steel-rimmed spectacles, yet sometimes holding a look of gentle melancholy, even of endurance. Ulrick, who could look like a poet, but could rasp out his words with the occasional venom of a disappointed schoolmaster. He was still sitting in one of the armchairs beside the fireplace, with the same book spread open on his closed knees. It didn't look like a legal tome. Langton found himself unreasonably curious to know what Ulrick was reading.

Drysdale Laud was looking out of the window with nothing of him visible but a perfectly tailored back. Now he turned. He didn't speak but gave a short interrogative twitch of his eyebrow and an almost imperceptible shrug. His face was perhaps paler than usual, but otherwise he looked as he always did, elegant, confident, relaxed. He was, thought Langton, easily the best-looking man in Chambers, perhaps one of the handsomest at the Bar, where confident good looks were not unusual before they hardened into the peevish arrogance of old age. The strong mouth was sculptured under the long straight nose, the hair a dark disciplined thatch flecked with grey above deep-set eyes. Langton found himself wondering what his relationship with Venetia had really been. Lovers? It seemed unlikely. And wasn't there a rumour that Venetia was sexually occupied elsewhere? A lawyer? A writer? A politician? Someone well known. He must have heard something more definite than this vague recollection of old gossip, perhaps even a name. If so, like so much else, it had escaped him. What else, he wondered, had been going on that he hadn't been aware of?

Lowering his eyes to look away from his colleagues and down at his own clasped hands, he thought: And what about me? How do they see me? How much do they know or guess? But at least so far in this emergency he had acted as Head of Chambers. The words had come when he had needed them. The event, so dramatic in its horror, had imposed its own response. Drysdale, of course, had almost taken over, but not quite, not altogether. He, Langton, had still been Head of Chambers; it was to him that Dalgliesh had turned.

Costello was the most restless. Now he got up from his chair, almost overturning it, and started again a deliberate pacing along the length of the table.

He said: "I don't see why we have to stay cooped up here as if we were suspects. I mean, it's obvious someone from outside got in and killed her. It doesn't mean it was the same person who decorated her with that bloody wig—bloody in more than one sense."

Looking up, Ulrick said: "It was an extraordinarily insensitive thing for anyone to do. It isn't particularly pleasant having blood taken. I very much dislike the needle. And there's always a risk, however small, of infection. Of course, I provide my own needles. Blood donors make out that the procedure is painless, and no doubt it is, but I have never found it agreeable. Now I shall have to cancel the operation and start all over again."

Laud said, half amused, half protesting: "For God's sake, Desmond, what does it matter? All you've lost, however inconvenient, is a pint of blood. Venetia's dead and we've got a murder in Chambers. I agree it would have been more convenient had she died elsewhere."

Costello stopped his pacing.

"Perhaps she did. Are the police sure that she was killed where she was found?"

Laud said: "We don't know what Dalgliesh is sure about. He's hardly likely to confide in us. Until he knows the time of death and the hours for which we are expected to provide alibis, I suppose we have to be considered suspects. But surely she was killed where she was found? I can't see a murderer carrying a dead body through the Middle Temple just to leave it in Chambers for the purpose of incriminating us. Anyway, how would he get in?"

Costello began again his vigorous pacing. "Well, that's not going to be difficult, is it? We're hardly security-conscious here, are we? I mean, you can't exactly describe this place as being secure. I frequently find the front door ajar or even standing open when I arrive. I've complained about it more than once but nothing gets done. Even the people with security buttons on their inner doors don't bother to use them half the time. Venetia and you, Hubert, have refused to have them fitted. Anyone could have got in last night—walked into the building and up to Venetia's room. Well, someone obviously did."

Laud said: "It's a comforting thought, but I don't somehow think Dalgliesh is going to believe that this murdering intruder knew where to find the full-bottomed wig or the blood."

Costello said: "Valerie Caldwell did. I've been wondering a bit about her. She was terribly upset when Venetia wouldn't take her brother's case." Looking round at their faces, suddenly stern, and Laud's disgusted, he said feebly: "Well, it was only a thought."

Laud said: "Best kept to yourself. If Valerie wants to mention it to the police then it's up to her. I certainly shan't. The suggestion that Valerie Caldwell could have had anything to do with Venetia's death is ludicrous. Anyway, with luck she'll have an alibi. We all will."

Desmond Ulrick said with a note of satisfaction: "I certainly haven't, that is not unless she was killed after seven-fifteen. I left Chambers just after seven-fifteen, went home to wash, leave my briefcase and feed the cat, then returned to have dinner at Rules in Maiden Lane. Yesterday was my birthday. I've had dinner at Rules on my birthday since I was a boy."

Costello asked: "Alone?"

"Of course. Dinner alone is the proper end to my birthday."

Costello sounded like a cross-examiner.

"Why bother to go home? I mean, why not go to the restaurant straight from here? A lot of trouble, wasn't it, just to feed the cat?"

"And to leave my briefcase. I never check it in when I have important papers and I greatly dislike leaving it under my chair."

Costello persisted: "Did you book?"

"No, I didn't book. I'm known at Rules. They usually manage to find me a table. They did last night. I was there by eight-fifteen, as the police will no doubt check. May I suggest, Simon, that you leave the police work to them?"

He returned to his book.

Costello said shortly: "I left Chambers just after you, Hubert, at six o'clock, went home and stayed at home. Lois can confirm it. What about you, Drysdale?"

Laud said easily: "This is all a bit pointless, isn't it, until we know the time of death? I too went home, and then to the theatre to see *When We Are Married* at the Savoy."

Costello said: "I thought that was at Chichester."

"It's been transferred to the West End for an eight-week run until November."

"You went on your own? Don't you usually go to the theatre with Venetia?"

"Not this time. As you say, I went on my own."

"Well, it was conveniently close anyway."

Laud kept his voice calm: "Conveniently close for what, Simon? Are you suggesting that I could have dashed out in the interval, killed Venetia and got back in time for the second act? I suppose that's something the police will check. I can just imagine one of Dalgliesh's minions leaping out of his seat, tearing down the Strand, timing it all to the minute. Frankly I don't think it could be done."

It was then that they heard the sound of wheels in the court. Laud moved to the window. He said: "What a sinister-looking van. They've come to take her away. Venetia leaves Chambers for the last time."

The front door was opened, they could hear masculine voices in the hall, the measured tread of feet on the stairs.

Langton said: "It seems wrong to let her go like this."

He pictured what was happening in the room above them, the corpse being zipped into the body bag, lifted onto a stretcher. Would they leave the bloody wig on her head or transport it separately? And didn't they tape the head and the hands? He remembered seeing that done last time he watched a crime series on television. He said again: "It seems wrong to let her go like this. I feel there's something we ought to do."

He moved to join Laud at the window and heard Ulrick's voice.

"Do what precisely? Do you want to find Harry and Valerie and then line us all up in a guard of honour? Perhaps we should be wearing robes and wigs to make the gesture more appropriate."

No one replied, but all except Ulrick stood at the window and watched. The burden was carried out and loaded into the van, swiftly and efficiently. The doors were quietly closed. They stood watching until the sound of the wheels had died away.

Langton broke the silence. He said to Drysdale Laud: "How well do you know Adam Dalgliesh?"

"Not well. I doubt whether anyone does."

"I thought you'd met."

"Once, at a dinner party given by the last Commissioner. Dalgliesh is the Yard's maverick. Every organization needs one, if only to reassure the critics that it is capable of inspiration. The Met doesn't want to be seen as a bastion of masculine insensitivity. A touch of controlled eccentricity has its uses, provided it's allied with intelligence. Dalgliesh certainly has his uses. He's adviser to the Commissioner to begin with. That could mean anything or nothing. In his case it probably means more influence than either would be willing to admit. Then he heads a small squad dignified with some innocuous name set up to investigate crimes of particular sensitivity. Apparently ours qualifies for that privilege. It's a device for keeping his hand in, presumably. He's a useful committee man too. At present he's just finished serving on that advisory group the Met set up to discuss how to assimilate the spies of MI-5 into conventional policing. There's a nice little pot of trouble brewing up there."

Unexpectedly, Ulrick looked up and asked: "Do you like him?"

"I don't know him well enough to feel any emotion as positive as like or dislike. I've a certain prejudice, irrational as prejudice usually is. He reminds me of a sergeant I knew when I was doing my spell in the Territorials. He was perfectly qualified to take a commission but preferred to remain in the ranks."

"Inverted snobbery?"

"More a kind of inverted conceit. He claimed that remaining a sergeant gave him a better chance of studying the men as well as greater independence. He was actually implying that he despised the officers too much to wish to join them. Dalgliesh could have been Commissioner or at least a Chief Constable, so why isn't he?"

Ulrick said: "There is his poetry."

"True, and that could be more successful if he put himself about, did a bit of publicity."

Costello said: "Will he realize that the work here has to go on, that's what I'm asking. After all, it's the beginning of the Michaelmas term. We've got to get access to our rooms. We can't see clients when there are heavy-footed detective constables stamping up and down the stairs."

"Oh, he'll be considerate. If he has to clamp the handcuffs on any of us he'll do it with a certain style."

"And if the killer has Venetia's keys, Harry had better arrange to have all the locks changed, and the sooner, the better."

They were too preoccupied to listen for noises outside the heavy door. Now it burst open and Valerie Caldwell almost tumbled in, white-faced.

She gasped: "They've found the weapon. At least they think it's the weapon. They've found Miss Aldridge's paper-knife."

Langton said: "Where, Valerie?"

She burst into tears and dashed towards him. He could hardly hear what she was saying. "In my filing drawer. It was in my bottom filing drawer."

Hubert Langton gazed helplessly at Laud. There was a second's hesitation in which he almost feared that Drysdale wouldn't respond, that he'd say, "You're Head of Chambers. You cope." But Laud went across to the girl and put an arm round her shoulders.

He said firmly: "Now, this is nonsense, Valerie. Stop crying and listen. No one is going to believe that you had anything to do with Miss Aldridge's death simply because the dagger has been found in your filing cabinet. Anyone could have put it there. It was the natural place for the murderer to drop it on his way out. The police aren't fools. So pull yourself together and be a sensible girl." He urged her gently towards the door. "What we all need now—and that includes you—is coffee. Proper coffee, fresh hot coffee and plenty of it. So be a good girl and see to it. We're not out of coffee, are we?"

"No, Mr Laud. I brought in a fresh packet yesterday."

"The police will probably be glad of some too. Bring ours in as soon as it's ready. And there must be some typing you have on hand. Keep busy and stop worrying. No one suspects you of anything."

Under the calming influence of his voice the girl made gallant attempts to control herself, even to manage a smile of thanks.

After the door closed behind her, Costello said: "She's feeling guilty, I suppose, because of that business with her brother. It was stupid to feel resentment over that. What the hell did she expect? That Venetia would present herself in a North London magistrate's court, complete with junior, to defend a boy accused of trading a few ounces of cannabis? Valerie shouldn't have asked."

Laud said: "I gather that Venetia made that only too obvious. She could have been more gentle about it. The girl was genuinely distressed. Apparently she's deeply devoted to the brother. And if Venetia couldn't or wouldn't help, someone here could have done something. I can't help feeling we let the girl down."

Costello rounded on him. "Do what, for Christ's sake? The boy had a perfectly competent solicitor. If he'd felt the need for a barrister and got in touch with Harry, one of us would have taken the case. Me, for example, if I'd been free."

"You surprise me, Simon. I didn't realize you were so happy to appear in the lower courts. A pity you didn't suggest it at the time."

Costello bristled but, before he could retort, Desmond Ulrick spoke. They turned to him as if surprised to find him still among them. Without looking up from his book, he said: "Now that the police have the weapon, do you suppose they'll let us back into our rooms? It really is most inconvenient being excluded. I'm not sure that the police have power to do it. You're a criminal lawyer, Simon. If I demand to have access to my room, legally has Dalgliesh the power to keep me out?"

Langton said: "I don't think anyone has suggested that, Desmond. This isn't a question of police powers. We're just trying to be reasonably co-operative."

Costello broke in: "Desmond's right. They've found the dagger. If they think that's the weapon, then there's no reason why we should stay cooped up here. Where is Dalgliesh, anyway? Can't you demand to see him, Hubert?"

Langton was saved from the need to reply. The door opened and Dalgliesh came in. He was carrying an object in a thin plastic bag. After taking it over to the table, he took it from the bag with his gloved fingers, then slowly drew the dagger from its scabbard while they watched as if this simple action had the intense fascination of a conjuring trick.

He said: "Could you confirm, Mr. Laud, that this is the steel paper-knife which you gave to Miss Aldridge?"

Laud said: "Of course. There would hardly be two. That's the paper-knife I gave Venetia. You'll find my initials on the blade, below the maker's name."

Langton gazed down at it, recognized it, knew it for what it was. He had seen it often enough on Venetia's desk, had even on some now forgotten occasion watched her using it to slit open a heavy envelope. Yet it seemed to him that he was seeing it for the first time. It was an impressive object. The scabbard was of black leather bound with brass, the handle and guard were brass, the whole made to a design that was both elegant and unfussy. The long steel blade was obviously very sharp. This was no toy. It had been made by a swordsmith and by any definition it was a weapon.

He said with a kind of wonder: "Can this really be what killed her? But it's so clean. It doesn't look any different."

Dalgliesh said: "It's been thoroughly wiped. There are no prints, but, then, we didn't expect any. We shall have to await the post-mortem report to be certain, but it looks as if this was the weapon. You've all been very patient. I'm sure you want now to get back to your rooms. And we shan't any longer need to tape off part of the court, which will be a relief to your neighbours. Before you leave Chambers it would be helpful if you would see one of my officers and let him or her know where you were last night from six-thirty onwards. If you could write the details down it would save time."

Langton felt the need to speak. He said: "I think we could all undertake to do that. Is there anything else you need?"

Dalgliesh said: "Yes. Before you go I'd like to know anything you can tell me about Miss Aldridge. The four of you here must have known her as well as anyone in Chambers. What was she like?"

Langton said: "You mean as a lawyer?"

"I think I know what she was like as a lawyer. As a woman, as a human being."

The four of them looked at Langton. He was swept by a wave of apprehension, almost of panic. He was aware that they were waiting, that something was expected of him. The moment required more than the platitudes of regret, but he wasn't sure what. It would be intolerably embarrassing to slip into bathos.

At last he said: "Venetia was a very fine lawyer. I put that first because that was the most important thing about her to the very many people who owe their liberty and their reputations to her skill. But I think she would have put that first herself. I don't think you can separate the lawyer from the woman. The law was what mattered most to her. As a member of Chambers she could be a difficult colleague. That isn't unusual; we have a reputation for being difficult. Chambers is a collection of intelligent, highly independent, idiosyncratic, critical and overworked men and women whose profession is argument. It's a dull set which doesn't contain its share of eccentrics and personalities who could be described as difficult. Venetia could be intolerant, over-critical, rebarbative. So can we all be at times. She was very greatly respected. I don't think she would have regarded it as a compliment if she'd been described as someone who was greatly loved."

"So she made enemies?"

Langton said simply: "I haven't said so."

Laud obviously thought it was time to speak. He said: "Being difficult in Chambers is practically an art form. Venetia brought it to a higher pitch than most, but we none of us like to live too peaceably. Venetia would have been a distinguished lawyer in any branch of the law. The criminal Bar suited her for some reason. She was a brilliant cross-examiner—but, then, you've probably heard her in court."

Dalgliesh said: "Sometimes to my discomfort. So there's nothing else you can tell me?"

Costello broke in impatiently: "What else is there to say? She prosecuted, she defended, she did her job. And now I'd like to get on with doing mine."

It was then that the door opened. Kate put her head in and said: "I have Mrs. Carpenter here for you, sir."

17

Dalgliesh had early learned not to judge in advance of the facts; this
applied as much to appearance as it did to character. Even so, he was
surprised and a little disconcerted when Janet Carpenter walked with
a quiet dignity across the reception room and held out her hand. He had got
to his feet as she entered and now took the outstretched palm, introduced
her to Piers, to whom she made a gesture of acknowledgement, and invited
her to sit down. She was composed, but the thin scholarly face was very pale
and his experienced eyes detected the unmistakable ravages of shock and
distress.

Watching her as she seated herself, he felt a small jolt of familiarity: he
had met her in various guises before, as much a part of his Norfolk childhood as the five-minute bell on Sunday mornings, the Christmas gift fair, the
summer fête in the rectory garden. She wore the clothes which were so familiar: the tweed suit with the long jacket and skirt with three front pleats,
the floral blouse discordant with the tweed, the cameo brooch at the neck,
the serviceable tights, a little wrinkled round the thin ankles, the sensible
walking brogues as polished as new chestnuts, the woollen gloves which she
now held in her lap, the felt brimmed hat. Here was one of Miss Barbara
Pym's excellent women, a dying breed no doubt, even in country parishes,
but once as much a part of the Church of England as sung evensong, an occasional irritant to the vicar's wife, but an indispensable prop to the parish;
Sunday-school superintendent, arranger of flowers, polisher of brass,
scourge of choirboys and comforter of favoured curates. Even the names
came back to him, a sad roll call of gentle nostalgic regret: Miss Moxon,
Miss Nightingale, Miss Dutton-Smith. For a second his mind amused itself
with the fancy that Mrs. Carpenter was about to complain about last Sunday's choice of hymn.

The brimmed hat made it difficult to see her face clearly, but then she looked up and her eyes met his. They were mild but intelligent, set beneath strong straight brows darker than the glimpse of grey hair under the hat. She was older than he had expected, certainly over sixty. Her face, devoid of make-up, was lined, but the jaw was still strong. It was, he thought, an interesting face but one which might defeat an Identikit to identify from a million others. She was holding herself with a controlled stillness, willing herself to contain the fear and distress which momentarily he saw in her eyes. He saw something else there too. For a fleeting second there was a tinge of shame or disgust.

He said: "I'm sorry we had to bring you back so urgently and, no doubt, so inconveniently. Inspector Miskin has told you that Miss Aldridge is dead?"

"She didn't say how." The voice, deeper than he expected, was not unattractive.

"We believe Miss Aldridge was murdered. We can't know until the post-mortem how exactly she died or the approximate time of her death, but it must have been sometime last night. Could you tell us what precisely happened here from the time you arrived? When was that?"

"Eight-thirty. It's always eight-thirty. I work Monday, Wednesday and Friday from then until ten."

"Alone?"

"No, normally with Mrs. Watson. She should have been here yesterday but Miss Elkington telephoned just after six o'clock to say that Mrs. Watson's married son had been involved in a road accident and was badly injured. She left at once for Southampton, where the family live."

"Did anyone except you and Miss Elkington know that you'd be working on your own yesterday night?"

"I don't see how they could know. Miss Elkington rang me as soon as she got the message. It was too late to find a substitute, so she told me to do what I could. Obviously she would make a deduction in the Chambers' monthly bill."

"So you arrived at the usual time. By what entrance?"

"The Judges' Gate at Devereux Court. I have a key to the gate. I take the tube from Earls Court to the Temple station."

"Did you see anyone you recognized?"

"Only Mr. Burch coming from Middle Temple Lane. He's Senior Clerk at Lord Collingford's Chambers. He sometimes works late and when I see him leaving we've got used to greeting each other. He said good-night. There was no one else."

"And what happened when you got to Pawlet Court?"

There was a silence. Dalgliesh had been watching Mrs. Carpenter's hands. Her body was still but her left hand had been methodically stretching the fingers of her gloves, finger by finger. Now she ceased this fidgeting, raised her head and gazed past him with the concentrated frown of someone trying to recall a complicated series of events. He waited patiently, aware of Kate and Piers sitting equally silent each side of the door. It had only been yesterday, after all. There was something histrionic about this apparently careful attempt at recollection.

Then she said: "There were no lights showing in any of the rooms when I arrived; only a light in the hall. That's generally left on. I unlocked the front door. The alarm hadn't been set but that didn't worry me. Sometimes the last person in Chambers forgets to set it. Everything else seemed usual. There is a secure entry device on the door to the reception and through to the clerk's office. I know the combination. Mr. Naughton tells me in advance when it's going to be changed, but they only do that about once a year. It's easier for everyone if they keep the same combination of numbers."

Easier, but hardly an effective safeguard, thought Dalgliesh, although he wasn't surprised. Security systems installed with enthusiastic zeal seldom survived the first six months of conscientious use.

Mrs. Carpenter went on: "Another three doors have similar devices, but most members of Chambers don't bother to use them. They each have keys to the front door and a key to the outer and inner doors of their rooms. Mr. Langton dislikes seeing security systems on the doors and so does—so did—Miss Aldridge."

"Did you see Miss Aldridge?"

"No. There was no one in Chambers, at least no one I saw or heard. Sometimes one of the lawyers or Mr. Naughton will work late, and then I leave their rooms till last, hoping to get in when they leave. But yesterday they had all left. At least, I thought they had all left."

"What about Miss Aldridge's room?"

"The outer door was locked. I thought, of course, that she'd already gone home and locked up after herself. She used to do that occasionally if she wanted to leave out private or important papers. Of course, it meant that her room didn't get cleaned, but I don't think a little dust worries lawyers. Some of them aren't very tidy, either. You have to get used to their ways if you have the job of cleaning Chambers."

"And you are sure there was no light visible from the room?"

"Quite sure. I'd have noticed when I arrived. Her room's at the front. The only light on was the one in the hall. I turned that off when I left, after I'd set the alarm."

"In what order did you clean the rooms? Perhaps it would be best if you talk us through your routine."

"I fetched my duster and polish from the cupboard in the basement. As Mrs. Watson wasn't with me I decided just to go over the floors with the carpet-sweeper and leave the vacuum cleaning. I saw to the carpet in the reception room and dusted and tidied there first. After that I cleaned the clerk's room. All that only took about twenty minutes, then I went upstairs and swept and dusted the rooms which were open. That's when I discovered that Miss Aldridge's room on the first floor was locked."

"What other rooms couldn't you get into?"

"Only hers and Mr. Costello's on the second floor."

"You heard no noise from either?"

"Nothing. If anyone was inside they had the light off and were very quiet. Last of all I went down to the basement and into Mr. Ulrick's room. I always do the basement last. There's nothing down there but Mr. Ulrick's room, the ladies' lavatory and the storeroom."

"Was it your job to clean Mr. Ulrick's refrigerator?"

"Oh yes, he likes me to clear it out occasionally and to see on Friday that nothing is left to get stale over the weekend. He uses it mostly for his milk, sometimes for his sandwiches and for his Malvern water and ice. If he buys food for his dinner he'll keep it in the fridge until he goes home. Mr. Ulrick is fastidious about cleanliness and freshness. Sometimes he keeps a bottle of white wine in it, but not often. And, of course, he's got his pouch of blood stored there ready for when he's called in for his operation. The blood's in a plastic bag, rather like a transparent hot-water bottle. I would have had quite a shock if he hadn't warned me."

"When did you first see the blood?"

"On Monday. He left a note on his desk addressed to me. It said: 'The blood in my refrigerator is for my operation. Please don't touch.' It was considerate of him to warn me, but it still gave me quite a shock. I thought the blood would be in bottles, not in a plastic pouch. Of course, he didn't need to tell me not to touch. I never touch papers, for example, even to tidy them, except the journals in the reception room. I certainly wouldn't touch anyone's blood."

Dalgliesh didn't pause before asking the crucial question and his voice, carefully neutral, gave no hint of its importance. "Was the pouch of blood in the refrigerator yesterday night?"

"Well, it must have been, mustn't it? Mr. Ulrick hasn't had the operation yet. I didn't look into the fridge yesterday. Because Mrs. Watson wasn't at work I had a struggle to get through the essentials. I knew I'd be clearing out the fridge on Friday anyway. Is there some problem? Isn't the blood there now? Are you saying someone has stolen it? That's extraordinary, surely. It wouldn't be of any use except to Mr. Ulrick, would it?"

Dalgliesh didn't explain. He said: "Mrs. Carpenter, I want you to think very carefully. While you were cleaning Chambers could anyone already here, perhaps in one of the locked rooms, have left the building without your noticing?"

Again there was that concentrated frown, then she said: "I think I would have noticed when I was cleaning the reception room. I had the door open and even if someone passed down the hall unnoticed, I think I would have heard the front door close. It's very heavy. I'm not sure about the time when I was cleaning the clerk's room. Someone could have left unnoticed then, I suppose. And of course, if anyone had been in Mr. Ulrick's room or any-where in the basement they could have left while I was cleaning the upper floors."

She paused, then said: "There is one thing I've just remembered. I don't know whether it's important. There must have been a woman in Chambers not long before I arrived."

"How can you be sure of that, Mrs. Carpenter?"

"Because someone had been using the ladies' lavatory in the basement. The basin was still damp and the soap was lying in a pool of water and was very wet. I've been meaning to bring in a soap dish for the ladies' lavatory. If the users don't wipe the basin after use—and, of course, they never do—the soap is usually left dissolving in a pool of water beside the tap and it's very wasteful."

Dalgliesh said: "How wet was the basin? Did you gain the impression it had been used very recently?"

"Well, it wasn't a hot night, was it? So it wouldn't dry very quickly. But the soak-away isn't working very efficiently either. The water takes a long time to drain. I've spoken to Miss Caldwell and Mr. Naughton about getting a plumber, but they haven't done anything about it yet. I think there was about half an inch of water in the bottom of the basin. I remember thinking at the time that Miss Aldridge must have used the room just before she left. She often worked late on a Wednesday. But, then, Miss Aldridge didn't leave, did she?"

"No," said Dalgliesh, "Miss Aldridge didn't leave."

He said nothing about the full-bottomed wig. It had been important to ask whether she had opened the fridge and seen the blood, but the less she knew about the details of Venetia Aldridge's death the better.

Dalgliesh thanked her for her help and let her go. She had sat through the interrogation with the docility of an applicant for a job, and now left as quietly and with as much careful dignity as she had come in with. But Dalgliesh sensed her relief in the more confident gait, the almost imperceptible relaxation of the shoulders. An interesting witness. She hadn't even asked directly how Venetia Aldridge had died. She had been totally without the ghoulish curiosity, the mixture of excitement and spurious horror so often found in those innocently caught up in murder. Violent death, like most disasters, afforded its satisfactions to those who were neither victim nor suspect. She was certainly intelligent enough to know that she had to be on his list of suspects, at least at this early stage. That alone could account for the nervousness. He wondered which of his colleagues, Kate or Piers, would say how much she differed from the usual image of a London daily cleaning woman. Probably neither. Both knew his dislike of that unthinking stereotyping of a witness which was as inimical to good policing as it was demeaning to the infinite variety of human life.

Piers spoke first. "She looks after her hands, doesn't she? You wouldn't guess that she earns her living cleaning. Wears rubber gloves, I suppose. Hardly significant, though, the gloves, I mean. Her prints can legitimately be found all over Chambers. Did you think she was telling the truth, sir?"

"The usual mixture, I think, some truth, some untruth, some things left unsaid. She's hiding something."

He had learned to be as wary of intuition as he was of superficial judgements, but it was hardly possible to be a long-serving detective officer and not know when a witness was lying. It wasn't always suspicious or even significant. Nearly everyone had something to hide. And it was optimistic to expect the whole truth at a first interview. A wise suspect answered questions and kept his counsel; only the naïve confused a police officer with a social worker.

Kate said: "It's a pity she didn't open that fridge, assuming, of course, that she was telling the truth. Odd that she didn't ask why we were so interested in Ulrick's blood. But if she did take it, then it was probably safer for her to say that she never looked in the fridge than to say that she did and the blood wasn't there. But if the blood hadn't been there, then at least we could be certain that Aldridge was dead in her room before Mrs. Carpenter arrived."

Piers said: "That's going a bit far. She could have been killed any time after she was last seen and the blood poured over her later. Two things we can be certain of, though: whoever decorated the corpse so dramatically

knew where the full-bottomed wig was kept and knew that there was Ulrick's blood in that fridge. Mrs. Carpenter must have known about the wig
and she admits she knew about the blood."

Dalgliesh turned to Kate. "How did she take the news when you and
Robbins broke it to her? Was she alone?"

"Yes, sir. She was in a small top-floor flat, one sitting-room, and one bedroom, I think, but we didn't get any further than the sitting-room. She was
alone and had her coat and hat on ready to go out to shop. I showed her my
warrant card and gave her the bare facts, that Miss Aldridge had been found
dead, apparently murdered, and that it would be helpful if she could come
back to Chambers and answer some questions. She was very shocked. She
looked at me for a second as if she thought I was mad, then went very pale
and swayed. I put out a hand to support her and led her to a chair. She sat
down for a few minutes, but recovered quickly. After that she seemed perfectly in control."

"Did you think that the murder was news to her? I realize that it's hardly
a fair question."

"Yes, sir. Yes, I did. I think Robbins will say the same."

"And she asked no questions?"

"Neither in the flat nor on the way here. She just said, 'I'm ready,
Inspector. I can start right away.' We didn't speak on the journey—oh, I
did ask if she was all right and she said she was. She sat in the car with her
hands folded in her lap looking down at them. She gave the impression of
thinking."

Sergeant Robbins put his head around the door.

"Mr. Langton is anxious to see you, sir. He's worried that the press will
get hold of it, or that the news will break in some way before he's had time
to tell the other members of Chambers. And he's asking how long Chambers
will have to be closed. Apparently they've got some solicitors arriving this
afternoon."

"Tell him I'll be with him in ten minutes. And you'd better ring Public
Relations. Unless some interesting news breaks tomorrow this is likely to
make the front page. And, Robbins, what was your impression of Mrs. Carpenter's reaction when she first heard the news?"

Robbins took his time; he always did. "Surprise and shock, sir." He
paused.

"Yes, Robbins?"

"I thought there was something else. Guilt perhaps. Or shame."

18

At three o'clock Dalgliesh had a meeting at the Yard of the working party set up to discuss the implications of the Security Services Act, but had arranged to meet Venetia Aldridge's solicitor at Pelham Place with Kate at six o'clock, and then to go on to Pimlico to see Mark Rawlstone.

Kate had spoken to the solicitor, a Mr. Nicholas Farnham, when the meeting was arranged. The man's voice had been deep and with some of the measured authority of late middle age, so that she was expecting to meet a long-standing family solicitor, cautious, conventional and probably inclined to keep a suspicious eye on any police activities in his client's house. Instead Nicholas Farnham, who came leaping up the steps as Kate rang the bell, was revealed as surprisingly young, vigorous, cheerful-faced and apparently not greatly distressed by the loss of a client.

Mrs. Buckley opened the door to them and told them that Miss Octavia was in the basement flat but would come up to see them later. Then she led them upstairs and showed them into the drawing-room.

When she had left, Dalgliesh turned to Nicholas Farnham. "We'd like to go through your client's papers now, if you have no objection. It's helpful having you here. Thank you for making the time."

Farnham said: "I've been here already, of course, late morning. I wanted to see if there was anything the firm could do for Miss Aldridge's daughter and assure her that we'd arrange for her to have money paid from the bank. It's almost the first thing the bereaved ask—'What do I do for money?' It's natural enough really. Death puts an end to a life. It doesn't put an end to the need to eat, settle the bills, pay the wages."

Dalgliesh asked: "How did you find her?"

Farnham hesitated. "Octavia? I suppose the conventional answer is bearing up remarkably well."

"More shocked than grieved?"

"I'm not sure that would be fair. How can you tell what people are feeling at a time like this? Her mother had only been dead a matter of hours. She had her fiancé with her, which didn't help. He asked most of the questions. Wanted to know the terms of the will. Well, I suppose that's natural enough, but it struck me as insensitive."

"Did Miss Aldridge consult you about her daughter's engagement?"

"No she didn't. Well, there was hardly time. And there wouldn't be much point, would there? I mean, the girl's of age. What could we or anyone else do? When I got her on her own for a few moments this morning I did murmur that it wasn't wise to make important decisions about one's future life when in a state of grief or shock, but the hint wasn't well received. It's not as if I'm an old family friend. The firm has acted for Miss Aldridge for twelve years but mostly it's been the divorce and conveyancing. She bought this place just after her divorce."

"What about the will? Did you draw that up?"

"Yes we did. Not the one drawn up when she married, but she revised it after the divorce and we acted for her then. There should be a copy in the desk here. If not, I can tell you the main provisions. It's very simple. A few bequests to legal charities. Five thousand pounds to the housekeeper, Rose Buckley, provided she's in her service at the date of death. Two of her pictures—the one in Chambers and the Vanessa Bell here—to Drysdale Laud. All the residue goes to her daughter, Octavia, in trust until she comes of age and then absolutely."

Dalgliesh said: "She is, I understand, now of age."

"Eighteen on the first of October. Oh yes, I forgot—there is a bequest of eight thousand pounds to her ex-husband, Luke Cummins. Considering that the total value of the estate apart from the house is three-quarters of a million, he may well feel it should either have been nothing or something more."

Dalgliesh asked: "Has he kept in touch with her or the child?"

"Not as far as I know. But, then, as I've said, I don't really know much about the family. I think he was pushed out of her life pretty effectively. Or maybe he didn't need pushing. There's something spiteful about that eight thousand quid and she never struck me as a petty or spiteful woman. But I didn't really know her. Of course, she was a very fine lawyer."

"That seems to be her epitaph."

Farnham said: "Well, you can't really wonder. Perhaps it's the epitaph she would have chosen herself. It was the most important thing about her. Look at this house, for example. It isn't exactly lived in, is it? I mean, you don't get much impression of the woman from these rather conventional rooms. Her real life wasn't here. It was in Chambers and the courts."

Dalgliesh drew up a second chair at the desk and Kate and he began their methodical search of the cubbyholes and drawers. Farnham seemed content to leave them to it, wandering round the room and inspecting each item of furniture with the air of an auctioneer assessing the possible reserve price.

He said: "Drysdale Laud should be happy with this Vanessa Bell. She could be a slovenly artist at times, but this is one of her best. Odd that Miss Aldridge was so keen on these Bloomsbury painters. I'd have expected her to go for something more modern."

The thought had crossed Dalgliesh's mind. The painting was an agreeable picture of a dark-haired woman in a long red skirt standing at the open window of a kitchen and gazing out over flat countryside. There was a dresser holding a variety of jugs and a vase of cornflowers on the windowsill. He wondered whether Drysdale Laud knew of the bequest; he wondered, too, why it had been made.

Farnham continued his pacing, then he said: "Odd job you have, grubbing through the leavings of a life, but I expect you get used to it."

Dalgliesh said: "Not altogether."

His and Kate's task was almost finished. If Venetia Aldridge had been able to predict the exact time of her death, she could hardly have left her affairs in better order. A locked drawer held the statements of her various bank accounts, her will and details of her investments. She paid her bills promptly, kept the receipts for six months, then obviously destroyed them. A manila file marked "Insurance" contained the policies for the house, its contents and her car.

He said: "I don't think there's anything we need to take away, and I don't think there's anything more we need to do here. I'd like to see Miss Cummins and Mrs. Buckley before I leave."

Farnham said: "Well, you won't need me for that, so I may as well be on my way. If there's anything else you want to know, give me a ring. I'd better have a word with Octavia before I leave. I've already told her the terms of the will but she may have questions and, of course, she'll probably need help and some support at the inquest and funeral. When is the inquest, by the way?"

"In four days' time."

"We'll be there, of course, although it'll probably be a waste of time. I assume you'll ask for an adjournment. Well, goodbye and good hunting."

He shook hands with Dalgliesh and Kate and they heard him bounding down the stairs, and caught his muttered words in the hall with Mrs. Buckley. He couldn't have spent long with Octavia. Within five minutes they heard footsteps and the girl came in. She looked pale but perfectly calm. She sat down on the edge of a chaise longue, rather like a child instructed how to behave in a strange room.

Dalgliesh said: "Thank you for your co-operation, Miss Cummins. It's been helpful to go through your mother's papers, but I'm sorry that we've had to bother you so soon after her death. There is one question if you feel able to talk to us."

She said rather sourly: "I'm all right."

"It's about the quarrel between your mother and Mr. Mark Rawlstone. Do you remember precisely what they said?"

"No I don't. I didn't hear what they said. I could only hear them quarrelling. I don't want to think about it and I don't want to remember it. And I'm not going to answer any more questions."

"I understand. This is a terrible time for you and we're very sorry. If you do remember more about it, please let us know. Is Mr. Ashe here? We rather expected that he would be."

"No he isn't. Ashe isn't very fond of the police. Do you wonder? You stitched him up for his aunt's murder. Why should he talk to you now? He doesn't have to. He's got an alibi. We've already explained all that."

Dalgliesh said: "If we need to speak to him, then I'll be in touch. I'd like to see Mrs. Buckley before I leave. Would you be good enough to tell her?"

"You could try her sitting-room. Top floor at the back. But I shouldn't take much notice of anything she tells you."

Dalgliesh, who was beginning to get up, sat down again and said in a voice of calm interest: "Wouldn't you? Why is that, Miss Cummins?"

She reddened. "Well, she's old."

"And therefore incapable of coherent thought, is that what you're telling us?"

"It's like I said, she's old. I didn't mean anything."

Kate saw with satisfaction the girl's angry discomfiture, then told herself quickly to control her dislike; antipathy could cripple judgement in a police officer as easily as partiality. And it was only hours since Octavia had learned of her mother's murder. Whatever their relationship, the girl must be in shock.

Octavia repeated sullenly her last words: "I didn't mean anything."

Dalgliesh's voice was gentler than his words.

"No? May I give you some advice, Miss Cummins? When you're talking to a police officer, particularly about murder, it's wise to ensure that your words do mean something. We're here to try to find out how your mother died. I'm sure that's what you want too. We'll find our own way up."

They mounted the staircase without speaking, Dalgliesh waiting for Kate to lead the way. She had noticed from her first day in the squad that he always did let her go first except when there was danger or unpleasantness to face. She saw it as an instinctive courtesy, but knew that she would have felt more comfortable with the macho thrusting of a typical male officer. Climbing the stairs, aware of him disconcertingly close behind her, she thought once again about the ambiguities of their relationship. She liked him—she would never allow herself a stronger word—she admired and respected him. She passionately needed his approval and sometimes resented that need. But she had never felt completely at ease with him, because she had never understood him.

The stairs to the top flight were carpeted, but Mrs. Buckley must have heard their footsteps. When they reached the top floor she was waiting for them, and welcomed them into her sitting-room as if they were expected guests. She was calmer than when Kate had first seen her, perhaps because she had recovered from the initial shock of the murder; perhaps, too, she was more at ease with them away from Octavia and on her own ground.

"It's rather crowded, I'm afraid, but I have three chairs. If Inspector Miskin doesn't mind taking this one—it's rather low. It was my mother's nursing chair. I was given the basement flat when I first arrived but Miss Aldridge explained that I might later have to move if her daughter needed it when she left school. That was only right, of course. May I offer you coffee? Miss Aldridge had this mini-kitchen made for me in what was a cupboard. I can make hot drinks and even cook a light meal in the microwave. It saves me the trouble of going down to the kitchen. If Miss Aldridge has—had—a dinner guest I could serve the main course and then come upstairs and eat here. If it was a large party she usually got in outside caterers. My job here isn't really arduous, just shopping, cooking the evening meal and a little light housework. We have a woman in twice weekly for the rough."

Dalgliesh asked: "How did you come to work for Miss Aldridge?"

"Forgive me if I wait until I've ground the coffee beans. One can't hear anything above the noise. That's better. The smell is wonderful, isn't it? That's one thing my husband and I never economized on, our coffee."

She busied herself with kettle and percolator while she told her story. In essentials it was common enough, and where she was reticent neither Dalgliesh nor Kate had difficulty in filling in the details. She was the widow of a country vicar who had died eight years previously. She and her husband had inherited a house in Cambridge from her grandmother but after her husband's death she had sold it in order to hand over a substantial sum to her son, and had moved into a cottage in rural Hertfordshire, the county in which she had been brought up. The son, an only child, had bought a house, sold it well within two years and had moved to Canada with the profit, apparently with no intention of returning. The country cottage proved to be a mistake. She was lonely among strangers and the village church on which she had pinned her hopes became uncongenial under the ministry of a new young vicar.

"I know that the church has to attract the young and there was a new housing estate on the fringes of the village which the vicar was anxious to bring in. We had a great deal of pop music and choruses, and we used to sing 'Happy Birthday to You' when anyone in the congregation had a birthday that week. The family communion was more like a concert than a service, and there really wasn't much for me to do in the parish. So I thought I might have a more fulfilled life if I came to London. I could let the cottage, that would bring in a little extra money. I read the advertisement for this job in *The Lady* and Miss Aldridge interviewed me. She agreed that I could bring some of my furniture with me, and my own things do help to make me feel at home."

The room, thought Kate, was indeed homely, if over-cluttered. The substantial desk at which Mrs. Buckley's husband must have written his sermons, the display cabinet crammed with patterned china, the small polished table crowded with family photographs in silver frames, the glass-fronted bookcase of leather volumes and the row of rather anaemic water-colours provided, even for her, a stranger, a sense of continuity and security, of a life which had known love. The single divan bed placed against the wall with a small shelf and a wall-mounted light above it, was covered by a patchwork quilt in faded silks.

Looking at Dalgliesh's grave face, at the long fingers curled round the coffee mug, Kate thought: He's perfectly at ease here. He's known women like this all his life. They understand each other.

He asked: "You have been happy here?"

"Contented rather than happy. I had hopes of evening classes, but it isn't really possible for an elderly woman to go out alone at night. My husband started his ministry in London but I hadn't realized how much has changed. But I do get to a matinée occasionally, and there are the galleries and the museums, and I'm close to St Joseph's and Father Michael is very kind."

"And Miss Aldridge. You liked her?"

"I respected her. She could be a little frightening at times, a little impatient. If she gave an instruction she didn't like to have to repeat it. She was very efficient herself and she expected it in others. But she was very fair, very considerate. A little remote, but, then, she advertised for a housekeeper, not a companion."

Dalgliesh said: "That call to her yesterday evening. Forgive me, but you are sure about the time?"

"Quite sure. I made it at seven-forty-five. I looked at my watch."

"Could you tell us about it, why you made it, what exactly was said?"

She was silent for a moment, and when she spoke it was with a pathetic dignity. "Octavia was quite right in what she said. It was to complain about her. Miss Aldridge disliked my telephoning her at Chambers unless it was really urgent, and that's why I hesitated. But Octavia and that young man, her fiancé, came up from the basement flat and demanded that I cook them dinner. She isn't a vegetarian but she decided that it had to be a vegetarian meal. The arrangement is that Octavia looks after herself in the flat. Of course, normally I wouldn't mind helping out, but she was very peremptory. I thought that if I gave way once she would expect me to cook for her on demand. So I came up from the kitchen into Miss Aldridge's study and telephoned Chambers, and explained the problem as briefly as I could. Miss Aldridge said, 'If she wants vegetables, cook her vegetables. I'll talk to her and sort it out when I get home. That will be in about an hour's time. I'll get my own dinner. I can't discuss it now, I have someone with me.' "

"And that was all?"

"And that was all. She sounded very impatient, but she never liked me to ring Chambers, and of course it wasn't a good time when she had someone with her. I went down to the basement kitchen and cooked a thick onion tart for them. It's one of Delia Smith's recipes and Miss Aldridge always liked it. But of course I had to make the pastry first and it's best to leave the dough in the fridge for half an hour while you prepare the filling, so it isn't a quick meal. Then afterwards they wanted pancakes with apricot jam. I made these after they'd had the onion tart, and served the pancakes straight from the pan."

Kate asked: "So you can be absolutely certain that both of them were in the flat the whole of the time from quarter to eight, when you made the call, until you went up to bed at about ten-thirty?"

"Oh absolutely sure. I was constantly in and out of their sitting-room, serving or clearing the plates. Both of them were under my eyes, so to speak, the whole evening. It wasn't very pleasant. I think Octavia was trying to show off in front of the young man. I didn't go downstairs again after I'd left them and come up here. I thought that Miss Aldridge would come up if she wanted to discuss anything that evening. I sat in my dressing-gown until after eleven in case she wanted me, and then I went to bed. In the morning I went in with her tea and found that the bed hadn't been slept in. That's when I rang Chambers again."

Dalgliesh said: "We need to know as much about her as possible. What about dinner parties? Did her friends come here often?"

"Not very often. She really lived a very private life. Mr. Laud came about once every month or six weeks. They liked to go to exhibitions or the theatre together. I usually cooked them a light meal before they went and he brought her home, but I don't think he stayed for more than a drink. And sometimes they went out to dinner together."

"And was there anyone else, anyone perhaps who stayed for more than a drink?"

She flushed and seemed reluctant to reply. Then she said: "Miss Aldridge is dead. It seems terrible even to discuss her, and more terrible to gossip about her life. We ought to protect the dead."

Dalgliesh said gently: "In a murder investigation to protect the dead can often mean endangering the living. I'm not here to judge her, I've no right. But I do need to know about her. I do need the facts."

There was a little silence, then Mrs. Buckley said: "There was another visitor. He didn't come very often but I think he did occasionally stay the night. It was Mr. Rawlstone, Mr. Mark Rawlstone. He's an MP."

Dalgliesh asked her when she had last seen him.

"It must be two or three months ago, perhaps more. Time passes so quickly, doesn't it? I can't really remember. But of course he may have come more recently, perhaps one night after I'd gone to my room. He was always gone early in the morning."

Before they left Dalgliesh asked: "What are you thinking of doing now, Mrs. Buckley? Staying on here?"

"Mr. Farnham, that very pleasant solicitor, suggested that I should take my time. His firm and Miss Aldridge's bank are the executors, so I suppose they'll be paying me for the time being. I don't think Octavia will want me to stay on—in fact, I'm sure she won't. But someone ought to be in the house with her and I suppose I'm better than nobody. She's spoken to her father but she doesn't want to see him. I don't think I can leave her even if she does resent me. But it's all so dreadful at the moment that I can't really think clearly."

Dalgliesh said: "Of course not. It's been an appalling shock for you. You've been very helpful, Mrs. Buckley. If there is anything else that comes to mind, please get in touch. This is the number. And if you find the media intrusive, let me know and I'll arrange some protection for you. I'm afraid you may be under siege when the news breaks."

She sat for a moment in silence. Then she said: "I hope you won't mind my asking. I hope you won't think it's vulgar curiosity. But can you tell me how Miss Aldridge died? I don't mean the details. I would just like to know that it was quick and that she didn't suffer."

Dalgliesh said gently: "It was quick and she didn't suffer."

"And there wasn't a lot of blood? I know it's silly but I keep on seeing blood."

"No," said Dalgliesh. "There wasn't any blood."

She thanked them quietly and saw them to the door, then stood at the top of the steps watching as they got into the car. Then, as they drove off, she raised her hand in a pathetic gesture of farewell, as if she were waving away a friend.

19

Just after one o'clock Valerie Caldwell was told by the police that they had finished questioning her for the present, and Mr. Langton suggested that she should go home. A message would be put on the answerphone to say that Chambers were closed for the day. She was glad of the chance to get away from a place in which everything familiar and comfortable now seemed strange, threatening and subtly different. It seemed to her that the people she worked with, liked and thought liked her, were suddenly suspicious strangers. Perhaps, she thought, they all felt the same. Perhaps this was what murder did, even to the innocent.

There was a problem about leaving so early. Her mother, who suffered from agoraphobia, complicated by depression since Kenny's imprisonment, would be worried if she arrived home in the afternoon without prior explanation. She would be worried still more on hearing the reason for it; even so, it was better to telephone in advance. To her relief it was her grandmother who answered. There was no knowing how Gran would take the news, but at least she'd be calm about it. Gran could break it to her mother, Valerie hoped tactfully, before she got home.

She said: "Tell Mummy I'll be home early. Someone broke into Chambers last night and killed Miss Aldridge. Stabbed to death. Yes, I'm all right, Gran. It's nothing to do with the rest of Chambers but we're closing for the day."

There was a brief silence while Gran took in the news, then she said: "Murdered, was she? Oh well, I can't say I'm surprised. Always mixed up with criminals, getting them off. I expect one she didn't get off has come out of prison and done for her. Your ma won't like it. She'll want you to leave that place, get a job locally."

"Gran, don't let her start all that again. Just tell her I'm all right and I'll be back early."

As usual she had brought sandwiches for her lunch, but she didn't want to eat them at her desk. Even to be seen with food was a desecration. So she walked down Middle Temple Lane, turned west and into Embankment Gardens and sat on a seat facing the river. She wasn't hungry, but there were sparrows who were. She watched their jerky peckings and sudden aggressive flurries, dropping an occasional crumb to the smaller, less assertive birds who were always too late for the pickings. But her mind was elsewhere.

She had told them too much, she realized that now. It had been the good-looking young detective and the woman officer who had interviewed her, and she had sensed that they were quietly sympathetic. But that of course had been deliberate. They had set out to get her confidence, and they had succeeded. And it had been a relief to talk to someone unconnected with Chambers about what had happened to Kenny, even if they were police officers. She had poured it all out.

Her brother had been arrested for selling drugs. But he hadn't been dealing, not like real drug barons, not like the people one read about in the papers. He hadn't got a job at present, but he shared a house with friends in North London and they smoked pot at their parties. Kenny said that everyone did. But it was Kenny who brought the drug, enough for the whole evening. And then the others paid him for their share. That was what everyone did. It was the cheapest way to get pot. But he had been caught and, desperate, she had asked Miss Aldridge for help. Perhaps she had asked at a bad time. She knew now that it hadn't been wise, hadn't even been right. Her cheeks burned as she remembered the response, the coldness in her voice, the contempt in her eyes.

"I don't propose to startle the North London Magistrate's Court by turning up complete with a junior to save your brother from his folly. Get him a good solicitor."

And Kenny had been found guilty and sentenced to six months.

The woman detective, Inspector Miskin, had said: "That's unusual for a first offence. He'd done it before, hadn't he?"

Yes, she admitted, he had done it before. But only once and in the same way. And what use was it sending him to prison? It had only made him bitter. He wouldn't have gone to prison if Miss Aldridge had defended him. She got people off who were far worse than Kenny—murderers, rapists, people accused of major fraud. Nothing happened to them. Kenny hadn't hurt anyone, hadn't cheated anyone. He was kind and gentle. He couldn't even stamp on an insect. Now he was in prison and her mother couldn't visit because of the agoraphobia, and Gran mustn't be told because Gran always criticized her mum about how she'd brought up her children.

The two detectives hadn't argued with her, hadn't criticized any more than they had been openly sympathetic. But somehow she had told them other things, things that weren't her business which they didn't need to know. She had confided about the gossip in Chambers over Mr. Langton's successor, about the rumour that Miss Aldridge was interested, the changes she might make.

Inspector Miskin had asked, "How do you know this?"

But of course she knew it. Chambers was a hotbed of gossip. People spoke in front of her. Gossip permeated the very air as if by a mysterious process of osmosis. She had told them about her friendship with the Naughtons. It was Harry Naughton, the Senior Clerk, who had got her the job. She and her mother and Gran lived close to him and his family, and she went to the same church. She had been looking for a job when the vacancy came up in Chambers and he had recommended her. At first she had been only the junior typist, but when Miss Justin retired after thirty years, she had been invited to take over her job and her own had been filled by a temp. The last temp hadn't been satisfactory, so, for the past two weeks, she had been managing on her own. She was still on trial, but she hoped her appointment as Chambers secretary would be confirmed at the next Chambers meeting.

It was Inspector Miskin who had asked: "If Miss Aldridge had been appointed Head of Chambers, would she have suggested you as secretary?"

"Oh no, I don't think so. Not after what happened. And I think she wanted to replace Harry with a practice manager, and if that happened the new practice manager would probably want a say in how the staff were organized."

She was amazed now how much she had confided to them. But there were two things she hadn't told them.

At the end she had said, trying not to cry, trying to retain some shreds of dignity: "I hated her for not helping Kenny. Or perhaps it was because she was so contemptuous about it—contemptuous to me. Now I feel awful because I did hate her and she's dead. But I didn't kill her. I couldn't."

Inspector Miskin had said: "We have reason to believe that Miss Aldridge was alive at a quarter to eight. You say you were home by seven-thirty. If your mother and grandmother confirm that, then you can't have killed her. Don't worry."

So they had never really suspected her. Then why so long in questioning? Why had they bothered? She thought she knew the answer and her cheeks burned.

It felt strange to be going home in the early afternoon. The tube was almost empty, and when it drew up at Buckhurst Hill Station only one person was waiting on the opposite platform for the London train. The street outside was as quiet and peaceful as if it were a country road. Even the small terraced house, at 3 2 Linney Lane, looked unfamiliar and a little forbidding, like a house in mourning. The curtains were drawn in the front downstairs room and across one other window. She knew what this meant. Her mother was upstairs resting—if lying taut, eyes open, staring into the darkness could be described as resting. Her gran was watching television.

She put her key in the lock and was met by a loud blare punctuated by shots. Gran loved crime films and had no inhibitions about sex and violence. As Valerie came into the sitting-room, she pressed the remote control. So it must be a video; Gran wouldn't otherwise interrupt her viewing.

Showing no interest in her granddaughter's arrival, she complained: "I can't hear what they're saying half the time. All they do is mutter-mutter at each other. And it's worse with those Americans."

"It's the way they act now, Gran. Naturalistic, like they'd talk to each other in real life."

"Fat lot of use that is if you can't hear a bloody word. And it's no use putting up the sound, it only makes it worse. And they keep dashing into nightclubs where it's so dark you can't see either. Those old Hitchcocks are better. *Dial M for Murder.* I wouldn't mind seeing that again. You can hear every word. They knew how to speak in those days. And why can't they hold the camera steady? What's the matter with the cameraman—drunk?"

"It's clever direction, Gran."

"Is that what it is? Too clever for me by half."

The television was Gran's entertainment, solace and passion. She approved of almost nothing she saw, but watched incessantly. Valerie sometimes wondered whether it provided a convenient focus for Gran's combative view of life. She could criticize the words, behaviour, appearance and diction of actors, politicians and pundits without fear of contradiction. Her granddaughter sometimes found it surprising that Gran seemed unable to see her own appearance with critical eyes. The hair, dyed an incongruous ginger above and around a seventy-five-year-old face which hardship had aged before its time into deep clefts and sagging skin, was embarrassingly grotesque, while a tight skirt an inch above the knee only emphasized the lean and mottled shanks. But Valerie admired her gran's spirit. She knew that they were allies even though she couldn't expect a word of appreciation or love. Together they coped with her mother's agoraphobia and depression, with the shopping Mrs. Caldwell couldn't do, with the cooking and housework, the paying of bills, the normal crises of everyday life. Her mother ate the food they placed in front of her but had no interest in how it had got on the plate.

And now there was the problem of Kenny. When he was sentenced, her mother had made her promise that Gran wouldn't be told, and she had kept that promise. It made it difficult to visit him in prison. She had only been able to go to him twice, and had had to devise complicated stories about visiting an old school friend which had seemed unconvincing even to herself.

Gran had said: "You're seeing a man, I suppose. What about the shopping?"

"I'll call in at the supermarket on my way home. It's open until ten on Saturdays."

"Well, I hope you have more luck with this one than you had with the other. I knew he'd throw you over once he got to university. It's always happening. And you didn't take much trouble to keep him, I must say. You need to show a bit more spirit, my girl. Men like it."

Gran, in her youth, had shown plenty of spirit and had known exactly what men liked.

As expected, Gran took the news of the murder in her stride. She seldom showed interest in people she hadn't met, and had long decided that Pawlet Court was her granddaughter's world, too remote from her life to be of interest. Real murder, particularly of someone she had never met, paled beside those bright, violent images which energized her life and provided all the excitement she craved. Seldom did Valerie come home to interested questions about what sort of day she'd had, what people in Chambers had said or done. But the unconcern was helpful when at last her mother's slow step was heard on the stairs and the news had to be broken.

Mrs. Caldwell was having a bad day. Preoccupied with her own misery, she seemed hardly to take in what she was being told. The physical death of a stranger could have no power over one who was enduring a living hell. Valerie knew what would happen, the cycle was predictable. Her mother's GP would increase the dosage of her drugs, she would break temporarily out of the depression, the reality of what had happened would break in on her, and then there would be the agitation, the worries, the reiteration that it would be so much better for everyone if Valerie could find a job locally, avoid the journey, get home earlier. But that was in the future.

The slow hours of the afternoon dragged into evening. At seven o'clock, with Gran and her mother both in front of the television, Valerie poured carrot soup from its carton and put the foil tray of canneloni into the oven. It was only when they had finished the meal and she had washed up, then seen her mother again seated with Gran in the front room, that she realized what she needed to do. She had to see the Naughtons. Harry would be home by now. She had to sit with him and Margaret in that warm homely kitchen where she had sat so often in childhood on her way home from Sunday school, and had been given home-made lemonade and chocolate buns. She needed the comfort and advice she had no hope of finding at home.

They made no demur about her leaving. Gran only said, "Don't be too late, now," without taking her eyes from the screen. Her mother didn't look round.

She walked the quarter-mile; it wasn't worth taking the car and the road was well lit. The street where the Naughtons lived was, despite its nearness, very different from Linney Lane. Harry had really done well for himself. Because the members of Chambers all called him Harry that was how she thought of him now. But when she spoke to him it was always Mr. Naughton.

They could have been expecting her. Margaret Naughton opened the door and drew her into the hall, enfolding her in warm arms.

"You poor child. Come in. What a day it's been for you both."

"Is Mr. Naughton home?"

"Yes, over two hours ago. We're in the kitchen, just clearing up after supper."

In the kitchen there was a savoury casserole smell, and the uneaten part of a home-made apple tart was on the table. Harry was loading the dishwasher. He had changed from his office suit into slacks topped with a knitted jersey and she thought how different it made him look, different and older. And when he drew himself up, leaning on the dishwasher for support, she thought: But he is an old man, much older than he was yesterday, and felt a rush of pity. Afterwards they moved into the sitting-room and Margaret brought in a tray with three glasses and a bottle of medium sherry, the kind Valerie liked. Totally at home, comforted and secure, Valerie poured out her worries.

"They were very kind, those two inspectors. I can see now that they were just trying to put me at my ease. I can't remember half I told them—about Kenny, of course, and how I hated Miss Aldridge, but that I hadn't killed her, I wouldn't kill anyone. And I told them about the gossip, that she might be next Head of Chambers and what that could mean. I shouldn't have said that. I shouldn't have said any of it. It isn't my business. And now I'm afraid Mr. Langton and Mr. Laud will find out and they'll know it was me and I might lose my job. I wouldn't blame them if they sacked me. I don't know how it happened. I always thought I could be relied upon—you know, relied upon to be discreet, not to talk about things I learned in Chambers. Miss Justin impressed that on me when I first came. You too, Mr. Naughton. You told me the same. And now I've blabbed to the police."

Margaret said: "You mustn't worry. It's their job to wheedle things out of people. They're good at it. And you only told them the truth. The truth can't hurt anyone."

But Valerie knew that it could. The truth was sometimes more fatal than a lie.

She said: "But there were two things I didn't tell them. I wanted to tell you."

She glanced at Harry, and saw that his face was suddenly suffused with anxiety and, for a second, something close to terror.

She went on: "It's about Mr. Costello—at least one of the things is. When Miss Aldridge came back from the Bailey on Tuesday, she asked if he was in Chambers. I said that he was. Then later I had to take some papers up to put on Mr. Laud's desk. Miss Aldridge was just opening Mr. Costello's door and they must have been standing close together. I could hear him speaking very loudly—well, shouting really. He said: 'It isn't true. None of it's true. The man's a liar trying to impress you with a juicy piece of calumny. He'll never prove it. And if you confront him with it, he'll deny it. What good will it do you, or anyone, to make a stink in Chambers?'

"I was on the top steps by then, so I quickly moved down the stairs and then came up again as noisily as I could. Miss Aldridge was closing the door by then. She passed me on the stairs without speaking, but I could see she was angry. The thing is, should I have told the police? What do I do if they ask me?"

Harry thought for a moment, then said quietly: "I think you were perfectly right to say nothing. If they ask you later whether you've ever heard Miss Aldridge and Mr. Costello quarrelling, then I think you have to tell them the truth. Don't make too much of it. You could have misunderstood. It could mean very little or nothing. But I think, if they ask you, you'll have to tell them."

Margaret said: "You said there were two things."

"The other's very odd. I don't know why it seems important. They asked me about Mr. Ulrick coming into Chambers this morning. Could I remember whether he was carrying his briefcase."

"What did you tell them?"

"I said I couldn't be sure because he was carrying his raincoat over his right arm, and it could have been hiding the case. But it was a funny question for them to ask, wasn't it?"

Margaret said: "I expect they had a reason. I shouldn't worry. You told them the truth."

"But it was odd. I didn't tell them—and it didn't occur to me till afterwards that it was funny—but Mr. Ulrick usually pauses in the door when he comes in and says good-morning. This morning he did call out, but he walked past as if he were in a hurry and I didn't have time to reply. It's such a small thing. I don't know why I worry about it. And there's something else. It's been so fine recently, almost like summer. Why was he carrying a rain-coat?"

There was a silence, then Harry said: "I don't think you should worry about details like that. All we have to do is to get on with our work as well as we can and answer questions from the police honestly. We don't have to volunteer information. That isn't our job. And I don't think we should gossip in Chambers about the murder. I know it's going to be difficult, but if we chatter and argue among ourselves and start putting forward theories, we could do great harm to the innocent. Will you promise me to be very discreet once Chambers reopens? There's bound to be gossip and speculation. We shouldn't add to it."

Valerie said: "I'll do my best. Thank you for being so kind. It's helped me, coming here."

They were kind. They didn't hurry her away, but she knew that she mustn't stay long. Margaret went to the door with her. She said: "Harry tells me you fainted when you heard the news this morning. I know it was a shock, but that isn't right, not in a young girl. Are you sure you're feeling well?"

Valerie confessed: "I'm all right, really I am. It's just that I've been rather tired lately. There's a lot to do at home and Gran isn't really fit for it. And there's the sneaking out to try and visit Ken at weekends without letting Gran suspect. And perhaps trying to do without a temp at work wasn't such a good idea. I think it's all been a bit of a strain."

Margaret put her arms round her. She said: "We'll try and see if we can get some help from Social Services. And I think you should speak to your gran. The old are much tougher than you think. And I wouldn't be surprised if she doesn't know about Ken already. There's not much you can keep from your gran. And you're lucky that she and your mother were at home yesterday night. I wasn't, I was at the parochial church council and then drove Mrs. Marshall home and stayed chatting. Of course, I'd left supper ready for Harry, but I wasn't back home until nine-thirty. You've got someone to confirm what time you got home. Harry hasn't. Now, if there's anything we can do to help, you will let us know, won't you?"

Reassured by the confident voice, the warm enfolding maternal arms, Valerie said that she would, and walked home comforted.

20

It was five past seven, a little past his normal time, when Hubert got back to the flat which he supposed he ought now to call home, but in which he still felt as ill at ease as a guest who is beginning to suspect that he has outstayed his welcome. The flat had something of the over-crowded look of an auction showroom; the furniture and pictures he had chosen to retain, far from providing a familiar and reassuring sense of continuance, looked as if they were waiting for the auctioneer's hammer to fall.

After his wife's death two years previously, his daughter, Helen, had moved in, both literally and figuratively, to help with the organization of his life. She was a woman in whom a certain sensitivity, acquired rather than innate, was at war with a natural authoritarianism. He was, of course, to be fully involved in all decisions. On no account should he be made to feel that others were taking over control of his life. While he still worked it would, of course, be sensible for him to live in London, preferably within easy travelling distance of the Temple. It would be ridiculously impractical—extravagant too—for a widower to keep on two homes. The message was communicated, and not subtly, that what was expected of his ageing generation was for the expensive family home to be sold, and for a proportion of its inflated value to be given to the grandchildren to enable them to mount the first rung of the property ladder. He offered no objection to arrangements made primarily for the benefit of others. What did occasionally irritate him was the assumption that he should be grateful.

The flat, chosen by Helen, was in a prestigious 1930s block in Duchess of Bedford's Walk in Kensington. Even after he had acquiesced in the purchase of the lease she continued irritatingly to reiterate its advantages.

"A good-sized drawing-room and dining-room and two double bedrooms—you won't need more. Twenty-four-hour porterage and a modern security system. No balcony, which is a pity, but a balcony always increases the risk of burglary. All the shops you need in Kensington High Street and you can go to Chambers from the High Street underground on the Circle Line. It only means a short walk downhill. If you go an extra station on the journey home and get out at Notting Hill Gate you can leave by the Church Street exit and avoid crossing either main road." There was the implication that Helen had arranged the London Underground system for his convenience. "And there's a supermarket close to both stations, and Marks and Spencer at the High Street, so that you can easily pick up any food you need. At your age there's no need to carry heavy loads."

It was Helen who, through one of her complicated networks of colleagues and acquaintances, found him Erik and Nigel.

"They're gay, of course, but that needn't worry you."

"No," he said, "it doesn't worry me. Why should it?" But neither his comment nor the question had been heard.

"They keep some kind of antique shop south of the High Street but they don't open before ten o'clock. They're prepared to come in first thing and cook breakfast, make your bed and do a little general tidying. You can have a daily woman for the heavy work. They offered to come back in the evening and give you dinner—well, 'supper' would be a more appropriate word, I suppose. Nothing complicated, simple well-cooked food. Erik, he's the elder, is reputed to be an excellent cook. He's Erik with a *k*, remember, he's particular over that. I can't think why, as he isn't Scandinavian. Born in Muswell Hill, I think he said. Nigel is a sweet boy, so Marjorie assures me. Very blond, but I suppose his mother rather liked the name and didn't know or care about derivations. Now, we'd better discuss pay. It will be a tie for them, of course. This kind of service doesn't come cheap."

He was tempted to say that he supposed the family would leave him enough from the sale of the house at Wolvercote to pay for part-time hired help.

It had worked well, was still working well. Erik and Nigel were kind, efficient and reliable. He wondered now how he had ever managed without them. Erik was a plump, dandyish fifty-year-old with a mouth too pink and perfectly formed above a rough beard. Nigel was slight, very fair and the more vivacious of the two. They worked always together, Erik doing the cooking, Nigel, his acolyte, preparing the vegetables, washing-up and providing vocal admiration. When they were in the flat he could hear from the kitchen their constant antiphonal voices: Erik's slower bass, Nigel's high enthusiastic treble. The sound was agreeably companionable, and when they were on holiday he missed that happy bird-like chatter. The kitchen had become their domain; even its smell was unfamiliar and exotic. He entered it as a stranger, wary of using his own pans and utensils in case he should mar their perfection, examining with curiosity the labels on the extraordinary variety of bottles and jars which Erik found necessary for his "good simple cooking": extra-virgin olive oil, sun-dried tomatoes, soy sauce. He would sniff half-guiltily the herbs in their pots set out in a row on the window-sill.

The food was beautifully served with a formality which complemented the quality of the meal. It was always Erik who brought in the supper, Nigel watching anxiously from the door as if to ensure the proper recognition of its perfection. Tonight Erik, putting down the plate, announced that he was to eat calves' liver and bacon with mashed potatoes, spinach and peas, the liver cut very thin and seared rather than cooked, just as he liked it. It was one of his favourite meals; he wondered how he would manage to eat it. He spoke the usual words: "Thank you, Erik, that looks excellent."

Erik permitted himself a brief, self-congratulatory smile, Nigel beamed. But something more must be said. Obviously they hadn't yet heard the news of the murder, but it would break tomorrow. It would look strange, suspicious even, if he came home and said nothing. But when he spoke, just as Erik had reached the door, he realized that, despite the careful nonchalance in his voice, he had said the wrong thing.

"Erik, can you remember what time I got home yesterday?"

It was Nigel who answered. "You were late, Mr. Langton. Three-quarters of an hour. We were a bit surprised that you hadn't telephoned. Don't you remember? You said you went for a walk after you left Chambers. It didn't matter, because Erik never begins cooking the vegetables until you're drinking your sherry."

Erik said quietly: "You got home just after seven-thirty, Mr. Langton."

Something more had to be said. When the news broke about the murder his question would be remembered, pondered over, its signifiance recognized. He reached for the bottle of claret, but realized in time that his hand wasn't steady. Instead he spread his napkin over his knees and kept his eyes on the plate. His voice was calm. Too calm?

"It may be of some importance. I'm afraid something very dreadful has happened. This morning, one of my colleagues, Venetia Aldridge, was found dead in Chambers. The police aren't sure yet how or when she died. There'll have to be an autopsy, but there is a strong possibility—almost a certainty— that she was murdered. If that is proved, then all of us in Chambers will have to account for our movements. A matter of police routine, nothing more. I wanted to be sure that my recollection was accurate."

He made himself look up at them. Erik's face was an impassive mask. It was Nigel who reacted.

"Miss Aldridge? You mean the lawyer who got off those IRA terrorists?"

"She defended three men accused of terrorism, certainly."

"Murder. But that's terrible! How ghastly for you. You didn't find the body, did you, Mr. Langton?"

"No, no. I've just explained. The body was discovered early in the morning, before I arrived." He added, "The Temple gates aren't closed until eight o'clock at night. Someone obviously got in."

"But the door to Chambers wouldn't be open, would it, Mr. Langton? It must have been someone with a key. Or perhaps Miss Aldridge let her murderer in. It could have been someone she knew."

This was awful. He said repressively: "I don't think it's helpful to speculate. As I said, the police haven't confirmed exactly how she died. It's a suspicious death. That's really all we know. But the police may ring or send someone to ask you what time I got home yesterday. If they do, obviously you must tell the truth."

Nigel opened his eyes very wide. He said: "Oh Mr. Langton, I don't think it's ever a good idea to tell the police the truth."

"It's a much worse idea to tell them a lie."

His voice must have been more impressive than he had intended. They left him without another word. Five minutes later they came briefly into the dining-room to say good-night and he heard the front door closing. He waited a few minutes to be safe, then took his plate and flushed the remainder of the meal down the lavatory. He cleared the table and left the dirty plates in the sink for Erik and Nigel to deal with next morning, rinsing them first to avoid overnight smells. It occurred to him, as it did every night, that he might as well finish the job, but this was not part of the domestic agreement drawn up by Helen.

Now he sat in the silence of his over-tidy drawing-room beside the "living-flame" gas fire which looked so realistic, gave so comforting a sense that someone had actually laid the kindling, carried the coals, and let the deadening weight of anxiety and self-disgust settle on his mind.

He found himself thinking of his wife. His marriage had endured, and if it had brought him no heart-healing joy, it had given him little keen unhappiness. Each had sympathized with rather than understood or shared the other's deepest concerns. The children and her garden had occupied most of Marigold's energy and in neither had he taken much interest. But now that she was dead, he mourned and missed her more than he would have thought possible. No adored wife could have bequeathed such a desolation of regret. Such a loss, he reasoned, might paradoxically have been easier to accept; death would have been seen as a rounding off, something achieved, something distinctively human, a perfection of loving which left no regrets, no hopes unfulfilled, no unfinished business. Now all his life seemed unfinished business. The horror, the abomination of that blood-bloated wig now seemed a grotesque but not unfitting comment on a career which had begun so full of promise but which, like a stream with too feeble a spring, had spent itself with a sad inevitability among the sandy shallows of unrealized ambition.

He saw the rest of his life with horrible clarity, that long future of humiliating dependence and inexorable senility. His mind, which he had thought was the best, the most dependable part of him, was turning traitor. And now, in his Chambers, there was this murder, bloody, obscene, with its overtones of madness and revenge, to demonstrate how fragile was that elegant, complicated bridge of order and reason which the law had constructed down the centuries over the abyss of social and psychological chaos. And somehow he, Hubert Langton, had to deal with it. He was Head of Chambers. It was he who must co-operate with the police, protect Chambers from the worst intrusions of publicity, steady the nerves of the frightened, find appropriate words to say to those who grieved or pretended to grieve. Horror, shock, disgust, astonishment, regret: those were the emotions common enough after the murder of a colleague. But grief? Who would feel genuine pain for the death of Venetia Aldridge? What was he feeling now but a fear close to terror? He had left Chambers just after six o'clock. Simon, leaving at the same time, had seen him. That was what he had told Dalgliesh when the police had interviewed each member of Chambers separately. He should have been home by six-forty-five at the latest. Where had he been during those missing forty-five minutes? Was this total loss of memory just the most recent symptom of whatever it was that afflicted him? Or had he seen something—worse still, done something—so terrible that his mind refused to accept its reality?

21

The Rawlstones lived in a stuccoed Italianate house on the eastern fringes of Pimlico. With its large portico, gleaming paintwork and brass lion's-head knocker polished almost to whiteness, the house gave an impression of stolid affluence just short of ostentation.

The door was opened by a young woman, formally dressed in a calf-length black skirt, high-buttoned blouse and cardigan. She could, thought Kate, have been a secretary, housekeeper, parliamentary researcher or general factotum. She received them with brisk efficiency but without smiling, and said in a voice which managed to convey a hint of disapproval: "Mr. Rawlstone is expecting you. Will you come up, please?"

The hall was wide, sparsely but impressively furnished, masculine, the only pictures a series of prints of historic London which covered both the hall and the staircase walls. But the first-floor drawing-room into which they were shown could have belonged to a different house. It was a conventional room, the dominant colour a soft greeny blue. The looped curtains framing the two tall windows, the linen covers of sofa and chairs, the small elegant tables, the richness of the rugs against the pale wood of the floor, all spoke of comfortable wealth. The oil over the fireplace was of an Edwardian mother, her arms round her two daughters, the sentimentality of the subject vindicated by the skill of the painter. Another wall held a series of watercolours, a third a miscellany of pictures, skilfully arranged but giving evidence of a personal taste indulged without much thought of artistic merit. There were Victorian religious scenes embroidered in silk, small portraits in oval frames, silhouettes and an illuminated address which Kate had to resist the temptation to go over and read. But the crowded wall saved the drawing-room from being too obviously a model of conventional good taste and gave it an individuality which was attractive because it was not self-conscious. One of the tables held a collection of small silver objects and the other a group of delicate porcelain figures. In the corner was a grand piano, the top covered with a silken shawl. There were flowers: smaller arrangements on the low tables and a large vase of uncut glass holding lilies on the piano. Their scent was pungent but, in this domestic ambience, not funereal.

Kate said: "How does he do this on an MP's salary?"

Dalgliesh was standing in front of the window, apparently in thought, and taking little interest in the details of the room. He said quietly: "He doesn't. His wife has money."

The door opened and Mark Rawlstone came in. Kate's first thought was that he looked smaller and less handsome than on the television. He had the strong clean-cut features to which the camera is kind, perhaps, too, the egotism which can psych itself up for a performance, producing an aura of confident glamour which, in the flesh, loses substance and vitality. She thought that he was wary but not particularly worried. He shook hands with Dalgliesh, briefly and without a smile, giving the impression, intentionally, Kate felt, that his thoughts were elsewhere. Dalgliesh introduced her, but all she received was a brief nod of acknowledgement.

Rawlstone said: "I'm sorry I've kept you waiting. I didn't expect to find you in here. My wife's drawing-room isn't really an appropriate place for the sort of conversation that we're likely to have."

It was the tone rather than the words which Kate found offensive.

Dalgliesh said: "We have no wish to contaminate any part of the house. Perhaps you would prefer to come to my office at the Yard?"

Rawlstone had too much sense to compound his mistake. He flushed slightly and gave a rueful smile. It made him look both more boyish and a little more vulnerable, and went some way in explaining his attractiveness to women. Kate wondered how often he used it.

He said: "Perhaps you wouldn't mind coming up to the library."

The library was on the floor above and at the back. When Rawlstone stood aside to let them in Kate was surprised to find a woman obviously waiting for them. She was standing in front of the single window but turned as they entered. She was slim and gentle-faced with fair hair intricately wound and plaited, looking too heavy for her delicate features and long neck. But the eyes which looked into Kate's with a first glance of almost frank curiosity were steady, unchallenging and not unfriendly. Kate was not deceived by her apparent fragility. Here was a woman of force.

The introductions made, Rawlstone said: "I think I can guess what this visit is about. I had a telephone call from a colleague in my Chambers just before you rang this afternoon. He told me the news about Venetia

Aldridge's death. As you can imagine, it got round the Inns of Court pretty quickly. It's both deeply shocking and unbelievable. But, then, violent death always is when it touches someone you know. I don't see how I can help but, obviously, if I can I shall be glad to. And there is nothing you can ask which can't be said in front of my wife."

Mrs. Rawlstone said: "Please sit down, Commander, Inspector Miskin. Is there anything you would like before we start? Coffee, perhaps?"

Dalgliesh thanked her but, looking across at Kate, declined for them both. There were four chairs in the room, one behind the desk, a single small armchair with a table and reading lamp beside it, and two solidly upright, their uncushioned seats and high carved backs promising little comfort. Kate thought: They've been brought in here for this interview. He always intended to have it in this room.

Lucy Rawlstone seated herself in the low armchair, but sitting well forward, her hands folded in her lap. Her husband took the chair behind the desk, leaving Dalgliesh and Kate to sit facing him. Kate again wondered if this was a ploy. They might have looked like two candidates before a prospective employer, except that it was impossible for her to see Dalgliesh as a supplicant. Glancing at him, she knew both that he had seen through the stratagem and that he was unworried by it.

Dalgliesh asked: "How well did you know Venetia Aldridge?"

Rawlstone took up a ruler from the desk and began rubbing his thumb along the edge, but his voice was calm and he kept his eyes on Dalgliesh.

"In one sense very well, for a time. About four years ago we began an affair. That was, of course, long after her divorce. It ended just over a year ago. I'm afraid I can't give you the precise date. My wife had known of the affair for about two years. She didn't, of course, condone it and about a year ago I promised her that it would end. Happily Venetia's and my wishes coincided. Actually it was she who ended it. If she hadn't brought matters to a head I suppose I should have taken the initiative. The affair can have no possible bearing on her death but you asked me how well I knew her and I have given you, in confidence, an accurate reply."

Dalgliesh asked: "So there was no bitterness about the ending of the affair?"

"Absolutely none. Both of us had known for some months that what we once had, or thought we had, was dead. Both of us had too much pride to scrabble over the carcass."

And that, thought Kate, is as carefully thought out a piece of justification as I've heard. And why not? He must have known why we wanted to see him. He's had plenty of time to get his act together. And it was clever of him not to have his lawyer present. But why should he need one? He knows enough about cross-examination to make sure that he makes no mistakes.

Rawlstone put down the ruler. He said: "It's clearer to me now how the affair happened. Venetia had—still has—an attractive man, Drysdale Laud, to squire her to theatres and dinners, but she occasionally wanted a man in her bed. I was available and willing. I don't think any of it had much to do with love."

Kate glanced across at Lucy Rawlstone's face. An almost imperceptible flush passed briefly over the delicate features and Kate detected a brief spasm of disgust. She thought: "Can't he see that she finds that crudity demeaning and humiliating?"

Dalgliesh said: "Venetia Aldridge has been murdered. Whom she did or did not need in her bed is no concern of mine unless it relates to her death." He turned to Rawlstone's wife: "Did you know her, Mrs. Rawlstone?"

"Not well. We met from time to time, mainly at law functions. I doubt that I exchanged more than a dozen words with her at any time. I thought that she was a handsome woman but not a happy one. She had a very beautiful speaking voice. I wondered if she was a singer." She turned to her husband: "Did she sing, darling?"

He said shortly: "I never heard her. I don't think she was particularly musical."

Dalgliesh turned again to Mark Rawlstone. He said: "You were with her at her house late on the Tuesday night, the day before she died. Obviously anything that happened during the days preceding her death is of interest to us. Why did you call on her?"

If Rawlstone was disconcerted by the question, he didn't show it. But, then, thought Kate, he must know that Octavia had seen him and heard part of the quarrel. To deny it would be futile; it would also be unwise.

He said: "Venetia called me around nine-thirty. She said she had something to discuss and that it was urgent. When I got there I found her in an odd mood. She said that she was thinking of trying for the Bench—did I think she'd make a good judge, and would it help if she took over from Hubert Langton as Head of Chambers? She hardly needed to ask me the latter. Obviously it would help. As to whether she'd make a good judge, I told her I thought she would, but was that really what she wanted and, more to the point, could she afford it?"

Dalgliesh said: "Did you think it strange that you should be called out at night to discuss something which she could have talked about with you or others at a more convenient time?"

"It was odd, certainly. Thinking about it on the way home, I decided that she probably had something quite different to discuss but had either changed her mind when I was on my way, or had decided after I arrived that I couldn't help and she wouldn't bother to raise it."

"And you've no idea what that could have been?"

"None. As I said, she was in a strange mood. But I left no wiser than when I arrived."

"But you did quarrel?"

Rawlstone was silent for a moment, then he said: "We had a disagreement, I would hardly call it a quarrel. I expect you've been talking to Octavia. You don't need me to tell you how unreliable that kind of information based on eavesdropping can be. It had nothing to do with the ending of the affair, or at least not directly."

"What was it about?"

"Politics mostly. Venetia wasn't a political creature, but she never pretended to me that she voted Labour. As I've said, she was in a strange mood that evening, and she may have been looking for a quarrel. God knows why. We hadn't seen each other in months. She accused me of neglecting human relations in pursuit of political ambition. She said that our affair would probably have lasted, that she wouldn't have been so keen to end it, if I hadn't always put her second to the Party. It wasn't true, of course. Nothing could have kept it alive. I replied the criticism was cool coming from her, that she'd neglected her daughter for her own career. It was that bit Octavia probably caught. We saw her standing at the open door. It's a pity, but she only heard the truth."

Dalgliesh said: "Can you tell me where you were between half past seven and ten o'clock yesterday?"

"I assure you I wasn't in the Temple. I left my Chambers in Lincoln's Inn shortly before six, met a journalist, Pete Maguire, in the Wig and Pen for a quick drink, and was home here shortly after seven-thirty. I had an appointment to meet four of my constituents in the Central Lobby of the House at eight-fifteen. They're keen on hunting and wanted to lobby me about the future of the sport. I left here at five minutes to eight and walked to the House down John Islip Street and through Smith Square." He put a hand into a desk drawer and took out a folded piece of paper. "I've written the names of my constituents here in case you feel the need to check. If so, I'd be glad if you'd do it with some tact. I had absolutely nothing to do with Venetia Aldridge's death. I shall regard it as a serious matter if gossip gets around that I had."

Dalgliesh said: "Gossip, if there is gossip, will not come through us."

Mrs. Rawlstone said quietly: "I can confirm that my husband arrived home just before seven-thirty and left for the House before eight. He was back for dinner an hour later. No one called during the evening. There were a couple of telephone calls, but they were for me."

"And there was no one here with you between seven-thirty and the time your husband returned about nine o'clock?"

"No one. I have one live-in cook and a daily woman. Wednesday is my cook's night off, and the daily woman leaves by five-thirty. I always cook dinner for my husband on Wednesday, that is if he hasn't an appointment elsewhere or isn't in the House. We prefer to dine at home rather than go out. We so rarely get the opportunity. And he didn't leave the house after I went to bed at eleven. He has to pass through my bedroom to get to the landing and I am a light sleeper. I should have heard him." She looked at Dalgliesh steadily and asked: "Is that what you want to know?"

Dalgliesh thanked her and turned back to Mark Rawlstone. "You must, of course, have known Miss Aldridge well over the four years of the affair. Were you surprised at her murder?"

"Very. I felt the usual emotions—horror, shock, grief at the death of someone who'd been close to me. But yes, I was surprised. It's always a surprise when something bizarre and horrible happens to someone you know."

"She had no enemies?"

"No enemies in the sense that she was hated. She could be difficult— well, we all can. Ambition in a woman, success in a woman, sometimes attracts envy, resentment. But I know of no one who wished her dead. I'm probably not the best person to ask. They can probably tell you more in Chambers. I know it sounds odd, but for the last two or three years we didn't see each other often, and when we did our talk—when we did talk— wasn't personal. We each had a private life and liked to keep it that way. She spoke about her friendship with Drysdale Laud and I knew she was having trouble with her daughter. But who doesn't have trouble with adolescent daughters?"

There was nothing else to be learned. They said their goodbyes to Lucy Rawlstone, and her husband went with them to the front door. Unlocking it, he said: "I hope it will be possible to keep this private, Commander. It concerns only my wife and myself, no one else."

Dalgliesh said: "If your relationship with Miss Aldridge has nothing to do with this inquiry, then it need not be known."

"There was no relationship. It had been over and done with for more than a year. I thought I'd made that clear. I don't want telescopic lenses aimed at my windows and my wife followed whenever she goes shopping, particularly now that sections of the press have become so intrusive and malicious. I suppose we are now entitled to believe that every press baron has lived an impeccable life of chastity before marriage, and of fidelity afterwards, and that the expense sheet of every journalist will bear the most scrupulous examination. Surely there has to be a limit to hypocrisy."

Dalgliesh said: "I've never found one. Thank you for your help."

But Rawlstone lingered at the door. He said: "How exactly did she die? Obviously there are rumours but no one seems to know."

There was no point in withholding at least some of the truth. The news would break soon enough.

Dalgliesh said: "We won't be absolutely sure until after the post-mortem, but it looks as if she was stabbed in the heart."

Rawlstone seemed about to speak, then changed his mind and let them go. As they turned the corner of the street, Kate said: "Not much sympathy shown there by either of them. But at least neither told us that she was a fine lawyer. I'm getting tired of that bleak epitaph. How much is that alibi worth, sir?"

"It won't be easy to break. But if you mean, did they conspire to murder Venetia Aldridge, I'd take a lot of convincing and so would a jury. Lucy Rawlstone is a paradigm of virtue: devout Roman Catholic, active on behalf of half a dozen charities mostly concerned with children, spends one day a week working in a children's hospice, self-effacing but efficient, generally regarded as the perfect MP's wife."

"And the perfect mother?"

"They haven't any children. I imagine that could be a grief to her."

"And incapable of lying?"

"No, who is? But Lucy Rawlstone would only lie for what she saw as an overwhelming reason."

Kate said: "Like keeping her husband out of prison? That story of why he was summoned by Aldridge doesn't ring true. She'd hardly ring him at night out of the blue just to ask his advice on whether she should become a judge. But he was clever when you pointed that out. His explanation was ingenious."

Dalgliesh said: "And could be true. It's more likely that she wanted to discuss something important and urgent and then thought better of it."

"Like Octavia's engagement. Then why didn't he suggest that as the reason? Oh, of course, if she didn't tell him, then he probably doesn't know about it yet. I suppose she could have had that in mind and then decided that he'd be useless to her. After all, what could he do? What can anyone do? Octavia's of age. But it sounds as if her mother was pretty desperate. She tried to get Drysdale Laud to help and got no joy."

Dalgliesh said: "I wish I knew when that affair ended. Over a year ago, as he claims, or on Tuesday night? Probably only two people know the answer. One of them isn't telling and the other is dead."

22

Desmond Ulrick usually worked late on Thursdays and saw no reason to vary his routine. The police had locked and sealed the murder room and had left, Dalgliesh taking with him a set of keys. Ulrick worked steadily until seven and then put on his coat, pushed the papers he needed into his briefcase and left, setting the alarm and locking the door behind him.

He lived alone in a charming small house in Markham Street, Chelsea. His parents had moved into it on his father's retirement from his job in Malaysia and Japan, and he had lived there with both his parents until their deaths five years earlier. Unlike most expatriates, they had brought nothing back with them as mementoes of those alien years except a few delicate water-colours. Few of these now remained. Lois had taken a fancy to the best of them; his niece had an almost regal skill in transferring to her ownership those items of value in Markham Street which caught her eye.

His parents had furnished the house by taking his grandparents' few pieces from store and buying what else they needed from the cheaper London auction houses. He was caged in by heavy nineteenth-century mahogany, by bulbous armchairs and cupboards so ornately carved and so heavy that it sometimes seemed that the delicate little house would collapse under their weight. Everything had been left as it was when the ambulance took his mother off to her last and final operation. He had neither the will nor the wish to change a ponderous legacy which he no longer noticed, and indeed seldom saw, since most of his time was spent in his study on the top floor. Here was the desk he had had since his Oxford days, a high-backed wing chair which was one of his parents' happier acquisitions, and his library, meticulously catalogued and arranged on shelves fitted from floor to ceiling and covering three walls.

Nothing here was touched by Mrs. Jordan, who cleaned for him three days a week, but the rest of the house received from her a rigorous attention. She was a large taciturn woman of ferocious energy. The furniture was waxed until the surfaces shone like mirrors, and the strong smell of the lavender polish she used met him whenever he opened his door, and permeated the whole house. Occasionally he wondered, but with little curiosity, whether his clothes smelt of it. Mrs. Jordan didn't cook for him. A woman who attacked mahogany as if physically to subdue it was unlikely to be a good cook, and she wasn't. That, too, didn't worry him. The district was well supplied with restaurants and he dined out and alone most evenings, greeted at either of his two favourites with a deferential welcome and shown to his usual secluded table.

When Lois dined with him—and until the arrival of the twins it had been weekly—they would eat at a restaurant of her choice, usually at an inconvenient distance, and would return to the house for coffee, which she would make. Carrying the tray into the drawing-room, she would say: "That kitchen is antediluvian. I must say Mrs. Jordan keeps it clean, but honestly! And, Duncs, darling, you really ought to do something about this room, get rid of all this old stuff of Granny's. It could look really elegant with different wallpaper and curtains and the right furniture. I know just the designer for you. Or I'll write down some ideas and a colour scheme and come shopping with you, if you like. We'd have fun."

"No thank you, Lois, I don't notice the room."

"But, darling, you should notice it. You'd love it once I'd done it, I know you would."

Thursday was one of Mrs. Jordan's days, and it seemed to him as though the hall smelt even more pungent than usual. There was a note on the hall table. "Mrs. Costello has rung three times. She says, please, to ring her." Simon must have telephoned home or to her office with the news of the murder. Well, of course he had. He wouldn't have waited until he got home. Probably she'd been reluctant to ring Chambers in case the police were still there.

He turned over the sheet of paper and, rummaging in his pocket for a pencil, wrote in his meticulous script: "Mrs. Jordan. Thank you. My operation arranged for Saturday has been postponed so I won't need you to come in on the extra days to feed Tibbles." He signed it with his initials and began slowly making his way up the stairs to his study, grasping the banisters like an old man.

On the top step of the first flight Tibbles lay stretched out in her usual pose, back legs extended, her paws across her eyes as if to shield them from the light. She was a white long-haired cat inherited from his parents and, after some unsuccessful excursions in the neighbourhood, had condescended to remain with him. She opened her small pink mouth in a soundless mew, but did not move. Mrs. Jordan had fed her as usual at five o'clock and no further demonstration of affection was necessary. Ulrick stepped over her and made his way up to the study.

The telephone rang as soon as he got inside the door. He lifted the receiver and heard his niece's voice.

"Duncs, I've been trying all day to get you. I didn't like to ring Chambers. I thought you'd be home early. Look, I haven't got long. Simon is with the twins but he'll be down any minute. Duncs, I need to see you. I'd better come round. I'll make some excuse to get away."

He said: "No, don't do that. I have work to do. I need to be on my own."

The note of anxiety bordering on panic came clearly across to him: "But we have to see each other. Duncs, darling, I'm frightened. We have to talk."

"No," he said again, "we don't have to talk. There's nothing either of us has to say. If you need to talk, talk to your husband, talk to Simon."

"But, Duncs, this is murder! I didn't want her murdered! And I think the police are going to come here. They're going to want to talk to me."

Ulrick said: "Then talk to them. And, Lois, I am capable of much folly, but did you really think that I'm capable of planning a murder, even for your convenience?"

He put down the receiver and then, after a moment, bent and pulled the plug from the wall. He said aloud, "Duncs." That was what she had called him from her childhood. Uncle Desmond. Duncs. Duncs, who could be relied upon for presents and meals and the odd cheque when needed, the cheque which Simon wasn't told about, and of course for other, less tangible marks of his besottedness. He placed his battered and bulging briefcase on the desk, selected from the bookcase the small leather-bound volume of Marcus Aurelius he would read at dinner and went down to the bathroom one flight below to wash his hands. Two minutes later he locked the front door behind him and set out to walk the fifty yards or so to his Thursday restaurant and his solitary dinner.

23

It was now just after ten o'clock. Dalgliesh, still at this desk in his office on the seventh floor of New Scotland Yard, closed the file he had been working on and for a moment leaned back and closed his eyes. Piers and Kate would be with him shortly for their review of the day's progress. He had left them to attend the post-mortem at eight o'clock, and Miles Kynaston had promised to fax through his report as soon as it was ready. He was aware for the first time of his tiredness. The day, like all days charged with a multiplicity of activity, physical and mental, seemed to have lasted for more than the fifteen hours he had been working. He reflected that, in defiance of popular opinion, time passes more quickly when the hours are filled with predictable routine.

Today had been anything but predictable. The afternoon meeting between senior officers of the Yard and their counterparts in the Home Office to consider yet again the ramifications of the Security Services Act had not been acrimonious—both sides had tiptoed with almost over-punctilious dexterity around the most dangerous ground—but it might have been easier if words, carefully unspoken, had actually been said. The co-operation had already proved its value in the recent success against the IRA; there was no wish on anyone's part to sabotage what was being painfully achieved; but, like two regiments in the process of amalgamation, both brought with them more than their insignia. There was a history, a tradition, a different way of working, a different perception of the enemy, even a different language and professional argot. And always there was the complication of class and snobbery present at every level of English society, the unspoken conviction that men could only work best with their own kind. The committee on which he served had, he thought, passed its interesting stage and was now slowly battling through the hinterland of boredom.

He had been glad to turn thought and energy again to the more straightforward rituals of a murder investigation, but even here he was becoming aware of unexpected complications. It should have been an easy enough case—a small community of people, the relatively secure building, an investigation not particularly difficult since the field of suspects was necessarily limited. But even after the first day he was beginning to suspect that it could turn into one of those cases which all detectives abhor: the inquiry in which the murderer is known but the evidence is never sufficient in the eyes of the DPP to justify prosecution. And the police team was, after all, dealing with lawyers. They would know better than most that what condemned a man was the inability to keep his mouth shut.

The office in which he waited was uncluttered, functional, a room which only a perceptive visitor might have found revealing of character, if only because of its occupant's obvious intention that it should be nothing of the kind. There was the minimum furniture prescribed by the Met as appropriate for a Commander: the large desk and chair, the two comfortable but upright chairs for visitors, the small conference table seating six, the bookcase. The shelves, in addition to the usual reference books, held volumes on police and criminal law, manuals, histories, a miscellany of recent Home Office publications, recent Acts of Parliament and Green and White Papers—a working library which proclaimed the job and defined its seniority. Three walls were bare, the fourth held a series of prints of policing in eighteenth-century London. They had been a happy find in a second-hand book-and-print shop off the Charing Cross Road, discovered by Dalgliesh when he was a detective sergeant, bought after anxious calculation of their affordability and now worth ten times what he had paid. He still liked them, but not as much as when he had first bought them. Some of his colleagues imposed on their offices an ostentatious celebration of masculine camaraderie, adorning their walls with badges from foreign forces, pennants, group photographs, cartoons, and their cupboards with cups and sporting trophies. For Dalgliesh the effect was depressingly contrived, as if a film designer, with a less than keen perception of his brief, had gone over the top. To him the office wasn't a substitute for a private life, a home, an identity. It was not the first office in the Yard he had occupied, probably it wouldn't be the last. It wasn't required to minister to any need except those of the job. And the job, for all its variety, its stimulus and its fascination, was that and no more. There was a world elsewhere; for Dalgliesh there always had been.

He moved over to the window and looked down over London. This was his city and he had loved it since he had first been brought as a birthday treat to spend a day's sightseeing with his father. London had laid its spell on him then, and though his love-affair with the city, as with all loves, had had its moments of disillusion, disappointment and threatened infidelity, the spell had remained. Through all the slow accretions of time and change there remained at its core, solid as the London clay, the weight of history and tradition which gave authority even to its meaner streets. The panorama beneath him never failed to enchant. He saw it always as an artefact, sometimes a coloured lithograph in the delicate shades of a spring morning, sometimes a pen-and-ink drawing, every spire, every tower, every tree lovingly delineated, sometimes an oil, strong and vigorous. Tonight it was a psychedelic water-colour, splashes of scarlet and grey layering the blue-black of the night sky, the streets running with molten red and green as the traffic lights changed, the buildings with their squares of white windows pasted like coloured cut-outs against the backcloths of the night.

He wondered what was keeping Kate and Piers. The day wasn't yet over for them, but both were young. They were buoyed along on a rush of adrenalin; a fifteen-hour day, with food eaten on their feet when it could be grabbed, was what they expected when an investigation was under way. It was also, he suspected, what they enjoyed. But he was worried about Kate. Since Daniel Aaron had left the force and Piers had taken his place in the squad, he had seen a change in her, a small alienation of confidence as if she was no longer sure why she was there or what she was supposed to be doing. He tried not to exaggerate the difference; occasionally he could believe that it wasn't there, that she was still the old confident, opinionated Kate who had combined the eager, almost naïve enthusiasm of a new recruit with the experience and tolerance which came with years of hands-on policing. Thinking that she might welcome time off from the job, he had suggested a few months earlier that she should apply for one of the university-entrance schemes and read for a degree, but she had stood for a moment without speaking and had then said: "Do you think it would make me a better police officer, sir?"

"That wasn't what I had in mind. I thought that three years at university might be an experience you'd enjoy."

"And give me a better chance of promotion?"

"That too, although it wasn't my first thought. A degree does help."

She had said, "I've policed too many student demonstrations. If I wanted to cope with screaming kids I'd apply to the Juvenile Bureau. Students seem to enjoy shouting down anyone they don't agree with. If a university isn't for free speech, what's the point of it?"

She had spoken as she always did, without apparent resentment, but there had been something close to it in her voice and he had detected a note of suppressed anger which surprised him. The suggestion had been more than unwelcome; it had been resented. He had wondered at the time whether her reaction was really to do with free speech and the spasmodic barbarism of the over-privileged, or was grounded in some more subtle, less easily articulated objection. Her present slight draining of enthusiasm might, he thought, be due to the loss of Daniel. She had been fond of him; how fond he had never thought it his business to inquire. Perhaps she resented the newcomer and, being honest and knowing the resentment to be unworthy, was trying to cope with it in her own way. He would watch the situation, more for the good of the squad than for hers. But he cared about her. He wanted her to be happy.

It was as he turned away from the window that they came in together. Piers was wearing his raincoat. It was swinging open. A bottle of wine was lodged in the inner pocket. Tugging it out, he placed it with some ceremony on Dalgliesh's desk.

"Part of my birthday present from a perceptive uncle. I thought we deserved it, sir."

Dalgliesh looked at the label. "Hardly a wine for casual tippling, is it? Save it for a meal which will do it justice. But we'll have coffee. Judy's left the things next door. See to it, will you, Piers?"

Piers gave Kate a rueful glance, pocketed the wine without comment and went out.

Kate said: "Sorry we're late, sir. Doc Kynaston was running late at the mortuary, but he should be reporting any minute."

"Any surprises?"

"None, sir."

They didn't speak again until Piers had come back with the cafetière, milk and three cups and set the tray down on the conference table. It was then that the fax chattered into life and they moved together over to the machine. Miles Kynaston had been true to his promise.

The report began with the usual preliminaries: the time and place of the post-mortem, the officers present, including members of the investigating team, photographer, scene-of-crime officer, laboratory liaison officer and forensic scientists and mortuary technicians. Under the instruction of the pathologist the external clothing was removed and the wig, suitably protected, handed to the exhibit officer. The lab would later confirm what they already knew: that the blood was Desmond Ulrick's. Then came the part of the report for which they were waiting.

The body was that of a well-nourished, middle-aged Caucasian female. Rigor mortis, fully developed when the body was first examined at ten that morning, had passed off in all muscle groups. The fingernails were of medium length, clean and unbroken. The natural head hair was short and dark brown. There was a single small puncture wound over the anterior chest wall, 5 cm. to the left of the midline. This injury lay approximately horizontally and measured 1.2 cm. in length. Dissection showed the track penetrated directly backwards into the chest cavity between the seventh and eighth ribs, entering the pericardial sac and penetrating into the anterior wall of the left ventricle, where it caused a 0.7 cm. injury. The track of the wound penetrated through the septum of the heart to a depth of approximately 1.5 cm. The injury itself and the pericardial sac showed minimal haemorrhage. It is my opinion that the injury was caused by the steel paper-knife, labelled Exhibit A.

There were no other external injuries except for a small bruise approximately 2 cm. square on the back of the skull. There were no defensive injuries to the hands or arms. The bruise is consistent with the deceased being pushed back against the wall or door with some force when the knife was inserted.

Then followed a long catalogue of Venetia Aldridge's organs, central nervous system, respiratory system, cardiovascular system, stomach and oesophagus, intestines. The words came up one after another, always with the comment that the organs were normal.

The report on the internal organs was followed by the list of samples handed to the exhibit officer, including swabs and samples of blood. Then followed the weights of the organs. It was hardly relevant to the inquiry that Venetia Aldridge's brain weighed one thousand three hundred and fifty grams, her heart two hundred and seventy grams and her right kidney two hundred grams, but the figures, baldly stated, were superimposed in Dalgliesh's mind upon the picture of Miles Kynaston's assistant, with his gloved and bloody hands, carrying the organs to the scales like a butcher weighing offal.

Then came the conclusions.

The deceased was a well-nourished woman with no evidence of natural disease that could have caused or contributed to death. The injury to the chest is consistent with a deep penetrating injury from a thin-bladed weapon which resulted in injury to the septum of the heart. The absence of bleeding along the wound track indicates that death occurred very rapidly following infliction of this injury. No defensive injuries were present. I give the cause of death as a stab wound to the heart.

Dalgliesh asked: "Did Doc Kynaston give any closer estimate of the time of death?"

It was Kate who replied: "Confirmed it, sir. Between seven-thirty and eight-thirty would be a working hypothesis. I don't think he'll be any more precise in court but privately he thinks she was dead by eight or very soon afterwards."

Estimating the time of death was always tricky, but Kynaston had never in Dalgliesh's experience been proved wrong. Whether by instinct or experience, or a mixture of both, he seemed able to smell out the moment of death.

They moved across to the table and Piers poured the coffee. Dalgliesh didn't intend to keep them long. There was no point in making an investigation into an endurance test, but it was important to review progress.

He asked: "So what have we got? Kate?"

Kate wasted no time on preliminaries but got straight to the murder. "Venetia Aldridge was last seen alive by the Senior Clerk, Harry Naughton, just before six-thirty, when he took up a brief received by messenger and a copy of the *Evening Standard*. She was alive at seven-forty-five, when her housekeeper, Mrs. Buckley, spoke to her to complain that Octavia Cummins had demanded that a vegetarian meal should be cooked for her. So she died after seven-forty-five, probably at about eight or soon after. When Mrs. Buckley spoke to her, Aldridge had someone with her. Obviously that person could be the killer. If so, it was either someone from Chambers or a man or woman Miss Aldridge had herself let in and had no reason to fear. No one from Chambers admits to being with her at seven-forty-five. Everyone claims to have left by then. Desmond Ulrick was the last out, he says just after seven-fifteen."

Piers spread out the map of the Temple on the table. He said: "If she died at eight, or thereabouts, the murderer must have been in the Temple before then. All the unmanned gates are closed at eight, so either Aldridge let him or her in or he or she was already in the Temple when the gates were locked. The Tudor Street entrance has a boom barrier and is manned twenty-four hours a day. No one got in there after eight. The Strand entrance, through the Wren Gate into Middle Temple Lane, is temporarily closed for reconstruction. That still leaves five possible gates, the most likely being the one from Devereux Court through the Judges' Gate, which most members of

Chambers use. But we've checked that they're all secure by eight o'clock. He or she would have needed a key. I refuse to go on saying 'he or she.' What are we going to call this murderer? I suggest MOAB—murderer of Aldridge, barrister."

Dalgliesh said: "How do we see the actual murder?"

Kate went on: "The murderer forced Aldridge back against the wall, bruising the back of her head, and stuck in the knife straight to the heart. Either he was lucky or he knew his anatomy. Afterwards he dragged the body across the carpet—there are heel marks in the pile—and put her in the chair. Her cardigan must have been unbuttoned when the knife went in. He buttoned it up, concealing the slit in her shirt, almost as if he was trying to make her look comfortably tidy. I find that odd, sir. He couldn't have hoped to make this look a natural death. He wrapped the knife in the coloured section of the *Evening Standard,* then probably took it down to the basement washroom to wash it, tearing up the paper and flushing the pieces down the lavatory. Before leaving, he put the knife in the bottom drawer of Valerie Caldwell's filing cabinet. At some time he, or someone else, took the full-bottomed wig from the tin in the clerk's office and the pouch of blood from Mr. Ulrick's refrigerator and decorated the body. If that was done by the killer, then we have a restricted list of suspects. The murderer knew where to find the knife, the wig and the blood, and the blood was only put in the refrigerator on Monday morning."

Piers said impatiently: "Look, it's obvious, surely, that the killer and the prankster are the same person. Why bother otherwise to drag the body and put it in the chair? Why not just let it drop to the ground and lie there? After all, the office was empty. She wasn't going to be found till next morning. There was no point in making it look as if she were sitting alive in the chair. He did it specifically so that he could decorate her with the wig and the blood. He was making a statement. MOAB killed Aldridge because of her job. The quarrel wasn't with the woman, it was with the lawyer. That ought to give us a lead on motive."

Dalgliesh said: "Unless that's precisely what we're intended to believe. Why was she killed near the door?"

"She could have been replacing a file in the cabinet to the left of the door, or showing the visitor out. On impulse he seizes the knife and lunges at her as she turns round. If so, it wasn't a member of Chambers. She wouldn't be showing out a colleague."

Kate objected: "She might in certain circumstances. They quarrel, she yells 'Get out of my room' and flings open the door. OK, that kind of dramatic outburst doesn't tie in with what we're told about her but it's perfectly possible. After all, she'd been in an odd mood recently."

"So who are our main suspects, assuming that the killer and the prankster are one and the same?"

Kate referred to her notebook. "There are twenty remaining members of Chambers. The City have done most of the alibi checking for us. All, of course, have keys to Chambers, but it looks as if sixteen are in the clear. We've got the names and addresses here. Three are on circuit, four work out of London at the Salisbury Annexe, the two international lawyers are in Brussels, five work from home and can account for their time from six-thirty onwards, one is ill in St Thomas's Hospital and one is in Canada visiting his daughter who's given birth to his first grandchild. We'll have to do some further checking on three of them to see if the alibis will hold. One of the pupils, Rupert Price-Maskell, has just got engaged and was at a dinner to celebrate from seven-thirty. The Connaught. As two of the guests were High Court judges and one a member of the Bar Council we can take it Price-Maskell's in the clear. Another pupil, Jonathan Skollard, is on circuit with his pupil-master. I haven't been able to see the third, Catherine Beddington, she's down with some bug or other. Oh, and the two assistant clerks are in the clear. One of the clerks at Lord Collingford's Chambers had his stag-night yesterday at a pub in the Earls Court Road. They were with him by seven-thirty and the party didn't break up until eleven."

Dalgliesh said: "So, if we're thinking at present of those people who had keys to Chambers, were there on Wednesday and knew where to lay hands on the wig and the blood, it brings us down to the Senior Clerk, Harold Naughton; the cleaner, Janet Carpenter; and four of the barristers: the Head of Chambers, Hubert St John Langton; Drysdale Laud, Simon Costello and Desmond Ulrick. Your priority tomorrow is to check more closely on their movements after seven-thirty. And you'd better check what time the Savoy has its interval, how long it lasts and whether Drysdale Laud could get to Chambers, kill Aldridge and be back in his seat before the play started again. Find out if he had a seat at the end of a row, and, if possible, who was next to him. Ulrick says he went home first to dump his briefcase and was at Rules for dinner by eight-fifteen. Check that with the restaurant and ask whether they remember if he had a briefcase with him, either at the table or checked in. And you need to see Catherine Beddington if she's well enough to be interviewed."

Kate asked: "What about Mark Rawlstone, sir?"

"At present we've no factual evidence to link him to the murder. I think we can take it he was at the House by eight-fifteen. He'd hardly persuade four constituents to lie for him and he wouldn't have given us their names if he wasn't confident they'd confirm his story. But have a word with the policeman on the gate to the Members' Entrance. He'll probably remember whether Rawlstone came by cab or was walking and, if so, from which direction. There's not much they miss. And there's something else you might fit in tomorrow if there's time. I had another look at Miss Aldridge's blue books before I left Chambers. Her notes on the Ashe case were instructive. It's extraordinary what trouble she took to know as much as possible about the defendant. Obviously she held the eccentric view for a lawyer that most cases are lost because of inadequacies in the defence. It makes a pleasant change. I'm not surprised that she was appalled by the engagement between Ashe and her daughter; she knew too much about that young man for any mother's peace of mind. And I was looking at her last case. GBH. Brian Cartwright. Apparently Miss Aldridge was in an odd mood when she returned from the Bailey to Chambers on Tuesday. It seems unlikely that Ashe and her daughter actually turned up at the Bailey to inform her of their engagement, so it's possible that something else happened. It's a long shot but it's worth seeing Cartwright to find out if anything happened at the end of the case. His address is in the blue book. And I'd like to know more about Janet Carpenter. The domestic agency may be able to help. We need to interview Miss Elkington anyway. After all, she and her cleaning women have keys to Chambers. And try Harry Naughton again. A night's sleep may have cleared his mind. It would be helpful if he could produce someone—anyone—who saw him on that journey home."

Kate said: "I've been thinking of the dagger. Why put it in that filing drawer? Hardly hidden, was it? If we hadn't found it pretty quickly, Valerie Caldwell would."

Dalgliesh said: "He dropped it in the most convenient place on his way out. He had a choice, leave it in Chambers or take it away. If he left it he'd have to wipe it clean of prints. If he took it away, perhaps with the idea of dropping it in the Thames, we'd still know that it was the weapon. There was no point in trying to conceal it effectively. That would take time, and he didn't have time. Mrs. Carpenter was expected at eight-thirty."

"So you think he knew when Mrs. Carpenter would arrive?"

"Oh yes," said Dalgliesh. "I think Piers's MOAB knew that."

Piers hadn't spoken for some minutes. Now he said: "Harry Naughton's the prime suspect for me, sir. He knew about the blood, he knew where to find the wig, he admits that no one saw him leave Chambers or arrive at his home station. And then there's his extraordinary behaviour this morning.

He's done that journey from Buckhurst Hill for—how long?—nearly forty years and he's always walked straight down Chancery Lane and into Chambers. So why does he suddenly find it necessary to go walkabout?"

"He said he had personal matters to think about?"

"Come off it, Kate. He'd had the whole journey from Buckhurst Hill to do his thinking. Isn't it possible that he just couldn't face going into Chambers? He knew damned well what was waiting for him. His behaviour this morning was totally irrational."

Kate said: "But people don't always behave rationally. And why pick on him? Are you saying that you can't believe a senior barrister would be guilty of murder?"

"Of course I'm not, Kate. That's bloody silly."

Dalgliesh said: "I think we'll call it a day. I shan't be in London for the first part of tomorrow. I'm going down to Dorset to see Venetia Aldridge's ex-husband and his wife. Aldridge seems to have called on Drysdale Laud for help about her daughter's engagement without success. Perhaps she tried Luke Cummins. In any case, they have to be seen."

Piers said: "An agreeable part of the country and it looks as if you're going to have a pleasant day for it, sir. I believe there's an interesting little chapel of ease at Wareham which you could probably find time to visit. And, of course, sir, you could take in Salisbury Cathedral." He glanced smilingly at Kate, his good humour apparently restored.

Dalgliesh said: "You could take in Westminster Cathedral on the way to Miss Elkington's Agency. What a pity you'll be too busy to find time for a quick prayer."

"What should I be praying for, sir?"

"Humility, Piers, humility. Well, shall we call it a day?"

24

It was just after midnight, time for Kate's invariable last ritual of the day. She tugged on the warmer of her two dressing-gowns, poured herself a modest whisky and unlocked the door to the balcony overlooking the Thames. Below her the river was empty of traffic, a heaving black waste of water quicksilvered with light. She had two views from her flat, one from the balcony which overlooked the huge shining pencil of Canary Wharf and the glittering glass-and-concrete city of Docklands, and this, her favourite, the river view. This was a moment she normally savoured, standing glass in hand, her head resting against the gritty brickwork, smelling the sea-freshness brought up with the tide, star-gazing on clear nights, feeling at one with the throb of the never-sleeping city and yet lifted up and apart from it, a privileged spectator, secure in her own inviolate world.

But tonight was different. Tonight there was no sense of contentment. Something, she knew, was wrong and she had to set it right, since it threatened both her private world and her job. It wasn't the job itself; that still held its fascination, still compelled her loyalty and her dedication. She had experienced the worst and the best of policing in London and was still able to feel something of her initial idealism, could still be convinced the job was worth doing. So why this unrest? The striving hadn't ceased. She was still ambitious for promotion when the opportunity came. So much had been achieved: senior rank; a prestigious job with a boss she liked and admired; this flat, her car, more money than she had ever before earned. It was as if she had reached some staging-post in which she could relax and look at the journey travelled, taking pleasure in the difficulties surmounted and finding strength for the challenges to come. Instead there was this nagging unrest, this sense of something which in the hard years she had been able to put out of mind, but which now must be faced and come to terms with.

She was missing Daniel, of course. He hadn't been in touch since he had left the Met, and she had no idea where he was, what he was doing. Piers Tarrant had taken his place, burdened with her resentment, a resentment which wasn't any easier to cope with because she knew it was unjust.

She had asked: "Why theology? Were you training to be a priest?"

"Good God no! Me a priest?"

"If you're not intending to go into the Church, what's the point of it? D'you find it useful?"

"Well, I didn't read it to find it useful. Actually, it's a very good training for a police officer. You cease to be surprised by the unbelievable. Theology isn't so very different from criminal law. Both rest on a complicated system of philosophical thought which hasn't much to do with reality. I read it because it was an easier way of getting into Oxford than choosing history or PPE, which were my other options."

She didn't ask what he meant by PPE but she resented it that he obviously thought she knew. She wondered whether she was jealous of Piers, not sexually jealous, which would be demeaning and ridiculous, but jealous of that unstressed camaraderie which he had with Dalgliesh and from which she felt that she, as a woman, was subtly excluded. Both men were perfectly correct towards her and towards each other. There wasn't anything definite to which she could point the finger, but the whole sense of being a team had gone. And she suspected that, for Piers, nothing was of overwhelming importance, nothing could be taken seriously because, for him, life was a private joke, one presumably shared between him and his God. She suspected that he found something risible, even slightly ridiculous, in the traditions, the conventions, the hierarchy of policing. She sensed, too, that this was a view which AD with part of his mind understood, even if he didn't share it. But she couldn't live her life like that, couldn't be lighthearted about her career. She had worked too hard at it, sacrificed too much for it, used it to climb out of that old life as an illegitimate motherless child in an inner-city high-rise flat. Was that at the heart of her present discontent—was she beginning for the first time to feel disadvantaged, educationally and socially? But she put that resolutely out of her mind. She had never given way to that insidious and destructive contagion of envy and resentment. She still lived by that old quotation, remembered but never identified:

> *What matters it what went before or after?*
> *Now with myself I will begin and end.*

But three days earlier, before the Aldridge case broke, she had gone back to the estate, to Ellison Fairweather Buildings, and, rejecting the lift, had climbed the concrete flights of stairs to the seventh floor, as she so often had in childhood when the vandalized lift had been out of use, doggedly mounting behind her complaining grandmother, listening to the old woman's laboured wheezings, laden with their shopping. The door of Number 78 was pale blue now, not the green she had remembered. She didn't knock. She had no wish to see inside even if the present owners were willing to admit her. Instead, after a moment's thought, she rang the bell at Number 79. The Cleghorns would be at home; with George's emphysema, they rarely risked finding the lift wouldn't work.

It was Enid who had opened the door, her broad face showing neither welcome nor surprise. She said: "So you've come back. George, it's Kate, Kate Miskin." And then, ungrudgingly, since hospitality must be offered, "I'll put on the kettle."

The flat was smaller than she remembered, but, then, it would be. She was used to her double sitting-room above the Thames. And it was more cluttered. The television set was the largest she had seen. The shelf to the left of the fireplace was heavy with videos. There was a modern sound system. The sofa and two chairs were obviously new. George and Enid were managing nicely on their two pensions and her carer's allowance. It wasn't lack of money which made their lives hell.

Over the tea Enid said: "You know who controls this estate, don't you?"

"Yes, the children."

"The kids, the bloody kids. Complain to the police or the council and you get a brick through your window. Tell 'em off and like as not you get an earful of foul language and burning rags through the letter-box next day. What are your lot doing about it?"

"It's difficult, Enid. You can't bring people to law without evidence."

"Law? Don't talk to me about law. What has the law ever done for us? Thirty million or so spent trying to nail that Kevin Maxwell, and the lawyers getting fat on it. And that last murder case you got mixed up in must have cost plenty."

Kate said: "It would be exactly the same if someone was murdered on the estate. Murder gets priority."

"So you're waiting for someone to get murdered? You won't have to wait long the way things are going."

"Haven't you a community policeman on the estate? There used to be one."

"Poor sod! He does his best but the kids laugh at him. What you want here is some dads on the estate who'll do a bit of clipping round the ears and bring out the strap now and again to keep the boys in order. But there aren't any dads. Poke the girl, breed the kid and be off, that's young men today. Not that the girls want them around, and who's to blame them? Better be on the welfare than get a bloody nose every Saturday when the old man's team doesn't win."

"Have you put in for a transfer?"

"Don't be daft. Every decent family on this estate has put in for a transfer, and there are decent families."

"I know. I lived here with Gran, remember? We were one of them."

"But you got away, didn't you? And stayed away. Monday's dustbin day, so they're out early kicking over the bins and strewing the muck up the stairway. Half of them don't know what a lavatory's for, or don't care. Have you smelled the lift?"

"It always smelt."

"Yes, but it was pee, not the other thing. And if they catch the little bastards and take them to youth court, what happens? Bloody nothing. They come home laughing. They're in gangs now by the time they're eight."

Of course they are, thought Kate. How else can they survive?

Enid said: "But they leave us alone now. I found a way. I whisper to them that I'm a witch. Upset me or George and you're as good as dead."

"Does that frighten them?" Kate found it difficult to believe that it could.

"It bloody well does, them and their mums. It started with Bobby O'Brian, a kid in this block with leukaemia. When they took him off in the ambulance, I knew he wouldn't be back. You don't get to my age without knowing death when you're looking it in the face. He was the worst of the kids till he got ill. So I chalked a white cross on his door and told the kids I'd put a curse on him and he'd die. He was gone quicker than I thought, within three days. I've had no trouble since. I tell 'em: Any bother from you and you get a cross on your door, too. I keep my eyes open. There's always a bit of trouble I can see coming and I'm ready with the chalk."

Kate sat for a moment in impotent silence, afraid that the disgust she felt at the exploitation of a child's pain, a child's death, must show in her face. Perhaps it did. Enid looked at her closely but said nothing. What was there to say? Like everyone else on the estate, Enid and George did what they needed to do to survive.

The visit hadn't done any good. Why had she ever thought that it would? You couldn't exorcise the past either by returning to it or by running away. You couldn't resolve to put it out of your mind and memory, because it was part of mind and memory. You couldn't reject it, because it had made you what you were. It had to be remembered, thought about, accepted, perhaps even given thanks for, since it had taught her how to survive.

Kate closed the door on the river and the night, and suddenly there came into her mind a picture of Venetia Aldridge, of the hands falling with graceful abandon over the arms of her chair, of that one dead open eye, and she wondered what luggage Venetia Aldridge had brought from her privileged past to that successful life, to that lonely death.

BOOK THREE

A LETTER FROM THE DEAD

25

The office of Miss Elkington's Domestic Agency, in a short street of neat early-nineteenth-century town houses off Vincent Square, was so unexpected in its location and appearance that, if it hadn't been for the neat brass name-plate above the two bell-pushes, Kate would have wondered whether they had been given the right address. She and Piers had walked the half-mile from New Scotland Yard, cutting through the noisy busyness of the Strutton Ground street market. The rails of gaudy-coloured cotton shirts and dresses and the clear bright gleam of the piled fruit and vegetables, the smell of food and coffee and the raucous camaraderie of one of London's villages going about its daily business seemed further to raise Piers's spirits. He was singing softly under his breath, a complicated and half-recognized tune.

She said: "What's that, last Saturday at Covent Garden?"

"No, this morning on Classic FM." He sang on, then said: "I'm rather looking forward to this interview. I have high hopes of Miss Elkington. It's surprising that she actually exists, for one thing. You'd expect to find that the original Miss Elkington died in 1890 and Elkington's is now just the usual boring domestic agency which has kept on the name. You know the sort of thing: glass-fronted premises, insalubrious street, depressed receptionist battered into submission by dissatisfied householders, the occasional sinister housekeeper looking for a rich widower with no relations."

"Your imagination's wasted on the police. You should be a novelist."

The top bell said "House," the lower "Office." Piers pressed it and the door was opened almost immediately. A cheerful-faced young woman, crop-haired and wearing a multi-striped jersey and a short black skirt, danced a small jig of welcome at the door and almost threw herself into Piers's arms as she ushered them in.

"Don't bother to show your warrant cards. Policemen always do, don't they? It must get very boring. We know who you are. Miss Elkington's expecting you. She'll have heard the bell, she always does, and she'll be down as soon as she feels like it. Have a seat. Do you want coffee? Tea? We've got Darjeeling, Earl Grey and herbal. Nothing? Oh well, I'll just get on with these letters. No good grilling me, by the way. I'm only the temp, been here just two weeks. Funny place, but Miss Elkington's all right if you make allowances. Oh sorry, I forgot. My name's Eager, Alice Eager. Eager by name, eager by nature."

Miss Eager, as if to justify the name, settled herself at her typewriter and began tapping the keys with a confident energy which suggested that she was at least good at part of her job.

The office, the walls painted a clear green, was obviously once the front sitting-room of the house. The cornice and ceiling rose looked original. There were fitted bookcases each side of an elegant fireplace where flames of gas licked the simulated coals. The floor was of stripped oak covered with two faded rugs. The room was sparsely furnished. To the right of the door were two four-drawer metal filing cabinets. Apart from Miss Elkington's desk and chair and the smaller, more functional desk of the typist, the only other pieces of furniture were two armchairs and a sofa against the wall. Here Kate and Piers seated themselves. The most incongruous objects were the pictures: framed and apparently original seaside posters from the 1930s; an exuberant fisherman in cap and sea boots bouncing across the beach at bracing Skegness; hikers in shorts and with rucksacks pointing their walking sticks at views of the Cornish cliffs; steam trains puffing through an idealized landscape of patchwork fields. Kate couldn't remember the last time she had seen such posters, but they were vaguely familiar. Perhaps, she thought, it had been on a school visit to an exhibition of life and art of the thirties. Looking at them, she felt drawn into an age remote, unknown and unknowable, but curiously comforting and nostalgic.

They had been waiting for precisely five minutes when the door opened and Miss Elkington stepped briskly into the room. They stood up as she entered and waited while she inspected their warrant cards, then looked keenly into each of their faces as if to satisfy herself by personal inspection that neither was an impostor. Then she motioned them back to the sofa and took her own chair behind the desk.

Her appearance was as subtly out of time as was the room itself. She was tall and thin, with a suggestion of gawkiness, and was dressed as if deliberately to accentuate her height. The fawn skirt in fine wool was narrow and almost ankle-length, topped by a matching silky cardigan over a high-necked blouse. Her shoes, with barred straps, were highly polished, narrow, long and slightly pointed. But it was her hairstyle which reinforced the impression of a woman dressed to personify, and perhaps celebrate, a less thrusting era. Above a face which was an almost perfect oval, with wide-spaced grey eyes, her hair was parted in the middle with a tight plait wound in an intricate whorl round each ear.

Alice Eager, busily dissociating herself from the business in hand, kept her eyes on the typewriter. Miss Elkington took an envelope from her right-hand drawer and, holding it out, said: "Miss Eager, would you be good enough to collect the new writing-paper from John Lewis? They telephoned yesterday to say that the order is ready. You can walk to Victoria and take the Jubilee Line to Oxford Circus, but you'll need a taxi to come back. The parcel will be heavy. Take ten pounds from petty cash. Don't forget to ask for a receipt."

Miss Eager departed with many enthusiastic bobbings and thanks. No doubt the prospect of an hour out of the office compensated for missing what could be an interesting conversation.

Miss Elkington got down to business with admirable promptness. "You said on the telephone that you were interested in the keys to Chambers and in the cleaning arrangements. Since the latter concerns two of my employees, Mrs. Carpenter and Mrs. Watson, I telephoned them early this morning to get their permission to give you any information you require about their arrangements with me. You must speak to them personally for anything you require to know about their private lives."

Kate said: "We have already spoken to Mrs. Carpenter. I believe that you hold a spare set of keys to Chambers."

"Yes, to the front door of Chambers and to the Devereux Court entrance. I have keys to ten of the offices we clean. It's useful in case one of the women unexpectedly can't do her hours and I need a replacement. Some offices are happy to provide a spare key for this purpose, others not. I keep all the keys in my safe. None is named, as you'll see. I can assure you that none has left my possession in the last month."

She walked over to the bookshelves to the right of the fireplace and, bending down, touched some knob under the lower shelf. The row of books, obviously false, swung open and behind was a small modern safe. Kate thought that the false books would hardly deceive even an inexperienced burglar, but the safe was a kind that she recognized. It was one not easily forced. Miss Elkington fiddled with the knob, opened the door and brought out a metal box.

She said: "There are ten sets of keys in here. This set belongs to Mr. Langton's Chambers. No one has access to these keys but myself. As you will see, they are numbered but not named. I keep the code in my bag."

Piers said: "Most of your cleaning ladies work in the Inns of Court, then?"

"The majority do. My father was a lawyer and it is a world of which I have some knowledge. What I provide is a service which is reliable, efficient and discreet. It is quite extraordinary how careless people are over their cleaning arrangements. Men and women who would never dream of lending their office keys even to their closest friends are quite happy to hand them over to their cleaning woman. That is why each of my employees is guaranteed to be honest and reliable. I take up and check all references."

Kate said: "As you did with Mrs. Carpenter. Could you tell us how she came to be employed?"

Miss Elkington went over to the nearby filing cabinet and took a file from the bottom drawer. She returned to her desk and opened it in front of her.

She said: "Mrs. Janet Carpenter came to me over two and a half years ago, on 7th February 1994. She telephoned the office and asked for an appointment. When she arrived she explained that she had recently come to live in Central London from Hereford, was a widow and required a few hours' domestic work each week. She thought she would like the Inns of Court, because she and her husband used to go regularly to hear morning service in the Temple Church. Apparently she called at Mr. Langton's Chambers and inquired whether they had a vacancy and someone—I imagine the receptionist—referred her to me. There was no vacancy in those Chambers but I was able to find her a place in the Chambers of Sir Roderick Matthews. She was there for about six months, but when I had a vacancy for her in Mr. Langton's Chambers she asked to be transferred."

Kate asked: "Did she give any reason for preferring that set?"

"None except she had been kindly received there when she inquired and apparently liked the look of the place. She was greatly valued by Sir Roderick's Chambers and they were sorry to see her go. She has been working with Mrs. Watson in her present Chambers for over two years. Both women work on Mondays, Wednesdays and Fridays from eight-thirty to ten. On Tuesdays and Thursdays Mrs. Watson carries out a less thorough cleaning on her own. And I understand that Mrs. Carpenter occasionally helps out at Pelham Place when Miss Aldridge's housekeeper is away or needs an extra pair of hands. But that is a private arrangement and does not go through my books."

Piers said: "And the references?"

Miss Elkington turned over some pages. "I had three, one from her bank manager, one from her parish priest and one from a local magistrate. They gave no personal details, but each wrote very highly of her honesty, probity, reliability and discretion. I asked her about her cleaning skills, but she pointed out that any woman who has effectively cleaned her own home and is house-proud is perfectly capable of cleaning an office, and this, of course, is true. I always ask the employer whether he is satisfied after a month, and both sets of Chambers have spoken most highly of her. She has told me that she wishes to give up working for the next month or two but I am hoping that she will return. No doubt the murder was a shock but I am a little surprised that a woman of her character and intelligence has allowed herself to be so upset by it."

Kate asked: "Isn't she a rather unusual person to be doing domestic work? I thought, when we interviewed her, that she was the sort of woman who would have looked for an office job."

"Did you indeed? I should have thought that, as a senior police officer, you would have been wary of making that kind of judgement. There aren't many advantages in office work for a mature woman. She has to compete with much younger women, and not all of us are enamoured of modern technology. The advantage of domestic work is that a woman can choose her hours, be particular about the firm she cares to work for and is unsupervised. It seems to me a perfectly natural choice for Mrs. Carpenter. And now, unless you have any other specific questions, I think I must get on with my own work."

It was a statement, and now there was no offer of coffee or tea.

Kate and Piers walked almost in silence until they reached Horseferry Road, then he said: "Doesn't it strike you that that place is a little too good to be true?"

"How do you mean?"

"It's hardly real. That woman, her office, the archaic gentility of the whole set-up. We could have been back in the 1930s. Pure Agatha Christie."

"I don't suppose you've ever read Christie, and what do you know of the thirties?"

"You don't have to read Christie to know her world, and actually I'm rather interested in the thirties. Their painters are under-valued, for one thing. But she isn't really thirties, is she? The clothes, I suppose, are closer to the 1910s. Whatever world she's living in, it isn't ours. She hasn't even a word processor. Miss Eager was using what must be one of the earliest electric typewriters. And think of the logistics of the exercise. How in the hell does she break even, let alone make a profit?"

Kate said: "It depends on how many women she has on the books. When she opened that filing drawer it looked pretty full to me."

"Only because some of the files are bulky. She seems to keep an eye on every detail. Who the hell, running a domestic agency, goes to that trouble? What's the point of it?"

"Useful for us that she did."

He was silent, obviously calculating, then he said: "Suppose she has thirty women on her books, and they work an average of twenty hours each a week. That's six hundred hours. They get paid six pounds, which is high, and if she takes fifty pence per hour, that's a total of three hundred pounds a week. Out of that she has to keep up the office and pay her assistant. It's just not viable."

"It's all surmise, Piers. You don't know how many women she's got on the books, and you don't know what commission she takes. But, OK, suppose she only clears three hundred, so what?"

"I'm wondering if it isn't a cover of some kind. It could be a nice little racket, couldn't it? A group of respectable women, all carefully vetted, placed in strategic offices, feeding back valuable information. I like it—I mean, I like the theory."

Kate said: "If you're thinking of blackmail, that doesn't seem likely. What are they going to pick up in legal offices?"

"Oh, I don't know. It depends what Miss Elkington is looking for. Some people would pay a great deal of money for copies of legal documents. Counsel's opinion, for example. Now, that's a possibility. And suppose Venetia Aldridge discovered the racket. Now, there's a motive for murder."

It was impossible to know whether he was being serious; probably not. But, glancing at his lively, amused face, she could believe that he was even now concocting some ingenious plot for his private entertainment, working out how he would organize the racket to maximize the gains and minimize the risk.

She said: "It's all too far-fetched. But perhaps we should have asked a few more questions. After all, she does have a key. We didn't even ask for her alibi. I'm not sure that AD will think we've made much of a job of it. We asked questions about Janet Carpenter but not about Miss Elkington. We certainly ought to have asked where she was on Wednesday night."

"So we go back?"

"I think so. No good leaving the job half done. Do you want to do the talking?"

"It's my turn."

"You're not proposing to ask her outright, I suppose, whether the Elkington agency is a cover for blackmail, extortion and murder?"

"If I did, she'd take it in her stride."

This time it was Miss Elkington who opened the door. She seemed unsurprised to see them and showed them into the office without speaking, then seated herself at her desk. Piers and Kate remained standing.

Piers said: "We're sorry to bother you again but there's something we forgot. The reason we overlooked it is because it's only a formality. We should have remembered to ask where you were on Wednesday night."

"You're asking me for an alibi?"

"You could certainly put it like that."

"I can't think of any other way to put it. Are you suggesting that I took my key and went over to Mr. Langton's Chambers on the off-chance that I might happen to find Miss Aldridge in her room and alone, in which case I could, of course, conveniently murder her before Mrs. Carpenter arrived?"

"We're not suggesting anything, Miss Elkington. We're only asking a simple question, one which we have to ask of anyone who has a key to Chambers."

Miss Elkington said: "As it happens I do have an alibi for most of Wednesday night. Whether or not you find it satisfactory is, of course, for you to say. Like most alibis it depends on the confirmation of another person. I was with a friend, Carl Oliphant, the conductor. He arrived at seven-thirty for dinner, which I cooked, and he left in the early hours. Since you haven't told me the approximate time of death, I don't know whether that is helpful. I shall, of course, get in touch with him and, if he agrees, I shall give you his number." She looked at Piers. "And that's all you came back for, my alibi?"

If she had hoped to intimidate Piers, she didn't succeed. He said, without a trace of embarrassment: "That's the reason why we came back, but there is something else I'd like to know. It's really only vulgar curiosity, I'm afraid."

Miss Elkington said: "Life must be difficult for you, Inspector, when you're anxious to know something but haven't any real justification for asking. I suppose with the frightened, the unimportant or the ignorant you just ask away and chalk it up to their future disadvantage if they tell you to mind your own business. Well, ask away."

"I was wondering how you managed to run a successful business by such eccentric methods."

"And is that relevant to your inquiry, Inspector?"

"It could be, anything could be. At the moment it doesn't seem likely."

"Well, at least you've given a reason for asking which I find convincing. 'Vulgar curiosity' is more honest than 'routine police procedure.' This business was left to me some ten years ago by a maiden aunt of the same name. It has been in the family since the 1920s. I keep it going partly from family piety, but principally because I enjoy it. It brings me into touch with interesting people, although no doubt Inspector Miskin would find that surprising, since most of them are content to do housework. I earn enough to supplement a small private income and enable me to employ one assistant. And now, if you'll excuse me, I have work to do. Give my compliments to Commander Dalgliesh. He should come on some of these routine inquiries himself occasionally. Had he done so, I would have had a question about one of the poems in his last volume. I hope he isn't falling into the fashionable error of incomprehensibility. And you can reassure him that I did not murder Venetia Aldridge. She was not on my list of people who, for the greater good of humanity, would be better dead."

Kate and Piers walked towards Horseferry Road in silence. She saw that he was smiling.

Then he said: "Extraordinary woman. I don't suppose we'll have any excuse for going back to her. That's one of the frustrations of this job. You meet people, question them, get intrigued by them, eliminate them from inquiries and never see them again."

"Most of them I'm only too happy not to see again, and that includes Miss Elkington."

"Yes, you didn't like each other much, did you? But didn't she interest you—as a woman, not as a prospective suspect or a provider of useful information?"

"She intrigued me. All right, she was playing a part, but who isn't? It would be interesting to know why that particular part, but it isn't important. If she wants to live in the 1930s—if that's what she's doing—then that's her concern. I'm more interested in what she told us about Janet Carpenter. She was pretty determined—wasn't she—to work in those particular Chambers. She was doing perfectly well with Sir Roderick Matthews. Why change? Why Pawlet Court?"

"I don't find that suspicious. She happened to call there, liked the clerk, liked the place, thought it might be an agreeable Chambers to work in. Then, when the opportunity came, she got a transfer. After all, if she'd set her heart on Langton's Chambers because she wanted an opportunity to kill Venetia Aldridge, why wait over two years? You're not telling me that

Wednesday night was the only time Mrs. Watson wasn't able to turn up at work."

Kate said: "And then she was apparently happy to work privately for Miss Aldridge when Mrs. Buckley needed an extra pair of hands. It looks as if Janet Carpenter was using every means to get close to Aldridge. Why? The answer could lie in her past."

"In Hereford?"

"Could be. I think someone should do a little nosing round. It's a small town. If there's anything to smell out it shouldn't take long."

Piers said: "City, not town. It's got a cathedral. I wouldn't mind a day in the country, but I suppose it had better be a sergeant and a woman DC from City Police. D'you want to wait until AD rings in?"

"No, we'll set it up at once. I've a feeling this could be important. You see to it, and I'll take Robbins to interview the conveniently sick Catherine Beddington."

26

Catherine Beddington lived in a narrow street of identical terraced houses tucked away behind Shepherd's Bush Green. Originally the street must have housed the respectable Victorian working class, but it had obviously now been colonized by young professionals attracted by its nearness to the Central Line and, for some in the media no doubt, to the BBC's television studios and headquarters. The painted doors and windows glistened, window boxes made their cheerful statement and the cars were so closely parked that Kate and Robbins had to circle for ten minutes before they could find a space.

The door of Number 19 was opened by a fat young woman wearing trousers and a voluminous blue shirt. Her frizzled hair, dark brown and parted in the middle, sprang like twin bushes each side of an amiable face. A pair of very bright eyes behind horn-rimmed spectacles summed up the visitors in a couple of quick glances. Before Kate could complete the introductions, she said: "All right, I don't need to see your warrant cards or whatever it is you flourish. I can recognize the police when I see them."

Kate said mildly: "Especially when they've telephoned in advance. Is Miss Beddington well enough to see us?"

"She says she is. I'm Trudy Manning, by the way. I'm halfway through my training contract. And I'm Cathy's friend. I suppose you've no objection if I sit in on the interview?"

Kate said: "None at all, if that's what Miss Beddington wants."

"It's what I want. Anyway you need me. I'm her alibi and she's mine. I expect it's an alibi you've come for. We all know what the police mean when they talk about helping with inquiries. She's in here."

The house was warm, and more accommodating than Trudy Manning's words. She led the way to a room to the left of the hall and stood aside while they entered. It ran the whole length of the house and was filled with light.

A conservatory fitted with white shelves had been built onto the rear and Kate could glimpse a small walled garden beyond the pots of geraniums, variegated ivies and lilies. A gas fire of simulated coals burnt in the period grate, the flames almost eclipsed by the strength of the sun. The room gave an immediate impression of comfort, warmth and security.

It was, Kate thought, an appropriate setting for the young woman who rose from her low chair before the fire to greet them. Here was a true blonde. The hair, drawn back tightly from the forehead and tied with a pink chiffon scarf, was flaxen, the eyes were a violet blue under curved brows, the features small and regular. For Kate, sensitive to beauty in either sex, there was something missing, that spark of eccentric individuality, a more positive charge of sexuality. The face was almost too faultless. It was, perhaps, the type of feminine beauty which fades quickly into prettiness and in old age into conventional nonentity. But now even anxiety and the dulling hand of recent illness couldn't destroy her serene loveliness.

Kate said: "I'm sorry you've been unwell. Are you sure you want to see us now? We could come back."

"No, please. I'd much rather you stayed. I'm all right. It was just a bad bilious attack, something I ate or one of those twenty-four-hour bugs. And I want to know what happened. She was stabbed, wasn't she? Mr. Langton did ring me Thursday afternoon with the news, and of course it's in the paper this morning, but they don't really tell us anything. Please, do sit down—I'm so sorry. The sofa's comfortable."

Kate said: "There isn't much to tell at present. Miss Aldridge was stabbed in the heart sometime after seven-forty-five on Wednesday evening, probably with her steel paper-knife. Do you remember seeing it?"

"The dagger? It was more like a dagger than a paper-knife. She kept it in the top right-hand drawer and used it to open her post. It was terribly sharp." She paused and whispered, "Murder. I suppose there's no doubt? I mean, it couldn't have been an accident? She couldn't have done it herself?"

Their silence was answer enough. After a pause she went on, her voice little more than a whisper. "Poor Harry. It must have been an appalling shock, finding her like that. Mr. Langton told me that it was Harry who found her. But it's worse for him—for Mr. Langton, I mean. And coming so near the end of his time. His grandfather was Head of Chambers before him. Eight, Pawlet Court, has been his whole life." The violet eyes brimmed with tears. She said: "This will kill him."

Perhaps to lighten the mood, or for some reason best known to himself, Robbins said: "I like this room, Miss Beddington. It's difficult to believe that you're only a few miles from Marble Arch. Do you own the house?"

It was a question Kate herself had wanted to ask, but she had been aware that there was little excuse for doing so: Miss Beddington's living arrangements were hardly the concern of the police. But it came better from Robbins, who might, she sometimes thought, have been recruited for the sole purpose of reassuring the timid or cynical that the Met was staffed by every mother's favourite son. He was a stalwart of his local Methodist church, a non-drinker and non-smoker, and a part-time lay preacher. He was also one of the most sceptical officers Kate had ever worked with; his presumed optimism about the redeemability of human nature was combined with an apparent ability to expect the worst and to accept it with non-judgemental but uncompromising calm. Very few questions asked by Robbins were resented; very few lying answers went undetected.

Trudy Manning, who had seated herself opposite her friend, obviously in the capacity of watchdog, looked as if she were about to protest and then thought better of it, perhaps feeling that it might be advisable to save her protests for the more objectionable questions which could be in store.

Miss Beddington said: "Actually it's Daddy's. He bought it for me when I started at university. I share it with Trudy and two other friends. We each have a bed-sitter and we share the basement kitchen and dining-room. Mummy and I chose it because it's convenient for the Central Line. I can get off at Chancery Lane and walk to Chambers."

Trudy said: "No point in giving your life history, Cathy. Don't you tell your clients that the less they say to the police the better?"

"Oh Trudy, don't be so stuffy. What does it matter if they know who owns the house?"

So I'm right, thought Kate. It was after all a common arrangement where students had rich fathers or private means. The house increased in value, Daddy made a profit on resale, the student avoided the machinations, financial or sexual, of landlords, and sharing the house covered the heating and maintenance costs and ensured that Daddy's girl lived with young people of her own kind. It was a sensible arrangement if you were lucky, and Catherine Beddington was one of the lucky ones. But Kate had known that as soon as she had entered the house. The furniture might be older pieces which could be spared from home, but they were carefully chosen, right for the proportions of the room. And the sofa, which was obviously new, hadn't been cheap. The polished oak floor was liberally covered with rugs, the family photographs on a side table were in silver frames, the divan set against the wall and covered with cream linen was plump with embroidered cushions.

Kate noticed that one of the photographs was of a young man in a cassock with Catherine Beddington standing beside him. A brother, she wondered, or a fiancé? She had noticed that Catherine Beddington was wearing an engagement ring, a cluster of garnets set in a small circle of diamonds in an old setting.

But it was time to get on with their business. Kate said: "Could you tell us where you were, what you were doing, from seven-thirty on Wednesday? These are questions we have to ask everyone who has a key to Chambers."

"I was in court at Snaresbrook with Miss Aldridge and her junior. We rose earlier than expected, because the judge didn't want to begin his summing up until the next morning. Miss Aldridge drove back to London and I caught the Central Line at Snaresbrook Station and got off at Chancery Lane. Daddy doesn't like me to drive in London, so I haven't a car."

"Why didn't you drive back with Miss Aldridge? Wouldn't that have been the normal thing?"

Catherine flushed. She looked at Trudy Manning and said: "I suppose it would. Actually, she did take it for granted that I'd drive with her, but I thought she would rather be on her own, so I said I was thinking of meeting a friend at Liverpool Street Station and would go by train."

"And were you?"

"No. I'm afraid it was a fib. I just felt I'd be more comfortable on my own."

"Did anything happen that day in court to upset you or Miss Aldridge?"

"Not really. At least not anything worse than usual." Again she flushed.

Trudy broke in: "You may as well know the truth of it. Venetia Aldridge was Cathy's sponsor. She is—well, was—a very fine lawyer, everyone will tell you that. I never met her, so I'm not competent to say, but I know her reputation. It didn't mean that she was good with people, particularly the young. She had no patience, a scathing tongue, and she expected a ridiculously high standard."

Catherine Beddington turned to her and said: "That's not quite fair, Trudy. She could be a wonderful teacher, but not to me. I was too frightened of her, and the more she scared me the more mistakes I made. It was my fault really, not hers. Because she was my sponsor I think she believed she ought to take an interest in me—although Mr. Costello is my pupil-master. QCs don't have pupils. Everyone said how lucky I was to have her as sponsor. She'd have been fine with someone who was clever and could stand up to her."

Trudy said: "Preferably male. She didn't like women. And you are clever. You got a Two-One, didn't you? Why the hell do women always under-rate themselves?"

Catherine turned on her friend: "Trudy, that isn't fair—I mean, about her not liking women. She didn't much like me, but that doesn't mean she was anti-women. She was just as fierce to the men."

"She didn't exactly support her own sex, did she?"

"She thought we ought to compete on equal terms."

"Oh, yeah? And since when have women enjoyed equal terms? Come off it, Cathy. We've had this argument before. She would have done everything she could to stop you getting a tenancy."

"But, Trudy, she was right. I'm not as bright as the other two."

"You're as bright, you're just not as confident."

"Well, that counts, doesn't it? What's the good of a lawyer who isn't confident?"

Kate turned to Trudy Manning: "You're one of the organizers of Redress, aren't you?"

If she had expected Trudy to be disconcerted by the question she was disappointed. The girl laughed.

"Oh that. I expect you found a copy of our newsletter in Venetia Aldridge's desk. Yes, that's me. I set it up with three friends, one of whom lets us use her house as an address. It's been quite a success—much more than we expected. Well, the country's practically run by vociferous pressure groups, isn't it? And this happens to be one I believe in. Not that women are a minority, that's what makes it all so irritating. What we're trying to do is to encourage employers to give women a fair crack of the whip and to suggest to women who've made it that they have a responsibility to support their own sex. After all, men do. We write to firms occasionally. Instead of replying that they have perfectly fair promotion procedures and will we please mind our own business, they send back long reports explaining exactly what they're doing in the cause of equal opportunities. But they won't forget that we've written. I mean, next time a promotion comes up, they'll probably think twice about rejecting a perfectly suitable woman in favour of a man."

Kate said: "You mentioned Venetia Aldridge by name in the newsletter. How did she respond to that?"

Again Trudy laughed. "She didn't much like it. She had a word with Catherine—she knows that we're friends—and talked darkly about libel. We weren't worried. She was much too intelligent to go down that road. It would be demeaning for one thing. But mentioning her by name in a newsletter was a mistake. We've stopped that now. It's dangerous and counter-productive. It's much more effective to send personal letters to people."

Kate said to Catherine: "Could we get back to Wednesday evening? You took the train from Snaresbrook Station?"

"That's right. The station's very convenient for the Crown Court. I was back in Chambers by about four-thirty. Then I worked in the library until just before six, when Trudy called for me. She'd brought my oboe from home and we both went to the rehearsal in Temple Church. I'm a member of the Temple Players. It's an orchestra mostly of people from the Temple. The rehearsal was called from six till eight but actually we finished just before eight. I suppose it was about five past by the time we left the Temple."

Kate asked: "What gate did you leave by?"

"The usual, the Judges' Gate at Devereux Court."

"And you were both in the church for the whole of the rehearsal?"

Trudy said: "Yes we were. I'm not a member of the orchestra, of course. I went because it's always entertaining to watch Malcolm Beeston rehearse. He sees himself as Thomas Beecham with a touch of the flamboyance of Malcolm Sargent. And they were playing the kind of music I can cope with."

Catherine Beddington said: "We're not bad really but we are amateurs. This time it was all English. Delius's *On Hearing the First Cuckoo in Spring,* Elgar's *Serenade for Strings,* and Vaughan Williams's *English Folk Song Suite.*"

Trudy said: "I sat well at the back so as not to be intrusive. I suppose I could have slipped out unnoticed, dashed through Pump Court and across Middle Temple Lane and into Pawlet Court, stabbed Venetia and then sneaked back into the church, but I didn't."

Catherine broke in: "You were sitting quite close to Mr. Langton, though, weren't you? He can probably confirm that you were there, at least for the first part of the rehearsal."

Kate asked: "So Mr. Langton was at the rehearsal, was he? Did that surprise you?"

"Well, it did a little. I mean, he's never attended a rehearsal before. He usually comes to the performance, but perhaps he won't be able to make it this year so he caught the rehearsal. Actually he didn't stay very long. When I looked up after about an hour, maybe a bit less, he'd gone."

Kate turned to Trudy: "Did he speak to you?"

"No. I hardly know him except by sight. Actually he looked pretty preoccupied. I don't know whether it was the music. At one time I thought he'd fallen asleep. Anyway, after about an hour he got up and left."

Robbins asked: "And after the rehearsal you went to supper?"

"That was the idea but it didn't happen. Cathy had been feeling queasy during the whole evening. We'd planned to eat at the Carvery in the Strand

Palace Hotel but when we got there she couldn't face a full meal. Cathy said she'd just have soup to keep me company, but the whole point of the Carvery is to stock up on protein for the next week. It's daft to pay a fixed price and eat nothing. The sensible thing was to get home, so that's what we did. As it counted as an emergency and we'd saved the cost of the meal, we took a taxi. The traffic was pretty heavy but we were back here in time to catch the nine o'clock news. At least I caught it, Cathy just about made it. She was violently sick and went straight to bed. I cooked myself some scrambled eggs and spent the rest of the night holding her head and bringing hot-water bottles."

Robbins asked: "In what order were the pieces rehearsed?"

"The Delius, the Vaughan Williams and last the Elgar. Why?"

"I'm wondering why you didn't leave early if you were feeling unwell. There is no woodwind in the Elgar. You wouldn't be wanted for the last part of the rehearsal."

Kate, surprised, half-expected the question to provoke either embarrassment or an angry retort from Trudy. But to her surprise the two girls looked at each other and smiled.

Catherine said: "It's obvious you haven't seen Malcolm Beeston rehearse. When he calls a rehearsal, he calls a rehearsal. You never know when he's going to switch pieces." She turned to Trudy. "Do you remember poor Solly, who sneaked out for a quick beer when he thought the percussion wouldn't be called?" She imitated a masculine voice, a high, petulant falsetto: " 'When I call a rehearsal, Mr. Solly, I expect all players to do me the courtesy of being present for the whole of the time. One more act of insubordination and you'll never play under my baton again.' "

Kate then asked Catherine about the wig and the blood. She admitted that she knew about both. She had been present in the hall when Mr. Ulrick had told Miss Caldwell that he had stored blood in his refrigerator. The girls were obviously surprised at the questions, but neither made any comment. Kate had thought hard before asking them; the police, as well as the barristers of Pawlet Court, had no wish for the spectacular desecration of the body to be made public. On the other hand, it was important to ascertain whether Catherine knew about the blood.

She asked her last question: "When you left by the Devereux Court gate at about five minutes past eight, did you see anyone in Pawlet Court or entering Middle Temple?"

Catherine said: "No one. Devereux Court and the passage out to the Strand were deserted."

"Did either of you notice whether there were any lights in Eight, Pawlet Court?"

The girls looked at each other, then shook their heads.

Catherine said: "I'm afraid we didn't notice."

There seemed nothing else to be learned and time was pressing. Trudy offered to make coffee but both Kate and Robbins declined, and they left soon afterwards. They didn't speak until they were in the car, then Kate said: "I didn't know you were musical."

"You don't have to be musical to know that Elgar's *Serenade for Strings* doesn't include oboes."

"It's odd that they didn't sneak off early. No one would have noticed anyway. The conductor would have been facing the orchestra and the orchestra would have had their eyes on him, not on the audience, such as it was. And Trudy Manning could certainly have gone out for ten minutes or so any time during the evening without people noticing. If both of them had left once the orchestra had started on the Elgar, would it have mattered? If Beeston tackled Beddington later she'd have had the excuse that she was taken ill. It was only a rehearsal, for God's sake, and she'd have been there when she was wanted. And it would only have taken a matter of minutes to get to Pawlet Court through the arch at Pump Court, linking Middle and Inner Temples. Beddington has a key to Chambers. She knew when Aldridge worked late. She knew about the blood and where to find the wig, and she knew exactly how sharp that dagger was. One thing is certain, if they did leave early, either separately or together, we'll never get Trudy Manning to admit it."

Robbins didn't reply. Kate said: "I suppose you're going to tell me that the fragrant Miss Beddington isn't the type of woman to commit murder?"

"No," said Robbins. "I was about to say that she's the type of woman other people commit murder for."

27

It was another perfect autumn day and Dalgliesh at last threw off the western tentacles of London with a sense of liberation. As soon as he saw green fields on each side of the road he drove the Jaguar onto the verge and put down the hood. There was little wind but as he drove the air tore at his hair and seemed to cleanse more than his lungs. The sky was translucent, with faint trails of white cloud dissolving like mist in the clear blue. Some of the ridged fields lay bare but others were flushed with the delicate green of winter wheat. He was not inhibited by Piers's remarks from stopping briefly at Salisbury Cathedral, as he had intended, despite the irritation and difficulty of finding somewhere to park the Jaguar. After an hour he pressed on through Blandford Forum, then south down the narrow country lanes, through Winterborne Kingston and past Bovington Camp towards Wareham.

But suddenly he was struck by an imperative need to glimpse the sea. Crossing the main road, he drove on towards Lulworth Cove. At the breast of a hill he stopped the car at a gate and climbed over into a field of shorn turf where a few sheep ambled clumsily away at his coming. There was an outcrop of rocks and he sat with one at his back and gazed out over the panorama of hills, green fields and small coppices to the wide blue stretch of the Channel. He had brought a picnic of French bread, cheese and pâté. Unscrewing the thermos of coffee, he hardly regretted the lack of wine. Nothing was needed to enhance his mood of utter contentment. He felt along his veins a tingling happiness, almost frightening in its physicality, that soul-possessing joy which is so seldom felt once youth has passed. After the meal he sat for ten minutes in absolute silence, then got up to go. He had had what he needed and was grateful. A drive of only a few miles towards Wareham brought him to his destination.

An arrow in white wood with the words "Perigold Pottery" painted in black was fixed to a post stuck into the grass of the verge. Dalgliesh took the turning indicated and drove slowly up a narrow lane between high hedges. The pottery came into view, an isolated white cottage with a tiled roof lying some fifty yards from the road on gently sloping ground. It was approached by a grassy path which widened into a parking-space for two or three cars. The Jaguar bumped almost silently over the lumpy ground. Locking it, Dalgliesh walked up to the cottage.

It looked peaceful, domestic, calmly deserted under the afternoon sun. In front was a stone patio furnished with an assortment of terra-cotta pots, the smaller ones clustered together. Two large pots, Ali Baba–shaped, stood each side of the door bearing apricot roses still with a few late buds. The hostas were finished, their brown-rimmed leaves slumped over the pot sides, but a fuchsia bush still flowered and the geraniums were woody but not yet over. To the right of the cottage he could see a vegetable garden and there came to him the country smell of manure. The canes of runner beans had been partly pulled out but there were rows of winter spinach, leeks and carrots behind a solid cluster of Michaelmas daisies. Behind the garden he could see the wired enclosure of a chicken-run and a few hens busily picking at the earth.

There was no sign of life but to the left of the cottage was a barn converted into living accommodation. He could see that the wide door was open and there came to him the gentle sound of a turning wheel. He had raised his hand to the door-knocker—there was no bell—but now let it fall and walked across the patio towards what was obviously the studio.

The room was full of light. It spilled over the red-tiled floor and filled every corner of the pottery with its soft effulgent glow. The woman bent over the wheel must have been aware of his presence but she gave no sign. She was wearing blue jeans heavily spattered with clay and a paler painter's smock. Her hair was covered with a green cotton scarf bound close to a high curved forehead and there was a single long plait of reddish gold hanging down her back. There was a child with her, a girl of about two or three with hair like white silk framing a delicate face. She was seated at a low table rolling a piece of clay and jabbering quietly to herself.

The woman at the wheel had just completed her pot. As Dalgliesh's tall figure darkened the doorway she lifted her foot and the wheel slowly stopped. Taking a wire, she sliced the pot from the wheel and carried it carefully over to a table. Only then did she turn and give him a long look. Despite the full concealing smock, he could see that she was pregnant.

She was younger than he had expected. Her eyes, calmly appraising, were widely spaced. The cheekbones were high and prominent; the skin was lightly tanned and freckled; her mouth was beautifully formed above a small cleft chin. Before either of them could speak the child suddenly got up from her chair and trotted across to Dalgliesh. She tugged at his trousers and then held up for his inspection an almost shapeless piece of clay. She seemed to be expecting either comment or approval.

Dalgliesh said: "You're very clever. Tell me what it is."

"It's a dog. Its name is Peter and my name is Marie."

"Mine is Adam. But it hasn't any legs."

"It's a sitting-down dog."

"Where's its tail?"

"It hasn't got a tail."

She went back to the table, apparently disgusted with the impossible stupidity of this new adult.

Her mother said: "You must be Commander Dalgliesh. I'm Anna Cummins. I was expecting you. But don't the police usually come in pairs?"

"Usually we do. Perhaps I should have brought a colleague. I was tempted by the autumn day and a need for solitude. I'm sorry if I'm early, sorrier if I spoilt the pot. I should have tried the door of the cottage but I heard the sound of your wheel."

"You haven't spoilt anything and you aren't early. I was busy and forgot the time. Would you like some coffee?" Her voice was low and attractive, with the trace of a Welsh lilt.

"Very much, if it isn't a trouble." He wasn't thirsty but it seemed kinder to accept than refuse.

She went over to a sink and said: "You want, of course, to speak to Luke. I don't think he'll be long. He's been delivering some pots to Poole. There's a shop there which takes a few every month. He should be back soon if he doesn't get held up. Sometimes people like to talk to him, or he may go for a coffee, and there was some shopping he had to do. Please sit down."

She indicated a wicker chair plump with cushions and with a high winged back. He said: "If you want to get on with your work, I could go for a walk and come back when your husband is likely to be here."

"I think that might be a waste of your time. He shouldn't be long. In the meantime I could probably tell you what you want to know."

For the first time he wondered whether her husband's absence had been planned. Both the Cumminses were taking his visit with extraordinary calmness. Most people, having made an appointment with a senior police officer, find it prudent to keep it on time, particularly when the time has been of their choosing. Had they wanted her to be here alone when he arrived?

He sat in the chair and watched while she set about making the coffee.

On either side of the sink were two low cupboards, one holding an electric kettle, the other with a two-ringed gas stove. He watched while she filled the kettle and plugged it in, reached up for two of her own mugs and a small jug from those lined up on a shelf, then bent to the cupboard and brought out a packet of sugar crystals, a carton of milk and a jar of ground coffee. He had seldom seen a woman who moved with such natural grace. No gesture was hurried, none was either studied or self-conscious. Far from resenting her detachment, he found it refreshing. The room was very restful, the wicker chair, with its high backrest and arms, enclosed him in a seductive comfort.

He let his eyes move from her bare, bespeckled arm as it bent to twist open the coffee jar, and studied the details of the studio. Apart from the wheel the dominant feature was a large wood-burning stove, the door open, the kindling laid ready for the evening's autumn chill. There was a roll-topped desk against the north wall with, above it, three shelves holding telephone directories and what looked like reference books and ledgers. The longest wall, opposite the door was fitted with shelves on which her pots were displayed: mugs, small bowls, beakers, jugs. The predominant colour was a greeny blue, the design pleasant but conventional. Below the shelves was a table holding larger artefacts: dishes, fruit bowls and platters. These showed a more individual, more experimental creativity.

She brought his mug of coffee over to him and placed it on the low table beside the chair, then seated herself in a rocking-chair and contemplated her child. Marie had demolished her menagerie and was now cutting a roll of clay into small pieces with a blunt knife and forming small bowls and plates. The three of them, only the child occupied, sat in silence.

It was obvious that no information would be volunteered. Dalgliesh said: "I want, of course, to speak to your husband about his late wife. I know they divorced eleven years ago, but it's possible he may have some information about her, her friends, her life, even an enemy, which could help. In a murder investigation it's important to learn as much as possible about the victim."

He could have added, That's my excuse for escaping out of London this wonderful autumn day.

She must have caught the unspoken thought. She said: "And you came yourself."

"As you see."

"I suppose finding out about people—even dead people—is fascinating if you're a writer, a biographer, but then it's always second-hand, isn't it? You can't know the whole truth about anyone. With some dead people, parents and grandparents, you never begin to understand them until they've died, and then it's too late. Some people leave more personality behind them than they seem to have had when they were alive."

She spoke without emphasis and as if she were divulging a private and newly discovered fact. Dalgliesh decided it was time for a more direct approach.

He asked: "When did you yourself last see Miss Aldridge?"

"Three years ago, when she brought Octavia here to stay with her father for a week. Venetia was only here for an hour. She didn't come to take Octavia home again. Luke put her on the train at Wareham."

"And she didn't come again—Octavia, I mean?"

"No. I thought—that is, we thought—that she should spend some time with her father. Her mother had custody but a child needs two parents. It wasn't a success. She was bored in the country and she was cross and rough with the baby. Marie was only two months old and Octavia actually struck her. Not a hard blow, but it was deliberate. After that, of course, she had to go."

It was as simple as that. The final rejection. She had to go.

He asked: "And her father agreed?"

"After she struck Marie? Of course. As I said, the visit wasn't a success. He was never allowed to be a father to Octavia when she was young. She was at prep school by the time she was eight and they rarely spent time together after the divorce. I don't think she ever really cared for him."

Dalgliesh thought: Or he for her. But this was dangerous and private ground. He was a police officer, not a family therapist. But it was part of that stark black-and-white sketch of Venetia Aldridge which he needed to fill in with living colour.

"And neither you nor your husband has seen Miss Aldridge since then?"

"No. Of course, I would have seen her on the night she died if she had come to the gate."

Her voice was gentle, unemphatic. She spoke as calmly as if making a comment on the strength of the coffee. Dalgliesh was trained not to show surprise when a suspect came out with the unexpected. But, then, he had never seen her as a suspect.

He put down his mug and said quietly: "You're telling me that you were in London that night? We're talking about this Wednesday, the ninth of October?"

"Yes. I went up to see Venetia at Chambers. It was at her suggestion. She was supposed to unlock that small door in the gate at the end of Devereux Court for me, but she never came."

The words shattered Dalgliesh's mood of almost indolent acquiescence in the seductive peace of the room, her undemanding fecund femininity. He had expected little from his visit but background information, the routine checking of an alibi which was never seriously in doubt. But now his self-indulgent excursion into rural peace was proving illusory. Could any woman really be as näive as this? He hoped that his voice was equally calm and uncensorious.

"Mrs. Cummins, didn't you realize that this is important information? You should have spoken to me earlier."

If she saw the words as a rebuke, she made no sign. "But I knew that you were coming. You telephoned. I thought it better to wait until you arrived. It was only a day's delay. Was that wrong?"

"Not wrong, perhaps. It was unhelpful."

"I'm sorry, but we're speaking now, aren't we?"

At that moment the child slipped from her chair and came over to her mother, showing on her plump outstretched palm what looked like the model of a flat tart filled with small pellets. Perhaps they were meant to be currants or cherries. She raised them to her mother, waiting for her approbation. Mrs. Cummins bent down and whispered in her ear, drawing the child to her. Marie, still without speaking, nodded, went back to her chair and began again her self-absorbed modelling.

Dalgliesh said: "Can you tell me exactly what happened from the beginning." It begged the question, what beginning? How far did the story go back? To their marriage? To the divorce? He added, "Why you went to London. What happened."

"Venetia telephoned. It was early on Wednesday morning, just before eight. I hadn't started working. Luke was getting into the truck to drive over to a farm outside Bere Regis to collect some manure he'd been promised for the garden, and was going to do some shopping in Wareham on the way home. I suppose I could have run out and stopped him, but I decided I wouldn't. I told Venetia that Luke had left, so she gave me the message. It was about Octavia. She was worried about this boy that Octavia had got involved with, someone Venetia had defended. She wanted Luke to intervene."

"How did she sound?"

"More cross than upset. And she was in a hurry. She said she had to leave for the Crown Court. If it had been anyone but Venetia I would have said she was in a panic, but Venetia doesn't allow herself to panic. But she said it was very urgent. She couldn't wait until Luke was home. I was to give him a message."

Dalgliesh asked: "What did she want your husband to do?"

"To put a stop to it. She said: 'He's her father, let him take some responsibility for a change. Buy Ashe off, take Octavia abroad for a time. I'll pay.' " Mrs. Cummins added, "The boy's name is Ashe, but I expect you know that."

"Yes," said Dalgliesh, "we know that."

"Venetia said, 'Tell Luke we have to talk about this. In person. I want to see him in my room at Chambers this evening. The gate to Middle Temple Lane is closed, but he can get in through the gate at the end of Devereux Court.' She gave me very detailed instructions exactly where it is. The passage—Devereux Court—is opposite the Law Courts and there's a pub called the George at the end. You go up the passage then take a small turn to the left, and then right, and opposite another pub, called the Devereux, there's a black studded gate with a small door in it. We agreed that Luke would be there at quarter past eight. Venetia said the gate would be locked by then, but that she'd come and let him in. She said, 'I shan't keep him waiting and I don't expect to be kept waiting myself.' "

Dalgliesh said: "Didn't it strike you as odd that the appointment was at Chambers, not at her house, and at eight-fifteen, after the gate would be locked?"

"She wouldn't want to see Luke at Pelham Place and he wouldn't want to go there. I expect she didn't want Octavia to know that she'd called in her father, not until they'd worked out a plan. And I was the one who fixed the time. I didn't see how I could catch a train before the seventeen-twenty-two which gets in to Waterloo at nineteen-twenty-nine."

Dalgliesh said: "So you had already decided that you would go to London, rather than your husband?"

"I decided that before we stopped talking. Then, when Luke returned, he agreed. I was afraid that Venetia would persuade him into something he didn't want to do. And what could he do? She had never treated him as a father when Octavia was small, and there was no point in calling for his help now. Octavia wouldn't have taken any notice, and why should she? And he can't take Octavia abroad even if she would go. His place is here with his family."

Dalgliesh said: "He is her father."

The comment was not intended to be censorious. Venetia's matrimonial affairs were not his concern except in so far as they were relevant to her death. But divorce legally separated husband and wife, not father and child. It was odd that a woman so obviously maternal as Mrs. Cummins should so casually reject Venetia's claim on her ex-husband's interest in his daughter's welfare. Yet she had spoken entirely without apology or apparent regret. She seemed to be saying: This is how things are; there is nothing now to be done about them. This is no longer our concern.

She said: "We couldn't both go to London, because of Marie and the studio. Customers expect to find us open when they turn up. I don't think those difficulties occurred to Venetia when she spoke."

"So how did Miss Aldridge react to the news that her ex-husband wouldn't appear?"

"I didn't tell her. I let her think that he would. It seemed the best way. Of course, she might refuse to see me, but I didn't think that was likely. I'd be there and Luke wouldn't. She wouldn't have much choice and I could explain what I felt—what we both felt."

"What did you feel, Mrs. Cummins?"

"That we couldn't impose ourselves on Octavia or interfere in her life. If she asked us for help we'd try to give it, but it was too late for Venetia to begin treating Luke as a father. Octavia's eighteen, she's an adult in law."

"So you went to London. It would be helpful if you could tell me exactly what happened."

"But nothing happened. As I said, she didn't come out to the gate. I caught the seventeen-twenty-two from Wareham. Luke drove me to the station with Marie. I knew it might not be convenient to get back that night. Luke couldn't leave Marie and I didn't want him to drive with her to Wareham Station long after her bedtime. I didn't want to spend money on a hotel—London is so expensive—but I have an old school friend who lets me use her flat near Waterloo Station when she isn't there. She's often abroad. I hardly ever use it, but when I do I telephone her neighbour to let him know I'll be arriving. That's in case he hears me in the flat and thinks Alice has burglars. I have a key so I can let myself in."

"Did he see you arriving?"

"No. But I did see him next morning, just before eight-thirty. I rang his bell to let him know I was leaving and that I'd put my sheets in the washing machine. He has a key too, and he said he'd go in later and put them in the drier. He's very helpful like that. He's an elderly bachelor who's fond of Alice and takes a proprietary interest in her flat when she's away. I told him, too, that I'd left some milk in the fridge, and I'd also left a small jug I'd made as a present for Alice."

So there was confirmation of her presence in the flat on the Thursday morning. That didn't mean she'd been alone. Her husband could have crept quietly out before eight-thirty. Whether this obliging neighbour would be able to say if he'd heard one or more people in the flat would depend on the thickness of the walls. But, then, there was Marie; she couldn't be left. If husband and wife had gone together to London someone would have had to look after the child, and it shouldn't be difficult to discover who. Or had they taken her with them? It would have been hard to conceal the presence of a child in the flat, however quiet. Had Mrs. Cummins stayed with Marie while her husband kept the appointment—kept it and killed? But what about the wig and the blood? He might possibly have known where to find the wig, but how could he have known about the blood? But that was to assume that the murderer had also desecrated the body. And what of motive? Dalgliesh had yet to meet Luke Cummins but presumed that the man was sane. Would a sane man have killed to avoid the inconvenient importunities of an ex-wife—ex by eleven years? Or for eight thousand pounds? That too was interesting. In relation to her estate the sum was almost insulting. Had Venetia Aldridge been saying: "You gave me some pleasure. It wasn't all disaster. I value it at a thousand a year"? A sensitive woman would have made it more or nothing. And what did this bequest say about their relationship?

The concatenation of theories sped through Dalgliesh's mind in seconds while Anna Cummins relaxed and, gently rocking in her chair, paused before going on with her story. But the room had lost its innocence and he was seeing her now through different, more critical eyes. The icon of comforting maternity and inward serenity was blurred now by a more insistent image: Venetia Aldridge's body, the dangling hands vulnerable and still, the bent head with its helmet of drying blood. He could, of course, have asked Marie if she'd been with her parents to London. But he knew that he couldn't and wouldn't. The whole idea of a joint murderous enterprise now struck him as bizarre.

The lilting voice went quietly on: "I took a piece of quiche and a pot of yoghurt with me to eat in the train so that I didn't have to bother about supper. I went straight to the flat from the station, left my overnight case at the flat and started out at once for the Temple. I wanted to be sure I was on time. I was lucky and picked up a taxi at once at Waterloo Bridge. I asked to be dropped opposite the Law Courts, crossed the road and found the passage, Devereux Court. It was perfectly simple. Oh I forgot. Before I set out from the flat I rang Chambers. I wanted to be sure Venetia was there. She answered the phone and I just said we were on our way and replaced the receiver. But she was there just after half past seven and I knew she was expecting me."

He asked the formal, necessary question. "And you are sure of the time?"

"Of course. I was keeping an eye on my watch the whole time to make sure I wasn't late. Actually I was early. I didn't want to make myself conspicuous loitering in the passage, so I killed five minutes walking along the Strand. I was outside the gate at ten past eight. I waited until eight-forty. Venetia never came."

Dalgliesh said: "Did you see anyone else come through the gate?"

"Three or four people, men. I think they were musicians. Anyway, they had instrument cases with them. I don't think I'd be able to recognize them. Then, at quarter past eight, there was one I might perhaps know again. He was strongly built and had bright-red hair. I remember him particularly because he unlocked the small door in the gate—he had a key—but was only in the Temple for about a minute. Then he came out again and went off down the passage. He was hardly in the Temple before he was out again. It was odd."

"And you think you'd recognize him if you saw him again?"

"I think so. There's a lamp above the gate. It shone on his bright hair."

Dalgliesh said: "I wish I'd known this earlier. You'd been told that Miss Aldridge was dead, probably murdered. Did it really not occur to you that this evidence was important?"

"I realized you'd need to know it, but then I thought you did know it. Didn't Octavia tell you? I thought that's why you'd arranged to see us, to verify her story."

"Octavia knew about your visit?" There was no point in pretending this was not news to him, but he kept his voice unsurprised.

"Yes, she knew. After I'd got back to Alice's flat I thought it was possible that Venetia hadn't come to the gate because she'd suddenly been taken ill. It didn't seem at all likely, but I wasn't happy about going to bed without alerting someone. Venetia had been so definite about the appointment. I rang Pelham Place. A man answered—a young man, I think—and then Octavia came on the line. I told her what had happened—not why I'd come up to London, but about the missed appointment. I suggested that she should ring to see if her mother was all right—that is, if she wasn't already at home. Octavia said, 'I expect she decided that she didn't want to see you. We none of us want to see you. And don't try to interfere in my life.' "

Dalgliesh said: "Which would suggest that she'd guessed what the appointment was about."

"It wouldn't be difficult to guess, would it? Anyway, I felt I'd done what I could and I went to bed. Next morning I left for home. Luke and Marie met me off the train. When we got back here Drysdale Laud telephoned. He'd been trying to reach us to tell us that Venetia was dead."

"And you did nothing? You still kept silent about your visit?"

"What could we do? Octavia knew the facts. We expected that the police would be in touch to confirm her story, and you did get in touch to say you'd be coming to see us. It seemed better to wait until you arrived. I didn't want to discuss it on the phone."

It was at that moment that they heard the approaching truck. Immediately the child ran from her seat and stood in the doorway, giving little jumps and squeaks of anticipatory joy. As soon as the engine stopped she dashed out as if in response to a signal. There was the slam of the truck door, the sound of a masculine voice, and a minute later Luke Cummins appeared, carrying his daughter on his shoulders.

His wife got up from her chair and stood quietly waiting. As he entered they moved soundlessly together. Gently releasing Marie, Cummins embraced his wife while the child, leaning against him, imprisoned his leg in her arms. For the moment they stood motionless in their private tableau, from which Dalgliesh felt an almost physical sense of exclusion. He studied Luke Cummins, trying to imagine him as Venetia Aldridge's husband, to see him as part of her world, of her over-driven obsessional life.

He was very tall, loose-limbed, with sun-bleached fairish hair and a boyish weather-tanned face, finely boned and sensitive but with a suggestion of weakness about the mouth. The thick corduroy trousers and roll-necked Aran sweater gave bulk to a body which looked as if in adolescence it had outgrown its strength. He glanced across at Dalgliesh over his wife's shoulder and gave a brief smile of acknowledgement before bending again to his family. Dalgliesh thought: He's mistaken me for a customer. He got up and moved over to the exhibition table, uncertain whether the move was prompted by a sudden whim to play the part, or the wish not to intrude on their privacy. His ears caught Cummins's softly spoken words.

"Good news, darling. They want another three cheese platters by Christmas, if you can manage it. Is that possible?"

"The garden scene with the geraniums and the open window?"

"One similar, the other two are commissions. The customers want to discuss with you what they'd like. I said you'd ring and make an appointment."

His wife's voice was anxious. "The shop won't put them on display together, will they? That always makes them look mass-produced."

"They understand that. They'll show only the one and then take orders. But it's cutting it fine, I don't want you stressed."

"I won't be."

It was only then that Dalgliesh turned round. Anna Cummins said: "Darling, this is Mr. Dalgliesh from the Metropolitan Police. Remember? We did know that he was coming."

Cummins came over and held out his hand. He could have been greeting a customer or a casual friend. The handshake was surprisingly firm, a gardener's hand, strong and hard.

He said: "I'm sorry I wasn't here when you arrived. I expect Anna has told you all we know. It isn't much. We haven't heard from my ex-wife for three years except for that telephone call."

"Which you weren't here to take."

"That's right. And Venetia didn't ring back."

And that, thought Dalgliesh, was in itself surprising. If the appointment had been so important, why had Miss Aldridge not confirmed it, spoken to Cummins herself? Surely she could have found a spare minute during the day. But she might later have half-regretted her call. It had sounded more like an impulse—panic even—than a reasoned response to her dilemma with Octavia, even though she wasn't a woman who panicked easily. She might have thought: I won't humiliate myself by ringing again. If he comes we'll talk; if not, nothing is lost.

Anna Cummins said: "Mr. Dalgliesh suggested earlier that he should take a walk. Why don't you go together up the field and show him the view, then you could come back for some tea before he leaves."

The suggestion, mildly voiced, had something of the force of command. Dalgliesh said that he'd like the walk, but would have to leave without waiting for the tea. Cummins put down his daughter and he and Dalgliesh set off through the garden, past the hen-house where a variety of fowl came squawking towards them, over a stile and into a field which stretched gently uphill. The winter wheat had recently been sown and Dalgliesh marvelled, as he always did, that such delicate shoots could push through so strong a soil. Between a high tangled hedge of brambles, gorse and bushes was a rough path wide enough for the two of them to walk abreast. The blackberries were ripe and from time to time Cummins would stretch out a hand to pick and eat them.

Dalgliesh said: "Your wife has told me about her visit to London. If the meeting had taken place it could hardly have been pleasant. I was a little surprised you let her go alone." He didn't add, "and when she was pregnant."

Luke Cummins reached up for a high branch and drew it down towards him. He said: "Anna thought it was best. I think she was afraid Venetia would bully me. It was rather the pattern." He smiled as if the thought amused him, then added: "We couldn't both go, because of Marie and the customers. Perhaps it would have been wiser if neither of us had, but Anna thought it would be better to make it plain once and for all that we couldn't get involved. Octavia is eighteen, an adult in law. She didn't take any notice of me when she was a child. Why should she now?"

He spoke without bitterness. There was no trace of apology, justification or excuse; he was simply stating a fact.

Dalgliesh asked: "How did you meet your first wife?"

It was hardly a relevant question, but Cummins showed no sign of resenting it.

"In the cafeteria of the National Gallery. It was very busy and Venetia was at a table for two. I asked if I might share it. She said yes, but hardly looked up at me. I don't suppose either of us would have spoken if a young man passing hadn't jerked our table and spilled her wine. He didn't apologize. She was angry at his bad manners and I helped by mopping up the mess and getting her another glass. After that we talked. I was teaching in London at the time at a comprehensive, and we spoke about the job, about the problems of discipline. She didn't tell me she was a lawyer but she did say that her father had been a schoolmaster. Oh, and we talked a bit about the pictures. Not much about ourselves. She was the one who suggested that we might meet again, I wouldn't have had the nerve. We were married six months later."

Dalgliesh asked: "Did you know that she's left you a bequest? Eight thousand pounds."

"The solicitor rang to tell me. I wasn't expecting it. I don't know whether it's a reward for marrying her or an insult for leaving her. She was glad when the marriage ended, but I think she would have liked to have been the one who walked out." He was silent for a moment, then said: "We thought at first that we'd refuse the bequest. I suppose you can refuse?"

"That might be awkward for the executors, but you don't have to use the money for yourselves if you've got scruples."

"That's what Anna thought, but I expect we shall take it in the end. One gets these fine ideas but there are usually second thoughts, aren't there? Anna does need a new kiln."

They walked on in silence for a few minutes, then he said: "How far is my wife involved in all this? I don't want her upset or bothered, particularly now, with the baby coming."

"I hope that she won't be. We'll probably need a statement."

"So you'll come back?"

"Not necessarily. Two of my colleagues may."

They were on the ridge of the field now and stood together looking down on the patchwork countryside. Dalgliesh wondered if Anna Cummins was watching them from the window. Then Cummins answered a question that Dalgliesh hadn't asked.

"I was glad to give up teaching, at least in London, glad to be rid of noise and violence and staff-room politics, and the constant fight to keep order. I was never any good at it. I do a little supply teaching here, it's different in the country. But mostly I do the garden and the studio accounts." He paused and then said quietly: "I didn't believe that anyone could be so happy."

They walked down the field together, this time in a silence which was curiously companionable. Approaching the studio, they could hear the whirl of the wheel. Anna Cummins was bent over a pot. The clay spun, rose and curved under her hands and, as they watched, her fingers delicately touched the rim, forming the lip of the vase. But suddenly, apparently without reason, she brought her hands together and the clay, like a living thing, twisted and collapsed into a slimy lump as the wheel slowed to a stop. Looking up at her husband, she laughed.

"Darling, your mouth! It's all smeared. Purple and red. You look like Dracula."

A few minutes later Dalgliesh said his goodbyes. Husband and wife with the child between them stood unsmilingly to see him off. He sensed that they were glad to see the last of him. Glancing back as they turned together into the studio, Dalgliesh felt the weight of a fleeting melancholy tinged with pity. That tranquil studio, the pots so unthreatening in design and execution, the small attempt at self-sufficiency represented by the garden and the henhouse: didn't they symbolize an escape, a peace as illusory as the dignified order of the eighteenth-century courts of the Temple, as illusory as all human seeking after the good, the harmonious life?

He felt no temptation to meander through the villages. Getting onto the main roads as soon as possible, he drove at speed. His pleasure in the beauty of the day was replaced by a dissatisfaction, partly with the Cumminses, but mostly with himself, which irritated him by its irrationality. If Anna Cummins had been telling the truth, and he thought that she had, there was at least one cause for satisfaction. The inquiry had progressed significantly. The time of death could now be placed between seven-forty-five, when Mrs. Buckley had rung Chambers, and eight-fifteen, when Venetia Aldridge had failed to appear to open the Judges' Gate in Devereux Court.

Some of Mrs. Cummins's evidence could be checked. Before leaving, he had taken the name and address of the friend who owned the flat at Waterloo and the name of the neighbour, but Luke Cummins had been unable to provide confirmation that he had been at the pottery. No customers had, in fact, called. Then there was the red-haired man Anna Cummins had seen entering and leaving the Temple. If she could positively identify Simon Costello, then it would be interesting to hear his explanation.

One question above all intrigued him: neither Luke Cummins nor his wife had asked whether the police had got anywhere with their inquiries, nor had they shown any curiosity about the identity of the killer. Was that really because they had deliberately distanced themselves from the unhappiness of the past and the violence of the present, from all that threatened their self-contained world? Or was it because they had no need to ask what they already knew?

After an hour's driving he drew into a lay-by and rang the incident room. Kate wasn't there but he spoke to Piers and they exchanged news.

Piers said: "If it was Costello Mrs. Cummins saw going into the Temple through the door from Devereux Court and then returning after a minute, it puts him in the clear. He would hardly have had time to get to Number Eight, let alone kill Aldridge. And if he'd killed her earlier he'd be a fool to return to the scene. Are you going to bring Mrs. Cummins up to London, sir, for a formal identification?"

"Not yet. First I'll speak to Costello and I'll see Langton at the same time. It's strange that he made no mention of attending that rehearsal. What did his two domestic helpers say?"

"We had a word with them, sir, at the antique shop they keep. They both say that Mr. Langton was later than usual on Wednesday but they can't say by how much. Their story is that they really can't remember. It's nonsense, of course. They were cooking dinner; they must have known almost to the minute how late he was. But he's an unlikely suspect, surely?"

"Very unlikely. Langton seems to be worried and I think it's personal, but if he has anything on his conscience I doubt it's the murder of Venetia Aldridge. Were you able to see Brian Cartwright?"

"Yes sir. He condescended to fit us in for five minutes after lunch at his club. No joy there, I'm afraid. He said that nothing happened after his trial at the Bailey and that Miss Aldridge seemed perfectly normal."

"Did you believe him?"

"Not altogether. I had a feeling he was holding something back, but, then, I may be prejudiced. I took against him. He was flirtatious with Kate and arrogant with me. But I did get the feeling, near the beginning of our interview, that he was weighing up whether it would be to his advantage to oblige the police by passing on information or prudent not to get involved. Prudence won. I don't think we'll get anything out of him now, sir. We can try again, be more pressing, if you think it's important."

Dalgliesh said: "It can wait. Your interview with Miss Elkington was interesting. You were right to send a couple of officers to Hereford. Let me know as soon as they report. Any news on Drysdale Laud's alibi?"

"That seems firm, sir, as far as it goes. We've checked at the theatre. The play began at seven-thirty and the interval was at eight-fifty. He couldn't have got to Chambers before nine. The foyer was never unattended and the box-office manager and doorman are both sure that no one left the theatre before the interval. I think the alibi holds, sir."

"That's if he went to the theatre at all. Did he remember the number of his seat?"

"The end of the fifth row of the stalls. I saw the plan for Wednesday night and there was a single seat there sold, but the girl couldn't remember whether it was to a man or a woman. I suppose we could show her a photograph of Laud, but I doubt we'd get any joy. It was an odd thing to do, though, wasn't it, going to see a play alone?"

"We can hardly arrest a man because he has an eccentric need of his own company. What about Desmond Ulrick's alibi?"

"We checked at Rules, sir. He was certainly there by eight-fifteen. He hadn't booked but he's a regular and they found him a table after only five minutes' wait. He checked in his coat and a copy of the *Standard* but no briefcase. The doorman was quite definite about it. He knows Ulrick well and they spent time chatting while he waited for his table."

"Right, Piers, I'll see you in a couple of hours."

"There's one other thing. An extraordinary little man turned up an hour ago wanting to see you. Apparently he knew Aldridge when she was a girl, worked as a teacher at a prep school kept by her father. He arrived clutching a large flat package to his chest, rather like a child with a present which somebody might snatch away from him. I suggested he talk to me or Kate, but he was adamant that he had to see you. You're tied up with the Commissioner and at the Home Office on Monday morning and there's the inquest in the afternoon. I know it's a formality and we'll ask for an adjournment, but I wasn't sure whether you'd want to be there. Anyway I told him to come along at six o'clock on Monday. It'll probably be a waste of your time but I thought you might want to see him. The name's Froggett. Edmund Froggett."

28

The squad had been working a sixteen-hour day since the murder but Saturday, with most of the suspects out of London for the weekend, was quieter, and Dalgliesh, Kate and Piers took Sunday as a rest day. None of the three confided in the others how they proposed to spend it. It was as if they needed a respite even from their colleagues' interest or curiosity. But with Monday the calm was broken. After a morning of meetings, a press conference was called in the early afternoon which Dalgliesh, greatly disliking them, attended because he thought it unfair not to take his turn. The intrusion of murder into the very heart of the legal establishment and the celebrity of the victim had a piquancy which ensured that media interest was intense. But somewhat to Dalgliesh's surprise, and greatly to his satisfaction, the news of the wig and the blood hadn't been leaked. The police said little more than that the victim had been stabbed and that no arrest was imminent. Any more detailed information at present would only hamper inquiries, but further news would be issued as soon as there was anything to report.

After the brief formality of the adjourned inquest which interrupted the late afternoon, he had temporarily forgotten his six o'clock visitor. But precisely on the hour Edmund Froggett was shown up, accompanied by Piers, not to a small interview room but to Dalgliesh's office.

He sat down on the chair which Dalgliesh had indicated, placed the large flat package, done up with string, carefully on the desk, took off his woollen gloves and laid them beside it, and began unwinding a long knitted scarf. His hands, delicate as a girl's, were white and very clean. He was an unprepossessing little man, but neither ugly nor repulsive, perhaps because of his air of quiet dignity, that of a man who expected little of the world but whose meek acceptance held nothing of servility. He was enveloped in a heavy coat of rough tweed, well cut and obviously originally expensive, but too large for his meagre frame. Below the sharply pressed edge of the gaberdine trousers the shoes were highly polished. The over-heavy coat, the thinner trousers and pale summer socks gave him an ill-assorted look, as if he and his clothes had been put together from the leavings of others. Now, having carefully folded his scarf over the back of the chair, he gave his attention to Dalgliesh.

Behind the pebble glasses his eyes were shrewd but wary. When he spoke his voice was high with an occasional stammer, a voice which it would be disagreeable to listen to for any length of time. He made no excuses or apologies for his visit. Obviously he felt that his insistence on seeing a senior officer would be justified.

He said: "You have been told, Commander, that I have come about the murder of Miss Venetia Aldridge, QC. I should explain my interest in this matter, but I expect you will first need my name and address."

"Thank you," said Dalgliesh, "that would be helpful."

Obviously he was expected to write it down. He did so, his visitor leaning forward to watch as if doubtful of Dalgliesh's ability to record it accurately. "Edmund Albert Froggett, 14 Melrose Court, Melrose Road, Goodmayes, Essex."

The surname was almost ludicrously appropriate to that long, downturned mouth, those exophthalmic eyes. No doubt in childhood he must have suffered from the cruelty of the young and had somehow grown his defensive carapace of self-regard and slight pomposity. How else could the unfortunate of the world survive? Come to that, thought Dalgliesh, how could anyone? We none of us present ourselves psychologically naked to the barbs of the world.

He said: "You have some information about Miss Aldridge's death?"

"Not directly about her death, Commander, but I have information about her life. With murder the two are indissolubly linked, but I don't need to tell you that. Murder is always a completion. I thought I owed it to Miss Aldridge, and to the cause of justice, to provide information which otherwise might not come your way, or which it would be time-consuming for you to obtain by other means. How far it is likely to prove useful is for you to say."

It was likely to be time-consuming to obtain it from Mr. Froggett at the present rate of progress, but Dalgliesh was capable of a patience which occasionally surprised his subordinates, except with the arrogant, the incompetent or the wilfully obtuse. Already he recognized in himself the familiar twinge of uncomfortable pity, a pity he half-resented and had never learned to discipline, but which with part of his mind he knew was a safeguard against the arrogance of power. This was likely to be a long session, but he was incapable of brutally hustling his visitor.

"Perhaps you could tell me from the beginning, Mr. Froggett, what information you have and how you came by it."

"Of course. I mustn't take up too much of your time. I said that I knew Miss Aldridge as a child. Her father—perhaps you already know this—kept a boys' prep school, Danesford in Berkshire. I was for five years his deputy headmaster, responsible for teaching English and history to the older boys. It was in fact intended that I should eventually take over the school, but events dictated otherwise. I have been interested in the law all my life, particularly criminal law, but I'm afraid I lack those physical and vocal attributes which contribute so much to success at the criminal Bar. But the study of the criminal law has been my main hobby and I used to discuss cases of particular forensic and human interest with Venetia. She was fourteen when we began our lessons. She showed even then a remarkable talent for analysing evidence and seizing on the fundamentals of the case. We used to have interesting discussions in her parents' drawing-room after dinner. They would sit listening to our arguments but took little part. It was Venetia who entered with real imagination and enthusiasm into these debates. Of course I had to be a little careful: not all the details of, for example, the Rouse case were suitable for a young girl to hear. But I have never known so good a judicial mind in one so young. I think I can say without conceit, Mr. Dalgliesh, that it was I who was chiefly responsible for making her a criminal lawyer."

Dalgliesh asked: "Was she an only child? We're not aware of any relations and her daughter says there are none. Children, of course, don't always know."

"Oh, I think that's correct. She was certainly an only child and so, I believe, were both her parents."

"A lonely childhood, then?"

"Very lonely. She attended the local high school but I had an idea that her friends, if she had any, weren't welcomed at Danesford. Perhaps her father thought that he saw enough of the young during his working day. Yes, I think you can say that she was a lonely child. Perhaps that is why our sessions together meant so much to her."

Dalgliesh said: "We found a volume of the *Notable British Trials* series in her room in Chambers. The Seddon case. It has her and your initials on the title page."

The effect on Froggett was extraordinary. His eyes brightened and his face glowed pink with pleasure. "So she kept it. And in Chambers. That is really gratifying, very gratifying. It was a small goodbye present when I left. The Seddon case was one we often discussed. I expect you remember Marshall Hall's words: 'The blackest case I have ever been in.' "

"Did you keep in touch after you left the school?"

"No, we never met again. There was never an opportunity, for one thing, and, for another, it wouldn't have been appropriate. We lost touch entirely. But that isn't really accurate; she lost touch, I never did. Not unnaturally, I have taken a lively interest in her career. I've made it my business to follow it closely. You could say that Miss Venetia Aldridge's career has been my hobby for the last twenty years. And that brings me to why I came. This parcel contains a cuttings book in which I have pasted such information as I have been able to obtain on all her important cases. It occurred to me that the mystery of her death might lie with her professional life: a disappointed client; someone she had successfully prosecuted; an ex-prisoner with a grievance. Perhaps I could show you?"

Dalgliesh nodded into eyes which now held a mixture of pleading and excitement. He couldn't bring himself to say that any information the police needed could be obtained from records in Chambers. Mr. Froggett had needed to show his book to someone who might be expected to have an interest in his achievement, and Venetia Aldridge's death had at least given him an excuse. Dalgliesh watched as the neat little fingers busied themselves with a surely unnecessary number of knots. The string drawn from the parcel was carefully wound into a skein. The treasure was revealed.

It was certainly a remarkable record. Carefully pasted under headings giving the date and name of each case were press photographs and cuttings, law reports, and magazine articles following the verdicts in the more notorious cases. Froggett had also included pages from a shorthand-writer's notebook which he had used after each trial to make his own comments on the conduct of the case, comments emphasized with underlinings and occasional exclamation marks. He had certainly listened to the evidence with the disciplined attention of a pupil in Chambers. Turning the pages, Dalgliesh saw that the earlier cases comprised mostly press cuttings but the last two years had been covered in detail. These were trials Froggett had obviously attended.

He said: "You must have had some difficulty in finding out when Miss Aldridge was next to appear. You seem to have been very successful in recent years."

The implied question was, he saw, unwelcome. There was a short pause before Mr. Froggett replied. "I have been lucky recently. I have an acquaintance in one of the listing offices and he has been able to give me details of pending cases. The public are, of course, allowed into trials, so I didn't regard the information as confidential. However, I would much prefer not to give you his name."

Dalgliesh said: "I'm grateful to you for bringing this along. I'll keep it for a little time, if I may? I will, of course, give you a receipt."

The little man's gratification was apparent. He watched while Dalgliesh wrote out the receipt.

Dalgliesh said: "You mentioned earlier that you were expected to take over the school, but that events intervened. What happened precisely?"

"Oh you haven't heard? Well, I suppose it's all old history now. I'm afraid Clarence Aldridge was something of a sadist. I protested to him many times about the frequency and indeed severity with which boys were beaten, but I'm afraid that, despite my senior position in the school, I had little influence over him. No one had. I decided that I couldn't happily continue to co-operate with a man for whom I was losing respect, so I gave in my notice. A year after I left there was, of course, the tragedy. One of the pupils, young Marcus Ulrick, hanged himself by his pyjama cord from the banisters. He was due to receive a beating next morning."

So here at least was information of value. And Dalgliesh would have missed it except for his patience. But he gave no sign that the name struck any chord.

Instead he asked: "And you haven't seen Miss Aldridge since?"

"Not since I left the school. I didn't think it right to get in touch or to approach her. It was perfectly easy to attend court without her seeing me. Happily she was a counsel who never glanced at the public benches and, of course, I took care not to sit in the front row. I wouldn't wish her to think that I have been, as it were, following her. She might even have thought that I was behaving like one of those stalkers. No, I have had no desire to intrude on her life in any way or to take advantage of our past friendship. And I need hardly say that I wished her nothing but good. But of course you have only my word for that, Commander. Perhaps I ought to provide an alibi for the night of her death. I can do so very easily. I was at evening classes from half past six until half past nine at the Wallington Institute in the City. I go every week. We study the architecture of London from six-thirty to eight, and then I have my Italian class from eight until nine. I am hoping to make my first visit to Rome next year. I can, of course, give you the names of the teachers of both classes, and they and anyone else present will be able to confirm that I was there for the whole time. It would have taken me at least half an hour to get from the Institute to the Temple, so if Miss Aldridge was dead by half past nine I think I can safely say I am in the clear."

He spoke almost with regret, as if disappointed that he wouldn't feature as a prime suspect. Dalgliesh thanked him gravely and got to his feet.

But his visitor still took his time. He slid the receipt for his book into a compartment of a rather battered wallet, replaced the latter carefully in an inner pocket of his jacket and patted it as if to make sure that it was safely lodged. Then he shook hands gravely with Dalgliesh and Piers, rather as if the three of them had just completed some complicated and highly confidential business. He cast a last look at the scrapbook lying on Dalgliesh's desk and seemed about to speak, perhaps just saving himself from the solecism of reminding Dalgliesh to keep it safely.

Piers saw him out. Bounding back into the room with his usual vigour, he said: "Extraordinary little man. God, he was weird! That's the oddest example of stalking I've ever seen. How do you think it started, sir?"

"He fell in love with her when she was a schoolgirl and it grew into an obsession—an obsession with her or with criminal law, or perhaps with both."

"Odd sort of hobby. Difficult to see what he gets out of it. He obviously regards her as his protégée. I wonder what she'd have thought of that. Not much, from what we know of her."

Dalgliesh said: "He wasn't doing her any harm. He took good care that she didn't know he was following her. Stalkers usually pester; he didn't. I thought there was something rather likable about him."

"I didn't see it. Frankly I thought he was a creep. Why doesn't he live his own life, instead of sucking at hers like some kind of bloated fly? OK, you can see it as pathetic, but I think it's obscene. And I bet those sessions didn't take place in her parents' drawing-room."

Dalgliesh was surprised at Piers's vehemence—usually he showed more tolerance than this frank disgust. But the reaction was close to his own. For any man who valued his privacy the thought that another human being could be living vicariously one's own closely guarded life was extraordinarily offensive. The stalker was disturbing enough; the secret stalker was an abomination. But Froggett had done his target no harm, had intended no harm. Piers was right to call his behaviour obsessional, but it had not been illegal.

Piers said: "Well, he's given us one piece of information which I doubt we'd have got any other way. It's an unusual name. If Marcus Ulrick was Desmond Ulrick's younger brother, at last it gives us a clear motive. That is, if it's the same family."

"Does it, Piers, after all these years? If Ulrick wanted to kill Aldridge in revenge for her father's actions, why wait over twenty years? And why blame her? She was hardly responsible. Still, it has to be followed up. Ulrick usually works late. Ring Chambers and see if he's there. If he is, say I'd like to see him. Langton and Costello, too, if they're in Chambers."

"This evening, sir?"

"This evening."

Dalgliesh began parcelling up Froggett's book. As Piers was about to leave Dalgliesh asked: "What's the news on Janet Carpenter?"

Piers looked surprised. Dalgliesh said: "I asked on Friday to be told if anything comes to light about her past life. Who went to Hereford, by the way? Who's looking into that?"

"Sergeant Pratt of the City and a WPC. I'm sorry, sir, I thought we'd reported. There's nothing criminal on record. She taught English before she retired. She's a widow and her only son died of leukaemia five years ago. She lived in a village outside the city with her daughter-in-law and her granddaughter. The granddaughter was murdered in 1993 and the daughter-in-law committed suicide shortly afterwards. Mrs. Carpenter wanted to cut herself free of all the old associations. It was the Beale case, I don't know if you remember it. He's doing life. The trial was at Shrewsbury Crown Court and Beale was defended by Archie Curtis. The case had nothing to do with London or with Miss Aldridge."

The tragedy explained something Dalgliesh had sensed in Mrs. Carpenter. The quiet resignation, the serenity which was evidence, not of inner peace, but of a private suffering patiently borne. He said: "How long has all this been known?"

"Since about nine this morning."

Dalgliesh's voice did not change. He said: "When I request information about a suspect, see that I get it when it's available, not when I happen to ask for it."

"Sorry, sir, it's just that other things seemed more important. She's got no record and the granddaughter's murder has nothing to do with London or with Aldridge. It's an old tragedy. It didn't seem relevant." He paused and said: "I'm sorry, there's no excuse."

"Then why make one?"

Piers paused, then said: "Do you want me to come to Chambers with you?"

"No, Piers, I'll see Ulrick alone."

After he had left, Dalgliesh paused for a moment, then he opened his drawer and took out his magnifying-glass and slipped it into his pocket. The door opened and Piers put his head round.

"Ulrick's in Chambers, sir. He says he'll be delighted to see you. I got the impression he was being sarcastic. He was about to leave but he says he'll wait. And Mr. Langton and Mr. Costello will be there until eight."

29

Dalgliesh asked: "Did you know that Venetia Aldridge was the daughter of Clarence Aldridge, who was headmaster of Danesford School?"

Ulrick did not at first answer and Dalgliesh waited patiently. The basement room, with three sections of the electric fire switched on, was over-heated for an autumn evening in which Dalgliesh, carrying Edmund Froggett's book, had walked through the court under the gentle glow of the gas lamps, and had seemed to feel emanating from the ancient stones the lingering warmth of late summer. Ulrick's room was an academic cell. The closely packed shelves of books seemed to press down on Dalgliesh from four walls. The desk was piled high with papers and Ulrick had to clear a chair before Dalgliesh could sit down. It was one of two high-backed chairs almost dangerously close to the fire and Dalgliesh had the sensation of being cushioned in the strong-smelling stickiness of hot leather.

As if sensing his visitor's discomfort, Ulrick knelt to turn off the top three bars of the fire. He did so with the deliberate carefulness of a man undertaking a complicated task requiring precision if disaster is to be avoided. Having satisfied himself that the glow of the bars was fading, he got to his feet and again seated himself, swivelling his chair to face Dalgliesh.

He said: "Yes, I knew. I knew that Aldridge had a daughter named Venetia and the age was right. I was naturally curious when she joined Chambers. I asked her. It was a matter of slight interest, no more."

"Can you remember the conversation?"

"I think so. It wasn't long. We were, of course, alone in her room at the time. I asked, 'Are you the daughter of Clarence Aldridge of Danesford?' She looked at me and said that she was. She seemed wary, but not particularly worried. I then told her that I was the elder brother of Marcus Ulrick. She made no comment for a moment, and then said: 'I thought there might be a relationship. It's not a common name. And he told me he had an elder brother.' I then said, 'I don't think either of us need talk about the past.' "

"How did she respond to that?"

"I don't know. I didn't wait to see. I left her room before she could reply. Neither of us mentioned Danesford again. This restraint required no resolution on my part. I hardly ever saw her. She has a reputation for being a difficult woman and I keep free of personalities in Chambers. I have no interest in the criminal law. Law should be an intellectual discipline, not a public performance."

"Would it distress you if I asked what happened about your brother?"

"Do you need to?" After a moment he added, "Do you need to for the purpose of your investigation?"

The voice was unemphatic, but the grey eyes met Dalgliesh's with something of the insistence of an interrogation.

Dalgliesh said: "I don't know. Probably not. It isn't easy with murder to know what will prove relevant. Most cases that go wrong do so because too few questions are asked, not too many. I've always felt the need to know as much about the victim as possible, and that includes her past."

"It must be gratifying to have a job which can be used to justify what in others might be called intrusive curiosity." He paused, then went on: "Marcus was eleven years younger than I. I wasn't sent to Danesford. Father was then prosperous enough to send me to his own prep school. But by the time Marcus was eight things had changed. My father was working overseas, I was at Oxford and Marcus was in the care of our paternal uncle during the holidays. Father had lost money and we were relatively poor. He wasn't a diplomat or working for an international corporation. School fees were not paid by the firm, although I believe his salary included a small compensatory payment. Danesford was cheap. The school was close to my uncle and aunt's home. It had a good reputation for getting boys into public schools with scholarships. The health record was satisfactory. My parents were impressed when they visited, although, given their circumstances, they would have found it inconvenient to have been unimpressed. It would have been particularly inconvenient to have discovered that Aldridge was a sadist."

Dalgliesh did not reply. Ulrick went on: "His perversion is so common that perhaps the word 'perversion' is inappropriate. He liked beating small boys. He had one refinement, which perhaps gave him claim to some originality. He would prescribe a certain number of strokes but would deliver them publicly at a set time every day for a week, usually after breakfast. It was that daily anticipation of humiliation and pain which Marcus couldn't face. He was a timid and sensitive boy. He hanged himself from the banisters with his pyjama cord. It wasn't a quick death, he suffocated. The public scandal which followed finished the school and finished Aldridge. I don't know what happened to him. That is a brief but, I trust, comprehensive account of what you wanted to know."

Dalgliesh said: "Aldridge and his wife are both dead." He thought, but did not add: Leaving a daughter who didn't like men, who competed successfully in their world, whose marriage ended in divorce, whose daughter disliked her. More to himself than to Ulrick, he said: "It wasn't her fault."

"Fault? That isn't a word I use. It implies that we have control over our actions, which I believe to be largely illusory. You're a policeman. You have to believe in free will. The criminal law rests on the premise that most of us can control what we do. No, it wasn't her fault. It was her misfortune, perhaps. As I said, we never discussed it. Private lives are best kept out of Chambers. Someone bears a heavy responsibility for my brother's death, but it wasn't—it isn't—Venetia Aldridge. And now I would like, please, to be allowed to go home."

30

Simon Costello occupied one of the smaller rooms at the front of the second floor. It was an untidy but comfortable office, the only personal object a large silver-framed studio photograph of his wife which he had on his desk. As Dalgliesh entered he motioned him to one of the two easy chairs placed, not in front of the fireplace, but each side of a small table by the window. Outside the leaves of the great horse chestnut, lit from below, made a pattern of black and silver against the pane.

Seating himself, he said: "I take it this is an official visit even though you've come alone. But, then, when is your arrival not official? How can I help?"

Dalgliesh said: "I went on Friday to Wareham to see Venetia Aldridge's ex-husband and his wife. She expected to meet Miss Aldridge at the Devereux Court entrance to the Temple at eight-fifteen on Wednesday night, but Miss Aldridge didn't turn up to let her in. But she says that she did see a strongly built man with bright red hair. I think it's very possible that, if we bring her up to London, she'll be able to identify you."

He didn't know how he had expected Costello to react. The man had seemed the most agitated by the Aldridge murder of all members of Chambers. He had certainly been the least co-operative. Faced with this new evidence he might bluster, deny the accusation or refuse to speak until his solicitor was present. Anything was possible. Dalgliesh knew that he had taken a risk in raising the matter without corroboration. But Costello's reaction was surprising.

He said quietly: "Yes, I was there. I saw a woman loitering in the passage, although obviously I didn't know who she was. She was there when I went in and there when I came out. No doubt she will confirm that I was in the Temple for less than a minute."

"Yes, that is what she told me."

"I was there because I decided on impulse to see Venetia. There were important matters I wanted to talk about. They related to the possibility that she would become Head of Chambers and the changes she proposed to make if she did. I knew that she worked late on Wednesdays, but, as I've said, the visit was somewhat on impulse. I walked into Pawlet Court and saw that her light was out. That meant, of course, that she must have left, so I wasted no more time."

"You told us when you were first questioned that you had left Chambers at six o'clock and gone home, and that your wife would confirm that you were in the house all evening."

"As she did. Actually, she was feeling unwell and was either in the nursery or in bed for an hour of the time. The police officer who called—I believe he was from the City Police—didn't ask her whether I was under her eye the whole time. She thought I was in the house the whole evening but in fact I wasn't. Nor, I may say, was I asked whether or not I had left the house. One of us—my wife—was mistaken. Neither of us deliberately lied."

Dalgliesh said: "You must have realized the importance of this evidence in fixing a time of death."

"I knew you'd already fixed the time of death, or near enough. You forget, Commander, that I'm a criminal lawyer. I advise my clients to answer police questions and to answer them honestly, but not to volunteer information. I took my own advice. If I'd told you that I'd been in Pawlet Court after eight you would have wasted valuable time concentrating on me as prime suspect, trying to ferret about in my private life to find something disreputable, distressing my wife, harming my marriage and probably destroying my professional reputation. Meanwhile, Venetia's killer would go undetected. I preferred not to take that chance. After all, I've seen what can happen to the innocent who are too confiding to the police. Will you want to make any more of this? It will be time-wasting if you do. I suppose, if you do want to pursue it, I ought to answer further questions in the presence of my solicitor."

Dalgliesh said, "That won't be necessary at present. But if there is anything else that you have concealed, half-told or lied about I suggest you remind yourself that this is a case of murder and that the offence of obstructing the police in the execution of their duty applies as much to members of the criminal Bar as it does to anyone else."

Costello answered calmly: "Some of your colleagues see my job as a defence counsel as obstructing the police in the execution of their duty."

There was nothing more at present which could be usefully said. As Dalgliesh made his way downstairs to Mr. Langton's room he wondered how many more lies he'd been told, what else had been concealed and by whom, and had again the uncomfortable conviction that this case might never be solved.

Hubert Langton was working at his desk. He rose and shook hands with Dalgliesh as if it were the first time they had met, then led him to one of the leather armchairs in front of the fireplace. Looking across at Langton's face, Dalgliesh thought again how much he had aged since the murder. The sharp dominant features seemed to be blurring into old age. The jaw was less firm, the pouches under the eyes were becoming pendulous, the flesh was becoming more mottled. But there were more than physical changes. The spirit was devitalized. Quietly Dalgliesh told him what Kate and Robbins had discovered during their visit to Catherine Beddington.

Langton said: "So that's where I was. At the rehearsal. I'm sorry I didn't tell you. The truth is that I didn't know. The best part of an hour out of Wednesday evening is missing from my life. You tell me that they saw me. I must have been there."

Dalgliesh thought that it was as difficult for him to make this admission as it would have been to accept a more damaging truth.

The tired voice went on. "I remember being about three-quarters of an hour late home, but that's all I remember. I can't understand what happened or why. I suppose I shall eventually find the courage to go to my doctor but I doubt whether he'll be able to help. It doesn't seem like any form of amnesia I've ever heard about." He smiled, then said: "Perhaps I'm secretly in love with Catherine. Perhaps that's why I can't accept that I spent the best part of an hour gazing at her—if that's what I did. Isn't that the kind of explanation a psychiatrist would come up with?"

Dalgliesh said: "Can you remember whether you went straight home when you left the church?"

"Not even that, I'm afraid. But I'm sure I was home before eight, and my two helpers should be able to confirm it. Venetia spoke on the telephone to her housekeeper—didn't she?—at a quarter to eight, so surely I'm in the clear."

Dalgliesh said: "I've never seen you as a suspect. What I did wonder was whether you saw anyone you knew in the church or in Pawlet Court when you left. Obviously, if you can't remember, there's no point in pursuing it."

"I can give you no help, I'm afraid." He paused and then said: "Old age can be very frightening, Commander. My son died young, and at the time it

seemed the most terrible thing that could happen to anyone in the world—
to him as well as to me. But perhaps he was one of the fortunate ones. I shall,
of course, be retiring as Head of Chambers at the end of the year, and retiring from work at the Bar. A lawyer whose mind is apt to go blank isn't just
inefficient, he's dangerous."

31

Dalgliesh was not yet ready to leave Chambers. There was something else he had to do. He went upstairs and unlocked Venetia Aldridge's room. It held no sense of her presence. He seated himself in her comfortable chair and swivelled it round to adjust the height to his six feet two. There came into his mind for a moment Naughton's description of finding the body, of the chair swinging round under his touch to confront him, of her dead upturned eye. But the room evoked no shudder of horror; it was just an empty office, elegantly proportioned, functional, waiting as it had for the last two hundred years for the next temporary occupant to move in, to spend brief working years there and finally close the door on success or failure.

He switched on the desk lamp and unwrapped and opened Edmund Froggett's scrapbook, turning the pages at first with casual interest, and then with a more deliberate attention. It was an extraordinary record. He had obviously made it his business in the last two years to attend every trial in which Venetia Aldridge was due to appear, whether, rarely, as prosecuting counsel or, more frequently, for the defence. He had noted the venue, the name of the defendant, the judge, counsel for the prosecution and for the defence, and had set out briefly the details of the case as presented by the prosecuting counsel. The arguments of both sides were also summarized with occasional comments.

The writing was very small and not always easy to read, the letters meticulously formed. The reports showed a remarkable grasp of the intricacies of the law. Froggett had concentrated on the performance of the object of his obsession. Sometimes his comments betrayed the pedagogue; he could have been a senior counsel assiduously monitoring the performance of a junior or a pupil. He must have had a small notebook with him and transcribed the details in court or as soon as he got home. Dalgliesh could picture the little man returning in solitude to his empty flat and sitting down to add a few more pages of analysis, comment and criticism to this record of a professional life. It was apparent, too, that he liked to embellish the record with pictures, some from newspaper accounts of the crime, published after the verdict. There were press photographs of judges processing to the service at the beginning of the new legal year, with a ring round whichever one had tried the case under review. There was even the occasional photograph, almost certainly taken by Froggett himself, of scenes outside the court.

It was these illustrations, so meticulously pasted in, labelled in that small precise handwriting, which began to induce in Dalgliesh the familiar uncomfortable mixture of pity and irritation. What would Froggett do with his life now that his passion had been brutally wrenched from him, his book becoming no more than a pathetic *memento mori*? Already some of the press cuttings were browning with age and exposure. And how much was he grieving? Froggett had spoken with a dignified regret that could be covering a more personal loss, but Dalgliesh suspected that the reality of Aldridge's death had yet to hit him. At present he was caught up in the excitement of it, the self-importance of bringing his record to the police, the sense that he still had a part to play. Or was his interest more in the criminal law than in the lawyer? Would he still go regularly to the Old Bailey in search of the drama which could give his life meaning? And what about the rest of that life? What had happened at the school? It was difficult to believe that Froggett had ever been deputy head. And what had Venetia Aldridge suffered with a sadist as a father, herself powerless to help his victims, growing up in that phobic world of terror and shame?

With half his mind on the past, he turned the next page almost without thinking. Then he saw the photograph. It was captioned: "Queue waiting outside the Old Bailey for the trial of Matthew Price, 20th October 1994." The snapshot showed a group of about twenty men and women photographed from across the road. And near the head of the queue was Janet Carpenter. Dalgliesh took out his magnifying-glass and scrutinized the image more clearly, but that first look had been enough. The photograph was so plain that he wondered whether Froggett had taken it to record her face rather than the size of the queue. It seemed unlikely that she had been aware of him. Her head was turned to the camera but she was looking over her shoulder as if something—a shout, a sudden noise—had attracted her attention. She was carefully dressed, and with no apparent attempt at disguise.

It could, of course, be a coincidence. Mrs. Carpenter might have had a sudden wish to experience a trial. She might have had some interest in the case. He went to the bookcase and began a quick search among the blue notebooks. The trial was easily found. Venetia Aldridge had defended a small-time crook who had unwisely moved into a more dangerous league and had attempted an armed robbery on a suburban jeweller's shop in Stanmore. Then one shot had injured but not killed the owner. The evidence had been overwhelming. Venetia Aldridge had been able to do little for her client except mount an impressive plea in mitigation which had probably taken some three years from the inevitably long sentence. Reading the details, Dalgliesh could see no possible connection either with Janet Carpenter or with the present case. So what was she doing there, patiently queuing outside the Old Bailey? Had there been another trial on that day in which she had a personal interest? Or was this tied up with her interest in Aldridge?

He resumed his careful study of the scrapbook. He was now about halfway through and then, turning a page, he saw not a face he knew but a name: Dermot Beale, convicted on 7 October 1993 at Shrewsbury Crown Court of the murder of Mrs. Carpenter's granddaughter. For a disorientating second the carefully printed name seemed to grow as he looked at it, the letters to blacken on the page. He went to the cupboard and found Miss Aldridge's notebook. The same name; an earlier trial. It wasn't the only time Dermot Beale had been accused of the rape and murder of a child. In October 1992, just a year earlier, Venetia Aldridge had successfully defended him at the Old Bailey. Dermot Beale had gone free, free to kill again. The two murders had been remarkably similar. Beale was a forty-three-year-old commercial traveller. In both cases a child had been knocked from her bicycle, abducted, raped and murdered. In both the body had been found some weeks later buried in a shallow grave. Even the accidental discovery had been the same; the family with their dogs taking a Sunday-morning walk, the sudden excitement of the animals, the scraping away of soft earth, the discovery of clothing and then of a small hand.

Sitting at the desk absolutely motionless, Dalgliesh pictured what might have happened, probably had happened. The pretended accident that was no accident, the rush to comfort, the suggestion that the child, dazed and wanting her mother, should get into the car and be taken home. He could picture the bicycle at the side of the road, the spinning wheels coming slowly to a stop. In the first case the defence had been brilliant. On the Aldridge blue notebook the main defence strategy was clearly set out. "Identification? Main prosecution witness easily muddled. Time? Could Beale have driven to Potters Lane in thirty minutes from the sighting in the supermarket carpark? Identification of car not positive. No forensic evidence linking Beale to the victim." But there would be no mention in Froggett's book, and no record among Miss Aldridge's blue notebooks, of that second trial in 1993 following the murder of Mrs. Carpenter's granddaughter. That had been held at Shrewsbury. The same crime but a different venue, a different defence counsel. But, of course, there would have been. Dalgliesh had heard that Miss Aldridge never defended the same man or woman twice on the same charge.

But what had she thought when she learned of that second murder? Had she felt any responsibility? Was this every defence counsel's private nightmare? Had it been hers? Or had she comforted herself with the thought that she had only been doing her job?

He replaced the Aldridge blue notebook in its place, then telephoned the incident room. Piers wasn't there but Kate answered. Succinctly he described the evidence he had found.

There was a pause, then Kate said: "It's the motive, sir. And now we've got the lot: motive, means, opportunity. But it's odd, I could have sworn that when I first saw her—that time in the flat—the murder was news to her."

Dalgliesh said: "It still could have been. But we're getting close to solving one part of the case. First thing tomorrow morning we'll see Janet Carpenter at her flat. I'd like you to come with me, Kate."

"Not tonight, sir? She's given up her job at Chambers. She won't be working till ten. We'll probably find her at home."

"Even so, it's late. It would be nearly ten before we arrived. And she isn't young. I want her to be rested. We'll take her in for questioning first thing tomorrow. It will be easier then for her to get a solicitor. She'll need one present."

Sensing Kate's impatience in her silence, he added, untouched by the slightest apprehension, or any premonition of impending disaster: "There's no hurry. She knows nothing of Edmund Froggett. And she isn't going to run away."

32

Some of Dalgliesh's early months as a police officer had been spent in South Kensington, and he remembered Sedgemoor Crescent as a somewhat raucous enclave of multi-occupied houses in a street chiefly remarkable for being difficult to find in the complicated urban maze between the Earls Court Road and Gloucester Road. It was a crescent of ornate stuccoed houses, their late-Victorian grandeur interposed with concrete blocks of undistinguished modern flats built to replace houses destroyed by enemy action. The far end of the crescent was dignified by the needle-sharp spire of St James's Church, an immense brick-and-mosaic monument to Tractarian piety much regarded by devotees of high-Victorian architecture.

The street seemed to have come up in the world since his last visit. Most of the houses had been restored, the gleaming white stucco and newly painted doors shining with almost aggressive respectability, while others with scaffolding erected against their discoloured and crumbling walls had boards advising their conversion to luxury flats. Even the modern blocks, once loud with the shrieks of children and the shouts of their parents across the balconies, and festooned with drying clothes, now held a subdued air of drab conformity.

Number 16, now named Coulston Court, had like most of the large houses been converted into flats. There was a bank of ten bells with the single word "Carpenter" on the card next to the bell-push, marked "10," indicating the top floor. Knowing the unreliability of some systems, Dalgliesh was patient, but after three minutes of trying he said to Kate: "We'll press all the bells; someone usually responds. They ought not to let us in without checking identity, but we could be lucky. Of course, most of them may have left for work."

He pressed the bells in succession. Only one voice, deep but female, replied. There was a low buzzing and the door clicked open to his touch. A heavy oak table was set against the wall, obviously there to hold the post. Kate said: "We had this arrangement at my first flat. Whoever came down first in the morning picked up the letters and put them on the table. Tenants who were punctilious or inquisitive set them out by name, but usually they were just left in a pile and you found your own. No one bothered to send on post and the circulars just accumulated. I hated having other people see my letters. If you wanted privacy you had to get up early."

Dalgliesh looked at the few letters left in the hall. One, in a window envelope, typed and bearing the words "Private and Confidential," was addressed to Mrs. Carpenter.

He said: "It looks like a bank statement. She hasn't collected her post. The bell could be defective. We'll go up."

The top floor, lit by a large skylight, was surprisingly light. Against the wall of the square landing was a wide storage cupboard with four numbered doors. Kate was about to press the doorbell of Flat Ten when they heard footsteps and, looking down the stairs, saw a girl looking up at them, anxious-eyed. She had obviously just woken. Her hair was a tousled mat fringing a face still bleared with sleep and she was enveloped in a man's large dressing-gown. As she looked at them her face lightened with relief.

"Was it you who rang? God, I'm sorry. I was asleep when the bell went. I thought it was my boyfriend. He works nights. They're always telling us, the weirdies on the Residents' Association, that we mustn't let people in without identification. The sound system isn't very clear and if you're expecting someone you don't always think. And I'm not the only one. Old Miss Kemp is always doing it, that is when she hears the bell. Do you want Mrs. Carpenter? She should be there. I saw her yesterday evening about six-thirty. She went out to post a letter—at least she was carrying one. And later I heard her TV on really loud."

Dalgliesh asked: "What time was that?"

"The TV? About seven-thirty, I suppose. She can't have been out long. I don't usually hear her. The flats aren't badly insulated and she's very quiet. Is anything wrong?"

"I don't think so. We're just calling."

She hesitated for a moment, but something in his voice reassured her or was taken as a dismissal. She said, "That's OK, then," and seconds later they heard her door close.

There was no reply to their ring. Neither Dalgliesh nor Kate spoke. Their thoughts were running on similar lines. Mrs. Carpenter could have left early, before the post, or after seven-thirty the previous night, perhaps to stay with a friend. It was premature to begin thinking of breaking down doors. But

Dalgliesh knew that this sudden weight of premonition, familiar from so many past cases and apparently intuitive, invariably had its basis in rationality.

There was a row of plants in pots outside Number Nine. He went over to them and found among the leaves of a lily a folded note. The note read: "Miss Kemp. These are for you to keep, not just to water for me. The calathea and the bird's-nest fern love humidity. I found they did best in the bathroom or kitchen. I'll drop in the keys before I leave in case of flood or burglary. I shall be away about a week. Many thanks." It was signed "Janet Carpenter."

Dalgliesh said: "There's usually a key-holder. Let's hope Miss Kemp's at home."

She was, but it took three rings before they heard the rasp of a bolt. The door was carefully opened on a chain and an elderly woman peered out at them into Dalgliesh's eyes.

Dalgliesh said: "Miss Kemp? We're sorry to trouble you. We're police officers. This is Detective Inspector Miskin and my name is Dalgliesh. We were hoping to have a word with Mrs. Carpenter but there's no reply and we want to check that she's all right."

Kate showed her warrant card. Miss Kemp took it and peered at it closely, silently mouthing the words. Then, for the first time, her eyes lit on the plants.

"So she's left them. She said she would. That's kind of her. Police officers, are you? Then I suppose it's all right. But she's not here. You won't find her at home. She told me she was going for a short holiday and she'd leave me the plants. I always water and feed them if she's away—not that she is very often. Just a weekend at the sea occasionally. I'd better take them in, no use leaving them out here."

She unchained the door and picked up the nearest pot with gnarled and shaking hands. Kate bent to help her. "I see there's a note. That'll be to say goodbye and to tell me about the plants too, I dare say. Well, she knows they're going to a good home."

Dalgliesh said: "If we might have the key, Miss Kemp."

"But I told you, she's not here. She's on holiday."

"We'd like to be sure."

Kate was holding two of the plants and, after a long look at her, Miss Kemp opened the door wide. Kate and Dalgliesh followed her into the hall.

"Set them down on the hall table. The saucers are clean at the bottom, aren't they? She never over-watered. Wait here."

She returned quickly with two keys on a ring. Thanking her, Dalgliesh wondered how he could persuade her to stay in her flat. But she showed no further interest in them or in their doings except to say again: "You won't find her. She isn't there. She's gone for a holiday."

Kate carried in the last two plants and the door was quickly and firmly closed.

He knew what he would find as soon as he turned the key and pushed open the door. Beyond the small entrance hall, the door to the sitting-room was open. The premonition of disaster isn't confined to violent death; there is always that instant of realization, however brief, before the blow falls, the car strikes, the ladder gives way. Part of his mind had been forewarned of the horror which smell and sight now confirmed. But not of its extent. Never that. Her throat had been cut. Strange that those five monosyllables could cover such an effusion of blood.

Janet Carpenter was lying on her back, her head towards the door, her legs splayed in a stiff decrepitude which looked somehow indecent. The left leg was grotesquely bent, the heel raised, the toe just touching the floor. Close to her right hand was a kitchen knife, the blade and handle heavily bloodstained. She was wearing a skirt in brown-and-blue-flecked tweed and a high-necked blue jumper with a matching cardigan. The left sleeve of both had been pushed up to reveal the forearm. There was a single cut across the left wrist and, above it on the inner side of the arm, some letters written in blood.

They squatted beside the body. The blood had dried into a brownish smear but the initials were plain, the date even plainer: "R v Beale 1992."

It was Kate who put the obvious into words, whispering as if to herself: "Dermot Beale. The murderer Aldridge defended in 1992 and got off. And a year later he raped and murdered again. This time it was Emily Carpenter."

Like Dalgliesh, Kate was being careful not to tread in the blood. It had spurted across the room to spot the ceiling, the wall, the polished wooden floor, and had seeped into the single rug on which she lay. Her jumper was stiff with it. The very air smelt of blood.

It was not, perhaps, the most terrible of violent deaths. It was quick enough, more merciful than most methods if one had the strength of hand and will to make that first incision deep and certain. But few suicides did. There were usually a few tentative slices of the throat or wrist. Not here, however. Here the preliminary cut on the wrist, which had provided the blood for the message, was superficial but purposeful, a single smudged thread beaded with dried blood.

He glanced at Kate as she stood quietly by the body. Her face was white but calm and he had no fear that she would faint. She was a senior officer; he could rely on her to behave like one. But whereas, with his male colleagues, their calm professionalism came from long experience, an acquired protective insensitivity and the stolid acceptance of the realities of their job, he suspected that with Kate it took a more painful discipline of the heart. None of his officers, male or female, was unfeeling. He rejected the callous, the incipient sadist, those who needed a crude graveyard humour to anaesthetize horror. Like doctors, nurses or the traffic police who extract the pulped bodies from the crushed metal, you couldn't do the job if your thoughts were centred on your own emotions. It was necessary to grow a carapace, however fragile, of acceptance and detachment if one was to remain competent and sane. Horror might enter, but must never be allowed to take a permanent lodging in the mind. But he sensed Kate's effort of will and he sometimes wondered what it was costing her.

With a part of his mind formed in early childhood, he wished for a moment that she was not there. His father had had a great respect and love for women, had desperately wanted daughters, had thought women capable of anything, short of actions requiring great physical strength, that a man could do. But he had seen them, too, as a civilizing influence without whose peculiar sensitivity and compassion the world would have been an uglier place. The young Dalgliesh had been brought up to believe that these qualities should be protected by chivalry and respect. In this as in other things his clerical father could not have been less politically correct. But he had never found it easy in a very different and more aggressive age to shake off this early indoctrination, nor in his heart did he really wish to.

Kate said: "A clean cut through the jugular. She must have more strength in her hands than you'd expect. They don't look particularly strong, but, then, the hands always do look frail." She added, "More dead than the rest of the body," and then blushed slightly, as if the comment had been stupid.

"More dead and sadder, perhaps because they are the busiest part of us."

Still squatting, and without touching the body, he looked carefully at each hand. The right was covered with blood, the left lying curled with the palm upwards. He gently pressed the mound of the flesh at the base of the fingers, then ran an exploring hand down each of her fingers. After a moment he got quickly to his feet and said: "Let's have a look at the kitchen."

If Kate was surprised, she didn't show it. The kitchen was at the end of the sitting-room and must originally have been part of it; the high curved window matched the two in the larger room and gave the same leafy view of the garden. The room was small but well fitted out and immaculately tidy. The double-drainer sink was set under the window and the working surface of simulated wood ran from it and then right down the whole length of the room with cupboards beneath and above. A ceramic hob was set into the working surface with, to its left, a large wooden chopping-board. To the left of this was a knife-block. One slot—the one on the left at the back, for the largest knife—was empty.

Dalgliesh and Kate stood in the doorway but did not go in. Dalgliesh asked: "Anything strike you as odd?"

"Not really, sir." Kate paused and looked more closely, then she said: "It all looks ordinary enough, except that I'd probably have put the washing-up liquid to the left of the sink. And that large chopping-board and the knives are a bit oddly placed. Hardly convenient in relation to the cooker, not as she's got them." She paused again, then said: "You think she was left-handed, sir?"

Dalgliesh didn't reply. He pulled out three of the drawers and looked inside, then shut them, dissatisfied. They returned to the sitting-room.

Dalgliesh said: "Take a look at her left hand, Kate. She did housework, remember."

"Only three nights a week, sir, and she wore gloves."

"There's a slight thickening of the skin, almost a callus, on the inner side of the second finger. I think she wrote with that hand."

Kate squatted and looked again carefully at the hand, but without touching it. After a second she said: "If she was left-handed, who would have known? She didn't arrive for work until most people in Chambers had gone, and they wouldn't have seen her writing."

Dalgliesh said: "Probably Mrs. Watson, who worked with her. But Miss Elkington is the one to confirm it. Mrs. Carpenter must have signed for her money. Phone her from the car, will you, Kate, and if she confirms what we suspect, get Dr. Kynaston, photographers, SOCO, the lot—and, of course, Piers. And in view of the pattern of the bloodstains it would be helpful if the lab could send a forensic biologist. And stay down there until some reinforcements arrive. I want someone on the door to see that no one leaves. Keep it discreet. The story is that Mrs. Carpenter has been attacked, not that she's dead. It will get out soon enough, but let's keep out the vultures while we can."

Kate went quietly without another word. Dalgliesh moved over to the window and stood looking out at the garden. He had disciplined his mind not to speculate; speculation in advance of the facts was always futile and could be dangerous.

These few minutes in the company of the undemanding dead seemed a bonus of time, stilled and inviolate, in which nothing was required of him but to wait. He could retire, less by an act of will than by an easy relaxation of mind and body, into that central privacy on which his life and his art depended. This was not the first time he had been alone with a dead body. The sensation, familiar but always forgotten until the next occasion, returned and took possession. He was experiencing a solitude, unique and absolute. A room empty except for himself could not have been more lonely. Janet Carpenter's personality could not have been more powerful in life than was its absence in death.

Below him the house shared his quietude. In these self-contained cabins the small business of daily life was going on. Curtains were being drawn, tea brewed, plants watered, the late-risers were stumbling to bathrooms or showers. All were unaware of the horror above. When the news did break, the response would be as varied as it always was: fear, pity, fascinated interest, self-importance; a surge of heightened energy at being alive; the pleasure of sharing the news at work, among friends; the half-shameful excitement of blood spilt which was not one's own. If this were murder the house would never escape its contamination, but it would be felt less here than in those desecrated Chambers of the Middle Temple. More had been lost there than a friend or colleague.

The ringing of his mobile telephone broke the silence and he heard Kate's voice. "Janet Carpenter was left-handed. There's no doubt about it."

So this was murder. But with part of his mind he had known this from the start. He asked: "Did Miss Elkington ask why you wanted to know?"

"No sir, and I didn't tell her. Doc Kynaston is expected in the hospital this morning but hasn't arrived. I left a message. Piers and the rest of the team are on their way. The lab can't send anyone until this afternoon. Sickness and two officers out on a case."

Dalgliesh said: "The afternoon will have to do. I'd like them to have a look at the pattern of the bloodstains. Don't let anyone leave the building without being interviewed. Probably most of them are at work, but we can get the names from the bells. I'd like you and Piers to get on with the interviews. Miss Kemp will probably be able to tell us most about her neighbour. And then there's that young woman who let us in. What time precisely did she hear the TV and when was it switched off? And let me know when you're coming up, Kate. There's an experiment I want to make."

It was five minutes before she rang again. "I've got Robbins and DC Meadows on the door now, sir. I'm coming up."

Dalgliesh left the flat and stood on the landing, flattening himself against the wall at the side of the cupboard. He heard Kate's quick footsteps. As she reached the landing and moved over to the door he came swiftly up behind her. She gave a gasp as she felt his hand on the back of her neck propelling her through the doorway.

Then she turned and said: "So that's one way he could have got in."

"It's possible. It would mean, of course, that he knew when she was expected home. She could have let him in, but would she do that for a stranger?"

Kate said: "She was less worried about security than most old people. Two locks, one a Banham, but no chain."

Miles Kynaston was first on the scene, with Piers and the photographers close behind him. He must have arrived at his hospital laboratory soon after Kate's call and come on immediately. He stood in the doorway, the calm eyes surveying the room, then coming to rest on the victim. His gaze was always the same, the momentary gleam of compassion, so fleeting that it would be missed by anyone who did not know him, and then the intense considering scrutiny of a man facing once again the fascinating evidence of human depravity.

Dalgliesh said: "Janet Carpenter. One of the suspects for the Venetia Aldridge murder. Discovered by Kate and myself forty minutes ago, when we came to interview her."

Kynaston nodded without speaking, then stood well clear of the body while the photographers, equally taciturn, moved past him, briefly acknowledging Dalgliesh, and got on with their work. In this charnel-house the position of the body and the pattern of the blood splatters were important evidence. The camera's eye came first, fixing the stark reality, before Dalgliesh and Kynaston risked even a small disturbance of the body. For Dalgliesh these preliminaries to the investigation, the careful manoeuvring of the photographers round the body, the lens focused impersonally on glazed, unreproachful eyes and the crude butchery of gaping flesh, was the first step in the violation of the defenceless dead. But was it really any worse than the dehumanizing routines which followed even a natural death? The almost superstitious tradition that the dead should be treated with reverence always failed at some point along that carefully documented final journey to the crematorium or the grave.

Ferris and his fellow SOCO arrived, their feet so silent on the stairs that the tap on the door was the first indication of their presence. Ferris watched avid-eyed at the door, frowning with anxiety as the photographers circled the body, anxious to get on with his search before the scene was contaminated. But he would have to wait. After the photographers had packed up with the same economic efficiency with which they had worked, Miles Kynaston took off his jacket and squatted to his task.

Dalgliesh said: "She was left-handed, but it always looked an unlikely suicide. There are those spatters on the ceiling and the top half of the wall. She must have been standing when her throat was cut."

Kynaston's gloved hands were busy with the body, gently, as if the dead nerves could still feel. He said: "A single cut, left to right, slicing the jugular. Superficial cut on the left wrist. He probably took her from behind, pulled the head back, one swift cut, then let the body gently down. Look at that ungainly twist to the leg. She was dead when she hit the floor."

"He'd be shielded by her body from the main spurt of blood. What about the right arm?"

"Difficult to say. It was quick and sure. Even so, I think the right arm would be fairly heavily stained. He'll have needed to wash before leaving. And if he was wearing a jacket the cuff and the lower part of the sleeve would be bloody. She'd hardly wait patiently while he stripped."

Dalgliesh said: "We may find blood traces in the U-bend of the sink or the bathroom, but it's unlikely. I think this killer knew his business. He'd have let the water run. The knife is from the kitchen block, but I don't think it's the one he used. This was a premeditated killing. I think he brought his own knife."

Kynaston said: "If he didn't use this knife it was one like it. So he killed her, washed the knife and himself, took a knife from the kitchen block, smeared it with her blood and pressed her hand round the handle. Is that how you see it?"

"It's a working hypothesis. Would it need much strength? Could a woman have done it?"

"With determination and a sharp enough knife. But it doesn't strike me as a woman's crime."

"Nor me."

"How did he get in?"

"The door was locked when we arrived. I think he probably stood concealed in the shadows by the landing cupboard and waited for her. When she opened the door he pushed in after her. It would have been easy enough to gain access to the building. You just push all the bells and wait for someone to respond. Someone always does."

"And then he waited. A patient man."

"Patient when he needed to be. But he may have known her routine, where she'd been, when she was likely to come home."

Kynaston said: "If he knew that much, it's odd he didn't know she was left-handed. The letters written in blood—I suppose they mean something?"

Dalgliesh told him. He added: "She was a prime suspect for the Aldridge murder. She had the means and the opportunity. That 1992 case, when Aldridge successfully defended Beale, gave her the motive. This was meant to look like suicide and if she'd been right-handed I don't think we could have proved otherwise. But it looked suspicious from the first, the throat cut standing when it would have been more usual to find her slumped over the bath or sink. She was a fastidious woman, she would have bothered about the mess. Odd how suicides often do. And why leave a message written in your own blood when you've got paper and pen? And she wouldn't have slit her throat. There are kinder, less brutal ways." But, however odd the circumstances, suspicion wasn't legal proof. Juries were apt to believe that suicides, having brought themselves to that one incredible act, were capable of any eccentricity.

Kynaston said: "The one fatal mistake. And it's usually the clever ones who make it."

He had finished his preliminary examination, wiping his thermometer and replacing it carefully in its box. Then he said: "Time of death, between seven and eight last night. That's judging by body temperature and the extent of rigor. I may be able to narrow it down after the autopsy. I suppose it's urgent? With you it usually is. I could fit it in tonight but it will be late, probably eight to eight-thirty. I'll give you a ring." He took a last look at the body. "Poor woman. But at least it was quick. This one knew what he was about. Hope you get him, Adam."

It was the first time Dalgliesh had ever heard Miles Kynaston express a hope about the success of a case.

As soon as Kynaston had left, the SOCOs set to work. Dalgliesh moved away from the body, leaving clear the vital area between it and the kitchen and bathroom. Kate and Piers were still interviewing the tenants. They had started with Miss Kemp but it was forty minutes since Dalgliesh had heard her door finally close and their footsteps descending the stairs. They were taking longer than he had expected and he hoped this meant that the chore was proving productive. He turned his own attention to the details of the flat.

The most prominent feature was the bureau set against the right-hand wall. It was obviously one Mrs. Carpenter had brought with her to the flat, a solid working desk in polished oak, disproportionate to the size of the room. It looked to be the only piece of furniture which wasn't new. The two-seater sofa against the wall, the round, drop-side table with four matching chairs, the single armchair facing the television set installed between the windows, all looked as unused as if they had just been delivered. They were modern, conventional and unexceptional in design, the kind of furniture one would expect in a three-star hotel. There were no pictures, no photographs, no ornaments. It was the room of a woman who had shed her past, a room which provided the essentials necessary for physical comfort and left the spirit free to inhabit its own unencumbered space. The small bookcase to the right of the desk held only modern editions of the major poets and classical novelists: a personal library, carefully selected to provide solid literary sustenance when required.

Dalgliesh moved into her bedroom. It was little more than nine feet square with a single high window. Here spare comfort had given place to austerity: a single bed covered with a light counterpane, an oak bedside cabinet with a shelf and a lamp, an upright chair, a fitted wardrobe. A plain brown handbag was on the floor beside the bed. Inside, it was as well ordered as Venetia Aldridge's had been, with nothing superfluous. He was surprised, however, to find that she had as much as £250 in crisp ten- and twenty-pound notes in her wallet. A dressing-gown in fine patterned wool hung from the single hook on the door. There was no dressing-table. She probably brushed her hair and made up in front of a mirror in the bathroom, but the bathroom was out of bounds until Ferris had finished with it. Except for the carpeted floor, the room could have been a nun's cell; he almost felt the lack of a crucifix above the bed.

He returned to the desk and, opening the lid, seated himself for a search, although with no clear idea of what he was looking for. This rummaging among the detritus of a dead life was for him a necessary part of the investigation. A victim died because of who she was, where she was, what she had done, what she knew. The clues to a murder lay always in the clues to a life. But it sometimes seemed to him that his search was a presumptuous violation of a privacy which the victim could no longer protect, and that his latex-gloved hands moved among her belongings as if merely by touching them he could hope to reach out to the core of her personality.

A much smaller desk would have sufficed for her leavings. Four of the six cubbyholes were bare. The last two held an envelope of bills awaiting payment, and a larger, buff one with the words "bills paid" lettered on it in careful script. It was apparent that she settled her bills promptly and kept the records only for six months. There were no personal letters. The similarity to Venetia Aldridge's desk, Venetia Aldridge's leavings, was almost uncanny.

Under the row of cubbyholes were two slim drawers. The right-hand one contained black plastic-covered folders stamped with the name of her bank, one with the statements of her current account, the slimmer one records of an instant-access deposit account showing a balance of £146,000. The latter showed the accumulation of comparatively low interest earned on the account, but there had been no further deposits and no withdrawals until 9 September of this year, when £50,000 had been transferred to her current account. He referred back to the statements for this account and saw that the sum had been credited and that, two days later, £10,000 had been withdrawn in cash.

He opened next the cupboard on the left of the kneehole, and then three main drawers on the right. The cupboard was empty. In the top drawer were only three telephone directories. The drawer beneath held a box of plain writing-paper and an assortment of envelopes. Only in the third and bottom drawer did he discover anything of interest.

Dalgliesh drew out a box-file and discovered, neatly arranged in chronological order, the explanation of the £146,000 in the deposit account. In December 1993 Janet Carpenter had sold the house in Hereford and bought the London flat; the history of the transactions was set out in letters from the estate agents and her solicitor, in surveyor's reports and estimates from a removal firm. A cash offer for the Hereford house, nearly £5,000 below the original asking price, had been quickly accepted. Her furniture, pictures and ornaments had been sold, not stored. Less valuable items had been given to the Salvation Army and the house finally cleared. There was a copy of a letter from her to her solicitor instructing him to ask the new owner to forward any post to him for onward transmission. No one was to be given her London address. She had cut herself free from her old life with ruthless efficiency and the minimum of fuss, as if the death of her granddaughter and of her daughter-in-law had severed more than their own lives.

But something other than the oak bureau had been brought with her. In the bottom drawer was a bulky manila envelope, unmarked and with the flap stuck down. Lacking a paper-knife, Dalgliesh insinuated his thumb under the flap and felt an irrational second of mixed guilt and irritation as the paper split into a jagged edge. Inside there was a letter on a single sheet of folded paper, a bundle of photographs and another bundle of birthday and Christmas cards held together with a rubber band. All the photographs were of the dead granddaughter, some formally posed, others amateur family snaps covering her life from babyhood in the arms of her mother until her twelfth birthday party. The young face, bright-eyed, confident, smiled obediently into the lens in a bright panorama of childish rites of passage: the first day at school, crisply uniformed, her smile a mixture of eagerness and apprehension; as bridesmaid at a friend's wedding, her dark hair crowned with a coronet of roses; a First Communion photograph, serious-eyed under the white veil. The birthday and Christmas cards were a complete set of those she had sent to her grandmother from the age of four until her death, the messages carefully written and obviously in her own words, a mixture of childish concerns, small triumphs at school, messages of love.

Lastly Dalgliesh took up the letter. It was handwritten. There was no address and no date.

Dearest Janet,

Please forgive me. I know what I'm doing is selfish. I know that I ought not to leave you. Ralph is dead and now Emily, and you only have me. But I wouldn't be any use to you. I know you're suffering too, but I can't help. I haven't even any love left to give, nothing to feel but pain. I long for the night when I can take my pills and sometimes I sleep. Sleep is like a little death, but there are the dreams too, and I hear her calling for me and I know I can't reach her, I'll never be able to reach her. And I always wake up, although I pray not to, and the pain comes down like a great black weight. I know it will never grow less, and I can't live with it any more. I could remember Ralph with love, even when remembering hurt most, because I was there with him when he died and I held his hand and he knew that I loved him, and we had known what it was to be happy. But I can't think of Emily's death without guilt and agony. I can't live with that imagined horror, with that pain, for the rest of my life. Forgive me. Forgive me and try to understand. I couldn't have had a better mother-in-law. Emily loved you very much.

Dalgliesh didn't know how long he sat as if in a trance, staring at the photographs laid out before him. Then he was aware of Piers at his shoulder and heard his voice.

"Kate is having a last word with Miss Kemp in case she may be more forthcoming to another female without me. Not that she's got anything more to tell. And the mortuary van's arrived. Is it all right for them to take her away?"

Dalgliesh didn't answer for the moment, but handed Piers the letter. Then he said: "The body? Oh yes, they can take her away."

The room was suddenly full of large masculine forms, subdued masculine voices. Piers nodded to them and then watched as the corpse, head and hands bagged with plastic, was zipped into a body bag. Piers and Dalgliesh could hear receding steps as the men manoeuvred their burden round the bend in the stairs, and a sudden laugh, like a bark, quickly suppressed. And now there was nothing left as witness to the horror but the bloodstained carpet under the spread of protective sheeting, the splattered ceiling and walls.

Ferris and his colleague were still in the bathroom, their presence there sensed rather than heard. Dalgliesh and Piers were alone.

Piers read the letter, then handed it back. He said: "Will you show this to Kate, sir?"

"Probably not."

There was a pause, then Piers said, his voice carefully neutral: "Did you show it to me because I'm the less sensitive or because you think I'm the one who needs a lesson?"

"A lesson in what, Piers?"

"I suppose in what murder can do to the innocent."

It was perilously close to questioning a superior's action, and if he expected a direct answer he didn't get it.

Dalgliesh said: "If you haven't learned that by now, would you ever learn it? This wasn't meant for either of our eyes."

He put the letter back in the envelope and began gathering up the photographs and cards. He said: "She's right, of course, the only immortality for the dead is in our remembrance of them. If that is tainted with horror and evil, then they're dead indeed. The bank statements and a file on her property sale and purchase are of more immediate interest."

He got up and left Piers studying them, and went to talk to Ferris. His search was over and, from the look on his face, had been disappointing. There were no discernible bloodstains carried from the body to the kitchen sink or the bathroom, no heavy footprints on the close pile of the carpet, no stain of oil, grease or dirt from alien shoes. Had the killer brought with him a cloth with which to wipe his shoes while he waited silently in the shadow of the landing? Had he been that careful?

As Ferris and his fellow SOCO with their meagre haul made ready to leave, Kate appeared and closed the door behind them. The three of them were alone.

33

Before Kate and Piers reported on their inquiries, Dalgliesh said: "See if there's any coffee in the kitchen, will you, Piers?"

There were coffee beans, a grinder and a percolator. Piers coped while Dalgliesh put Kate in the picture. The coffee when it came was black and strong, brought in on a tray in green Denby mugs.

Piers said: "I don't think she'd begrudge us her coffee. There isn't any whisky. If there had been I must say I'd have been tempted."

Dalgliesh sat in the one easy chair, Piers and Kate on the sofa. They drew up a small table and sat, relaxed and companionable, as if they had taken over the flat. After the constant comings and goings it seemed preternaturally quiet. Uniformed police were keeping a discreet watch on the door. Any tenants arriving would be checked in and questioned by Sergeant Robbins and the detective constable. But little activity could be expected until people began coming home from work, and the news of the murder still hadn't spread beyond Coulston Court. They had a sense of inhabiting a short hiatus in time between bouts of feverish activity, during which it was possible to take stock.

Dalgliesh said: "So what have we got so far?"

Kate was swallowing a mouthful of coffee and it was Piers who got in first. He had obviously decided to give a résumé of the case.

"Mrs. Janet Carpenter, a widow. Lives with her daughter-in-law and granddaughter just outside Hereford. Three years ago the child is raped and murdered. The murderer, Dermot Beale, is convicted and is now serving a life sentence. He had previously been tried in 1992 for an almost identical rape and murder. The evidence was less compelling and he was acquitted. The defending counsel was Venetia Aldridge. Emily's mother, distraught with grief, kills herself. After her suicide Janet Carpenter sells her house, moves anonymously to London, cuts herself free from her old life.

"She sets out to gain access to Venetia Aldridge's Chambers by working as a cleaner. It isn't difficult. She's respectable, obviously competent, can provide references. She has to start with another set of Chambers but she asks for a transfer and gets it. She also offers to do occasional and temporary cleaning in Miss Aldridge's house and buys a flat within two stations' travelling distance by tube of where Miss Aldridge lives. She only works three nights a week. That in itself is odd; if you're going to look to housework for an income, you can hardly earn much in three nights. But three nights are sufficient for her needs. All she wants is access to Chambers.

"On Wednesday, 9th October, Venetia Aldridge is murdered. Stabbed in the heart with an ornamental dagger which she used as a paper-knife. A full-bottomed wig is stuck on her head and blood stored in a basement refrigerator poured over the wig. Mrs. Carpenter cleaned Miss Aldridge's room. She knew about the dagger. She knew that the blood was stored in Mr. Ulrick's room. She knew where the full-bottomed wig was kept. She had the means, motive and opportunity. She has to be chief suspect still for the Aldridge killing."

At this point Kate broke in: "But now we've got her murder. That alters everything. Whoever killed her wrote those letters in her blood. It was a definite attempt to pin the Aldridge murder on her. Why bother to do that if she's already the prime suspect? And she was a prime suspect, I'll give you that, but it isn't as straightforward as you make out. If she took the job in Chambers to give her the opportunity to kill Aldridge, why wait for over two years? There must have been other nights when Mrs. Watson wasn't with her. Anyway, she had a key to Chambers. She could have got in any time. And why choose a method which she must have known would make her chief suspect? It was hardly certain. If Mrs. Carpenter did it, she acted like a fool, and I don't think that she was a fool. There's another thing. I was the first to interview her after the murder. I could swear she was surprised. She was more than surprised, she was deeply shocked."

Piers said: "That's not evidence. I'm constantly amazed at the acting ability of the general public. You've seen it often enough, Kate. There they are on television, eyes full of tears, voice broken, pleading for the return of the loved one, when they know bloody well that the loved one's under the floorboards and they put her there. Anyway, what about the money? How do you explain the withdrawal of that ten thousand pounds?"

"The obvious explanation would be blackmail, but she drew it out before the murder, not after, so that's out. Or she could have wanted to pay someone to do the murder, but that seems unlikely. Where would a woman like that look for a contract killer? Anyway, the Aldridge murder wasn't a contract job. Contract killers use guns and a getaway car. That murder was an inside job. And you can't get over the fact that this second murder is a deliberate attempt to pin the first onto Janet Carpenter. If she hadn't been left-handed it might have succeeded."

Now that the body had been taken away and the experts had done their jobs and departed, the flat had become less claustrophobic, but the dead, polluted air was still oppressive, as if the living had sucked it dry. Dalgliesh went over to the window and pushed up the bottom pane. The morning breeze came in, cleansing, coldly autumnal. He almost believed that he could smell the grass and the trees. They sat together and felt no sense of intrusion, perhaps because there was so little in that spare, underfurnished space to bring the dead alive.

He asked: "Any joy from the tenants?"

Piers left it to Kate. "Not a great deal, sir. Miss Kemp can't tell us much more than she has already. She didn't hear anything last evening, but, then, she's very deaf. She says the last time she saw Mrs. Carpenter was yesterday afternoon, when she knocked on the door to tell Miss Kemp that she was going away and would leave her the pot plants and her keys. She says she didn't know Mrs. Carpenter well. She's never been in this flat, for example, nor Mrs. C. in hers. But they met on the stairs occasionally and chatted briefly. That's how Mrs. Carpenter knew her neighbour liked pot plants. And they keep each other's spare keys when they're away from home. That's been agreed by the Residents' Association. Apparently last year a flat was left with a tap running and no one could get in to stop the flood. Miss Kemp only goes out when her nephew occasionally calls to take her to his home or for a drive. She leaves her spare keys with Mrs. Carpenter all the time. She walks about twice a week to the corner shop and she's afraid that someone will snatch her purse. It's a comfort to know that Mrs. C. has her spares. She'd like them back, please, if Mrs. C. is in hospital. She seems more concerned about the keys than about the accident. She didn't even ask what had happened or how it had happened. I think she assumes that Mrs. C. fell over. Falling over and getting mugged are her two main fears. I think she regards one or both of them as more or less inevitable."

Dalgliesh asked: "Did she know when Mrs. Carpenter put her spare keys through the door?"

"They weren't there when she checked on the bolt last evening but that was early, before she settled down to her evening viewing at six. She found them on the mat this morning, when she went to check whether the post had arrived. Mrs. Carpenter usually collected her post for her and put it through her letter-box. The hall's carpeted, so she wouldn't have heard the keys fall."

"Did Mrs. C. usually just drop them through the letter-box without a note?"

"No she didn't. They were usually in a strong envelope, stuck down and with Mrs. Carpenter's name, flat number and the date she expected to be back. If the keys were wanted in a hurry it would be safer to have them labelled."

Piers said: "But this time they weren't. My God, this killer had it handed to him on a plate. She'd already written the note to place with the plants. He reads it, puts the plants outside, locks the door when he leaves, puts the keys through the letter-box of Number Nine. He couldn't have reckoned on that amount of luck."

Dalgliesh said: "What about the rest of the tenants?"

It was Piers who replied. "One of the two basement flats is unoccupied and we didn't get any reply from four of the others. I suppose they're out at work. The girl we saw this morning, the one who let us in, wasn't helpful. Her boyfriend's home now and he's no lover of the police. And they guessed we weren't here because of a break-in. She'd hardly let us in when she said, 'It's murder, isn't it? That's what you've come about. Mrs. Carpenter's dead.' There seemed no point in denying it, but we didn't confirm it either. After that they were both pretty cagey, although I don't think it's because they're hiding anything, at least not about the murder. It's just funk and a wish not to get involved. The girl—her name's Hicks—won't even stand by her story that Mrs. C.'s TV was on very loudly at about seven-thirty. She's not sure now whether it was television or radio or where the noise came from. When we left she was insisting that the boyfriend go out immediately to buy a strong bolt for the inside of the door while imploring him not to leave her alone in the flat."

"Did she let anyone in through the street door last night?"

"She says not, and she's pretty definite about it, but she may be lying. On the other hand we haven't spoken to the other tenants, who are at work. One of them could have released the door. The couple in the basement flat are unemployed. She's just finished her teacher-training and is applying for jobs. He's been made redundant from a law firm. They were still in bed and none too pleased to see us. Apparently they were at a party until the early hours. Nothing of any use there, I'm afraid. They only bought the flat two months ago and say they didn't even know that Mrs. C. was a tenant. They're adamant that they didn't let anyone in last night. They claim that they'd left for the party by half past eight."

Kate added: "We did get something from the last flat we tried. Mrs. Maud Capstick, a widow living alone. She only knew Mrs. C. because Mrs. C. attended a meeting of the Residents' Association when they were discussing the cost of external painting—the only time she did attend. They sat together and Mrs. Capstick rather took to her, thought they might have things in common, but it never came to anything. She did issue an invitation to coffee from time to time but Mrs. C. always had an excuse. She didn't hold it against her, she too likes her privacy. She said that Mrs. C. was always pleased when they did meet, but it wasn't often. Mrs. Capstick's flat is the garden flat at the back, so there was no occasional passing on the stairs."

Piers broke in. "You should meet Mrs. Capstick, sir. She's the garden expert on one of the glossy monthlies. My aunt takes it and I recognized her from her photograph in the mag. She sees herself as the Elizabeth David of gardening journalists—reliable advice and elegant, original writing. My aunt swears by her. Mrs. Capstick writes about her magnificent garden in Kent. She admitted to me that she hasn't got a garden in Kent and never has had. It's a garden of the imagination. That way, she claims, her readers get a better garden and so does she."

An unseen listener might have been surprised to hear him speak with such amused detachment, but his colleagues were grateful to Maud Capstick for the eccentricity which, for a moment, had lightened their mood.

Intrigued, Dalgliesh asked: "What about photographs? Aren't the articles illustrated?"

"She takes them herself using partial views of gardens she visits, clumps of plants from London parks. That's half the fun, she says, finding a suitable shot, one that won't be recognized. She never actually states that the photographs are of her garden. The one she has here is about six feet by eight, a patch of rough grass much visited by local dogs, a flower bed which provides a useful scrape for cats, and about three indistinguishable shrubs which the local children have vandalized."

"I'm surprised she admitted to all this."

Kate said, more tolerantly than Dalgliesh would have expected: "He just sits there with that look of boyish sympathy. It usually does the trick."

"Well, I did recognize her. I asked how often she was in Kent. I think she'd been keeping it as a secret for years and just wanted to tell someone. That's the fascination of policing. People are either concealing secrets or pouring them out. I wish you'd been there, sir. She said, 'You should avoid living too much in the real world, young man. It isn't conducive to happiness.' "

"I hope she's sufficiently in the real world to answer questions reliably.

When you weren't exchanging homespun philosophy or discussing herba-
ceous borders, did she have anything useful to tell?"

"Only that she definitely didn't let anyone in last night. Her bell did ring
just after seven but she was in the shower and by the time she got to the door
to answer it there was no one there. She wasn't expecting a caller. She says
she often gets non-productive calls. Sometimes it's the local kids pressing the
bells, sometimes it's someone who's mistaken the number."

Kate said: "It could have been the murderer. By the time she got to the
door someone could have let him in."

Dalgliesh said: "Someone did. If we can get them to admit it we will at
least know when he arrived—provided, of course, that he got in that way.
Was that all?"

Kate answered: "We asked Mrs. Capstick when she'd last seen Mrs. Carpenter. It was Sunday at half past three. Mrs. Capstick was coming home
from lunch with a friend and saw Mrs. C. going into the church at the end
of the crescent, St James's. So she was alive then. But it doesn't get us any
further. We knew that already."

It could, thought Dalgliesh, be of no importance except as a piece of
somewhat surprising information. There was nothing in the flat to suggest
that Mrs. Carpenter was a churchgoer, but, then, there was nothing in the
flat to throw any light on her interests or her personality, except that she was
essentially private. No life could be as uncluttered as this living-space. But
Sunday afternoon was an odd time to visit a church unless, unusually surely,
there was a service. It was possible that she was using it as a meeting-place.
It wouldn't be the first time in his experience that one of these quiet empty
places had been used for an assignation or for the passing on of a message.
If she had wanted to talk privately without the risk of inviting a visitor to
her flat, the church was an obvious place to choose.

Kate asked: "Is it worth calling in, sir? I suppose there's a chance it will
be open."

Dalgliesh went over to the bureau and took out a photograph of Mrs.
Carpenter with her granddaughter. He studied it carefully for half a minute,
his face giving nothing away, then placed it in his wallet.

"A good chance. It's usually kept open. I know the parish priest, Father
Presteign. If Father Presteign is involved in all of this we may have complications."

Glancing at him, Kate saw his rueful, half-amused smile. She would have
liked to have asked more but felt herself on uncertain ground. Was there any
world, she wondered, in which AD didn't feel at home? Well, he was said to
be the son of a parson. That gave him a familiarity with a part of life which

was to her as unfamiliar as if St James's had been a mosque. Religion, whether as a practical guide to life, a source of legend and myth, or a philosophical concept, had never entered that seventh-floor flat in Ellison Fairweather Buildings. Her moral training had at least had the benefit of simplicity. Certain actions—reading when she should be cleaning the flat, forgetting items from the shopping list—were inconvenient or abhorrent to her grandmother, and were therefore wrong. Others were accepted as illegal and therefore dangerous. On the whole the law had seemed both a more sensible and a more consistent guide to morality than her grandmother's eccentric self-interest. Her large inner-city comprehensive school, attempting to accommodate the religious affiliations of seventeen different nationalities, had been content to instil the belief that racism was the greatest if not the only unforgivable sin, and that all faiths were equally valid—or invalid, as you chose to believe. The minority ones, their feasts and their ceremonies, received most attention, presumably on the grounds that Christianity had had an unfair head start and could be left to look after itself. Kate's personal moral code, never discussed with her grandmother, had in childhood been instinctive and in adolescence worked out without reference to any power beyond herself. She sometimes found it bleak, but it was all she had.

Now she wondered why Mrs. Carpenter had visited the church. To pray? There was presumably a particular grace, and therefore a greater hope of success, if one prayed in church. To take a short rest? Surely not; she was within eighty yards of her home. To meet someone? That was possible; a large church could be a good place for an assignation. But she expected nothing of use from the visit to St James's.

The young constable on duty in the hall saluted as they left and ran down the steps to the car. Dalgliesh said: "Thank you, Price, we'll walk." Then he turned to Piers: "Get back to the incident room, will you, Piers, and set up the inquiry. Then go on to break the news at Pawlet Court. Tell them as little as you need. This will be hard on Langton."

Piers was following through his own thoughts: "I can't see it, sir. They're not butchers. This is a very different murder."

Kate said with a touch of impatience: "Not the same delicate touch. But they're connected. They have to be. If we're right, if the motive was to set up Carpenter for the Aldridge killing, then we're back at Pawlet Court."

"Only if the first murder really was an inside job. I'm beginning to wonder. If we separate the actual killing from the business with the wig and the blood . . ."

Kate broke in: "In my book it had to be an inside job and Carpenter was, and still is, the prime suspect. She had it all, means, motive, opportunity."

Dalgliesh said: "We already know one thing: three members of Chambers have an alibi for the Carpenter killing, Ulrick, Costello and Langton. I was speaking with them last evening and there's no way any of them could have got to Sedgemoor Crescent by seven-thirty. Kate and I will call in at the church since we're so close, then come on later."

The crescent was almost deserted. The news of the murder hadn't yet broken in the neighbourhood. When it did, there would be the usual small crowd of onlookers standing with careful nonchalance at a prudent distance, trying to give the impression that they were loitering there by chance.

Dalgliesh said, almost as if he were talking to himself: "Father Presteign is a remarkable man. He's reputed to know more secrets both in and out of the confessional than any other man in London. He's become a kind of personal chaplain to writers who are High Anglicans—novelists, poets, scholars. They would hardly consider themselves properly baptized, married, shriven or buried without Father Presteign's assistance. It's a pity he'll never be able to write his autobiography."

The church was open. The great oak door swung easily inward to Dalgliesh's push and they passed into a cavernous sweet-scented dimness pierced with a momentary flicker of candles like distant stars. As Kate's eyes grew accustomed to the darkness the great church took shape and she paused for a moment in amazement. Eight slender marble pillars rose to a roof set with medallions of red and blue, and flanked by carved angels, crimp-haired, their wings outstretched. Behind the high altar was a gilded reredos; in the glow of a crimson lamp she could just make out the haloes of saints and the mitres of bishops rank on golden rank. The south wall was completely covered with a fresco in pink and blue. It looked like an illustration to Scott's *Ivanhoe*. The opposite one was similarly adorned, but the work had stopped halfway, as if the money had run out.

Dalgliesh said: "One of Butterfield's later efforts, but I'm not sure he didn't go too far this time. What do you think of it?"

The question, unexpected and unlike him, disconcerted her. After a moment's thought, she said: "I suppose it's impressive, but I don't feel at home in it."

The answer had been honest. She wished it didn't sound inadequate.

"I wonder if Mrs. Carpenter was—at home in it."

The only other person visible was a cheerful-faced, middle-aged woman who was polishing and dusting the stand which held prayer books and guides to the church. She gave the visitors a brief smile intended, Kate thought, to welcome them while reassuring them that they wouldn't be bothered and that their devotions, if any, would be tactfully ignored. The English, thought Kate, obviously regarded praying much as they did a necessary physical function, something best done in private.

Dalgliesh apologized for interrupting her work: "We're police officers and I'm afraid we're here on police business. Were you in church, I wonder, when a Mrs. Carpenter came in on Sunday afternoon?"

"Mrs. Carpenter? I'm afraid I don't know her. I don't think she's a regular member of the congregation, is she? But I was here on Sunday between services. We try to keep the church open, which means having a rota of people who can come in for a few hours every day. I'm doing two days this week, because Miss Black is in hospital. I may have seen her. Is she in any trouble—Mrs. Carpenter, I mean?"

"I'm afraid that she's been attacked."

"And badly injured? I am sorry." The cheerful face expressed a genuine concern. "Mugged, I suppose. And soon after she left here? That's terrible."

Taking out the photograph of Mrs. Carpenter, Dalgliesh handed it to her. She said at once: "So that's who you mean. Yes, she was here on Sunday afternoon. I remember her very clearly. There were only three people for confession and she was one of them. Confessions are from three to five on Sundays. Father Presteign will be terribly distressed to know she's been hurt. He's in the vestry now, if you want to see him."

Dalgliesh thanked her gravely and put away the photograph. As he and Kate walked together up the side aisle she glanced back. The woman was standing, duster drooping from her hand, looking after them. Meeting Kate's glance, she bent again and began a vigorous polishing, as if caught out in an unseemly curiosity.

The vestry was a large room to the right of the high altar. The door was open and, as they darkened the entrance, an elderly man turned to meet them. He had been standing at a cupboard with a heavy leather-bound book in his hand. Now he placed it on a shelf, shut the cupboard door and said without a trace of surprise: "It's Adam Dalgliesh, isn't it? Please come in. It must be six years since we last met. It's good to see you. You're well, I hope?"

He was less immediately impressive than Kate had envisaged. Somehow she had expected someone taller and with the thin aesthetic face of a scholarly celibate. Father Presteign could be no more than five feet five inches. He was old but gave no impression of weakness. The grey hair was still thick, but cropped rather than shaped, round a moon-shaped face more suited, she felt, to a comedian than to a priest. His mouth was long and humorous. But the eyes behind the horn-rimmed spectacles were as shrewd as they were gentle, and when he spoke she thought that she had seldom heard a more attractive human voice.

Dalgliesh said: "I'm well, thank you, Father. May I introduce Detective Inspector Kate Miskin? I'm afraid we're here on police business."

"I thought you might be. How can I help?"

Dalgliesh again took out the photograph. "I understand that this woman, Mrs. Janet Carpenter, came to confession Sunday afternoon. She lived in Coulston Court, at Number Ten. We found her this morning in her sitting-room with her throat cut. Almost certainly it was murder."

Father Presteign looked at the photograph but did not take it. Then he crossed himself unobtrusively and stood for a moment silently with his eyes closed.

"We need any information you can give which will help us to discover why she was killed and who killed her." Dalgliesh's voice was calm, uncompromising, but gentle.

Father Presteign had expressed neither horror nor surprise, but now he said: "If I can help, then of course I shall. That would be a matter of duty as it would be my wish. But I never met Mrs. Carpenter before Sunday. Everything I now know about her was told to me under the seal of the confessional. I'm sorry, Adam."

"That was rather what I expected, and what I feared."

He made no protest. Was that, thought Kate, all they were going to get? She tried to control her frustration and an emotion closer to anger than disappointment. She said: "You know, of course, that the QC, Venetia Aldridge, has also been murdered. The two deaths are almost certainly connected. Surely you can tell us whether we should still be looking for Miss Aldridge's killer?"

His eyes looked into hers and she saw in them a pity which she thought was as much for her as it was for the two dead women. Resenting it, she resented, too, the implacable will which she knew couldn't be broken.

She said more roughly: "It's murder, Father. Whoever killed these two could kill again. Surely you can tell us that one thing. Did Mrs. Carpenter confess to killing Venetia Aldridge? Are we wasting our time looking for someone else? Mrs. Carpenter's dead. She can't care now whether you break faith with her. Wouldn't she want you to help? Wouldn't she want her murderer to be caught?"

Father Presteign said: "My child, it isn't Janet Carpenter I'd be breaking faith with." Then he turned to Dalgliesh. "Where is she now?"

"She's been taken to the mortuary. The PM will be held later today, but the cause of death was apparent. As I said, her throat was cut."

"Is there someone I should see? She lived alone, I believe."

"As far as we know she lived alone and there's no family. But you must know more about her than I, Father."

Father Presteign said: "If there's no one else to take responsibility, I will help with the funeral arrangements. I think she would like a requiem. You will keep in touch, Adam?"

"Of course. In the meantime we will get on with our inquiries."

Father Presteign walked down the nave with them. When they reached the door he turned to Dalgliesh. "There may be a way in which I can help. Before she left the church, Mrs. Carpenter said that she would write me a letter. After I'd read it I could make what use of it I thought right, including showing it to the police. She may have changed her mind: no letter may exist. But if she did write it, and if as she promised that letter gives me the authority to pass on to you whatever it contains, then I shall consider doing so."

Dalgliesh said: "She did post a letter yesterday evening. To be accurate, she was seen leaving the house with an envelope in her hand."

"Then perhaps that is the letter she promised to write. If she sent it by first-class post, it may arrive tomorrow morning, although one can never be sure. It's rather strange that, being so close, she didn't put it through the church door, but perhaps she thought the post would be safer. The letters are usually delivered shortly after nine o'clock. I shall be here by eight-thirty to say an early Mass. The church will be open, if you care to come back then."

They thanked him and shook hands. There was, thought Kate, nothing more to be said.

34

It was six o'clock of the same day. In his room in Chambers, Hubert Langton stood at the window looking out over the gas-lit court.

He said to Laud: "I was standing here—remember?—two days before Venetia died and we talked of her becoming Head of Chambers. It seems an eternity away and yet it's only eight days. And now this second murder. Horror heaped on horror. It may have been Venetia's world, but it isn't mine."

Laud said: "It's nothing to do with Chambers."

"Inspector Tarrant seemed to think that it was."

"He also seemed to think—although we had difficulty prising it out of him—that Janet Carpenter died between seven and eight. If so most of us here have got the best of alibis—Adam Dalgliesh in person. It's over now, Hubert. At least the worst is."

"Is it?"

"Of course. Janet Carpenter killed Venetia."

"The police don't seem to think so."

"It may not suit them to think so, but they'll never prove otherwise. They've got their motive now. Tarrant more or less admitted that when he told us who Mrs. Carpenter was. I can picture exactly how it happened. Mrs. Watson was unexpectedly absent. Mrs. Carpenter found herself alone in Chambers with only Venetia still working. She couldn't resist the opportunity of confronting her, accusing her of being indirectly responsible for the death of her granddaughter. I can imagine how Venetia would have responded. She had been opening letters. The paper-knife was there on the desk. Carpenter seized it and drove it in. She may not have meant to kill, but kill she did. She would almost certainly have got away with manslaughter if it had ever come to trial."

"And this second murder?"

"Can you see anyone in Chambers cutting a woman's throat? Leave Janet Carpenter's death to the police, Hubert. Solving murder is their job, not ours."

Langton didn't answer at once. Then he said: "How is Simon taking it?"

"Simon? Relieved, I imagine, as we all are. It was uncomfortable knowing oneself to be a suspect. The experience had its initial interest, if only as a novelty, but it became tedious when prolonged. Incidentally, Simon seems to have taken against Dalgliesh. I can't think why, the man was perfectly civil."

He was silent for a moment, looking across at Langton, then said more gently: "Hadn't we better settle the agenda for the 31st? Are you happy with the main items and with the order? Rupert and Catherine are offered the two places in Chambers. Harry gets a year's extension with the possibility of a second. Valerie is confirmed as Chambers secretary and we advertise for a permanent second girl to help her out. Harry tells me she's been too pressed recently. You announce your retirement at the end of the year and it's agreed that I take over. And I suggest that for the benefit of the Salisbury contingent you begin with a brief statement about Venetia's death. As the police don't exactly confide in us there's not much to tell, but Chambers will expect a statement. Don't let it get out of hand. We don't want questions, conjecture. Keep it short and factual. And are you sure you want to announce your retirement at the end of the meeting, not the beginning?"

"At the end. We don't want to waste time on formal expressions of regret, however insincere."

"Don't under-rate what you've done for Chambers. But there'll be a more appropriate time to say a formal goodbye. By the way, I had a telephone call from Salisbury. They think we should begin the meeting with two minutes' silence. I tried the suggestion out on Desmond. He said he would so far subjugate principle as to present himself suitably attired for any service we care to arrange in the Temple Church, but that there were some hypocrisies which even Chambers ought to jib at."

Langton didn't smile. He came over to his desk and picked up the draft agenda written in Laud's elegant hand. He said: "We haven't begun to think of the memorial service. Venetia isn't even cremated yet, and next week everything she opposed will be agreed. Does nothing of us last once we are dead?"

"For the lucky ones, perhaps love. Influence, maybe. But not power. The dead are powerless. You're the churchman, Hubert. Remember Ecclesiastes? Something about a living dog being better than a dead lion?"

Langton said quietly: " 'For the living know that they shall die: but the dead know not any thing, neither have they any more a reward; for the memory of them is forgotten. Also their love, and their hatred, and their envy, is now perished; neither have they any more a portion for ever in any thing that is done under the sun.' "

Laud said: "And that includes decisions in Chambers. If you're happy, Hubert, I'll take the agenda and get it typed and copied. I suppose some people will complain that it should have been circulated earlier, but we've had other things on our minds."

He moved over to the door, then turned and looked back. Langton thought: Does he know, is he going to tell me, or is he going to ask?—and realized that Laud was thinking exactly the same of him. But nothing further was said by either of them. Laud went out and closed the door behind him.

35

It was Kate whom Dalgliesh asked to accompany him to the church next morning, leaving Piers to get on with the inquiries at the Middle Temple. It seemed to Kate that this second murder had for a time eclipsed the first, had produced in the team a sense of added urgency and more immediate danger than the death of Miss Aldridge. If the same man was responsible—and she had little doubt that the murder of Mrs. Carpenter had been the work of a man—then he was one of that dangerous breed who are prepared to kill and kill again.

Father Presteign was at the church before them and answered the side door to Kate's ring. Leading them down the short passage and into the vestry, he asked: "Would you care for some coffee?"

"If it isn't a trouble, Father."

He opened a cupboard and took down a large jar of ground beans, a packet of sugar and two mugs. Filling the kettle and switching it on, he said: "The milk will be here soon. Joe Pollard brings it with him. He serves at Mass on Wednesdays. He and I will have ours later. That'll be him now. I think I can hear his bike."

A young man made immense by a motorcycling outfit more appropriate for a ride across Antarctica than for an English autumn day, burst into the vestry and took off his helmet.

"Morning, Father. Sorry I cut it fine. It's my day to get the kids' breakfast and the traffic's hell on Ken High Street."

Introducing him, Father Presteign said: "Joe always complains of the traffic but I've never known it inconvenience him when I ride pillion. We dodge and weave between the buses in the most exhilarating fashion, followed, I have to say, by imprecations."

Joe, having shed leathers, scarves and jumpers with extraordinary speed, had buttoned himself into a cassock and pulled a cotta over his head with the ease of long practice.

Father Presteign silently robed and said: "I'll see you after Mass, Adam."

The door closed behind them. It was a solid door of iron-bound oak and they could hear nothing beyond it. Presumably, thought Kate, a congregation of sorts had assembled. She pictured the early-morning faithfuls: a few old women, fewer men, perhaps some of the homeless finding the door open and seeking warmth. Had Mrs. Carpenter been one of them? She thought not. Hadn't Father Presteign said she wasn't a regular member of the congregation? So what had brought her into the church to seek his advice, to make her confession, to receive absolution? Absolution from what? Well, with luck they would know before they left the building. That was, of course, if Mrs. Carpenter had written the promised letter. Perhaps they were investing too much hope in what Father Presteign had said. She had been seen leaving the flats with a letter in her hand; it could have been to anyone.

Kate disciplined herself to sit in patience. It was obvious that Dalgliesh didn't intend to talk and she had learned very early to be sensitive to his moods and to be silent when he was silent. Usually it wasn't difficult. He was one of the few people she knew who could produce by their silence not embarrassment but a sense of quiet relief. But now she would have welcomed talk, an acknowledgement that he shared her impatience and anxieties. He was sitting very still, the dark head bent over his mug of black coffee, his fingers cupped round it but not touching it. He could have been waiting for it to cool, or perhaps he had forgotten it was there.

At last she said, getting up: "We won't hear the post from here. I think I'll wait by the door."

He didn't reply. She went out into the narrow passage, which led to the side door, mug in hand. The minutes passed with infuriating slowness. But away from Dalgliesh she could at least indulge her impatience by a vigorous pacing and by constant glances at her watch. Nine o'clock. Hadn't Father Presteign said that the post came at nine or shortly after? "Shortly after" could mean anything. They could be waiting for half an hour. Five past nine. Seven minutes past. And then it came. She heard no footsteps outside the heavy door, but the letter-box was thrust open and the post fell through with a thud: two large manila envelopes; a couple of bills; a large, bulky white envelope marked "Private" and addressed to Father Presteign, an educated hand, the hand of someone who wrote with confidence. She had seen envelopes of this size and make in Mrs. Carpenter's flat. This was surely what they were waiting for. She took it back to Dalgliesh and said: "It's come, sir."

He took the letter and laid it on the table, then placed the rest of the post in a neat pile beside it.

"It looks like it, Kate."

She tried to conceal her impatience. The letter, looking preternaturally white against the dark oak of the table, lay there like a portent.

"How long is it likely to take, sir, the Mass?"

"Low Mass with no sermon or homily, about half an hour."

She glanced surreptitiously at her watch; just over fifteen minutes to go.

But it was a little before the half-hour that the door opened and Father Presteign and Joe reappeared. Joe disrobed, clambered into his multi-layered biking gear and became metamorphosed into a huge metallic insect.

He said: "I'll not wait for coffee this morning, Father. Oh, I forgot now, Mary asked me to tell you that she'll be doing the flowers for Our Lady on Sunday as Miss Pritchard is ill. You did hear that she'd had her op, Father?"

"Yes, I heard, Joe. I'll be visiting her this afternoon if she's well enough for visitors. Thank Mary for me, will you?"

They went out together, Joe still talking. The outer door closed with a clang. Kate had a sense that with Joe's departure the normal world, the world she lived in and understood, had left with him, leaving her mentally isolated and physically ill at ease. The smell of incense had suddenly become oppressive, the vestry itself claustrophobic and oddly threatening. She had an irrational urge to pick up the letter and take it out into the fresh air to be read for what it was—a letter, important, perhaps even vital to their investigations, but still only a letter.

Father Presteign had returned. He took it up and said, "I'll leave you for a moment, Adam," and went out again into the church.

"You don't think he'll destroy it?" Kate wished the words unsaid as soon as they had left her mouth.

Dalgliesh replied: "No, he won't destroy it. Whether he gives it to us will depend on what's in it."

They waited. It was a long wait. Kate thought: He must give it to us. It's evidence. He can't conceal evidence. There must be a way of compelling him to hand it over. You can't bind a letter under the seal of the confessional. And why is he taking so long? It can't take him over ten minutes to read a letter. What is he doing out there? Perhaps he's in front of the altar praying to his God.

There came into her mind for no reason she could imagine snatches of another conversation she had had with Piers about his curious choice of academic subject. She wondered now at his patience under her questioning.

"What does this theology do for you? After all, you spent three years on it. Teach you how to live? Answer some of the questions?"

"What questions?"

"The big questions. The ones there's no sense in asking. Why are we here? What happens when we die? Have we really free will? Does God exist?"

"No, it doesn't answer questions. It's like philosophy, it tells you what questions to ask."

"I know what questions to ask. It's the answers I'm after. And what about learning how to live? Isn't that philosophy too? What's yours?"

The reply had come easily but, she had thought, with honesty: "To get as much happiness as I can. Not to harm others. Not to whine. In that order."

It was as reasonable a basis for living as any she'd heard. Effectively it was her own. You didn't need to go to Oxford to learn that. But what did it say when confronted with a tortured and murdered child, or with that body lying like a butchered animal, the throat cut to the bone? Perhaps Father Presteign thought he had the answer. If so, could it really be found in this dim, incense-laden air? Well, you had to believe in your job whether you were a priest or a policeman. You had at some point to say: This is what I choose to believe. To this I shall give my loyalty. With her it had been the police service. Father Presteign had chosen a more esoteric commitment. It would be difficult for both of them if their loyalties were to conflict.

The door opened and Father Presteign came in. He was very pale. He held out the letter to Dalgliesh. He said: "She has authorized me to give it to you. I'll leave you to read it in peace. You'll need to take it, I assume."

"Yes, we shall need to take it, Father. I will, of course, give you a receipt for it."

Father Presteign had not replaced it in the envelope.

Dalgliesh said: "It's longer than I expected. I suppose that's why she didn't catch the Monday post. It must have taken her at least a day to write."

Father Presteign said: "She was an English teacher. Written words were as companionable to her as speech. And I think she needed to write it, to set down the truth, as much for herself as for us. I'll be back before you go."

He went again into the church and closed the door.

Dalgliesh spread the letter out on the table. Kate drew up a chair beside him and they read it together.

36

Janet Carpenter had wasted no time on preliminaries. This was written out of a need which went beyond any promise to Father Presteign.

Dear Father,

It was almost a relief to me when Rosie killed herself. I know that's a terrible thing to write; it was a terrible truth to have to confess. But I don't think I could have gone on living with her grief and stayed sane. She needed me there, I couldn't have left her. We were shackled together by grief—the grief for my son, the death of her daughter—but it was Emily's death that killed her. And if she hadn't hoarded those Distalgesic tablets, washed them down with that bottle of red wine, she would have died in the end, of grief, but more slowly. She moved about the house like the walking dead, dull-eyed, performing small household tasks as if she had been programmed to do them. Her occasional smile was like a twitch of the mouth. Her uncomplaining docile silence was almost more terrible than the outbursts of wild sobbing. When I tried to bring comfort by silently enclosing her in my arms, she didn't resist or respond. There were no words. Neither of us had any words. Perhaps that was the trouble. I knew only that her heart was broken; and I know now that the phrase isn't a sentimental exaggeration; everything that made her Rosie was broken. She lived every waking hour in the black horror of Emily's murder. I'm only surprised that, so drained, so depersonalized, she found the strength and the will to end the torment and to write me that last coherent note.

I grieved with her and for her. Of course I did, I had loved Emily too. I wept for Emily, for the Emily I knew and for all dead, violated children. But for me, grief was subsumed in anger—a terrible, all-consuming anger—and from the start this anger focused on Venetia Aldridge.

If Dermot Beale hadn't been found guilty I might have planned somehow to make him pay. But Beale was in prison with a recommended minimum sentence of twenty years. I would be dead before he got his freedom. Instead my hatred found its target, its necessary release, in the woman who had defended him at his first trial. She had defended him brilliantly; it had been for her a great forensic triumph, a masterly cross-examination of the Crown witnesses, another personal accolade. And Dermot Beale had gone free to kill again. This time it was Emily who, cycling home from the village less than a mile away with her basket piled with groceries, had heard the sound of his car wheels on that lonely road. And this time Aldridge wasn't available for the defence. I have heard that she never represents the same client twice. Perhaps even she wouldn't have the arrogance for that. This time he didn't get off.

I don't think that my hatred for Aldridge was naïve. I knew the argument, knew what any of her fellow defence lawyers would say on her behalf. She was doing her job. An accused man, however obvious his guilt may appear to be before the facts are known, however heinous the crime, however unprepossessing his appearance or repellent his character, is entitled to a defence. His lawyer is not required to believe in his innocence, only to test the evidence against him and, if there is a hole in the case for the Crown, to enlarge it so that he can crawl through it to safety. She was playing a lucrative game according to complicated rules designed, or so it seemed to me, to disadvantage her opponents, a game that was sometimes won at the cost of a human life. All I wanted was for her just once to pay the price of victory. Most of us have to live with the results of what we do. Actions have consequences. That's one of the earliest lessons we have to learn as children, and some of us never learn it. She won her victories and that, for her, was the end; others have had to live with the consequences, others have paid the price. This time I wanted her to pay.

It was only after Rosie's death that this resentment and anger grew into what I now have to accept was an obsession. Perhaps this was partly because, relieved of the need to try to care and comfort Rosie, my mind and heart were free to brood on the events. It may also have been because after Rosie's death I lost my faith. I don't mean my Christian faith, that High Church Tractarian tradition of sacramental worship in which I had been brought up and in which I had always found a natural home. I no longer believed in God. I wasn't angry with Him, that at least would have been understandable. God must be used to human anger. After all, He invites it. I just woke up one morning to the same grief, the same dull daily tasks, and knew with certainty that God was dead. It was as if all my life I had been hearing the beating of an unseen heart which was now for ever stilled.

I wasn't aware of regret, only of an immense solitude and a great loneliness. It felt as if the whole living world had died with God. I began to have a recurrent dream from which I would wake up, not terrified and screaming as Rosie would start up from her nightmares of Emily's death, but weighed down with a profound sadness. In the dream I would be standing on a lonely beach at sunset with a great sea rolling and tumbling over my ankles and sucking the shingle from under my feet. There would be no birds and I knew that the sea was without life, that the whole earth was without life. Then they would begin walking out of the sea, passing me without looking or speaking, a great army of the dead. I saw Ralph and Emily and Rosie walking with them. They didn't see me or hear me, and when I called out to them and tried to touch them they were cold sea mist in my hands. I would stumble downstairs and switch on the BBC World Service desperate to hear a reassuring human voice. It was out of this emptiness, this loneliness, that my obsession grew.

At first it was as simple as wishing that someone would kill Aldridge's daughter and then go free, but that was for my private imaginings. It wasn't something I could arrange, nor was it something that in my heart I really wanted. I hadn't become a monster. But from that private fantasy there grew a more realistic imagining. Suppose that a young man accused of a serious crime, murder, rape, robbery, was successfully defended by Aldridge and then, after the acquittal, set out to seduce, even perhaps to marry, her daughter? I knew that she had a daughter. There had been a picture of them together after one of her most successful cases, in one of those mother-and-daughter articles which had become popular in the weekend supplements. The photograph, unsentimental but carefully posed, had shown the two of them together, the girl, Octavia, staring at the camera, scarcely troubling to hide her embarrassed reluctance. It told me more than the whole article, carefully written, obviously approved by its main subject. Here, under the pitiless eye of the camera, was the old story, the beautiful successful mother, the plain resentful daughter.

If this was something I might be able to contrive I would need money. The young man would have to be bribed, and bribed with a capital sum in cash that he couldn't resist. I would need to move to London to get to know Venetia Aldridge's life, her routine, where she and her daughter lived, in which court she was next to appear. I would have to attend as many of her trials as possible, whenever the crime was serious and the defendant a young male. All of this seemed possible. I had already decided to sell the house I had shared with Rosie and Emily and which I owned. The mortgage had long ago been paid off. The sale would provide enough for me to buy a small convenient flat in London and have more than enough left for the bribery. I would try to find a cleaning job in the Middle Temple in the hope of moving eventually to Aldridge's Chambers. It would all take time, but I was in no hurry. The girl, Octavia, was still only sixteen. My plan required that she should be of age; I didn't want her mother making her a ward of court in order to prevent an unsuitable marriage. And I had to choose the right man. On that choice depended the whole success of the enterprise. There was no room for failure here. I had one great advantage: I had been a schoolteacher for more than thirty years, for much of the time teaching adolescents. I thought I would be able to recognize the qualities I was looking for: conceit, acting ability, unscrupulousness, greed. And, once I had a job in her Chambers, I would have access to Venetia Aldridge's papers. I would know more about his life, his past, than he would ever know of mine.

It all went according to plan. The details don't matter; the police will know them by now anyway. They have spoken, I know, to Miss Elkington. I ended where I had hoped to end, with a flat in London where I could expect to be private, a job in Aldridge's Chambers, occasional access to her home. It all went so smoothly that I felt that, were I superstitious, I would be able to believe that my great revenge was pre-ordained, my small craft launched among clouds of propitiatory incense. I didn't use the word "revenge" then. I saw myself in a less ignoble role, setting out to redress an injustice, to teach a lesson. I know now that what I was planning was revenge and the satisfaction of revenge, that my hatred of Venetia Aldridge was both more personal and more complicated than I was willing to admit. I know now that it was wrong, it was evil. I also know that it kept me sane.

From the beginning I think I accepted that success would be largely a matter of chance. I might never find a suitable young man, or if I did he might not succeed with Octavia. This knowledge that events weren't entirely under my control seemed paradoxically to make the enterprise more rational and feasible. And I wasn't changing my whole life for a caprice. I needed to sell the house, to get away, to free myself from the curious glances of strangers and the embarrassed sympathy of friends, that overworked word which can conveniently cover anything from love to the mutual tolerance of neighbours. When I told them, "Don't write, I need a few months absolutely alone, free of the past," I could see the relief in their eyes. They had found it hard to cope with an overwhelming grief. Some friends, particularly those with children, made no attempt but, after a single letter or visit, distanced themselves as if I were infectious. There are some horrors, and the murder of a child is one, which probe our deepest fears, fears we hardly dare acknowledge in case a malignant fate senses the depths of our imagined horror and strikes triumphantly to make it real. The egregiously unfortunate have always been the lepers of the earth.

And then I met Mr. Froggett. I still don't know his first name. He will always be Mr. Froggett to me, and I Mrs. Hamilton to him. I used my maiden name, feeling that its familiarity would at least prevent me from giving myself away. I didn't confide in him my name, my past, where I lived or where I worked. We first met in the public gallery of Number Two Court at the Old Bailey. There are regulars who go to important or interesting trials, particularly at the Old Bailey, and after that first meeting I saw him every time I went, an unassuming little man of about my own age, always neatly dressed, who, like me, would sit patiently through the longueurs of the trial when the sensation-seekers had departed in search of livelier entertainment and, from time to time, would make notes with his small delicate hands, as if he were monitoring the performance of the chief actors. And what we were seeing was a performance, that was its fascination. It was a play in which some of the characters knew their words and the plot, some were awkward amateurs, making their first appearance on a frightening, unfamiliar stage, but all had their roles assigned in a performance which afforded the ultimate audience satisfaction: no one knew the end.

After we had seen each other about half a dozen times, Mr. Froggett began to greet me with a tentative good-morning, but he didn't speak until I was overcome with a sudden faintness during the prosecution's opening speech in a particularly horrible case of child cruelty and abuse. It was the first of such cases I had sat through. I had told myself that there would be times when I would find it hard to go on, but I had never envisaged a case like this: the gowned and bewigged prosecuting counsel, in his quiet educated voice, outlining without embellishment, and apparently without emotion, the torture and degradation of young boys in care. And that case was no use to me. I early realized that most sex cases weren't. The men concerned were either repellent or more often pathetic creatures whom I could reject as unsuitable for my purpose as soon as they appeared in the dock. Now I put my head between my knees and the worst of the faintness passed. I knew I had to leave and I did so as unobtrusively as I could, but I was in the middle of a tightly packed bench and inevitably I caused a disturbance.

When I reached the concourse I found the little man at my side. He said: "Please forgive the intrusion but I saw that you were ill and that you have no one with you. Could I offer assistance? Perhaps you would permit me to take you for a cup of tea. There is a respectable little café I use which is quite close. It's really very clean."

The words, the tone, the careful formality amounting to diffidence were essentially out of date. I remember that I had a ridiculous picture of us standing together on the deck of the *Titanic*: "Please permit me, madam, to offer you my protection and to assist you into this lifeboat." Looking into eyes which were genuinely concerned behind the thick glass of his spectacles, I had no distrust of him. My generation knows by instinct—one lost to young women of today—when we can trust a man. So we went together to the respectable little café, one of those innumerable eating places catering for office workers or tourists, where you can get freshly made sandwiches made up from a variety of fillings set out in dishes under the counter—eggs, mashed sardines, tuna fish, ham—together with good coffee and strong tea. He led me to a square table in the corner covered with a checked red-and-white cloth, and then fetched two cups of tea and two chocolate éclairs. Afterwards he walked with me to the underground station and said goodbye. We exchanged names, but nothing more. He didn't ask whether I had far to travel or where I lived, and I sensed in him a natural reluctance to seem to pry, a concern that I shouldn't feel that he was intruding, using his act of kindness to force on me an intimacy which I might not want.

And so began our acquaintanceship. It wasn't friendship—how could it be when I confided so little?—but it had some of the comforts of friendship without its commitment. We got used to having tea together after the court rose at the same café or at one similar. At our first meeting I was worried, not that he would become inquisitive, but that it would increasingly seem odd to him that I was so uncommunicative, and even odder that I should sit there week after week listening to the sad, often predictable recital of human weakness—weakness and wickedness. But that, it appeared, was the last thing to worry him. He was obsessed with the criminal law, nothing seemed more natural to him than that I should share this compelling interest. He confided much about himself and seemed not to notice that I told so little. On our third meeting he told me something which, for a minute, terrified me, until I realized that it posed no real danger, and that it could even be one more auspicious sign that my enterprise would succeed. He had taught at a prep school owned by Venetia Aldridge's father, had known her well as a child. He claimed—and this was the first time I detected in him evidence of a certain conceit which, once noticed, seemed to be part of his personality—that it was he who had given her the taste for law, had set her on the first steps of her brilliant career. My hand shook as I raised my cup of tea, spilling a little bit in the saucer. I waited a second until the spasm of shaking passed, then calmly poured it back. Not looking at him, I made my voice steady, the question no more than one of casual interest.

"Do you see her now? I expect she'd be grateful to know you're still interested in her career. She'd probably arrange for you to have a seat in the court."

"No, I don't see her. I'm careful not to place myself where I might catch her eye—not that there's much danger of that. But it might seem like pushing myself forward. It was a long time ago, she may have forgotten me. But I try not to miss any of her cases. It's my hobby now, watching her career, but of course it isn't always easy finding out where she's appearing."

I said on impulse: "I could probably help. I have a friend who works in her Chambers. Of course, she wouldn't ask directly, she's in quite a humble capacity, but there must be court lists. I could probably find out for you when Miss Aldridge is next due to appear and at what court."

Mr. Froggett was genuinely, almost pathetically, grateful. He said,

"You'll need my address," and, taking out his notebook, wrote it down, keeping his small hands close together like paws. Then he carefully tore out the page and handed it to me. If he thought it odd that I didn't, in a reciprocal gesture of confidence, give him my address, he made no sign. I saw that he lived—I expect he still lives—in a flat in Goodmayes, Essex, I imagine in one of those modern blocks of small identical characterless apartments. After that I would send him a postcard from time to time, just with a date and a place on it— Winchester Crown Court, 3 October—and sign it with my initials, J.H. I didn't always see him in court, of course. If the defendant was a woman, or was obviously unsuitable for my purpose, I didn't bother to turn up.

But those shared half-hours or so of undemanding companionship became some of the happiest interludes of my obsessed life. Perhaps "happiest" is too positive a word. Happiness is not an emotion I feel now, nor ever expect to feel. But there was a kind of contentment, a restfulness and a sense of belonging again to the real world, which I found comforting. We must have looked a strange couple to anyone interested, but, of course, no one was interested. This was London, the city workers chatting together before they began their journeys home, the tourists with their cameras, their maps, their foreign jabber, the occasional solitary drinker of tea, they came in without a glance in our direction. It is all so recent, and yet it already seems a distant memory: the rhythmic groan of the city breaking against the windows like the roar of a distant sea, the hiss of the coffee machine, the smell of toasted sandwiches and the clatter of cups and beakers. Against this background we would talk over the details of the day, comparing our views of the witnesses, assessing their veracity, discussing the conduct of counsel, the possible verdict, whether the judge was hostile.

Only once did I get close, perhaps dangerously close, to my own obsession. The day had been given up to the prosecution evidence. I said: "But she must know that he's guilty."

"It isn't important. It's her job to defend him whether she thinks he's guilty or not."

"I know that. But surely it helps if you believe your client is innocent."

"It may help, but it can't be a necessary qualification to take on the job." Then he said: "Look at me. Suppose I were accused— wrongly accused—of some criminal offence, perhaps an act of inde-

cency against a young girl. I live alone, I'm solitary, I'm not very pre-
possessing. Suppose my solicitor had to go begging from one set of
Chambers to another, desperately seeking a barrister who believed
me innocent before I could mount a defence. Our law rests on the
presumption of innocence. There are countries where an arrest by the
police is taken as a sign of guilt and the subsequent court procedures
are little more than a recital of the case for the prosecution. We
should be grateful not to live in such a country."

He spoke with extraordinary force. For the first time I sensed in
him a personal belief, emotional and deeply felt. Up till then I had
seen his obsession with the law as no more than an overwhelming intellectual interest. Now, for the first time, I saw signs of a passionate
moral commitment to an ideal.

Although Mr. Froggett travelled to any Crown court where Venetia Aldridge was due to appear, he liked it best when she prosecuted
or defended at the Old Bailey. No other place, for him, had the romance of Court Number One at the Bailey. "Romance" seems an odd
word to use of a place whose origins go back to Newgate, to the horrors of those early prisons, the public executions, the pressing yard
where prisoners endured the torture of being pressed to death by
weights to safeguard the inheritance of their families. Mr. Froggett
knew about these things, the history of criminal law fascinated but
never seemed to oppress him. His obsession may have had its element
of morbidity—it was, after all, the criminal law which enthralled
him—but I never detected ghoulishness and would have found his
company disagreeable if I had. His was essentially an intellectual obsession. Mine was very different and yet, as the months passed, I
began to understand his passion, began even to share it.

Occasionally, when there was a case of particular interest in
Number One Court, I would join him there even if Venetia Aldridge
wasn't the defending counsel. It was important that I did; he must
never suspect that I was interested only in the defence. So, time after
time, I joined the queue at the public entrance, went through the security screen, climbed the seemingly never-ending bare stairs to the
hall outside the public gallery, took my seat and waited for the appearance of Mr. Froggett. Often he was there before me. He liked to
sit in the second row and thought it odd of me not to share this pref-
erence until I realized that there was little chance of Miss Aldridge
looking up, let alone of her recognizing me. I always wore a hat with
a brim and my smartest coat; she had seen me only in my working

overalls. There was no real risk, yet it was several weeks before I first felt happy sitting so close to the front.

My view of the court was almost as good as that of the judge. Below, to the left, was the large dock with its glass screen at the back and the sides, opposite us the jury, to the right the judge, and below us the barristers. Mr. Froggett told me that the front row in the public gallery was the place from which the only photograph of a defendant being sentenced to death had been taken. The people in the dock had been Crippen and his mistress, Ethel Le Neve. The photograph had been printed in a daily paper and it was this that had led to the new law that there could be no photography in court.

He was full of these snippets of history and information. When I commented on the smallness of the witness box, the neat wood stand with a canopy above it like a minuscule pulpit, he explained that the canopy was a relic of the days when courts were held in the open air and a witness needed protection. When I wondered aloud why the judge, splendid in his scarlet, never sat in the centre seat, he told me that this was reserved for the Lord Mayor of London, the Chief Magistrate of the City. Although he no longer presides at trials, he arrives in state four times a year and processes through the Grand Hall to Number One Court, the procession headed by the City Marshal, the Sheriffs, the Swordbearer and the Common Cryer carrying the sword and mace. Mr. Froggett spoke with regret; it was a procession he would have liked to have seen.

He told me too that this was the court in which some of the greatest criminal trials of the century had been held. Seddon, found guilty of murdering his lodger, Miss Barrow, with arsenic; Rouse of the Blazing Car Murder; Haigh, who had dissolved his victims in acid—all had been sentenced to death in that dock. The stairs beneath it had been trodden by men and women in the throes of a desperate hope or filled with the terror of death; some had been dragged down screaming or moaning. Somehow I had expected the very air of the courtroom to be polluted by the faint, half-imagined taint of terror; but I breathed it feeling nothing. Perhaps it was the very ordered dignity of the court—smaller, more graceful, more intimate than I had imagined, the richness of the splendid carving of the royal coat of arms behind the dais, the sixteenth-century Sword of Justice of the City, the robes and wigs, the courteous formality, the unraised voices; all imposed a sense of order and reason, and of the possibility of justice. And yet it was an arena; it was as much an arena as if the floor had

been strewn with blood-soaked straw and the antagonists had entered to the sound of trumpets, half naked, with their breastplates and swords, to make their obeisance to Caesar.

And it was in Court Number One at the Old Bailey that my search ended. It was here that I first saw Ashe. By the third day of the trial I knew that I had found my man. If I could still have prayed, I would have been praying for an acquittal. But I felt no real anxiety. This, too, was pre-ordained. I watched him day after day as he sat there, motionless and upright, his eyes on the judge. I sensed the power, the intelligence, the ruthlessness, the greed. My concentration on him was so intense that, when, for the only time, he looked up at the public gallery and scanned us with a glance of contempt, I felt a momentary fear that he had guessed my purpose there and was seeking out my face.

I left the court as soon as the verdict was announced. Mr. Froggett was, I know, hoping that we might have tea together and talk about the finer points of the defence. As I pushed my way out, he was on my heels saying: "You know the point when she won the case, don't you? You recognized that fatal question?"

I told him that I had to hurry, that I had someone arriving for the evening and must get home to cook. But we walked together to the Central Line at St Paul's Station, he to go east, I west. I had it all planned. First the train to Notting Hill Gate, then by the District or Circle Line to Earls Court, a few minutes in my flat to write the two notes to Ashe, and then off at once to his address. The notes—one for the front door, one for the back—took only minutes. I had decided weeks ago what I would say: the subtle flattery, the appeal to curiosity, the bribe which might not make him co-operate but would certainly make him open the door. I wrote it carefully but didn't print it: it had to be personal. Rereading it, I didn't think I could do better.

"Dear Mr. Ashe. Forgive me for intruding on you in this way but I have a proposal to put to you. I'm not a journalist and I have no connection with officialdom, the police, social services, or any other busybodies. I have a job I need doing and you are the only one who can do it successfully. If you succeed, the payment is twenty-five thousand pounds in cash. The job isn't illegal or dangerous but it does require skill and intelligence. It is, of course, confidential. Please see me. If your answer is no I won't bother you again. I am waiting outside."

I had planned that, if there were lights in the house, I would put the letter through the front-door letter-box, ring or knock and then

quickly conceal myself. He had to read the note before he saw me. If he wasn't at home I would put a note through both the front and back doors and await his return, preferably in the garden if I could gain access.

I had his address, but until the trial was over I didn't visit the house; it would have been too like tempting fate; but I knew that it was on Westway stretching out from Shepherd's Bush. It wasn't a road I normally used. If there were buses that went there, I had never needed to take them. So, to save time and energy, I decided on a taxi, giving the driver a house number twenty away from the one I needed. I would walk the last hundred yards or so, arriving without attracting the notice of neighbours. And by now it was getting dark. I needed the darkness.

But when the cab turned off the main road, onto a slip road, and then drew up, I thought for a moment that something was wrong with the engine and that he had been forced to stop. Surely no one could still be living in this wasteland? Right and left, floodlit in the glare of the overhead lamps as if it were a film set, stretched an urban desolation of boarded-up windows and front doors, peeling paint and crumbling stucco. The house before which I stood had part of its roof missing, where demolition had already begun, whilst to the left of it the destruction had been completed and no roofs were visible behind the high boarding. On the boarding, beside the official notice announcing the road-widening scheme, were painted the forceful expressions of contemporary protest and the obscene scribbles of incoherent rage, all of them saying, Look at me! Listen to me! Take note of me! I am here! I walked under that hard glare between the dead condemned houses and the ceaseless roar of the uncaring traffic and felt that I was walking through an urban hell.

But when I reached Number 397 I saw that it was one of the few still showing signs of occupation. It was on a corner, the last of a long line of identical semi-detached houses. The three panes of the bay window to the right of the porch were boarded with what looked like reddish-brown metal, as was the smaller window to the left, but the door looked as if it were still in use and there were curtains at the upstairs window. What had once been a small front garden was now a patch of weeds and tufted grasses. The front gate, the wood splintered, swung on its rusted hinges. I could see no lights. Standing in the shelter of the porch, I pushed open the letter-box and put my ear

to the aperture. I could hear nothing. Then I put one of my notes through the slot and thought that I heard it drop.

Next I tried the gate at the side of the house. It was bolted from the other side and too high to climb. There was no access this way. But I preferred to wait at the back of the house rather than loiter in the street. I went back to the road, walked to the corner and turned left down the side street. Here I was luckier. The garden was fenced and, moving slowly down it and putting out an exploring hand, I found a place where a plank had been broken. I kicked it vigorously, choosing a moment when the noise from the road was particularly loud. The wood splintered inward with a crack which I feared would alert the whole street, but all was silent. I leaned against the adjoining planks with all the strength I could muster and heard the nails giving way. The fence was old and the supports swayed as I leaned against them. Now I had a gap just wide enough to squeeze through. I was where I wanted to be: in the back garden.

I didn't need to conceal myself—no eyes could be watching at those dead, boarded-up windows. On each side the homes had been dark since the first crash of the demolition crane's swinging ball. The small garden was a wasteland, grass almost waist-high. Still, I felt happier out of sight, and I squatted between the black wall of the shed and the boarded-up kitchen window.

I had come well prepared: a warm coat, a woolly cap into which I'd tucked my hair, a torch and a paperback copy of twentieth-century poetry. I knew that the wait might be long. He could be out celebrating with friends, although I didn't think of Ashe as a boy who had friends. He could be drinking, and I hoped that he wasn't. Our negotiations would be delicate enough. I needed him sober. He could be looking for sex after the months of deprivation. I didn't think he was. I had seen him only for those few weeks, but I felt that I knew him and this meeting was predestined. Once I would have rejected such a thought as sentimental irrational nonsense. Now, at least with part of my mind, I knew that fate or luck had led me to this moment. I knew that in the end he would come home. Where else could he go?

I sat there, not reading but waiting and thinking, in a silence and seclusion that seemed absolute. I had the feeling, always agreeable to me, that I was absolutely alone since no one in the world knew where I was. But the silence was internal. The world around me was full of noise. I could hear the constant rhythmic boom of the traffic on Westway, seeming sometimes as close as a wild and threatening sea, and at others an almost reassuring memory of that ordinary and safer world of which I had once been part.

I knew when he had come home. The kitchen window, like the others, had been boarded up, but only partly, enough to ensure security. There was a narrow slit at each end. Now a light shone through and I knew that he was in the kitchen. Slowly I drew myself up, feeling the ache of my muscles, and stared at the door willing him to open it. But I knew that he would. Curiosity if nothing else would compel him. And now, at last, the door opened and I saw him, a black silhouette outlined in bright light. He didn't speak. I shone the beam of my torch upwards on my face. Still he didn't speak. I said:

"I see you got my note."

"Of course. Wasn't I meant to?"

I had heard his voice before: those two firmly spoken words in court, "Not guilty," and his answers in examination and cross-examination. It wasn't unattractive but was somehow unnatural, as if he had acquired it by practice and wasn't yet sure whether he wanted to keep it.

He said, "You'd better come in," and stood aside.

I smelt the kitchen before I saw it. These were old, sour smells embedded in wood and walls and in the corners of cupboards, never to be got rid of now until the house crashed down in rubble. But I saw that he had made an attempt to clean up and I found this disconcerting. And then he did something else that surprised me. He took a clean handkerchief from his pocket—I can remember now the size and whiteness of it—and flicked it over a chair seat before motioning me to sit. He sat down opposite and we regarded each other across the stained and torn vinyl that covered the kitchen table.

I had thought of all the ploys I might need. How to appeal to his vanity and his greed without making it obvious that I judged him to be vain and greedy. How to compliment without being suspiciously fulsome. How to offer money without suggesting that he was being patronized or too easily bought. I had expected to be frightened; I would, after all, be alone with a murderer. I'd sat through the whole of the trial. I knew that he had killed his aunt, and killed her no more than yards from where I was sitting now. I had thought about what I'd do if he threatened violence. If I became unduly frightened I would say that someone I trusted knew where I was and would send the police if I didn't return within the hour. But, sitting opposite him, I felt curiously at ease. He didn't at first speak, and we sat in a silence that was neither oppressive nor embarrassing. I had expected him to be more volatile, trickier than he was proving to be.

I put my proposition to him simply and without emotion. I said: "Venetia Aldridge has a daughter, Octavia, who is just eighteen. I'm willing to pay you ten thousand pounds to seduce her and another fifteen thousand if she agrees to marry you. I've seen her. She's not particularly attractive and she isn't happy. That last should make it easier. But she is an only child and she does have money. For me it's a matter of revenge."

He didn't reply, but the eyes looking into mine grew blank, as if he had retreated into a private world of calculation and assessment.

After a minute, he got up, filled and switched on a kettle and took down from a cupboard two mugs and a jar of instant coffee. There was a plastic shopping bag beside the sink. He had called at a super-market for food and a carton of milk on his way home. When the water boiled he poured it onto a heaped teaspoonful of coffee in each of the mugs, placed one in front of me and pushed the sugar and the carton of milk towards me.

He said: "Ten grand to fuck her, another fifteen if we get engaged. Revenge comes dear. You could have Aldridge killed for less."

"If I knew who to hire. If I was willing to risk blackmail. I don't want her killed, I want her to suffer."

"She'd suffer if you kidnapped the girl."

"Too complicated and too risky. How would I do it? Where would I hold her? I don't have access to people who manage these things. The beauty of my revenge is that no one can touch me for it even if they find proof. But they won't find proof. They won't be able to touch either of us. And she'll mind it more than a kidnapping. Kid-napping would gain her sympathy, good publicity. This will hurt her pride."

I knew from the second that the words left my mouth that they were a mistake. I shouldn't have suggested that an engagement to him would be demeaning. I saw the mistake in his eyes, the second of blankness and then the pupils seeming to widen. I saw it in the tens-ing of his body as he leaned across the table towards me. I smelt for the first time his masculinity as I might smell a dangerous animal. I didn't speak too quickly; he mustn't see that I'd recognized my error. I let my words drop into the silence like stones.

"Venetia Aldridge likes to be in control. She doesn't love her daughter, but she wants her to conform, to do her credit, to be respectable. She'd like her to marry a successful lawyer, someone she's chosen and approves of. And she's a very private woman. If you and Octavia are romantically linked it will make a good story for the tabloids; they'll pay good money for it. You can imagine the headlines. It's not the kind of publicity she'd welcome."

It wasn't enough. He said very quietly: "Twenty-five grand for a bit of social embarrassment. I don't believe it."

He was demanding the truth. He knew it already but he was insisting that I put it into words. And if I didn't, then there would be no bargain. It was then that I told him about Dermot Beale and my granddaughter. But I didn't tell him Emily's name. I couldn't bring myself to speak it in that house.

I said: "Aldridge thinks that you killed your aunt. She believes you to be a murderer. That's how she gets her kicks, defending people she thinks are guilty. There's no triumph in defending the innocent. She doesn't love her daughter, that's her guilt. How do you think she'll feel if Octavia gets engaged to someone her mother believes is a killer, someone she defended? She'll have to live with that knowledge—but she won't be able to do a thing about it. That's what I want. That's what I'm willing to pay for."

He said: "And what do you believe? You were at the trial. Do you think I did it?"

"I don't know and I don't care."

He leaned back. I could almost believe that I heard the satisfied release of his breath.

He said: "She thinks she got me off. Is that what you think?"

And now to risk the flattery. "No, you got yourself off. I heard your evidence. If she'd kept you out of the witness box you'd be in prison now."

"That's what she wanted to do at first, keep me out of the box. I told her, no way."

"You were right, but she has to take all the credit. It has to be her victory, her triumph."

Again that curiously companionable pause. Then he said: "So what are you paying for? What do you want me to do?"

"Sleep with the daughter, make her love you. In the end, marry her."

"And what do you want me to do with her after I've married her?"

It was only when he spoke those words that I began to realize what I was dealing with. He wasn't being ironic or sarcastic. The question was perfectly simple. He could have been speaking of an animal, an article of furniture. If I'd been capable of turning back, I would have turned back then.

I said: "You do what you like. Fly to the Caribbean, take her on a cruise, go to the Far East and dump her, buy a house and settle down. You could separate whenever you wanted, divorce without consent after five years. Or her mother would probably pay you off, if that's what you want. You won't lose anyway. After I've paid over the last of the money I shan't be in touch with you again."

I had realized by then that he was both more perceptive and more intelligent than I had expected. That made him more dangerous, but paradoxically it made him easier to deal with. He had summed me up, had known that I wasn't some elderly freak, that the offer was genuine, the money there for the taking. And once he'd known that, then his decision was made.

And that was how it was done, in that stinking kitchen over that stained table, two people without conscience bargaining over a body and soul. Except, of course, that I didn't believe that Octavia had a soul or that there was anything in that room except the two of us, or any power which would alter or influence what we said and did and planned. The bargaining was perfectly amicable, but I knew that I had to let him win. He mustn't be humiliated, even by a minor defeat. Equally, he would despise me for a too-easy capitulation. In the end I gave way to an extra thousand on the preliminary payment and an extra two on the final sum.

He said: "I'll need something to start with. I can get money, I can always get money, but I haven't any yet. I can get it when I want it, but it takes a bit of time."

I heard it again in his voice, the childish swagger, the dangerous mixture of conceit and self-doubt.

I said: "Yes, you'll need money if you're going to take her out, get her interested. She's used to money, she's had it all her life. I've brought two thousand pounds in cash with me. You can take that now and I'll set it off against the preliminary sum."

"No, it has to be extra."

I paused, and then said: "All right, it can be extra."

I'd had no fear that he would take the money from me, perhaps kill me. Why should I fear? He was after much more than two thousand pounds. I bent down to my bag and took out the money. It was in twenty-pound notes.

I said: "It would have been easier if I'd brought fifties, but they're rather suspect at present. There've been so many forgeries. Twenties are safer."

I didn't count them out in front of him, but handed over the four bundles of five hundred pounds each in a rubber band. He didn't count them either. He left them in front of him on the table, and then said: "What about the arrangement? How shall I report progress? Where shall we meet when I'm ready to collect the first eleven thousand pounds?"

Ever since the first day of the trial I had been wondering about this. I thought of the church at the end of Sedgemoor Crescent, St James's, which is kept open for most of the day. My first idea was that it would be convenient to meet there—but then I decided against it for two reasons. A young man entering alone, particularly Ashe, would be noticeable to anyone keeping watch in the church. And I found, despite my loss of faith, that I had a reluctance to use a sacred building for a purpose I knew in my heart to be evil. I had thought of large empty spaces, perhaps at one of the statues in Hyde Park, but that might be inconvenient for Ashe. I didn't want to risk his not turning up. In the end I knew that I would have to give him my telephone number. It seemed a small risk. After all, he would still not know my address and I could always change the number if it proved necessary. So I wrote it down and handed it to him. I told him to telephone me at eight o'clock in the morning whenever he needed to, but to begin with at least every other day.

He said: "I'll need to know something about her, where to find her."

I gave him the Pelham Place address and told him: "She lives with her mother but in a separate basement flat. There's also a housekeeper, but she won't be any trouble. Octavia's not doing a job at present as far as I know, so she's probably bored. Once you've got some kind of relationship established I'll need to see you together. Where will you take her? Have you got a favourite pub?"

"I don't go to pubs. I'll ring you and let you know when I'll be leaving the house with her, probably on my bike. You'll be able to see us together then."

I said: "I shall have to be fairly discreet. I can't loiter. Octavia knows me. I work occasionally at the house. How long do you think this will take you?"

"As long as it needs to take. I'll tell you as soon as I have news. I may need more money to be going on with."

"You've got the two thousand pounds. You can have the rest in instalments as and when you need it, and the final payment when you're married."

He looked at me with his dark withdrawn eyes and said: "Suppose I get married and then you refuse to pay?"

I said: "Neither of us is a fool, Mr. Ashe. I have a greater regard for my own safety than to think of doing that."

After that I got up and left. I don't remember that he said another word, but I do recall his dark figure against the light from the kitchen as he stood at the door and watched me go. I walked all the way to Shepherd's Bush, unaware of the distance, of my tiredness, of the dazzle and swish of the passing traffic. I was conscious only of a heady exhilaration, as if I was young again and in love.

He didn't waste any time, but, then, I didn't expect him to. As arranged, he rang me two days later at eight o'clock in the morning to tell me he had established contact. He didn't tell me how and I didn't ask. Then he rang again to say that he and Octavia planned to go to the Old Bailey on 8 October, when her mother was due to appear, and would together see her after the case and tell her that they were engaged. If I wanted proof I could hang about the Old Bailey and see them together for myself. But that I knew would have been too risky; besides, I already had the proof I needed. Ashe had told me a day earlier when I could see them both leaving Pelham Place on his motorcycle. It was ten o'clock in the morning. I was there; I saw them. I had also telephoned Mrs. Buckley, ostensibly just for a chat, and inquired about Octavia. She had told me little, but that little was enough. Ashe was established in Octavia's life.

And now I come to the part of this letter which will most concern the police: the death of Venetia Aldridge.

On the night of 9 October I got to Chambers at the usual time. I was, as it happened, alone—it was purely chance that Mrs. Watson had been called to her injured son. Had she been with me one thing at least would have been different. I set about the cleaning, but less thoroughly than when there were the two of us. After finishing the ground-floor offices I went up to the first floor. Miss Aldridge's outer door was shut but unlocked. The inner door was ajar but with the key in her side of the lock. The room was in darkness, as were all rooms of Chambers when I arrived except for the hall. I pressed down the switch.

At first I thought she was asleep in her chair. I said, "I'm so sorry," and drew back, thinking I'd disturbed her. She didn't reply, and it was then I knew that something was wrong and moved up to her. She was dead. I knew that at once. I put my finger gently against her cheek. It was still warm but her eyes, wide open, were dull as dry stones and when I felt her pulse it was lifeless. But I needed no confirmation. I know the difference between the living and the dead.

It never occurred to me that the death was other than natural. Why should it have? There was no blood, no weapon, no sign of violence, not even any disturbance of the room or of her clothes. She was sitting relaxed in her chair, her head bent on her chest, and she looked perfectly peaceful. I thought it was probably a heart attack. And then the reality of it swept over me. She had cheated me of my great vengeance. All that planning, all that expense, all that trouble, and now she had escaped for ever. It was some consolation that at least she had known of Ashe's presence in her daughter's life, but the knowledge had been for so brief a time, the revenge so meagre.

It was then that I fetched the blood and the wig and made my last gesture. I knew of course where to find the full-bottomed wig—Mr. Naughton's cupboard was never locked. I didn't bother about fingerprints; I was still wearing the thin rubber gloves I always put on before starting my cleaning. I think I realized—I must have done—that my action would cause trouble in Chambers, but I didn't care. I hoped that it would. I went out, locking both doors of her room behind me, put on my coat and hat, set the alarm and left Chambers. I took her key-ring with me and dropped it in the Thames just across the Embankment from Temple Station on my way home.

It was only after Inspector Miskin called the next morning to take me back to Chambers that I learned that the death wasn't natural. My first thought was to protect myself, and it was only when I returned home that morning that I began for the first time to face the reality of what I had done. I took it for granted that Ashe must be involved, and it was only after I'd rung Mrs. Buckley that I was told of his alibi. But I knew now that it had to end, the whole charade. When I'd poured that blood over Venetia Aldridge's head it was as if I'd poured out all the hatred. What had seemed an act of appalling desecration had become one of liberation. Venetia Aldridge was out of my reach for ever. I could at last let go, and in letting go of my obsession I faced the truth. I had conspired with evil to do evil. I, who had lost a grandchild by murder, had deliberately put another child into a murderer's power. It had taken her mother's death to show me the enormity of the sin into which my obsession had drawn me.

That is why I came to you, Father, and made my confession. That had to be the first step. The second will be no easier. You have told me what I have to do and I shall do it, but in my own way. You said I must go at once to the police. Instead, when Ashe rings me, as he will on Tuesday morning, I shall tell him to bring Octavia to see me that evening at half past seven. If he refuses, then I shall go to see her. But I would prefer that our talk should be here in my flat, one she need never enter or see again. That way her home won't be tainted with the memory of my perfidy. Then I shall go away, just for a week. I know that this escape is cowardice, but I have to be alone.

I give you authority to show this letter to the police. I suspect that they already know that I was responsible for desecrating Venetia Aldridge's body. I know that they will want to interview me but that can wait for a week. I shall be back in seven days. But now I have to get away from London to decide what I shall do with the rest of my life.

You made me promise to tell the police and the police will be told. You said that I must put things right with Octavia and I shall. But I must be the one to tell her. I don't want it done by a police officer, however sympathetic. And it will be difficult to tell her, that is part of the penance. It may be that she is so committed to Ashe that nothing will shake her faith. She may not even believe me. She may still want to marry him, but if she does it must be with the knowledge of what he is and what he and I together have done.

There was nothing else but the signature.

Dalgliesh read a little faster than Kate and would wait the few seconds until she nodded before turning the page. The writing had been easy to read, strong and upright. When they had finished, Dalgliesh, folding the letter, was silent.

37

It was Kate who broke the silence. "But she was crazy to make that assignation. Did she really expect him to bring Octavia?"

"Perhaps. We don't know what was said between them when he rang. He may even have told her that he was happy for Octavia to know the truth. He may have persuaded her that he could convince Octavia that what had begun as a deception on his part had ended for him in love. There was unfinished business between them."

"But she knew he was a murderer."

"Of his aunt, not of Venetia Aldridge. And even when she saw that he was alone she may have let him in. That would account for the turning up of the TV. He'd hardly have had time to do that if he'd burst in upon her."

"If it was he who turned up. We can't be sure."

"We can't be sure of anything except that she's dead and he murdered her." And perhaps, at some deep level of the mind, unacknowledged, subconscious, Janet Carpenter might not even have cared whether what he brought with him was Octavia or death.

Kate said: "He turned up for the appointment, waited in the shadow of the cupboard, knew when she'd be home. Or perhaps he rang the bell and overpowered her when she opened the door. Or was Octavia with him? Were they in it together?"

"I don't think so. It's in his interest that the marriage goes ahead. She's an heiress of sorts, after all. She may think she's in love, but presumably she has some sense of self-preservation. I doubt whether he'd risk committing murder in front of her, and it was a messy killing. No, I think he came alone. But he'll probably rely on her for an alibi and she may be besotted enough to give it. I want a watch on the Pelham Place house, now. But see that it's kept discreet. And ring Mrs. Buckley. Check that the two of them are at home. Tell her we'll be with her in half an hour. Don't say why."

"It could be we're wrong, sir. Did he kill Miss Aldridge? Can't we break that alibi?"

"No, he didn't kill Aldridge. That rests where we always thought it did—in Chambers."

"If that priest had told us on Sunday everything he knew, she'd still be alive."

"If we'd gone to interview her early Monday evening she'd still be alive. I should have realized that her granddaughter's murder had to be significant. We had a choice, Father Presteign didn't."

He left Kate to get on with it and went into the church. At first he thought that it was empty. The congregation had left and the great door was closed. After the warmth and light of the vestry the incense-heavy air struck chill. The marble pillars rose into a black nothingness. It was strange, he thought, how spaces designed for people—theatres, churches—always held when empty this sense of a bereft expectant air, a sense too of the pathos of irretrievable years, of voices stilled and footsteps long faded. To his right he saw that two fresh candles had been lit before the statue of the Virgin and wondered what hope or desperation was held in their steady burning. The statue, despite the pristine blue of the robe, the golden curls of the child with the chubby hand outstretched to bless, was less sentimental than most of its kind. The face, gravely carved, expressed in its perfection a Western ideal of untouchable femininity. He thought: Whatever she had looked like, that unknowable Middle Eastern girl, it was never like this.

A shape moved among the shadows, and took form as Father Presteign came out of the Lady Chapel. He said: "If I had persuaded her to go to you immediately after she left the church, if I had insisted on accompanying her, she'd be alive today."

Dalgliesh said: "If I had interviewed her as soon as I learned of her granddaughter's murder, she would be alive."

"Perhaps. But you couldn't know then that Ashe was in any way concerned. You made a reasonable operational decision, I made an error of judgement. It's strange that the consequences of a misjudgement can be more destructive than the consequences of a mortal sin."

"You are the expert in these matters, Father, but if an error of judgement counts as sin we are all in a perilous state. I must keep the letter, at least for the present. Thank you for handing it over. I'll ensure that it is read by as few people as possible."

Father Presteign said: "That is what she would have wished. Thank you." They began to move back towards the vestry.

Dalgliesh half-expected Father Presteign to say that he would pray for them, but then he realized that this would not be put into words. Of course the priest would pray for them; that was his business.

They were almost at the vestry door when it suddenly opened and Kate confronted them. Their eyes met. She said, trying to keep her voice level, unemotional: "He's not there. He left late yesterday night on the motorbike without saying where he was going. And he's got Octavia with him."

At Pelham Place Mrs. Buckley greeted them with as much relief as if they were friends whose arrival had been long expected.

"I'm so glad to see you, Commander. I was hoping you'd find time to drop in. That sounds foolish when I know how busy you are, but I've had no news. Octavia tells me nothing and it's been a dreadful week."

"When did they leave, Mrs. Buckley?"

"Yesterday evening at about ten-thirty. It was very sudden. Ashe said that they wanted to be alone for a time, that they needed to get away from the press. Well I can understand that, it was particularly bad for the first two days. We kept the door locked and that nice policeman was very helpful, but it really was like being under siege. Luckily Miss Aldridge had an account at Harrods so that I could telephone for food to be delivered and didn't have to shop. But Ashe and Octavia didn't seem worried at the time, and it did get better. But now they've suddenly decided that they have to get away."

They had moved from the hall and down the stairs to the basement flat. The door didn't open to Mrs. Buckley's hand. She said: "They've locked it on the inside. We'll have to go through the garden basement entrance. I've got a spare key. Miss Aldridge insisted on my having one in case of fire or flood in the flat. I won't keep you a moment."

They waited in silence. Kate tried to suppress her impatience. With every hour Ashe and Octavia could be travelling further, abandoning the motorcycle, making it more difficult to find them. Yet she knew that Dalgliesh was right in not hurrying Mrs. Buckley. She had information they needed, and too many inquiries go wrong, Kate knew, because the police had acted in advance of the facts.

The housekeeper was quickly back and they went into the garden and down the basement steps. She unlocked the door and led them into a narrow hall. It was dim, and when Mrs. Buckley switched on the light, Kate saw with surprise that half the wall had been pasted with a collage of illustrations from magazines and books. The dominant colours were brown and gold and the arrangement, although initially startling, was not displeasing.

Mrs. Buckley led them into the sitting-room to the right of the hall. It was surprisingly tidy, but otherwise was much as Kate had expected, typical, she thought, of many a basement flat converted by the prosperous middle class for the use of their adolescent children. The furniture was comfortable but not valuable; the walls were left bare to allow for private taste. Octavia had hung a collection of posters. The divan against the left wall was presumably also a spare bed.

Seeing her glance towards it, Mrs. Buckley said simply: "He used to sleep there. I know because I clean in here now. I thought he'd be sleeping with Octavia. The young do, even if they're not engaged." She paused and said: "I'm sorry, I shouldn't have said that. It's nothing to do with me."

Kate thought: Clever of Ashe, puzzling Octavia, making her wait, proving that he's different.

The central table was covered with newspapers and this was obviously where they had been working at the collage. There was a large pot of glue and a heap of magazines, some already mutilated, others as yet untouched. Illustrations had been torn out of books as well, and Kate wondered whether these had been taken from the shelves upstairs.

Dalgliesh said: "What happened last night? Did they leave in a hurry?"

"Yes they did, it was very odd. They were down here cutting up pictures to paste on the wall and Ashe came up to the kitchen to ask for a second pair of scissors. That was at nine o'clock. I gave him a pair from the drawer, but he was back within minutes, very angry. He said he couldn't use them. It was only then that I realized I'd given him the pair Mrs. Carpenter left here when she'd been helping out during my holiday. I'd been meaning to give them to Miss Aldridge to take into Chambers—scissors are so difficult to pack and send by post—but somehow I didn't like to ask as she was so busy. Actually, I'm afraid I'd forgotten we had them. But of course he couldn't use them, they're special scissors. Mrs. Carpenter was left-handed."

Dalgliesh asked quietly: "What did Ashe do when you told him?"

"That's what's so extraordinary. He went very white and stood absolutely still for a moment, then he gave a cry. It was almost as if he was in pain. He took hold of the handles and tried to pull the scissors apart. He couldn't do it, they were too strong. So he closed the blades and drove the point down into the table. When we go upstairs I can show you the mark. It's quite deep. It was extraordinary, rather frightening—but, then, he always frightened me."

"In what way, Mrs. Buckley? Was he aggressive, threatening?"

"Oh no, he was perfectly polite. Cold, but not threatening. But he was always watching me, calculating, hating. And Octavia was the same. He influenced her, of course. It isn't happy living in a house where you're resented and hated. She really needs help and kindness, but I can't give it. You can't give love where you're hated. I'm glad that they've gone."

"And you've no idea where? They never spoke of taking a holiday, or said where they might go?"

"No, never. Ashe said that they would be away for a few days. They didn't leave an address. I'm not sure they knew where they were going. And they never spoke before of taking a holiday, but, then, we didn't speak much. Mostly it was Octavia giving me orders."

"Did you see them go?"

"I watched them through the drawing-room window. They were gone by ten-thirty. Afterwards I came down to the flat to see if they'd left a note, but there was nothing. But I think they meant to camp out. They took nearly all the tins from my kitchen cupboard. I could see that Octavia, on the pillion, had her backpack, the one Miss Aldridge bought her when she went on a school hike some years ago. And she had a sleeping-bag."

They went upstairs and into the kitchen. There Dalgliesh asked Mrs. Buckley to sit down and gently broke the news to her about Janet Carpenter's murder.

She sat very still, then said: "Oh no. Not again. What is happening to us, to our world? She was such a nice woman, kind, sensible, ordinary. I mean, why would anyone want to kill her? And in her own flat, so it wasn't a mugger."

"Not a mugger, Mrs. Buckley. We think it could have been Ashe."

She bent her head and whispered: "And he's got Octavia with him." Then she looked up and gazed straight into Dalgliesh's face. Kate thought: She isn't thinking first of herself, and felt an increased respect.

Dalgliesh said: "Was he here early on Monday evening?"

"I don't know. During the afternoon they were both out on the bike. They very often were. And, of course, they were working on their collage by nine o'clock, but I don't know whether they were in the basement earlier that evening. I think Octavia must have been, because I could smell cooking—spaghetti bolognese, I think. But they were very quiet. Of course, I can't hear when anyone goes down to the flat, but I usually hear the bike."

Dalgliesh explained that the house would be kept under police surveillance and that he was arranging for a WPC to sleep there at night. For the first time Mrs. Buckley seemed to be aware of the possible danger.

Dalgliesh said: "Don't worry. You're his alibi for the murder of Miss Aldridge. He needs you to be kept safe, but I shall be happier if you aren't alone."

As they left, Kate asked: "Will you put out a general call, sir?"

"I must, Kate. He's already killed once, probably twice, and it looks as if he's panicked, which makes him doubly dangerous. And he's got the girl.

But I don't think she's in immediate danger. She's still his best chance of an alibi for Monday night, and he won't give up his chance of marriage and her money unless he has to. We won't give out her name. It'll be enough to say that he's wanted for questioning and that he may have a young woman with him. But if he comes to believe that he stands a better chance alone, do you think he'd hesitate to kill her? We need to contact the Suffolk police and the care authority, find out the addresses of every foster parent he had, every children's home he was in. If he's hiding out he'll almost certainly go back to a place he knows. We need to find the care assistant who spent most time with him. His name is in Venetia Aldridge's blue notebook. We need to find a Michael Cole. Ashe called him Coley."

BOOK FOUR

THE REED BEDS

38

As she had neither spoken nor stopped until they reached the house on Westway. She was surprised that they were to stop there, but he gave no explanation. They dismounted and he wheeled the Kawasaki into the back garden, heaved it onto the centre stand, then unlocked the kitchen door.

He said, as she dismounted: "Wait in the kitchen. I won't be long."

Octavia had no wish to follow him. They hadn't been back to the house since that first visit when he had shown her the photograph. The smell of the kitchen, stronger than she remembered but dreadfully familiar, was like a contagion, the darkness beyond presaged a horror which surprised her by its immediacy and its power. Only a thin wall divided her from that single divan which she saw, in her mind's eye, no longer decently covered, ordinary, innocent, but soaked with blood. She could hear it dripping. After a second of disorientating terror she identified the slow plop of water from the kitchen tap and turned it off with shaking fingers. The image of that pale slashed body, the gaping mouth and dead eyes, which she had been able either to banish, or to recall with little more than a shiver of half-induced terror, now took possession with greater reality than on first sight. The black-and-white print took shape again before her eyes, but this time in lurid images of crimson blood and pale disintegrating flesh. She wanted to get out of the house, never to see it again. Once they were on the road, speeding through the clean night air, all the bad images would be swept away. Why didn't Ashe come? She wondered what he was doing upstairs, straining her ears for any sound. But the wait wasn't long. She heard his footsteps and he was with her again.

There was a large canvas backpack slung over his shoulder and in his right hand, held aloft on his clenched fist as if it were a trophy, a blond wig. He shook it gently and the curls trembled in the light of the single unshaded bulb, and seemed for a moment to become alive.

"Put it on. I don't want us to be recognized."

Her revulsion was immediate and instinctive, but he countered it before she could speak. "It's new. She never wore it. Look for yourself."

"But she must have put it on. She put it on when she bought it."

"She didn't buy it. I bought it for her. I'm telling you, she never wore it."

Octavia took it from him with a mixture of curiosity and repugnance, and turned it over. The lining of what looked like fine net was pristine. She was about to say, "I don't want to wear anything that belonged to her," when she looked into his eyes and knew that he was the stronger. She had taken off her crash helmet and placed it on the kitchen table. Now, with a sudden gesture, as if urgency could overcome distaste, she pulled the wig over her head and tucked in the strands of her dark hair.

He said, "Take a look," and, holding her firmly by the shoulders, turned her towards a mirror of glass tiles stuck to the cupboard door.

The girl who stared back at her was a stranger, but one to whom she would turn in the street with a start of recognition. It was difficult to believe that this contraption of blond curls could so extinguish personality. Then there came a second of fear as if something already precarious, nebulous, had been further diminished. She saw him reflected over her shoulder. He was smiling with a critical, speculative gaze, as if the transformation had been his creation, born of his cleverness.

He asked: "How do you like it?"

She put up her hand and touched the hair. It felt unnatural, stronger and slimier than real hair. She said: "I've never worn a wig before. It's weird. It'll be hot under that helmet."

"Not in this weather. I like it. It suits you. Come on, we've got a way to go before midnight."

"Are we coming back here?" She tried to keep the revulsion out of her voice.

"No. We're never coming here again. Not ever. We've finished with this place for good."

"Where are we going?"

"Somewhere I know. Somewhere secret. Somewhere we can be absolutely alone. You'll see when we get there. You'll like it."

She asked no further questions and there was no more talk. He drove westward out of London, then joined the M25. She had no idea where they were going, except that by now she thought they must be travelling northeast. Once London was behind them Ashe chose the secondary roads. For Octavia the ride was without thought, without anxiety, a journey taken out of time in which she was aware of nothing but the exhilaration of power and speed, of a rushing air which tore from her shoulders all the weight of her nothingness. Poised on the pillion, her gloved hands loosely round his waist, she relinquished everything but the sensation of the moment: the surge of the evening air, the throb of the engine, the darkness of country roads where the hedges seemed to close in on them, the wind-blown trees no sooner visible than dissolving into a black limbo, the white lines endlessly disappearing under their wheels.

At last they were nearing a town. Hedges and fields gave way to terraced houses, pubs, small shops, closed but still with lighted windows, the occasional larger house set back behind railings. He turned down a side road and stopped the engine. Here there were no houses. They had stopped outside what looked like a small urban park near a children's playground with swings and a slide. Opposite was a commercial building, perhaps a small factory. A name which meant nothing to her was painted on the blank windowless wall. Dismounting, he took off his helmet and she did the same.

She said: "Where are we?"

"Outskirts of Ipswich. You're going to spend the night in a hotel I know. It's only just around the corner. I'll be back for you in the morning."

"Why can't we stay together?"

"I told you, I don't want anyone to recognize us. I want us to be private. They'll be looking for two of us together."

"Why should they be looking?"

"Maybe they won't, but I'm not taking the risk. You've got money?"

"Of course. You said to bring plenty of cash. And I've got my credit cards."

"The hotel's round the corner, about fifty yards further on. I'll show you. Go in and tell them you want a single room for one night only. Say you want to pay at once because you have to leave very early to catch the first train to London. And pay cash. Register in any name you like, as long as it isn't yours. Give a false address. Got that?"

"It's terribly late. Suppose they haven't got a room?"

"They'll have a room, but I'll wait here for ten minutes. If you come back there are other places I know. When you've registered, go straight up to your room. Don't eat in the dining-room or bar. They'll be closed anyway. Ask them to send up sandwiches. Then meet me here at seven o'clock tomorrow morning. If I'm not here, walk up and down the road until I come. I don't want anyone to see me waiting."

"Where will you go?"

"I know places, or I can sleep rough. Don't worry about me."

"I don't want to be parted. I don't see why we can't be together."

She was aware that her voice had become querulous. He wouldn't like that. But he was trying to be patient.

He said: "We shall be together. That's what this is all about. We shall be together and there'll be no one to bother us. There'll be no one in the world who'll know where we are. I need to be alone with you just for a few days. There are things we need to talk about." He was silent, and then said with gruff intensity, as if the words were forced out of him: "I love you. We're going to be married. I want to make love to you, not in my aunt's house, not in your mother's house. We have to be alone."

So that was what it was all about. She felt a spring of happiness and re-assurance, and, moving over to him, put her arms round him and lifted her face to his. He didn't bend his head to kiss her, but he clasped her tightly in a hug that was more like a violent restraint than an embrace. She could smell him—his body, his breath—stronger even than the leather of his jacket.

He said: "All right, darling. Until tomorrow."

It was the first time he had called her "darling." The word sounded strange on his lips and she had a second's disorientation, as if he were speaking to someone else. Walking beside him to the end of the road, she put out her ungloved hand to hold his. He didn't look at her but responded with a grip that crushed her fingers. It seemed to her that nothing mattered now. She was loved, they were going to be alone together, everything would be all right.

39

As she had reorganized their baggage to make her backpack less bulky but had said that she must take it in with her. The hotel would be suspicious of a guest with no luggage even if she paid in advance. She said: "Suppose they won't have me?"

"They'll have you. They'll be reassured as soon as you open your mouth. Haven't you ever heard yourself?"

And there it had been again, that small note of resentment, like a pinprick, so slight, so quickly felt that it was easy to pretend that it had been imaginary.

There was no one behind the desk when she entered the lobby, which was small with a mean fireplace, the grate filled with a large vase of dried flowers. Above the mantelpiece was a vast oil of an eighteenth-century sea battle, the paint so grimy that little of the scene was decipherable except the lurching ships and small puffballs of smoke from their guns. The few remaining pictures were animal and child prints of a revolting sentimentality. A high rail running the length of each wall held a display of plates which looked like the relics of smashed dinner services.

Octavia was hesitating, wondering whether to clang the bell on the desk, when a girl little older than herself came in through the door marked "Bar" and slammed open the hatch. Octavia spoke the words she had been given.

"Have you a single room just for tonight? If so, I'd like to pay now. I want to be up early to catch the first train to London."

Without replying, the girl turned to an open cupboard and took down a key from the keyboard. "Number Four, first floor at the back."

"Has it got a bathroom?"

"Not *en suite*. We've only got three rooms *en suite* and they're taken. That'll be forty-five pounds if you want to pay now, but there'll be someone on duty from six o'clock."

Octavia said: "Forty-five pounds including breakfast?"

"Continental. Cooked is extra."

"Can I have some sandwiches now, in my room? I don't think I'll bother with breakfast."

"What do you fancy? There's ham, cheese, tuna or roast beef."

"Ham, please, and a glass of half-skimmed milk."

"The milk comes skimmed or normal."

"Well, normal, then. I'll pay cash now for the food as well as the room."

It was as easy as that. The girl showed as little interest in the transaction as she had in Octavia. The key was handed over, a receipt ripped from a machine, the hatch was lifted again and slammed, and she disappeared into the bar, leaving the door open. The noise billowed out in a cacophony of male voices. The bar must be closed by now but it sounded as if they were playing pool. She could hear the clash of the balls.

The room was small but clean. The bed felt comfortable to her probing hand. The bedside lamp worked and the wardrobe stood steady and had a door that closed. The bathroom, which she found at the end of the passage, was unluxurious but adequate, and when she turned on the tap the water, after a few unpromising spurts, ran hot.

When, ten minutes later, she returned to her room, there was a plate of sandwiches and a glass of milk on the bedside table, each covered with a paper serviette. The sandwiches, besides being remarkably cheap, were freshly cut and the filling was generous. She was surprised to find herself hungry and for a moment was tempted to venture down and ask for a second plate, but then she remembered Ashe's instructions:

"Be businesslike, ordinary. You want a room; they're in the business of supplying rooms. You're of age and you can pay. They won't ask any questions, hotels don't. Anyway it's not that kind of place and it's none of their business. Don't be furtive, but don't make yourself conspicuous. Keep out of the public rooms."

She had stuffed a pair of pyjamas in the top of her pack but no dressing-gown. Ashe had needed as much space as possible for the tins of food and the bottles of water. The cupboards in the house kitchen and in her flat had been emptied and he had stopped for additional supplies at a late-night supermarket on the way. The room struck suddenly chill and she would have liked to have lit the gas fire, but there was a slot machine at the side which took only pound coins and she hadn't the right change. She slid carefully between the taut sheets, as she had on her first night at boarding school, when she had feared that even to disturb the bedclothes was to risk disapproval from that pervasive but mysterious authority which from now on would govern her life.

The room was at the back but was not quiet. She lay stiffly between detergent-smelling sheets and identified the distant sounds: the voices now soft, now raucous, breaking into guffaws of laughter as the last customers left, cars revving up, doors slamming, the distant barking of a dog, the background swish of cars on the side road. Gradually her legs grew warm and she relaxed, but her mind was too stimulated for sleep. She was possessed by a mixture of excitement, anxiety and a strange disorientating sense that she had moved out of her familiar world into a limbo of time in which nothing was recognizable, nothing real except Ashe. She thought: No one knows where I am. I don't know where I am. And now Ashe was no longer with her. Suddenly she pictured herself next day moving out of the quiet hotel into the dim light of the October morning to find that he wasn't where he'd promised to wait, that the bike wasn't there, that she waited and he still didn't come.

The thought wrenched her stomach and, when the spasm passed, left her feeling cold again and a little sick. But there was still a vestige of common sense and she held on to it. She told herself that it wouldn't be the end of the world. She had money, she wasn't in danger, she could take a train back home. But she knew that it would be the end of her world, that there was no safety now except with him, and that the home to which she returned had never been a home to her and never would be without him. Of course he would be there, he would be waiting for her. He would be there because he loved her, they loved each other. He was taking her somewhere private, somewhere special, somewhere only he knew about where they could be together, away from Mrs. Buckley's accusing, worried eyes, away from that basement flat which had never really been hers, had always been grudged, away from death and murder and inquests, insincere condolences and her own overwhelming sense of guilt, the feeling that everything, including her mother's murder, was her fault and always had been.

They would have to go back to London eventually, of course, they couldn't stay away for ever. But when they went back everything would be different. She and Ashe would have made love, they would belong to each other, would get married, would move away from the past, find their own life, their own home. She would never, ever, be unloved again.

She was glad that they hadn't made love in London, that he had wanted to wait. She couldn't remember when her interest in him, in his mysteriousness, his silences, his power, had grown into fascination, but she knew the precise moment when fascination had sharpened into desire. It had been when that half-developed print, floating gently in the developing fluid as if it were coming alive, had suddenly become clear and they had gazed together at the lineaments of horror. And she knew now why he had taken that photograph even before he had called the police. He had known that, one day, he would have to face that horror again before he could exorcise it and put it out of his memory for ever. He had chosen her to share that moment so that the worst terror he had ever known would be her terror too. There would be nothing secret between them. After that realization it had become difficult not to touch him; the need to put a hand to his face, to lift her mouth for the kiss which, when it came, had been so formal, so transitory, had at times been overwhelming. She loved him. She needed to know that he loved her. He did love her. She clung to that certainty as if it alone could bring her out of the dead years of rejection into a shared life. Under the bedclothes, she pressed the ring hard against her finger as if it were a talisman.

And now her body warmth was returning, the noise was becoming muted and she felt that first slow dropping into the borderlands of sleep. When at last sleep came, it was dreamless.

40

She awoke early, long before it was light, and lay almost rigid, looking at her wristwatch every ten minutes, waiting for six o'clock, when she told herself that it would be reasonable to get up and make tea. There was a tray in her room set with two large thick cups and saucers, a bowl containing tea bags, sachets of coffee and sugar and a couple of biscuits. There was a small kettle but no teapot. She supposed she was expected to make the tea in the cup. The biscuits were wrapped but still tasted stale, but she made herself eat them, not knowing when she would have the chance of a meal. Ashe had said: "Don't draw attention to yourself by going down to breakfast. It'll be too early anyway. We can stop and get something on the road."

She understood the need to get away from London, from the concerned faces, the inquisitive eyes, Mrs. Buckley's undisguised antagonism. She understood all that. But it still seemed strange that Ashe should be so concerned that they shouldn't be seen together on the journey, that he should worry about her being recognized in this small insignificant hotel. She had slung the blond wig on the back of an upright chair, the only one in the room. The wig looked ridiculous. The thought of putting it on again was repulsive. But she had arrived at the hotel as a blonde. She would have to leave as a blonde. When they arrived at Ashe's secret place she would take it off for ever and be herself again.

By six-forty-five she was dressed and ready to go. She had become so infected with Ashe's caution that she found herself creeping downstairs as if she were sneaking out without paying her bill. But that had been settled the night before. There was nothing to worry about, no one to watch her go except an elderly porter in a long striped apron who was shuffling across the hall as she made for the door. She put her key on the desk and called out to him, "I'm just leaving. I have paid," but he took no notice and passed through the swing doors into the bar.

Carrying her helmet and with her backpack slung across her shoulder, she turned left off the main road to where he had said he would be waiting. But the side road was empty. For a second her heart seemed to miss a beat. Disappointment rose bitter as bile on her tongue. And then she saw him.

He was riding slowly towards her, coming out of the darkness and the morning mist, bringing with him the remembered surge of excitement, the reassurance that everything was under control, that her one night alone was the last time on the journey when they would be separated. He drew up and clasped her briefly to him, then kissed her cheek. Without speaking, she mounted behind him.

He said: "Was it all right, the hotel? Were you comfortable?"

Surprised at the concern in his voice, she said: "It was all right."

"They didn't ask you any questions, where you were going?"

"No, why should they? I couldn't have told them anyway. I don't know, do I?"

He restarted the engine. Above the noise he said: "You'll know soon. It isn't far now."

And now they were riding along the A12 towards the sea. The dawn came in pale reds and pinks, solid as a range of gleaming mountains against the eastern sky, the yellow light streaming down its slopes and spilling into the crevasses. There was little traffic, but Ashe rode well within the speed limit. Octavia longed for him to go faster, to ride as he so often had over the South Downs in great surges of sound, so that the air ripped at her body and stung her face. But this morning he was cautious. They rode through sleeping villages and small towns under the brightening sky, between low windtorn hedges and the flat landscape of East Anglia. And now they turned south and were riding through a forest with straight paths leading between the tall firs into a green darkness. And then that too ended, and there was heathland, gorse and small clumps of silver birch. The road here was narrow as a track. The light was strengthening and she thought she could smell the salt tang of the sea. Suddenly she was aware of hunger. They had passed a number of brightly lit roadside cafés, but either Ashe wasn't hungry or he had decided not to risk a stop. But surely they would arrive soon. They had packed plenty of food. There would be time then to have a picnic breakfast.

To their right the road was fringed with woodland. And now he was riding almost at a walking pace, looking to each side of the road as if searching for a landmark. After about ten minutes of this crawl he found what he was looking for. There was a holly bush on the eastern side of the road and, opposite it, a few yards of broken wall.

Dismounting, he said: "This is the place. We have to get through the wood."

He wheeled the Kawasaki under the boughs of the holly and into the trees. There must, she thought, once have been a path, but it was long overgrown, obstructed by hanging boughs and encroaching shrubs. Sometimes they had to bend double to get beneath the branches. From time to time Ashe would make her go ahead to hold back the springing boughs so that he could force the bike through the thickets. But he seemed to know where he was going. They didn't speak. She listened for his commands, obeyed them, and was glad of the protection of her gloves and leathers against the thorn and matted brambles. And then, suddenly, the wood became less dense, the soil sandier. There was a fringe of silver birch and then, miraculously, the wood ended and she saw stretching before them a green sea of reeds, hissing and sighing and gently waving their frail tops, as far as the eye could see. They stood for a moment, panting with exertion, gazing out over the tremulous waste of green. It was a place of utter loneliness.

Filled with excitement, she asked: "Is this it? Is this the place?"

"Not quite. That's where we're going. Over there."

He pointed over the reed beds. About two hundred yards ahead and a little to the right she could just see the top of a clump of trees barely visible above the reeds.

Ashe said: "There's a derelict house there. It's on a kind of island. No one ever goes near it. That's where we're going."

He was looking towards it and it seemed to her that his face was alight with happiness. She couldn't ever remember seeing him like this. He was like a child who knows at last that the longed-for present is within his grasp. She felt a pang that it was a place and not she who had brought that brightness to his face, that joy.

She asked: "How can we get there? Is there a path? What about the bike?" She was anxious not to sound discouraging, not to spoil the moment by making objections.

"There's a path. It's very narrow. We'll have to wheel the bike for the last part."

He left her for a moment and went to the edge of the reed beds, walking along the fringes searching for a remembered place. Then he returned and said: "It's still here. Get on the pillion, we can ride for the first part. It looks firm enough."

She said: "Can't I take the wig off now? I hate it."

"Why not?" He almost tore it from her head, then tossed it behind him.

It caught on the bough of a young fir tree and hung there, brightly yellow against the dark green. He turned to her and smiled, his face transformed. "This is the last part. We're nearly there."

He wheeled the bike to the beginning of the track and she mounted behind him. The ridge was little more than a yard wide, a sandy narrow path through the reeds. On either side they grew so high that the tops waved six inches above their heads. It was like riding slowly through an impenetrable forest of whispering green and pale gold. He rode warily but without fear. Octavia wondered what would happen if he swerved from the path, how deep the water was on either side, whether they would thrash about among the reeds, struggling to pull themselves up onto the narrow ridge. From time to time, when the pathway became sodden and even narrower, or the edges had crumbled into the water, he would dismount and say: "I'd better push the bike here. You walk behind."

Sometimes the track became so narrow that the reeds brushed both her shoulders. She had the sense that they were closing in on her, that soon there would be nothing ahead but a wall, insubstantial but impenetrable, of green-and-pale-gold stalks. The path seemed endless. It was impossible to believe that they were making their way towards their goal, that they would ever reach that far island. But she could hear the sea now, a faint rhythmic rumble that was curiously comforting. Perhaps that was how the journey would end, the reeds would suddenly part and she would see in front of her the grey trembling expanse of the North Sea.

It was just when she was wondering whether she dare ask Ashe how much further they had to go that the island came suddenly into view. The reed beds opened up and she saw the clumps of trees, firm sandy soil, and behind the trees the glimpse of a derelict cottage. There was an expanse of about thirty feet of water, reed-free, between the island and where they stood. It was spanned by a ramshackle bridge two planks wide and supported in the middle by a single wooden post, blackened with age. Once there had been a handrail on the right, but this had rotted away and only the uprights and a foot of the rail still remained. There must once have been a gate barring the entrance to the bridge; one of the posts was intact and there were three rusted hinges embedded in the wood.

Octavia shivered. There was something oppressive, even sinister, about the stretch of still, olive-dark water and the broken bridge.

She said, "So this is the end," and the words struck chill, as if they were a portent.

Ashe had been wheeling the bike. Now he propped it on its side-stand and moved over to the bridge, walking cautiously to the middle, then testing it by jumping up and down. The planks sagged and groaned but held firm.

Still gently jumping, he spread his arms, and she saw again that happy transforming smile. He said: "We'll unpack and carry our stuff across. Then I'll come back for the bike. The bridge should hold."

He was like a boy relishing a first longed-for adventure.

He came back and unpacked the bike. Encumbered by two sleeping-bags and the leather side-panniers, he handed her one of the rucksacks. Laden with that and her own pack, she followed him over the bridge, then under the low branches of the tree, and saw the cottage clearly for the first time. It had long been derelict. The tiled roof was still partly in place, but the front door hung open on broken hinges, its base embedded in the soil. They moved into what was originally one of two ground-floor rooms. There was no glass in the one high window. The door between the rooms had gone and only a deep sink, stained and scarred, under a tap wrenched from the wall, showed that the further room had once been a kitchen. The back door, too, was missing and she stood looking out over the expanse of reeds towards the sea. But it was still out of sight.

Disappointed, she asked: "Why can't we see the sea? I can hear it. It can't be far away."

"About a mile. You can't see it from here. You can't see it from anywhere on the reed beds. At the end of the reeds there's a high bank of shingle and then the North Sea. It isn't very interesting. Just a stony beach."

She would have liked to be there, to get away from this claustrophobic greenness. But then she told herself that this was Ashe's special place; she mustn't let him know that she was disappointed. And she wasn't disappointed, not really. It was just that everything was so strange. She had a sudden vision of the garden at the convent, the wide well-tended lawns, the flower beds, the summer-house at the end of the garden overlooking a meadow, where they could sit in warm weather. It was the kind of country she was used to, English, ordered, familiar. But she told herself that they wouldn't be here for long, probably just overnight. And he had brought her here to his own special place. Surely this was where he meant to make love.

Now, like a child, he asked: "What do you think of it? Good, isn't it?"

"It's secret. How did you find it?"

He didn't answer. Instead he said: "I used to come here when I was in that home outside Ipswich. No one knows it's here except me."

She said: "Were you always alone? Didn't you have a friend?"

But again he didn't reply. Instead he said: "I'll go and get the bike. Then we'll unpack and have some breakfast."

The thought lightened her spirits immediately. She had forgotten how hungry, how thirsty she was. She watched from the water's edge as he went back over the bridge, kicked back the prop-stand, and wheeled the Kawasaki backwards.

She called: "You're not going to ride it, are you?"

"It's the easiest way. Stand clear."

He mounted the bike, revved up and drove furiously towards the bridge. The front wheels were nearly on dry land when, with a crack which sounded to her like an explosion, the centre post gave way, the two near planks splintered and fell and the struts of the side rail were flung into the air. At the first crack Ashe had stood up and leapt for the island, reaching it with inches to spare, slithering on the sandy earth. She dashed forward to help him up. Together they turned and watched as the purple Kawasaki slowly disappeared under the brackish water. Half the bridge had collapsed. There was nothing now but the two further planks, their shattered ends sinking in the water.

Octavia looked at Ashe's face, terrified of an explosion of rage. She knew that the rage was there. He had never shown it with her but she had always been aware of those smouldering depths of feeling held so tightly under control. But instead he gave a great shout of laughter, harsh, almost triumphant.

She couldn't keep the dismay out of her voice. "But we're cut off. How are we going to get home?"

Home. She used the word un-self-consciously. Only now did she realize that the house in which for so many years she had felt alien and unwanted was her place, her home.

He said: "We can take off our clothes, then swim for it, holding them out of the water. Then we'll dress and make for the road. We've got money. We can hitch into Ipswich or Saxmundham and take a train. And we don't need the bike any more. After all, we've got your mother's Porsche. That's yours now. Everything she had is yours. You know what that solicitor told you."

She said sadly: "I know what he told me."

She heard his voice, eager, the voice of a new, a different Ashe. "There's even an old outside lavatory in the garden. Look, it's here."

She was wondering about that. She had never liked squatting behind bushes. He pointed to a wooden shed, black with age, the door almost too stiff on its hinges to open. Inside was an earth closet. It smelt perfectly fresh, the smell of soil and old wood, and sweet sea-scented air. Beyond the shed was a clump of elder and dry half-dead bushes, a gnarled tree and grass almost knee-high. Octavia walked on and saw again the shimmering vale of reeds, saw too another narrow ridge of firm tussock grass.

She asked: "Where does that lead? To the sea?"

"Nowhere. It's only about a hundred yards long and then it peters out. I go there when I want to be alone."

Away from me, she thought, but didn't speak. She felt again a momentary churning of the heart. She was with Ashe. She should be feeling happy, exultant, sharing his pleasure in the peace, the silence, the knowledge that this isolated island was their special place. Instead she was aware of a moment of claustrophobic unease. How long did he mean to stay here? How were they to get back? It was easy to talk about swimming the ten yards or so, but what then?

In the cottage he was unpacking the bags, shaking out the bedding, setting out their provisions on the one shelf to the right of the fireplace. She moved over to help him, feeling at once happier. He had thought of everything: tins of fruit juice, beans, soup, stew and vegetables, half a dozen bottles of water, sugar, tea bags, instant coffee and chocolate. There was even a small paraffin stove and a bottle of fuel, and two cooking-tins with detachable handles. He boiled water for their coffee, cut slices of bread, buttered them and made two thick ham sandwiches.

They took their coffee and picnic outside and sat together, their backs against the wall, gazing out over the reeds. The sun was strengthening now, she could feel it warm on her face. The food was the most wonderful she had ever tasted. No wonder she had experienced that moment of depression. It was due to hunger and thirst. Everything was going to be all right. They were together, that was all that mattered. And tonight they would make love; that was why he had brought her here.

Daring at last to question him, she asked: "How long are we going to stay here?"

"A day, maybe two. Does it matter? Don't you like it here?"

"I love it. I just wondered—I mean, without the bike it's going to take us longer to get home."

He said: "This is home."

41

Kate had been afraid that the local-authority records would be incomplete, that they would have difficulty in tracing Ashe's moves from foster home to foster home. But a Mr. Pender in the Social Services Department, surprisingly young and with a look of premature anxiety, was able to produce a shabby and voluminous file.

He said: "It isn't the first time Ashe's records have been asked for. Miss Aldridge wanted a sight of the file when she defended him. Obviously we asked his consent first, but he said she could see it. I'm not sure what help it was."

Kate said: "She liked to know as much as possible about the people she defended. And his background was relevant. She made the jury sorry for him."

Mr. Pender gazed down at the closed file. He said: "I suppose you could be sorry for him. He didn't have much of a chance. If your mother throws you out before you're eight, there's not a lot Social Services can do to compensate for that rejection. There were numerous case conferences about him, but he was hard to place. No one wanted to keep him for long."

Piers asked: "Why wasn't he put up for adoption? His mother had rejected him, hadn't she?"

"It was suggested while we were in touch with her, but she wouldn't agree. I suppose she had some idea of taking him back. These women are odd. They can't cope and they put their lover before their child, but they don't like the idea that they'll actually lose the child. By the time his mother died Ashe had become unadoptable."

"We'll need a list of all the people he was placed with. May I take the file?"

Mr. Pender's face changed. "I don't think I can go as far as that. These are confidential social and psychiatric reports."

Piers broke in: "Ashe is on the run. Almost certainly he's killed one woman. We know he has a knife. He also has Octavia Cummins. If you want the responsibility for a second murder on your conscience, that's up to you. Hardly the kind of publicity the Social Services Committee will welcome. Our job is to find Ashe, and we need information. We have to talk to people who might know his special places, where he could be hiding out."

Mr. Pender's face was a mask of indecision and anxiety. Reluctantly, he said: "I think I could get authority to let you have the records. It may take time."

Kate broke in. "We can't wait."

She held out her hand. Mr. Pender still didn't push the file towards her.

After a moment Kate said: "All right. Give me a list of all the names and addresses where he was placed, children's homes and foster parents. I want it at once."

"I can't see any objection. I'll dictate the information now if you'll wait. Would you like coffee?"

He spoke rather desperately, as if anxious to find something which he could offer without reference to higher authority.

Kate answered: "No thank you. Just the names and addresses. And there was someone called Cole or Coley who apparently spent a lot of time with Ashe. We found a mention of him in the notebook Miss Aldridge used at the time of the trial. It's important to trace him. He was on the staff of one of your children's homes, Banyard Court. We'll start there. Who's in charge now?"

Mr. Pender said: "I'm afraid that will be a waste of time. Banyard Court was closed three years ago, after it was burnt down. Arson, I'm afraid. We're fostering children now whenever we can. Banyard Court was for particularly difficult young people but who didn't require secure accommodation. I'm afraid it wasn't very successful. I don't think we have any record of where the staff are now, except the ones who were transferred."

"You may know where Coley is. He was accused by Ashe of sexual abuse. Haven't you an obligation in those cases to inform future employers?"

"I'll look at the file again. As I remember he was exonerated after an inquiry, so we had no further responsibility. I may be able to give you his address, if he agrees. It's a difficult matter."

Piers said: "It will be if anything happens to Octavia Cummins."

Mr. Pender sat for a moment in worried silence. He said: "I went through the papers after you telephoned. They make depressing reading. We didn't do well by him, but I don't know that anyone could have done better. We placed him with a schoolmaster and he stayed there the longest—eighteen months. Long enough to do well at the local grammar school. They had hopes of GCSEs. After that he made sure he was kicked out. He'd got what he wanted out of the placement and it was time to go."

"What did he do?" Kate asked.

"Sexually assaulted the fourteen-year-old daughter."

"Was he prosecuted?"

"No. The father didn't want to put her through the trauma of a court appearance. It wasn't a full rape but it was unpleasant enough. The girl was extremely distressed. Naturally Ashe had to go. It was then that we admitted him to Banyard Court."

Piers said: "Where he met Michael Cole?"

"Presumably. I don't think they'd met before. I'll telephone the ex-headmaster of the court. He's retired now, but he may know where Cole is. If so, I'll ring the man and ask if I can give you his address."

At the door he turned and said: "The foster mother who got closest to understanding Ashe was a Mary McBain. She takes five children of all ages and seems to be able to cope. All done by love and cuddles. But even she had to let Ashe go. He stole from her. Small amounts from the house-keeping purse at first, and then persistently. And he began to ill-treat the other children. But she said something perceptive when he left: that Ashe couldn't bear people to get close to him; that it was when they began to show affection that he had to do the unforgivable. I suppose it was the need to reject before he was rejected. If anyone could have coped it was Mary McBain."

The door closed behind him. The minutes slowly passed. Kate got up and began pacing the room. She said: "I suppose he's ringing the County Solicitor to make sure he's in the clear."

"Well you can't wonder. Bloody awful job. I wouldn't have it for a million a year. No thanks if things go right and plenty of stick if they go wrong."

Kate said: "Which they often do. It's no use trying to make me feel sorry for social workers. I've seen too many of them. I'm prejudiced. And where the hell is Pender? It can't take more than ten minutes to type out a dozen names."

But it was a quarter of an hour before he returned and said apologetically: "Sorry it took so long but I've been trying to find out if we have an address for Michael Cole. No luck, I'm afraid. It's some years ago now, and he didn't give an address when he left Banyard Court. No reason why he should, really. He resigned, he wasn't sacked. As I said, the home's closed now, but I've given you the address of the last headmaster. He may be able to help."

Once in the car, Kate said: "We'd better phone half these names through to the Suffolk searchers. We'll take the headmaster. I've a feeling Cole is probably the only one who'll be able to help."

The rest of the day, and the morning and afternoon of the next, were frustrating. They drove from foster parent to foster parent, following with increasing despair Ashe's self-destructive trail. Some were as helpful as they were able to be; others only needed to hear the name Ashe before making it only too plain that they wished the police away. Some foster parents had moved and couldn't be located.

The schoolmaster was at work, but his wife was at home. She refused to speak about Ashe except to say that he had sexually assaulted their daughter Angela, and that his name was never mentioned in the house. She would be grateful if the police did not return that evening. Angela would be home and mention of Ashe would bring it all back. She had no idea where Ashe could be now. The family had gone on outings when he was with them, but it was to places of educational interest. None of them could possibly have provided a hiding-place. That was all she was prepared to say.

The address they had been given for the former headmaster of Banyard Court was on the outskirts of Ipswich. They had tried there first but got no reply to their ringing. They kept returning throughout the day, but it wasn't until after six o'clock that they were successful in finding someone at home. This was his widow, returned from a day in London. A tired, harassed-looking woman in late middle age, she told them that her husband had died of a heart attack two years earlier, then welcomed them in—the first person who had done so—and offered them tea and cake. But there wasn't time to stop. It was information they desperately needed, not food.

She explained: "I worked at Banyard Court myself as a kind of relief under-matron. I'm not a social worker. I knew Michael Cole, of course. He was a good man and wonderful with the boys. He never told us that he and Ashe went off together when he had a day's leave, but I don't think it was other than completely innocent. Coley would never have hurt a child or young person, never. He was devoted to Ashe."

"And you've no idea where they went?"

"None at all. I don't think it can have been too far from Banyard Court, because they bicycled and Ashe was always back before dark."

"And you don't know where Michael Cole went when he left Banyard Court?"

"I can't give you the address, I'm afraid, but I think he went to a sister. I have a feeling that her name was Page—yes, I'm sure it was. And I think she was a nurse. If she's still working you may be able to trace her through the hospital—that is, if she's still living in the area."

It seemed a small chance but they thanked her and went on their way. It was now half past six.

And this time they were lucky. They telephoned three hospitals in the district. The fourth, a small geriatric unit, said that they had a Mrs. Page on their staff but that she had taken a week's leave because one of her children was sick. They made no difficulty about giving out her address.

42

They found Mrs. Page in a semi-detached house on a modern estate of red-brick-and-concrete houses outside Framsdown Village, a development typical of the not uncommon intrusion of suburbia into what had been unspoilt, if not particularly beautiful, countryside. At the entrance to the cul-de-sac the garish street lamps shone down on a small deserted playground with swings, a slide and a climbing-frame. There were no garages, but every house and flat seemed to have a car or caravan, parked in the roadway or on hard-standing where front gardens had been paved over. There were lights behind the drawn curtains, but no sign of life.

The bell at Number 11 set up a musical jingle and almost at once the door was opened. Outlined against the hall light stood a black woman with a child on her hip. Without waiting for Kate or Piers to show a warrant card, she said: "I know who you are. The hospital phoned. Come in."

She stood aside and they passed her into the hall. She was wearing tight black slacks with a grey short-sleeved top. Kate saw that she was beautiful. Her graceful neck rose to a proudly held head capped by shorn hair. Her nose was straight and fairly narrow; the lips were strongly curved, the eyes large and full-lidded, but clouded now with anxiety.

The front room into which she led them was clean but untidy, the new furniture already showing signs of the depredations of small sticky hands and vigorous play. There was a play-pen in the corner caging an older child who was engaged in pulling herself up to reach the row of coloured bells fixed along the top rail. At their entrance she flopped down and, grasping the bars, gazed at them with immense eyes, grinning a welcome. Kate went over to her and held out a finger. It was immediately grasped with remarkable strength.

The two women, Mrs. Page still holding the younger child, sat down on the sofa with Piers in the chair opposite.

He said: "We're looking for your brother, Mr. Michael Cole. I expect you know that Garry Ashe is wanted for questioning. We're hoping that Mr. Cole may have some idea where he could be hiding."

"Michael isn't here." They could hear the anxiety in her voice. "He left early this morning on his bicycle—at least the cycle isn't in the shed now. He didn't say where he was going but he left a note. It's here."

She struggled up and took it from behind a small toby jug on the top of the television. Kate read: "I'll be away for the whole day. Don't worry, I'll be back by six o'clock for supper. Please ring the supermarket and say I'll be in for the night shift."

Kate asked: "When exactly did he leave, do you know?"

"After the eight o'clock news. I was awake then and could hear it from my room."

"And he hasn't rung?"

"No. I waited for the meal until seven, and then ate on my own."

Piers asked: "When did you begin to get worried?"

"Soon after six. Michael's so reliable about time. I was going to ring round the hospitals and then the police if he wasn't back by tomorrow morning. But it's not as if he's a child. He's a grown man. I didn't think the police would take it seriously if I rang too soon. I'm getting really worried now. I was glad when the hospital rang to say you were looking for him."

Kate asked: "And you've no idea where he could have gone?"

Mrs. Page shook her head.

Kate asked her about her brother's relationship with Ashe. "We know that Ashe lied about his relationship with your brother. We don't know why. Is there anything you can tell us about their friendship? Where they went to-gether, the sort of things they liked to do? We feel that Ashe is likely to be hiding in a place he knows."

Mrs. Page shifted the child in her lap and for a moment bent her head low over the tight curls in a gesture maternal and protective. Then she said: "Michael was working at Banyard Court as a care assistant when Ashe was admitted. Michael was fond of him. He told me something about Ashe's past, how he'd been rejected by his mother and the man she was living with. He'd been beaten and generally ill-treated by one or both of them before he was taken into care. The police wanted to prosecute but each adult blamed the other and they couldn't get enough evidence. Michael thought he could help Ashe. He believed that everyone is redeemable. He couldn't help, of course. Perhaps God can redeem Ashe, a human being can't. You can't help people who are born evil."

Piers said: "I'm not sure what that word means."

The great eyes turned on him. "Aren't you? And you a police officer."

Kate's voice was persuasive. "Think very hard, Mrs. Page. You know your brother. Where would he be likely to go? What did he and Ashe enjoy doing?"

She thought for a moment before answering, then said: "It was on Michael's rest days. He'd go off on his cycle and meet Ashe somewhere on the road. I don't know where they went but Michael was always back before dark. He took food and his camping stove. And water, of course. I think he'd have gone to open country. He doesn't like dense woodland. He likes wide spaces and a great expanse of sky."

"And he would tell you nothing?"

"Only that he'd had a good day. I think he'd promised Ashe that the place would be their secret. He'd come back full of happiness, full of hope. He loved Ashe, but not in the way they said. There was an inquiry. They exonerated Michael because there wasn't any real evidence, and they knew how Ashe lied. But these things don't get forgotten. He won't get another job with children. I don't think he'd want one. He's lost confidence. Something died in him after what Ashe did, the accusations, the inquiry. He works at the supermarket in Ipswich now, doing night work, stocking the shelves. We manage with his wage and mine. We're not unhappy. I hope he's all right. We all want him back. My husband was killed last year in a road accident. The children need Michael. He's wonderful with them."

Suddenly she was crying. The beautiful face didn't alter but two large tears sprang from her eyes and rolled down over her cheeks. Kate had an impulse to move along the sofa and enfold mother and child in her arms, but resisted it. The action might be resented, even repulsed. How difficult it was, she thought, to make a simple response to distress.

She said: "Try not to worry, we'll find him."

"But you think he could be with Ashe, don't you? You think that's where he's gone."

"We don't know. It's possible. But we will find him."

She went with them to the door. She said: "I don't want Ashe here. I don't want him near my children."

Kate said: "He won't be. Why should he come here? But keep the door on the chain, and if he does get in touch, ring us at once. Here's the number."

She stood looking after them, child on hip, as the car moved away.

In the car Piers said: "So you think Cole has really gone to look for Ashe, without telling anyone, without ringing the police?"

"Oh yes, that's where he's gone. He heard about Ashe on the eight o'clock news and then left. He's gone to try a little private redemption again, God help him."

They stopped outside the village and Kate rang to report to Dalgliesh. He said: "Hold on a moment." She heard the rustle of a map being opened. "Banyard Court was just north of Ottley Village, wasn't it? So he and Ashe started out from there or nearabouts. Assume that they cycled between twenty and thirty miles to get to their special place. Up to four hours cycling, coming and going. Tough, but it's possible. Better take a thirty-mile radius. There isn't much wooded country except for Rendlesham and Tunstall forests. If his sister's right and he didn't like enclosed spaces, he'd probably head for the coast. Stretches of it are desolate enough. Start the helicopter search at first light and concentrate on the coast. I'll see you at the hotel by ten tonight."

Kate told Piers: "He's coming down."

"Why, for God's sake? Suffolk's being co-operative. We've got it all organized."

"I suppose he wants to be there at the end."

"If there is an end."

"Oh there'll be an end. The question is what and where."

43

That morning they slept late, each cocooned in a sleeping-bag, side by side but not touching. Ashe woke first. He was at once instantly alert. He could hear beside him her soft regular breathing, broken by low mutters and little snorts. He imagined that he could smell her, her body, her breath. There came into his mind the thought that he could release his arm and stretch over to clamp a hand over that half-open mouth and silence it for ever. He indulged the fantasy for a few minutes, then lay rigid, waiting for the first light. It came at last and she stirred and turned her face towards him.

"Is it morning?"

"Yes, it's morning. I'll get the breakfast."

She wriggled out of her sleeping-bag and stretched.

"I'm hungry. Doesn't the morning smell wonderful here! The air never smells like this in London. Look, I'll get breakfast. You've done all the work so far."

She was trying to sound happy, but there was something false in her over-bright voice.

"No," he said. "I'll do it."

There must have been an insistence in his voice for she didn't persevere. He lit two candles and then the stove, then opened a tin of tomatoes and one of sausages. He was aware of her eyes, anxious and questioning, following his every move. They would eat and then he must get away from her. He would go to his own place among the reeds. Even Coley had never followed him there. He had to be alone. He had to think. They spoke little during the meal; afterwards she helped him wash the plates and mugs in the water. Then he said, "Don't follow me. I won't be long," and went out through the kitchen door.

He pushed his way through the bushes to the familiar path leading to-

wards the distant sea. The track was narrower even than the first. He had almost to grope his way, pushing the reeds apart, feeling them stiff and cold
against his palms. The ridge wound as he remembered it, now firm and
lumpy, now grassy and starred with a few daisies, now squelchy under his
feet so that he was afraid it wouldn't hold his weight. But at last it ended.
Here was the grassy knoll he remembered. There was just room for him to
sit, knees bent against his chest, arms tight around them, an inviolable ball.
He closed his eyes and listened to the familiar sounds, his own breathing, the
eternal whispering of the reeds, the far-off rhythmic moaning of the sea. For
a few minutes he sat absolutely still, his eyes closed, letting the tumult which
possessed his mind and body subside into what he thought of as peace. But
now he had to think.

He had made a mistake, the first since he had killed his aunt. He should
never have left London. It was a bad mistake but it needn't be fatal. The decision to go, the hurried preparations, persuading Octavia, the journey itself—what had it all amounted to but panic? And he had never panicked
before. But it could be put right. The police would have found the body by
now and they would know that it was murder. Someone would tell them that
she had been left-handed—that bitch Buckley, for one. But he couldn't be the
only person who hadn't known it. The police would surely reason that she
had been killed to make them think that she had murdered Aldridge and
done away with herself out of remorse or guilt, or because she could no
longer live with the horror of what she'd done. And that alone should be
enough to put him in the clear. He had an alibi for the Aldridge killing, he
wasn't a suspect. Why should he kill Carpenter? He had no need to set up a
second victim to divert suspicion. There was no suspicion. Whoever had
killed Aldridge, he was in the clear.

So they had to go back. They would do so openly. Once they were on
the road he would ring Pelham Place and explain what had happened, that
they were now on their way back but had lost the bike and been marooned.
The story was true; it could all be verified. And he hadn't left London without an explanation. They'd told Buckley that they were planning a short
break from London, from the trauma of Aldridge's murder. There at least he
hadn't made a mistake. This had been no unexplained flight. The story
held together.

But there was something more. He needed an alibi for the Carpenter
murder. If he could persuade Octavia to give him that, to say that they had
been together in her flat, then nothing and no one could touch him. And
Octavia would do what he wanted, say what he told her to. What had happened between them last night, that coupling which he had dreaded but had

known would have to happen, had bound her to him for ever. He'd get his alibi. She wouldn't renege on him now. And he needed her for more than that. Without her he couldn't get at the money. More than ever the marriage was necessary, and as soon as possible. Three-quarters of a million, and the house, which must be worth another half-million at least. And hadn't that solicitor said something about life assurance? How could he ever have thought of killing her? It had never been a serious option, not now—perhaps it wouldn't be for months, even years. But as they had lain, side by side but distanced, he had pictured her death, her body weighted with old cans filled with stones so that it sank beneath the reeds and was lost for ever. No one would find it, not in this desolate place. But his mind had quickly seized on the objection. If they did find her, the heavy tins slung round her body would prove it was murder. Better simply to drown her, to hold her head under the water and then push her, face downwards, out among the reeds. Even if she were found what would the police have but a drowned body? It could have been an accident, or suicide. He could return alone to London today and say that they had parted on the first day, quarrelled, that she had taken the bike and left him.

But he knew that it was all a fantasy. He needed her alive. He needed that marriage. He needed the money, money that could make money, wealth which would wipe out all the humiliations of the past and make him free. They would go back today.

And then he saw the hands. They moved like a shoal of pale fishes stretching out towards him through the reeds. But the reeds entangled them and held them back. There were forgotten hands and the hands he remembered too well. Hands that thumped and punched and wound belts lovingly through their fingers, over-busy hands that tried to be tender and made his nerves creep, exploring hands—soft, moist, or hard as rods—that came under the bedclothes at night, hands over his mouth, hands moving about his rigid body, doctors' hands, social workers' hands, the schoolmaster's hands with their square white nails and the hair like silk threads on the back of the fingers. That is how he thought of him, the schoolmaster, nameless, the one he had stayed with the longest.

"Sign here, boy, this is your savings book. Half of your local-authority pocket money should be put by, not squandered." Printing his name carefully, aware of those critical eyes. "Garry? That isn't a name. It's spelt with one *r*—it's short for Gareth."

"That's how it is on my birth certificate."

His birth certificate. A short certificate. No father named. One of that official file which, growing by the year, was the record that he existed. He had said: "I like to be called Ashe." He was called Ashe. That was his name. He needed no other.

And with the names came the voices. Uncle Mackie, who wasn't an uncle, roaring at his mother while he watched, and heard and crouched in the corner, waiting for the blows.

"Either that fucking kid goes or I go. You take your choice. Him or me."

He had fought Uncle Mackie like a wild cat, scratching, kicking, spitting, tearing at his hair. He had left his marks on that bastard.

And now the voices filled the air, drowning even the rustling of the reeds. The worried voices of social workers. The determinedly cheerful voice of yet another foster parent hoping to cope. The schoolmaster had thought that he could cope. There were things Ashe had wanted from the schoolmaster: to copy how the family spoke, to watch how they ate, how they lived. He remembered the smell of freshly washed linen as he got into bed, or pulled a clean shirt over his head. One day he would be rich and powerful. There were things it was important to know. Perhaps he should have stayed longer with the schoolmaster, taking those examinations which were supposed to be so vital. They wouldn't have been difficult; none of the work at school was difficult. He heard again the schoolmaster's voice: "The boy is obviously intelligent. An IQ well above the normal. He needs discipline, of course, but I think I'll be able to make something of him." But the schoolmaster's house had been almost the worst of all his prisons. In the end he had needed to get away and the going had been easy. He didn't smile, but inwardly he relished the memory of Angela's screams, her mother's appalled face. Did they really think he wanted to fuck their stupid po-faced daughter? He had had to take gulps of the sherry in the dining-room before he could make himself do it. He had needed drink then, but he didn't need it now. That one episode had taught him that drink was dangerous. To need alcohol was as fatal as to need people. He remembered the frantic telephone calls, the social workers asking why he'd done it, the sessions with the psychiatrist, Angela's mother weeping.

And then there had been Banyard Court and Coley. It was Coley who had shown him the reed beds, Coley who spoke little and who at first had made no demands, who could cycle for twenty-five miles without getting tired, who knew about making fires and cooking a meal out of tins. But in the end he had been the same as all the others. Ashe remembered their conversation, sitting outside the cottage looking out over the reeds towards the sea.

"You'll be sixteen in three months and out of care. I thought I might look for a flat to rent, perhaps somewhere near Ipswich. Or maybe I could find a country cottage. You could look for a job and we could live together, just as friends, just as we are now. And you could make a life for yourself."

But he had a life. He had had to get rid of Coley. And Coley, too, had gone. Suddenly there came over him a wash of self-pity. If only they would leave him alone. Nothing he'd ever done would have been necessary if only they'd left him alone.

It was time to go back, back to the cottage, back to Octavia, back to London. She would give him an alibi for the Carpenter murder, they would marry, he would be rich. With a clear two million—and it must surely be that—everything was possible.

And then he heard it, the last voice, his aunt's voice, shouting at him across the wilderness of reeds.

"Go away? What d'you mean, you want to go away? Go where for Christ's sake? Who'll have you except me? You're mad. Fucking crazy. Don't you know that by now? That's why they all chucked you out after a couple of weeks. And what's so bloody wrong with this place? You get your food, clothes, a roof. You get your presents, the camera, that bloody Kawasaki. That cost a bomb. And all I ask is what any man who was half a man would be glad to give. Plenty are, and they pay good money for it."

The voice went on, cajoling, insinuating, shrieking. He put his hands over his ears and squeezed himself into a tighter ball. After a few minutes the voice stopped, cut off as, with that one final slash, he had thought to cut it off for ever. But the anger remained. Thinking of her, making himself remember, he fuelled it so that, when he rose to go, he carried it back with him to the cottage like a burning coal in his breast.

44

Octavia watched him until he was out of sight, swallowed up by the reeds, then passed through the cottage and stood looking across the thirty feet of water towards the path leading to the wood. She could see the cluster of trees in the distance and, when the sun suddenly broke through, thought she could glimpse the gold of the wig dangling from the bough like an exotic bird. The trees seemed very far away and she felt for the first time a longing to feel the strength of their boughs above and around her, to be free of this wilderness of hissing green. The wind was rising now in erratic gusts and she could see the sluggish surface of the water beginning to crease. The motorcycle must have leaked some oil or petrol, which moved on the surface in patterns of iridescent colour. The wind strengthened. The sibilant rustling of the reeds rose to a crescendo and, as she watched, they bent and swayed and swept in great circles of changing light. She stood there and thought of the night that had passed, the chilly morning.

Was that all there was to it? Had that really been love? She wasn't sure how she had pictured their first love-making except that they would be lying entwined together, every inch of skin yearning for the touch of the other's body. Instead it had been as impersonal as a medical examination. He had said, "It's too cold to undress," and they had taken off the minimum of clothes, without helping or looking at each other, without loving ceremony. And not once during that brief, almost brutal taking had he kissed her. It was as if he couldn't bear the touch of her lips; any intimacy, any lewdness was possible, but not that. But it would be better next time. He was worried, they had been uncomfortable and cold. She couldn't give up loving because their first night had been less wonderful than she had imagined. And the day had been happy, exploring the cottage together, arranging their provisions on the shelves, playing at keeping house. She loved him. Of course she loved him. If she deserted him now—and for the first time she thought of it as a desertion—what would become of her?

And then she heard it, even above the rustling of the reeds. Someone was coming up the path towards her. No sooner had her ears detected that first soft footfall than he appeared out of the reeds like an apparition, black, tall and slim, not young but not yet middle-aged. He was wearing a belted jacket open at the neck to show a thick high-necked jersey. She stared across at him, but she wasn't afraid. She knew at once that he came meaning no harm.

He called softly across to her: "Where is he? Where's Ashe?"

"In his special place, among the reeds." She jerked her head towards the sea.

"When did he go? How long?"

"About ten minutes. Who are you?"

"My name's Cole. Look, you've got to come away. Now, before he returns. You mustn't stay with him. You know the police are looking for him, that he's wanted for murder?"

"If it's about my mother, we've seen the police. He hasn't done anything. We're going back anyway when he's ready."

Suddenly he flung off the jacket, pulled the jersey over his head and plunged into the water. She gazed at him in amazement as he swam vigorously towards her, his eyes still fixed on her face. Gasping, he staggered up the bank, and instinctively she ran to his aid and held out a hand.

He said: "Swim across now with me. You can do it. It's nothing, only about thirty feet. I'll help you. Don't be afraid. I've got a bicycle hidden by the road. You can ride on the crossbar and we'll be in the nearest village before he's after us. You'll be cold and wet for a time, but anything's better than staying here."

She cried: "You're mad. Why should I come? Why?"

He had moved closer to her now as if to compel her by the force of his presence. The water ran from his hair and over his face. He was shivering violently. His white vest clung to his body and she could see the pulsing of his heart. They were almost hissing at each other.

He said: "Janet Carpenter is dead. Murdered. Ashe did it. Please, you must come away. Now. Please, he's dangerous."

"You're lying. It isn't true. The police sent you to trick us."

"They don't know I'm here. No one knows."

"How did you know where to find us?"

"I brought him here. It was a long time ago. This was our special place."

She said: "You're Coley."

"Yes. But it doesn't matter who I am. We can talk later. Now you must come. You can't stay with him. He needs help but you can't give it. Neither of us can."

She almost cried out, "No, no," but she was trying to convince herself, not him. The power of him, the urgency of that dripping body, the pleading in his eyes were compelling her towards him.

And then they heard Ashe's voice: "You heard what she said. She's staying here."

He had come up silently. Now he moved towards them out of the dimness of the cottage into the sunlight and she saw in his hand the glitter of a knife.

After that it was a confusion of horror. Coley made a move to shield her, then rushed at Ashe. But the reaction was a second too late. Ashe's hand jerked forward and the knife sank into Coley's stomach. Wild-eyed, rooted with horror, Octavia heard his cry, a low shuddering cry between a grunt and a moan. Then, as she watched, the red stain spread over his vest and he sank almost gracefully to his knees and keeled over. Ashe bent over him and drew the knife across his throat. She saw the great rush of blood and it seemed to her that the dark eyes, still with that look of pleading, gazed into hers and slowly dulled as his life drained away into the sandy earth.

She couldn't scream. Something had happened to her throat. Instead she heard a high-pitched wailing and knew that it was her voice. She stumbled into the cottage and threw herself down on her sleeping-bag, twisting and turning, grasping and tearing at the cotton. She couldn't breathe. She gave great wrenching sobs that tore at her chest but still there was no air. Then, exhausted by the paroxysm, she lay panting and sobbing. She heard his voice and knew that he stood above her.

"It's his fault. He shouldn't have come. He should have left me alone. Come and help me shift him. He's heavier than I thought."

"No, no. I can't. I won't," she gasped.

She heard him moving about the room. Turning her head, she could see that he was collecting some of the tins.

He said: "I'll need these to weigh him down. I'm taking the heaviest. I'll get him away from here, down the path into the reeds. I'll fetch his clothes later. Don't worry. We'll have enough food to see us through."

Now he was lugging the body through the cottage. She shut her eyes, but she could hear every gasp of his harshly drawn breath, the drag of the corpse. And then she found enough strength for action. She scrambled to her feet, ran to the water and waded in. But he was too quick for her. Before she could recover from that first stinging cold on her legs, his arm was out to jerk her back. She had no strength to resist as he pulled her out on to the bank, dragging her back into the cottage through Coley's blood. He carried her, half fainting, and propped her against the wall, then took off his belt and, twisting her arms behind her, bound them tightly. He bent over Coley's body and removed his trouser belt, then came over and fastened her ankles.

In a voice which was curiously gentle, almost sad, he said: "You shouldn't have done that."

Octavia was crying now, crying like a child. She could hear his laboured breathing as he dragged the body through the cottage and out towards the path between the reeds. Then there was silence.

She thought: He'll come back and kill me. I tried to run away. He won't forgive that. I can't appeal to his pity or his love. There isn't any love. There never has been.

He had bound her left wrist tightly over the right but she still had movement in her fingers. Now, still sobbing, she began to work the little and third fingers of the right hand round the ring and at last got sufficient purchase to slide it off. It was strange that the falling of so small an object should release such a flood of relief. She had freed herself from more than a ring.

Fear was like a pain. It swept over her, receded into a few minutes of blessed peace, then returned stronger and more terrible than before. She tried to think, to plan, to scheme. Could she persuade him that running away had been instinctive, that she had never meant to leave him, that she loved him and would never betray him? But she knew that it was hopeless. What she had seen had killed her love for ever. She had been living in a world of fantasy and delusion. This was reality. It would be impossible to pretend, and he knew it.

She thought: I won't even be able to die bravely. I'll scream and plead but it will make no difference. He'll kill me like he did Coley. He'll push my body out among the reeds like his and no one will ever find us. I'll lie there until I'm bloated and stinking and no one will come, no one will care. I won't exist any more. I never have existed, not really. That's why he could deceive me.

From time to time she sank into a brief unconsciousness. Then she heard him returning. He was standing over her, looking down, not speaking.

She said: "Please let me lie under the sleeping-bag. I'm so cold."

Still he didn't reply, but he lifted her in his arms, set her down by the empty grate and pulled the sleeping-bag over her. Then he left her again. She thought: He can't bear to be here with me. Or is he deciding what to do, whether to kill me or let me live?

She tried to pray, but the words learnt at the convent came out in a meaningless jumble. But she did pray for Coley. "Eternal rest grant him, O Lord, and let light perpetual shine upon him." That sounded right. But Coley hadn't wanted eternal rest. Coley had wanted life. She wanted life.

She didn't know how long she had lain there. The hours passed. Darkness fell and Ashe returned. He came quietly and her eyes were closed, but she knew he was there with her. He lit three candles and then the stove, made coffee and heated some beans. He came over to her, propped her upright and fed them into her mouth bean by bean. She tried to say that she wasn't hungry, but she swallowed them. Perhaps if she let him feed her he would feel some pity. But still he didn't speak. When the candles burned out he got into his own sleeping-bag and soon afterwards she heard his regular breathing. For the first hour he turned restlessly, muttering, and once he cried out aloud. From time to time in the hours of that seemingly endless night she would drop into a fitful sleep. But then the cold and the pain in her arms would waken her and she would lie quietly sobbing. She was eight years old again, lying in that bed in her first boarding school, crying for her mother. The sobbing was curiously comforting.

She was woken by the first light. She was conscious first of the terrible cold, the icy compress of her wet trousers, of the pain in her strained arms. She saw that he was already up. He lit one candle, but it was only when he bent over that momentarily she saw his face. It was the same face, stern and resolute, the face she thought she had loved. Perhaps it was the softness of the candlelight that for a second gave it a look of terrible sadness. Still he didn't speak.

Her own voice came out in a plea between a sob and a gibber. "Please light the fire, Ashe. Please. I'm so cold."

He didn't reply. Instead, he lit another candle, then a third, then sat with his back against the wall looking into the flames. The minutes passed.

She said again, "Please Ashe. I'm so cold," and heard the tears in her voice.

Then he moved. She watched as he went to the shelf and began tearing the labels from the tins, crunching them in his hands. He laid them in the grate. Next he went outside. She could hear him moving about among the bushes, and within minutes he was back with an armful of twigs, dried leaves and larger pieces of bough. He went over to what had been the window and tore at the rotting wood of the lintel. A spar of wood cracked and came apart in his hands. And then he moved across to the fireplace and began building his fire methodically, with loving care, as he must have done when he first came here with Coley. He placed the smallest twigs round the paper, then built up a pyramid with the bark and stouter pieces of dead bough. Finally he lit a match and the paper flamed and caught at the twigs. Smoke billowed into the room, filling it with its sweet autumnal smell, then rose up the chimney as if it were a living thing and had found the way out. The whole room was full of the crackle and hiss of burning wood. He lodged the piece of window lintel across the grate and that too caught fire. The glorious warmth came out to her like the promise of life and painfully she edged her way towards it and felt its benison on her cheeks.

Ashe went across to the window and again tore at the lintel, then he returned to the fire and crouched there, carefully tending it, as if, she thought, it were a ceremonial or sacred flame. Some of the wood was damp. Her eyes smarted with the smoke. But the fire strengthened, the little room became warm. She lay silently weeping with relief. She was safe now. He had lit the fire for her. Surely that meant he didn't mean to kill her? She lost account of time, lying there with the fire on her face as, outside, the wind gusted and the fitful autumnal sun laid swaths of light over the stone floor.

And then she heard it, faint at first and then approaching in a rattle until it circled overhead, seeming to shake the cottage. Hovering above them was a helicopter.

45

He heard them coming before she did. He came over and lifted her to her feet. Standing behind her he commanded: "Hop to the door."

She tried but couldn't move. The warmth of the fire had yet to reach her feet and the strap had made them numb. She sagged against him, every muscle drained of strength. With the knife in his right hand, he grasped her body with his left and lifted her before him out of the cottage into the bright morning air.

And then she both heard and saw. She was too confused to count, but there were so many of them: large men in waders; men in thick jackets and woollen caps; a tall man, hatless, his dark hair stirred by the breeze; and a woman. Those two looked different from how she remembered but she recognized them, Commander Dalgliesh and Inspector Miskin. There they waited, a little distanced from each other, as if each had decided exactly where he should stand, and looked across at Ashe. He jerked her closer to his body, holding her by the belt round her wrists. She could feel against her back the pounding of his heart. She was beyond either terror or relief. What was happening was between Ashe and those watching eyes, those silent waiting figures. She had no part in it. She felt the cold blade of the knife pressing against her chin. She shut her eyes. And then she heard a male voice—surely Dalgliesh's?—clear and commanding.

"Throw down the knife, Ashe. Enough is enough. This isn't going to help you."

Ashe's voice was soft in her ear. It was the gentle voice which he used so rarely but which she had loved.

"Don't be frightened. I'll be quick and it won't hurt."

As if he had caught the words, Dalgliesh called out: "All right, Ashe, what is it you want?"

His reply was a great cry of defiance. "Nothing that you can give."

She opened her eyes as if she needed to see, for the last time, the brightness of the day. She felt an instant of terror beyond belief, the coldness of the steel, a searing pain. And then the world exploded around her in a great crack of sound, the cottage, the reed beds, the bloodstained earth disintegrating in a shrieking of wildly beating wings. With the report echoing in her ears she fell forward with Ashe's body crushing her own, and felt across the back of her neck the warm pulsating stream of his blood.

And now the air was filled with masculine voices. Hands lifted the weight of his body from her. She could breathe again. A woman's face was close to hers, a woman's voice was in her ear. "It's all right, Octavia. It's all right. It's over now."

Someone was pressing a pad against her throat. Someone was saying, "You're going to be fine." And now they were lifting her onto a stretcher and she was being covered with a blanket and strapped down. She was dimly aware that there was a small boat. She could hear sharply spoken words of command and warning and felt the boat rocking beneath her as they loaded the stretcher. And now she was being carried, gently swaying, between the reeds. Above her, their trembling heads made a restlessly changing pattern of green, but she could glimpse through them the scudding clouds and the clear blue of the sky.

46

It was three days later. Dalgliesh was reading at his desk as Kate came in. He half-rose as she entered, which always disconcerted her. She stood in front of the desk as if she had been summoned.

She said: "I've had a message from the hospital, sir. It's Octavia. She wants to see me. She says not as a police officer."

"Kate, your only relationship with her is as a police officer."

She thought: Yes, I know all that. I know the policy. We were taught it in preliminary training school. "You aren't a priest, a psychiatrist or a social worker—particularly the last. Don't get emotionally involved." She thought, too: If Piers can speak his mind, so can I. She said: "Sir, I've heard you speak to people, innocent people who've been caught up in murder. I've heard you say things that helped, that they needed to hear. You weren't speaking as a police officer then."

She nearly said, but stopped herself in time, "You did it once with me," and there came into her mind a vivid image of that moment after her grandmother's death in which, sobbing wildly, she had buried her head against his jacket, smearing it with her bloody hands, and he had stood there holding her in his strong clasp among the shouting voices, the commands, the sounds of scuffling. But that was in the past.

Now he said, and she thought she detected a coldness in his voice: "Saying the comforting word that they want to hear is easy. It's the continuing commitment that's difficult, and that's what we can't give."

Kate wanted to say, "But would you be able to give it even if we could?" and knew that that was a question even Piers wouldn't have had the courage to ask. Instead she said: "I'll remember, sir."

She was at the door when, on impulse, she turned back. She had to know. Aware that her voice was harsh, she asked: "Why did you tell Piers to shoot?"

"Instead of you?" He looked at her with dark unsmiling eyes. "Come, Kate, are you really telling me that you wanted to kill a man?"

"Not that. But I thought I could have stopped him without killing him, sir."

"Not from where you were placed, not with that line of fire. It was difficult enough for Piers. It was a remarkable shot."

"But you're not forbidding me to see Octavia?"

"No, Kate, I'm not forbidding you."

The hospital to which Octavia had been transferred from the emergency department at Ipswich was one of London's newest and looked as if it had originally been intended as a hotel. In the immense entrance hall a silver-barked tree, looking artificial in its bright gleaming greenness, spread wide branches towards the roof of the atrium. There was a flower-and-fruit stall, a newsagent's shop and a large café in which the customers, who looked to Kate's eyes neither particularly anxious nor ill, were chatting over their coffee and sandwiches. The two young women presiding over the reception desk would have looked at home behind the reception desk of the Ritz.

Kate walked past them. She knew the name of the ward she needed and had confidence in following the direction signs. She was borne upwards with other visitors and staff on escalators each side of the wide lifts. Suddenly she was aware for the first time of the distinctive antiseptic hospital smell. She had never been admitted to hospital but she had kept watch at too many bedsides—suspects and victims waiting to be questioned, prisoners receiving treatment—to feel intimidated or ill at ease. Even the ward complex was familiar: the combined air of quietly purposeful activity and meek acquiescence, the gentle rattling of bed curtains, the mysterious rituals carried on behind them. Octavia was in a small private room at the end of the ward complex, and the staff was meticulous in checking Kate's identity before she was admitted.

The story had, of course, broken. Even the efforts of the Met's public-relations branch hadn't been able to prevent the press from sensationalizing the drama. "Police Shoot Suspect Dead" was the kind of publicity the police could always do without. And the story had broken at a bad time. There had been no public scandal, no fresh gossip about the Royal Family to divert the press's attention from the hunt and its sequel. And there had been no arrest for Venetia Aldridge's murder. Until that case was solved or forgotten Octavia would always be partly in the public eye. Kate knew that the Reverend Mother of the convent Octavia had once attended had written to offer her hospitality as soon as the inquest into Ashe's death was over. It seemed a sensible solution, if Octavia would accept. In the convent she would at least be safe from the more rapacious journalists.

Her small room was a bower of flowers, the side-locker, the window-sill and an over-bed table crowded with them. There was even a spectacular bouquet in a large vase in a corner on the floor. A line of greetings cards slung on a long cord adorned the wall opposite the bed. Octavia was watching television but switched it off with the remote control as Kate came in. She was sitting up in bed and looked as fragile and vulnerable as a sick child. The bandage round her throat had been replaced by a dressing fixed with plaster.

Kate pulled forward a chair and sat beside the bed. There was a moment's silence, then Octavia said: "Thanks for coming. I thought they might have stopped you."

"No, they didn't do that. How are you feeling?"

"Better. They're sending me out tomorrow. It should be today but they want me to see a counsellor. Do I have to?"

"Not if you don't want to. Sometimes it's helpful. I suppose it depends on who you get."

"Well, I won't get anyone who knows about murder. I won't get someone who's watched their lover being killed. If they haven't, I don't see what use they'd be."

"That's what I've always felt, but we could be wrong. It's your choice."

There was a silence. Octavia said: "Will that detective, Inspector Tarrant, get into trouble for shooting Ashe?"

"I don't think so. There has to be an inquiry, but he was obeying orders. I think it will be all right."

"For him. It wasn't all right for Ashe."

Kate said gently: "Perhaps it was. He wouldn't have known anything about it. And the future was terrible for him, long long years in prison. Could he have stood that? Would he have wanted that in exchange for life?"

"He didn't get the choice, did he? And he wouldn't have killed me."

"We couldn't take that risk."

"I thought he loved me. It was as silly as thinking that Mummy loved me. Or Daddy. He's been to see me, but it wasn't any good. Nothing has changed. Well it doesn't, does it? He came to visit me, and on his own too, but he doesn't really want me. He loves that woman and Marie."

Kate thought: Love, always love. Perhaps that's what we're all looking for. And if we don't get it early enough we panic in case we never shall. Easy to say to Octavia: Stop bleating for love, love yourself, take hold of your own life. If you get love it's always a bonus. You've got youth, health, money, a home. Stop feeling sorry for yourself. Stop looking to others for love and affection. Heal yourself. But the child had some right to self-pity. Perhaps there were things she could say which would help. If so, she ought to say them; Octavia deserved honesty.

She said: "My mother died having me and I never knew who my father was. I was brought up by my grandmother. I thought she didn't love me, but afterwards, when it was too late, I realized that she did, that we'd loved each other. It was just that we weren't very good at saying so. But I knew after she died that I was on my own, that we're all on our own. Don't let what's happened spoil your life; it doesn't have to. If help is offered, take it if you want it. But in the end, find the strength to take hold of your own life and make what you want of it. Even the bad dreams fade in time."

She thought: I've said the wrong thing. Perhaps she hasn't that kind of strength and never will have. Am I laying on her a burden which she'll never be able to carry?

They were silent for a moment, and then Octavia spoke: "Mrs. Buckley has been really kind since I've been ill. She's visited several times. I thought perhaps she could move back into the basement flat. She'd like that. I suppose that's why she comes to see me, because she wants the flat."

Kate said: "Perhaps that's part of the reason, but it isn't the whole. She's a nice woman. She seems capable too. You need someone you can trust in the flat to keep an eye on things when you aren't there. She needs a home, you need someone reliable. It seems a good arrangement."

"I might not be there all the time. I have to think about getting a job. I know I'll have Mummy's money but I can't live all my life on that. I'm not qualified for anything, so I thought I ought to get some A levels. That would be a start."

Kate said carefully: "I think that's a good idea, but you don't have to make any decisions in a hurry. There are plenty of good places in London where you could study for A levels. You need to decide what you're interested in. I expect they'll be able to advise you about the A levels while you're staying at the convent. You'll be going there when you leave here, won't you?"

"Just for a time. Reverend Mother wrote to invite me. She said come home and be with your friends for a little time. Perhaps it will feel like that when I get there."

"Yes," said Kate, "perhaps it will."

She thought: You'll be offered love of a kind there, the love that Father Presteign deals in, and, if love is what you want more than anything, it's as well to look for it where you can be sure it won't let you down.

As she rose to go, Octavia said: "If I want to talk to you again, would you be able to come? I don't want to be a nuisance. I was rude to you when we first met and I'm sorry."

Kate said: "I'll come if I can. Police officers never really know when they'll be free, so you might want to see me when I'm on duty and can't come. But if I can, I will."

She was at the door when Octavia suddenly spoke again.

"What about Mummy?"

It was the first time Kate had noticed Octavia calling Venetia Aldridge "Mummy," and it made her sound very young. Kate went back to the bedside.

Octavia said: "It will be easier to catch the murderer, now that you know it was Mrs. Carpenter who put on that wig and poured the blood. You'll find him, won't you?"

Kate thought: She has a right to the truth—or at least part of it. After all, it was her mother. She said: "We can separate the killing from what happened to your mother's body afterwards. That's an advance, but actually it widens the field of suspicion. Anyone could have killed her who had a key to Chambers, anyone whom your mother might have thought it safe to let in."

"But you're not going to give up?"

"No, we won't give up. We never give up on murder."

"And you do suspect someone, don't you?"

Kate said cautiously: "Suspicion isn't enough. We have to have the evidence, evidence that will stand up in court. The police don't prosecute. That decision is for the Director of Public Prosecutions and she needs to be satisfied that there is at least a fifty-per-cent chance of getting a conviction. Taking hopeless cases to court wastes time and money."

"So sometimes the police can be sure that they've got the right man and still aren't able to take him to court?"

"That happens quite often. It's frustrating when it does. But it's not for the police, it's for the court to decide guilt or innocence."

"And if you arrest him, he'll have someone like Mummy to defend him?"

"Of course. That would be his right. And if his lawyer is as clever as your mother was, he may be acquitted."

There was a pause, then Octavia said: "It's a funny system, isn't it? Mummy tried to explain it to me, but I wasn't interested. I never even went to hear her in court except for one time with Ashe. She never said anything, but I think she minded. I was horrid to her most of the time. She thought I only went with Ashe to annoy her. But I didn't. I thought I loved him."

Ashe and Octavia. Ashe and Venetia Aldridge. Octavia and her mother. This was an emotional minefield and Kate had no intention of being drawn onto that dangerously explosive terrain. She went back to what Octavia had first said, and spoke of what she knew.

"It is a funny system, but it's the best we have. We can never expect perfect justice. We have a system which sometimes lets the guilty go free so that the innocent can live in safety under the law."

"I thought you were so keen to catch Ashe that you'd forgotten about Mummy."

"We hadn't forgotten. Officers were working on the case while we were trying to find you."

Octavia put out her thin hands and began to pull at the heads of flowers on her over-bed table. The petals fell like blobs of blood. She said quietly: "I know now that he didn't love me, but he did care a little. He lit that fire. I was terribly cold and I begged him to light it. He knew that it was dangerous, that the smoke might be seen. But he did light it. That was for me."

If that was what she wanted to believe, why not let her? Why make her face the truth? Ashe had lit the fire because he knew that, for him, the end had come. He had died exactly as he had planned to die. He knew the police wouldn't come unarmed. The only question was whether he had intended to take Octavia with him. But was there really any doubt? That first cut had been deep enough. As if she had guessed Kate's thoughts, Octavia said: "He wouldn't have killed me. He wouldn't have cut my throat."

"He did cut your throat. If Inspector Tarrant hadn't fired you'd be dead."

"You don't know that really. You don't know him. He never had a chance."

Kate wanted to cry out: "For God's sake, Octavia, he had health, strength, intelligence and food in his belly. He had more than three-quarters of the world can ever hope to have. He had a chance."

But it wasn't as easy as that, and she knew it. How did you apply logic to a psychopath, that convenient word devised to explain, categorize and define in statute law the unintelligible mystery of human evil? Suddenly she remembered a visit paid a year ago to the Black Museum at Scotland Yard, the high shelf with the rows of death masks—only they had been death heads—of executed criminals, the blackness of the heads, the encircling mark of the rope with the deeper impression of the thick leather washer behind the ear. The masks had been taken to test Cesare Lombroso's theory that there was a criminal type which could be identified by studying physiognomy. That nineteenth-century theory had been discredited, but were we any closer to knowing the answer? Perhaps for some people it lay in the incense-laden air of St James's Church. If so, it had never been open to her. But the altar table was, after all, only an ordinary table covered with gorgeous cloth. The candles were wax candles. The statue of the Virgin had been made by human hands, painted, bought, fixed in place. Under his cassock and his robes Father Presteign was only a man. Was what he offered part of some complicated system of belief, richly adorned, embellished with ritual and music, pictures and stained glass, designed, like the law itself, to bring men and women to the comforting illusion that there was an ultimate justice and that they had a choice?

She was aware that Octavia was still speaking. "You don't know where he was born. He told me about it. I'm the only one he did tell. In one of those high-rise estates in North-West London. It's a terrible place. No trees, no green, just concrete towers, shouting, ugliness, stinking flats, broken windows. It's called Ellison Fairweather Buildings."

It seemed to Kate that her heart gave a great leap and then began a drumming which surely even Octavia would be able to hear. For a moment she couldn't speak, only her mind seemed to have power. Was this deliberate? Did Octavia know? But of course she didn't. The words had been spoken with no malicious intent. Octavia wasn't even looking at her, she was plucking at the sheet. But Dalgliesh knew, of course he did; there wasn't much about Garry Ashe that he hadn't learned from Venetia Aldridge's notebooks. But he hadn't shown them to her, hadn't told her that she and Ashe had shared a past, separated in years but rooted in the same childhood memories. What was AD trying to do? Spare her embarrassment? Was it as simple as that? Or had he feared to reactivate a memory which he knew was painful and, by reactivating it, load it with additional trauma. And then she remembered. Surely that resolution made as she stared out over the Thames wasn't about to be so quickly forgotten. The past had happened. It was part of her now and for ever. And had it been so much worse than the childhoods of millions of others? She had health, she had intelligence, she had food in her belly. She had had her chance.

They shook hands. It was a curiously formal goodbye. Kate wondered for a moment whether what Octavia really needed were her arms about her, but that was something she couldn't give. Travelling down the escalator, she felt a spasm of anger, but whether it was against herself or, irrationally, against Dalgliesh, she was unable to decide.

47

The next day Dalgliesh went for the last time to Eight, Pawlet Court. He walked into the Temple from the Embankment entrance. It was late afternoon, but already the day was fading. A thin wind crept up from the river, bringing with it the first frigid breath of winter. As he reached the door of Chambers, Simon Costello and Drysdale Laud were coming out together.

Costello gave him a hard, long look of undisguised hostility and said: "That was a bloody business, Commander. I should have thought a posse of police could have arrested one man without blowing his head off. But I suppose we should be grateful. You've saved the country the expense of keeping him in prison for the next twenty years."

Dalgliesh said: "And you or one of your colleagues the task of having to defend him. He would have proved an unrewarding and not particularly lucrative client."

Laud smiled as if secretly enjoying an antagonism which he didn't share. He asked: "Any news? You haven't come to make an arrest, I take it. Of course not, there would be at least two of you. There should be a Latin tag about it. *Vigiles non timendi sunt nisi complures adveniunt.* I leave the translation to you."

Dalgliesh said, "No, I haven't come to make an arrest," and stood aside to let them out.

Inside Chambers, Valerie Caldwell was at her desk, with Harry Naughton bending over her holding an open file. Both looked happier than when Dalgliesh had last seen them. The girl smiled at him. He greeted them, then asked after Valerie's brother.

"He's settling in much better, thank you. That's a funny way of talking about prison, but you know what I mean. He's concentrating on earning his remission and getting out. Not long now. And my gran knows about him and that makes visiting easier. I don't have to pretend."

Harry Naughton said: "Miss Caldwell has been promoted. She's our Chambers secretary now."

Dalgliesh congratulated her and asked whether Mr. Langton and Mr. Ulrick were in Chambers.

"Yes, they're both here, although Mr. Langton said that he'd be leaving early."

"Will you tell Mr. Ulrick that I'm here, please?"

He waited until she had telephoned, then made his way down the stairs. The basement room was as claustrophobic and as over-heated as on his first visit, but the afternoon was cooler and the heat of the fire less oppressive. Ulrick, seated at his desk, didn't get up but motioned him to the same armchair, and Dalgliesh felt again the warm stickiness of the leather. Among the old furniture, the books and papers piled on every surface, the archaic gas fire, the stark white refrigerator set against the wall was a discordant intrusion of modernity. Ulrick swung his chair round and gravely regarded him.

Dalgliesh said: "When we last spoke in this room we talked of your brother's death. You said that someone bore a heavy responsibility but that it wasn't Venetia Aldridge. I thought afterwards that you might mean yourself."

"That was percipient, Commander."

"You were eleven years older. You were at Oxford, only a few miles away. An elder brother, particularly one so much older, is often hero-worshipped or at least looked up to. Your parents were overseas. Did Marcus write to you about what was happening at school?"

There was a silence before Ulrick replied, but when he did his voice was calm, unworried. "Yes, he wrote. I should have gone to the school at once, but the letter came at the wrong time. I played cricket for my college. There was a match that day and a party in London afterwards. Then three more days passed quickly, as they do when you're young, happy, busy. I intended to go to the school. On the fourth day I received a telephone call from my uncle with the news that Marcus had killed himself."

"And you destroyed the letter?"

"Is that what you would have done? Perhaps we are not so unalike. I argued that it was unlikely that anyone at the school knew of the letter's existence. I burned it, more I think in panic than after careful thought. There was, after all, enough evidence against the headmaster without it. Once the dam breaks nothing can hold back the waters."

Again there was a silence, not awkward but curiously companionable. Then Ulrick asked: "Why are you here, Commander?"

"Because I think I know how and why Venetia Aldridge died."

"You know, but you can't prove it and you never will be able to prove it. What I'm telling you now, Commander, is a little for your satisfaction, perhaps more for my own. Think of it as fiction. Imagine as our protagonist a man, successful in his career, reasonably content if not happy, but who loved only two people in his life: his brother and his niece. Have you ever experienced obsessive love, Commander?"

After a moment, Dalgliesh replied: "No. I was close to it once, close enough, perhaps, to have some understanding of it."

"And close enough to feel its power and draw back. You are armoured, of course, by the creative artist's splinter of ice in the heart. I had no such defence. Obsessive love is the most appalling, the most destructive of all love's tyrannies. It is also the most humiliating. Our protagonist—let us use my name and call him Desmond—well knew that his niece, despite her beauty, was selfish, greedy, even a little silly. Nothing made any difference. But perhaps you would like to go on with the story, now that we have the characters and the beginning of the plot."

Dalgliesh said: "I think, although I have no evidence, that the niece telephoned her uncle and told him that her husband's career was in jeopardy, that Venetia Aldridge had acquired information which might prevent him ever becoming a QC, might even destroy him as a lawyer. She pleaded with her uncle to put a stop to it, to use his influence to see that it didn't happen. She was, after all, used to coming to her uncle for advice, for money, for help, for support—for anything she wanted. Always he had provided it. So I see him going upstairs to reason with Venetia Aldridge. That couldn't have been easy for him. I see him as a proud and private man. Venetia Aldridge and he are the only two people in Chambers. She was taking a telephone call when he entered and he could tell by her voice that it was a bad time to choose. She had recently learned of her daughter's affair with a man she had defended but knew was a particularly brutal murderer. She had looked for advice and support from men who might have been expected to help and had found none. I don't of course know what was said, but I imagine that it was a bitter rejection of our protagonist's plea for mercy or restraint. And there was something which she could use, some knowledge which she could throw in his face. I think she did use that knowledge. I think it was Venetia Aldridge who posted Marcus Ulrick's letter. Letters at prep schools are invariably censored. How else could he get it out unless he gave it to Venetia to post on her way to school?"

Ulrick said: "We are, of course, devising fiction, inventing a plot. This isn't a confession. There will be no confession and no admission of anything that is said between us. That is an ingenious sophistication of our plot. Let us assume that it is true. What then?"

Dalgliesh said: "I think it's your turn now."

"My turn to continue this interesting fabrication. So let us suppose that all the suppressed emotions of an essentially private man come together. Long years of guilt, disgust with himself, anger that this woman whose family have already harmed his so irrevocably should be planning more destruction. The paper-knife was on the desk. She had moved to the door, a file in her hand to replace in the cabinet. It was a way of saying that she had work to do, that the interview was over. He seized the dagger, rushed at her and struck. It must, I think, have been an amazement to him that he was capable of the deed, that the dagger went in so cleanly, so easily, that he had actually killed a human being. Astonishment rather than horror or fear would have been the first emotion.

"After that I think he would have moved quite quickly, dragging the body across and arranging it in her swivel chair. I remember reading somewhere that this attempt to make the body look normal, even comfortable, is typical of killers who didn't intend their deed. He decided to leave the room unlocked, with the key still in place. That way it would be assumed that the killing was the work of an intruder. Who would be able to prove otherwise? The wound, to his relief, did not bleed, and the dagger, when he withdrew it, was remarkably clean. But even he knew that it would be tested for prints. He extracted with care the middle portion of the evening paper to wrap the dagger, took the weapon downstairs to the basement cloakroom, washed it thoroughly, then wound a length of toilet tissue round the handle. He tore up the newspaper and flushed the pieces down the lavatory bowl. He then returned to his own room and turned off the gas fire. Does this recital, so far, seem to you a convincing hypothesis, Commander?"

"It's what I believe happened, yes."

"Our putative Desmond is happily ignorant of the minutiae of the criminal law but he does know that malefactors find it convenient to supply the police with an alibi. For a man without an accomplice and one who lives alone this presented a difficulty. He decides to go at once to Rules in Maiden Lane, a short walk only, leaving his briefcase in his room. Mrs. Carpenter, who usually cleans his room, must not be allowed a sight of it, so he pushes it into the bottom drawer of his desk. His plan is to say that he left Chambers at seven-fifteen, not just after eight, and went home first to wash and leave his case. He realized that there would be a difficulty next morning, but the carrying of a raincoat over his arm and a more hurried entry than usual should deal with that little problem. I think he was rather pleased with his alibi. It was, of course, important to make sure that Pawlet Court was empty before he left the shelter of the doorway of Number Eight. There was no problem about his non-arrival home until after dinner. A neighbour if questioned might be able to attest that he came home at the usual time, but not that he didn't. He dropped the dagger in Valerie Caldwell's filing cabinet, scrunching the toilet tissue in his pocket for disposal in the first rubbish bin he found, and he remembered not to set the alarm system. But he made one mistake. Criminals usually do, I believe. Under stress, it is difficult to think of everything. On leaving, perhaps from long habit, he double-locked the front door. It would, of course, have been wiser to have left it open, thus casting suspicion on an outsider rather than on members of Chambers. The subsequent furore has, however, had its interest to a student of human nature. His own indignation and disgust on viewing the body next morning were unfeigned and, presumably, convincing. He did not place the full-bottomed wig on her head, nor did he waste his own blood."

Dalgliesh said: "That was Janet Carpenter."

"I thought it might be. So, Commander, we have devised a plausible solution to your problem. What a pity for you that it is unprovable. There isn't a single piece of forensic evidence to link our protagonist with the crime. It's much more likely that Janet Carpenter stabbed Miss Aldridge before decorating her with the wig, symbol of her profession, and the blood, which metaphorically she had shed. I am told she has confessed only to the desecrations, but could a woman like Janet Carpenter ever have brought herself to confess to murder? And if not Carpenter, why Desmond? How much more likely that someone from outside Chambers had gained entry and killed out of revenge or hatred. More likely, even, that it was Ashe. Ashe had an alibi, but alibis are meant to be broken. And Ashe, like Carpenter, is dead.

"You have nothing to reproach yourself with, Commander. Console yourself with the thought that all human justice is necessarily imperfect and that it is better for a useful man to continue to be useful than to spend years in gaol. But it wouldn't happen, would it? The DPP would never allow so flimsy a case to be brought. And if it were brought, it wouldn't need a Venetia Aldridge to defend it successfully. You are used to success, of course. Failure, even partial failure, must be galling, but perhaps salutary. It is good for us to be reminded from time to time that our system of law is human and, therefore, fallible and that the most we can hope to achieve is a certain justice. And now, if you'll forgive me, I have this Opinion to write."

They parted without another word. Making his way upstairs, Dalgliesh left his keys to Chambers with Harry Naughton, who came to show him out. As he walked across the court, Dalgliesh saw that Hubert Langton was just ahead of him. The Head of Chambers was walking without a stick but with the shuffling gait of an old man. He heard Dalgliesh's footsteps, paused and seemed about to look back. Then, quickening his step, he walked resolutely on. Dalgliesh thought: He doesn't want to speak. He doesn't even want to see me. Does he know? He slackened his pace to let Langton get ahead, then slowly followed. Carefully distanced, they made their way through the gas-lit court, then down Middle Temple Lane towards the river.

A NOTE ABOUT THE AUTHOR

P. D. James is the author of fourteen previous books, nine of which have been filmed and broadcast on television. She spent thirty years in various sections of the British Civil Service, including the Police and Criminal Law Departments of the Home Office. She has served as a magistrate and as a governor of the BBC. P. D. James is the recipient of many prizes and honors, and in 1991 was made Baroness James of Holland Park. She lives in London and Oxford.

A NOTE ON THE TYPE

The text of this book was set in Sabon, a typeface designed by
Jan Tschichold (1902–1974), the well-known German typog-
rapher. Because it was designed in Frankfurt, Sabon was
named for the famous Frankfurt typefounder Jacques Sabon,
who died in 1580 while manager of the Egenolff foundry.
Based loosely on the original designs of Claude Garamond
(c. 1480–1561), Sabon is unique in that it was explicitly
designed for hot-metal composition on both the Monotype
and Linotype machines as well as for film composition.

Composed by ComCom,
an R. R. Donnelley & Sons Company,
Allentown, Pennsylvania

Printed and bound by R. R. Donnelley & Sons,
Harrisonburg, Virginia

Typography and binding design
by Dorothy S. Baker